THE SEATS OF THE MIGHTY

THE SEATS OF THE MIGHTY

BEING THE MEMOIRS OF CAPTAIN ROBERT MORAY, SOMETIME AN OFFICER IN THE VIRGINIA REGIMENT, AND AFTERWARDS OF AMHERST'S REGIMENT

BY

GILBERT PARKER

AUTHOR OF PIERRE AND HIS PEOPLE
WHEN VALMOND CAME TO PONTIAC
THE TRAIL OF THE SWORD
THE TRESPASSER
ETC

NEW YORK ... D. APPLETON AND COMPANY ... MDCCCCII

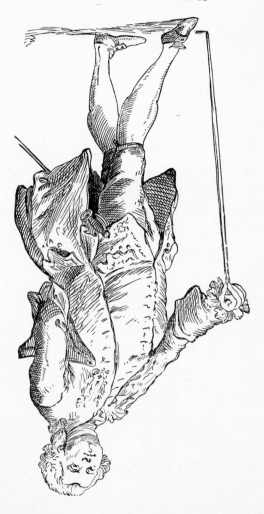

M. François Bigot, the Intendant.

To the Memory of
Madge Henley.

PREFATORY NOTE.

THIS tale would never have been written had it not been for the kindness of my distinguished friend Dr. John George Bourinot, C. M. G., of Ottawa, whose studies in parliamentary procedure, the English and Canadian Constitutions, and the history and development of Canada have been of singular benefit to the Dominion and to the Empire. Through Dr. Bourinot's good offices I came to know Mr. James Lemoine, of Quebec, the gifted antiquarian, and President of the Royal Society of Canada. Mr. Lemoine placed in my hands certain historical facts suggestive of romance. Subsequently, Mr. George M. Fairchild, Jr., of Cap Rouge, Quebec, whose library contains a valuable collection of antique Canadian books, maps, and prints, gave me generous assistance and counsel, allowing me " the run " of all his charts, prints, histories, and memoirs. Many of these prints, and a rare and authentic map of Wolfe's operations against Quebec are now reproduced in this novel, and may be considered accurate illustrations of places, people, and events. By the insertion of these faithful historical elements it is hoped to give more, vividness to the atmosphere of the time, and to strengthen the verisimilitude of a piece of fiction which is not, I believe, out of harmony with fact.

GILBERT PARKER.

CONTENTS.

LIST OF ILLUSTRATIONS.

The Château Saint-Louis, 1620–1834.

THE SEATS OF THE MIGHTY.

PRELUDE.

To Sir EDWARD SEAFORTH, Bart., of Sangley Hope in Derbyshire, and Seaforth House in Hanover Square.

DEAR NED: You will have them written, or I shall be pestered to my grave! Is that the voice of a friend of so long standing? And yet it seems but yesterday since we had good hours in Virginia together, or met among the ruins of Quebec. My memoirs—these only will content you? And to flatter or cajole me you tell me Mr. Pitt still urges on the matter. In truth, when he touched first upon this, I thought it but the courtesy of a great and generous man. But indeed I am proud that he is curious to know more of my long captivity at Quebec, of Monsieur Doltaire and all his dealings with me, and the motions he made to serve La Pompadour on one hand, and, on the other, to win from me that most perfect of ladies, Mademoiselle Alixe Duvarney.

Our bright conquest of Quebec is now heroic memory, and honour and fame and reward have been parcelled out. So I shall but briefly, in these memoirs (ay, they shall be written, and with a good heart), travel the trail of history, or discourse upon campaigns and sieges, diplomacies and treaties. I shall keep close to my own story; for that, it would seem, yourself and the illustrious minister of the

1

King most wish to hear.   Yet you will find figuring in it great men like our flaming hero General Wolfe, and also General Montcalm, who, I shall ever keep on saying, might have held Quebec against us, had he not been balked by the vain Governor, the Marquis de Vaudreuil; together with such notorious men as the Intendant Bigot, civil governor of New France, and such noble gentlemen as the Seigneur Duvarney, father of Alixe.

I shall never view again the citadel on those tall heights where I was detained so barbarously, nor the gracious Manor House at Beauport, sacred to me because of her who dwelt therein—how long ago, how long! Of all the pictures that flash before my mind when thinking on those times, one is most with me: that of the fine guest-room in the Manor House, where I see moving the benign maid whose life and deeds alone can make this story worth telling.   And with one scene therein, and it the most momentous in all my days, I shall begin my tale.

I beg you convey to Mr. Pitt my most obedient compliments, and say that I take his polite wish as my command.

With every token of my regard, I am, dear Ned, affectionately your friend,

ROBERT MORAY.

I.

AN ESCORT TO THE CITADEL.

WHEN Monsieur Doltaire entered the salon, and, dropping lazily into a chair beside Madame Duvarney and her daughter, drawled out, "England's Braddock—fool and general—has gone to heaven, Captain Moray, and your papers send you there also," I did not shift a jot, but looked over at him gravely—for, God knows, I was startled —and I said,

"The General is dead?"

I did not dare to ask, Is he defeated? though from Doltaire's look I was sure it was so; and a sickness crept through me, for at the moment that seemed the end of our cause. But I made as if I had not heard his words about my papers.

"Dead as a last year's courtier, shifted from the scene," he replied; "and having little now to do, we'll go play with the rat in our trap."

I would not have dared look towards Alixe, standing beside her mother then, for the song in my blood was pitched too high, were it not that a little sound broke from her. At that I glanced, and saw that her face was still and quiet, but her eyes were shining anxiously, and her whole body seemed listening. I dared not give my glance meaning, though I wished to do so. She had served me much, had been a good friend to me, since I was brought a hostage to Quebec from Fort Necessity. There, at that

3

little post on the Ohio, France threw down the gauntlet, which gave us the great Seven Years' War. And though it may be thought I speak rashly, the lever to spring that trouble had been within my grasp. Had France sat still while Austria and Prussia quarrelled that long fighting had never been. The game of war had lain with the Grande Marquise—or La Pompadour, as she was called— and later it may be seen how I, unwillingly, moved her to set it going.

Answering Monsieur Doltaire I said stoutly, "I am sure our general made a good fight; he had gallant men."

"Truly gallant," he returned—"your own Virginians among others" (I bowed); "but he was a blunderer, as were you also, monsieur, or you had not sent him plans of our forts and letters of such candour. They have gone to France, my captain."

Madame Duvarney seemed to stiffen in her chair, for what did this mean but that I was a spy? and the young lady behind them now put her handkerchief to her mouth as if to stop a word. To make light of the charges against myself was the only thing, and yet I had little heart to do so. There was that between Monsieur Doltaire and myself—a matter I shall come to by and by— which well might make me apprehensive.

"My sketch and my gossip with my friends," said I, "can have little interest in France."

"My faith, the Grande Marquise will find a relish for them," he said pointedly at me. He, the natural son of King Louis, had played the part between La Pompadour and myself in the grave matter of which I spoke. "She loves deciding knotty points of morality," he added.

"She has had will and chance enough," said I boldly, "but what point of morality is here?"

"The most vital—to you," he rejoined, flicking his handkerchief a little, and drawling so that I could have stopped his mouth with my hand. " Shall a hostage on parole make sketches of a fort and send them to his friends, who in turn pass them on to a foolish general ? "

" When one party to an Article of War wilfully breaks his sworn promise, shall the other be held to his ? " I asked quietly.

I was glad that at this moment the Seigneur Du-varney entered, for I could feel the air now growing colder about Madame his wife. He at least was a good friend ; but as I glanced at him I saw his face was trou-bled and his manner distant. He looked at Monsieur Doltaire a moment steadily, stooped to his wife's hand, and then offered me his own without a word. This done, he went to where his daughter stood. She kissed him, and, as she did so, whispered something in his ear, to which he nodded assent. I knew afterwards that she had asked him to keep me to dinner with them.

Presently turning to Monsieur Doltaire, he said in-quiringly, " You have a squad of men outside my house, Doltaire ? "

Doltaire nodded in a languid way, and answered, " An escort—for Captain Moray—to the citadel."

I knew now, as he had said, that I was in the trap ; that he had begun the long sport which came near giving me the white shroud of death, as it turned white the hair upon my head ere I was thirty-two. Do I not know that the indignities, the miseries I suffered, I owed mostly to him, and that at the last he well-nigh robbed England of her greatest pride, the taking of New France ?—For chance sometimes lets humble men like me balance the scales of fate ; and I was humble enough in rank, if in spirit always something above my place.

I was standing as he spoke these words, and I turned to him and said, " Monsieur, I am at your service."

" I have sometimes wished," he said instantly, and with

2

a courteous if ironical gesture, "that you were in my
service—that is, the King's."

I bowed as to a compliment, for I would not see the
insolence, and I retorted, "Would I could offer you a
company in my Virginia regiment!"

"Delightful! delightful!" he rejoined. "I should
make as good a Briton as you a Frenchman, every whit."

I suppose he would have kept leading on to such silly
play, had I not turned to Madame Duvarney and said, "I
am most sorry that this mishap falls here; but it is not
of my doing, and in colder comfort, Madame, I shall recall the good hours spent in your home."

I think I said it with a general courtesy, yet, feeling
the eyes of the young lady on me, perhaps a little extra
warmth came into my voice, and worked upon Madame,
or it may be she was glad of my removal from contact
with her daughter; but kindness showed in her face, and
she replied gently, "I am sure it is only for a few days
till we see you again."

Yet I think in her heart she knew my life was perilled:
those were rough and hasty times, when the axe or the
rope was the surest way to deal with troubles. Three
years before, at Fort Necessity, I had handed my sword
to my lieutenant, bidding him make healthy use of it,
and, travelling to Quebec on parole, had come in and out
of this house with great freedom. Yet since Alixe had
grown towards womanhood there had been marked change
in Madame's manner.

"The days, however few, will be too long until I tax
your courtesy again," I said. "I bid you adieu, Madame."

"Nay, not so," spoke up my host; "not one step:
dinner is nearly served, and you must both dine with us.
Nay, but I insist," he added, as he saw me shake my
head. "Monsieur Doltaire will grant you this courtesy,
and me the great kindness. Eh, Doltaire?"

Doltaire rose, glancing from Madame to her daughter. Madame was smiling, as if begging his consent; for, profligate though he was, his position, and, more than all, his personal distinction, made him a welcome guest at most homes in Quebec. Alixe met his look without a yes or no in her eyes—so young, yet having such control and wisdom, as I have had reason beyond all men to know. Something, however, in the temper of the scene had filled her with a kind of glow, which added to her beauty and gave her dignity. The spirit of her look caught the admiration of this expatriated courtier, and I knew that a deeper cause than all our past conflicts—and they were great—would now, or soon, set him fatally against me.

"I shall be happy to wait Captain Moray's pleasure," he said presently, "and to serve my own by sitting at your table. I was to have dined with the Intendant this afternoon, but a messenger shall tell him duty stays me. . . . If you will excuse me!" he added, going to the door to find a man of his company. He looked back for an instant, as if it struck him I might seek escape, for he believed in no man's truth; but he only said, "I may fetch my men to your kitchen, Duvarney? 'Tis raw outside."

"Surely. I shall see they have some comfort," was the reply.

Doltaire then left the room, and Duvarney came to me. "This is a bad business, Moray," he said sadly. "There is some mistake, is there not?"

I looked him fair in the face. "There is a mistake," I answered. "I am no spy, and I do not fear that I shall lose my life, my honour, or my friends by offensive acts of mine."

"I believe you," he responded, "as I have believed since you came, though there has been gabble of your doings. I do not forget you bought my life back from those wild Mohawks five years ago. You have my hand in trouble or out of it."

Upon my soul, I could have fallen on his neck, for the blow to our cause and the shadow on my own fate oppressed me for the moment!

At this point the ladies left the room to make some little toilette before dinner, and as they passed me the sleeve of Alixe's dress touched my arm. I caught her fingers for an instant, and to this day I can feel that warm, rich current of life coursing from finger-tips to heart. She did not look at me at all, but passed on after her mother. Never till that moment had there been any open show of heart between us. When I first came to Quebec (I own it with shame) I was inclined to use her youthful friendship for private and patriotic ends; but that soon passed, and then I wished her companionship for true love of her. Also, I had been held back because when I first knew her she seemed but a child. Yet how quickly and how wisely did she grow out of her childhood! She had a playful wit, and her talents were far beyond her years. It amazed me often to hear her sum up a thing in some pregnant sentence which, when you came to think, was the one word to be said. She had such a deep look out of her blue eyes that you were hardly drawn from them to see the warm sweet colour of her face, the fair broad forehead, the brown hair, the delicate richness of her lips, which ever were full of humour and of seriousness—both running together, as you may see a laughing brook steal into the quiet of a river.

Duvarney and I were thus alone for a moment, and he straightway dropped a hand upon my shoulder. " Let me advise you," he said, " be friendly with Doltaire. He has great influence at the Court and elsewhere. He can make your bed hard or soft at the citadel."

I smiled at him, and replied, " I shall sleep no less sound because of Monsieur Doltaire."

" You are bitter in your trouble," said he.

I made haste to answer, " No, no, my own troubles do not weigh so heavy—but our General's death ! "

" You are a patriot, my friend," he added warmly. " I could well have been content with our success against your English army without this deep danger to your person."

I put out my hand to him, but I did not speak, for just then Doltaire entered. He was smiling at something in his thought.

" The fortunes are with the Intendant always," said he. " When things are at their worst, and the King's storehouse, the dear La Friponne, is to be ripped by our rebel peasants like a sawdust doll, here comes this gay news of our success on the Ohio ; and in that Braddock's death the whining beggars will forget their empty bellies, and bless where they meant to curse. What fools, to be sure ! They had better loot La Friponne. Lord, how we love fighting, we French ! And 'tis so much easier to dance, or drink, or love." He stretched out his shapely legs as he sat musing.

Duvarney shrugged a shoulder, smiling. " But you, Doltaire—there's no man out of France that fights more."

He lifted an eyebrow. " One must be in the fashion ; besides, it does need some skill to fight. The others—to dance, drink, love : blind men's games ! " He smiled cynically into the distance.

I have never known a man who interested me so much—never one so original, so varied, and so uncommon in his nature. I marvelled at the pith and depth of his observations ; for though I agreed not with him once in ten times, I loved his great reflective cleverness and his fine penetration—singular gifts in a man of action. But action to him was a playtime; he had that irresponsibility of the Court from which he came, its scornful endurance of defeat or misery, its flippant look upon the world, its scoundrel view of women. Then he and Duvarney talked, and I sat thinking. Perhaps the passion of a cause grows in you as you suffer for it, and I had suffered, and suffered most by a bitter inaction. Governor Dinwiddie, Mr. Washington (alas that, as I write the fragment chapters of my life, among the hills where Montrose my ancestor fought, George leads the colonists against the realm of England!), and the rest were suffering, but they were fighting too. Brought to their knees they could rise again to battle; and I thought then, How more glorious to be with my gentlemen in blue from Virginia, holding back death from the General, and at last falling myself, than to spend good years a hostage at Quebec, knowing that Canada was for our taking, yet doing nothing to advance the hour!

In the thick of these thoughts I was not conscious of what the two were saying, but at last I caught Madame Cournal's name; by which I guessed Monsieur Doltaire was talking of her amours, of which the chief and final was with Bigot the Intendant to whom the King had given all civil government, all power over commerce and finance in the country. The rivalry between the Governor and the Intendant was keen and vital at this time, though it changed later, as I will show. At her name I looked up and caught Monsieur Doltaire's eye.

He read my thoughts. "You have had blithe hours here, monsieur," he said—"you know the way to probe us; but of all the ladies who could be most useful to you, you left out the greatest. There you erred. I say it as a friend, not as an officer, there you erred. From Madame Cournal to Bigot, from Bigot to Vaudreuil the Governor, from the Governor to France. But now——"

He paused, for Madame Duvarney and her daughter had come, and we all rose.

The ladies had heard enough to know Doltaire's meaning. "But now—Captain Moray dines with us," said Madame Duvarney quietly and meaningly.

"Yet I dine with Madame Cournal," rejoined Doltaire, smiling.

"One may use more option with enemies and prisoners," she said keenly, and the shot struck home. In so small a place it was not easy to draw lines close and fine, and it was in the power of the Intendant, backed by his confederates, to ruin almost any family in the province if he chose; and that he chose at times I knew well, as did my hostess. Yet she was a woman of courage and nobility of thought, and I knew well where her daughter got her good flavour of mind.

I could see something devilish in the smile at Doltaire's lips, but his look was wandering between Alixe and me, and he replied urbanely, "I have ambition yet—to connive at captivity"; and then he gazed full and meaningly at her.

I can see her now, her hand on the high back of a great oak chair, the lace of her white sleeve falling away, and her soft arm showing, her eyes on his without wavering. They did not drop, nor turn aside; they held straight on, calm, strong—and understanding. By that look I saw she read him; she, who had seen so little of the world, felt what he was, and met his invading interest firmly, yet sadly; for I knew long after that a smother was at her heart then, foreshadowings of dangers that would try her as few women are tried. Thank God that good women are born with greater souls for trial than men; that given once an anchor for their hearts they hold until the cables break.

When we were about to enter the dining-room, I saw,

to my joy, Madame incline towards Doltaire, and I knew
that Alixe was for myself—though her mother wished it
little, I am sure. As she took my arm, her finger-tips
plunged softly into the velvet of my sleeve, giving me a
thrill of courage. I felt my spirits rise, and I set myself
to carry things off gaily, to have this last hour with her
clear of gloom, for it seemed easy to think that we should
meet no more.

As we passed into the dining-room, I said, as I had
said the first time I went to dinner in her father's house,
" Shall we be flippant, or grave ? "

I guessed that it would touch her. She raised her eyes
to mine and answered, " We are grave ; let us seem flippant."

In those days I had a store of spirits. I was seldom
dismayed, for life had been such a rough-and-tumble
game that I held to cheerfulness and humour as a hills-
man to his broadsword, knowing it the greatest of weapons
with a foe, and the very stone and mortar of friendship.
So we were cheerful, touching lightly on events around us,
laughing at gossip of the doorways (I in my poor French),
casting small stones at whatever drew our notice, not forgetting a throw or two at Château Bigot, the Intendant's
country house at Charlesbourg five miles away, where
base plots were hatched, reputations soiled, and all clean
things dishonoured. But Alixe, the sweetest soul France
ever gave the world, could not know all I knew ; guessing
only at heavy carousals, cards, song, and raillery, with far-
off hints of feet smaller than fit in cavalry boots dancing
among the glasses on the table. I was never before so
charmed with her swift intelligence, for I have ever lacked
great nimbleness of thought and power to make nice play
with the tongue.

" You have been three years with us," suddenly said
her father, passing me the wine. " How time has flown !
How much has happened ! "

"Madame Cournal's husband has made three million francs," said Doltaire, with dry irony and truth.

Duvarney shrugged a shoulder, stiffened; for, oblique as the suggestion was, he did not care to have his daughter hear it.

"And Vaudreuil has sent to Versailles bees buzzing of Bigot and Company," added the impish satirist.

Madame Duvarney responded with a look of interest, and the Seigneur's eyes steadied to his plate. All at once I divined that the Seigneur had known of the Governor's action, and maybe had counselled with him, siding against Bigot. If that were so—as it proved to be—he was in a nest of scorpions; for who among them would spare him: Marin, Cournal, Rigaud, the Intendant himself? Such as he were thwarted right and left in this career of knavery and public evils.

"And our people have turned beggars; poor and starved, they beg at the door of the King's storehouse—it is well called La Friponne," said Madame Duvarney, with some heat; for she was ever liberal to the poor, and she had seen manor after manor robbed, and peasant farmers made to sell their corn for a song, to be sold to them again at famine prices by La Friponne. Even now Quebec was full of pilgrim poor begging against the hard winter and execrating their spoilers.

Doltaire was too fond of digging at the heart of things not to admit she spoke truth.

> "La Pompadour et La Friponne!
> Qu'est que cela, mon petit homme?"
> "Les deux terribles, ma chère mignonne,
> Mais, c'est cela—
> La Pompadour et La Friponne!"

He said this with cool drollery and point, in the patois of the native, so that he set us all laughing, in spite of our mutual apprehensions.

Then he continued, " And the King has sent a chorus to the play, with eyes for the preposterous make-believe, and more, no purse to fill."

We all knew he meant himself, and we knew also that so far as money went he spoke true ; that though hand-in-glove with Bigot, he was poor save for what he made at the gaming-table and got from France. There was the thing to have clinched me to him, had matters been other than they were ; for all my life I have loathed the sordid soul, and I would rather, in these my ripe years, eat with a highwayman who takes his life in his hands than with the civilian who robs his king and the king's poor, and has no better trick than false accounts nor better friend than the pettifogging knave. Doltaire had no burning love for France, and little faith in anything ; for he was of those Versailles water-flies who recked not if the world blackened to cinders when their lights went out. As will be seen by and by, he had come here to seek me and through me to serve the Grande Marquise.

The evening was well forward when Doltaire, rising from his seat in the drawing-room, bowed to me, and said, " If it pleases you, monsieur ? "

I rose also, and prepared to go. There was little talk, yet we all kept up a play of cheerfulness. When I came to take the Seigneur's hand, Doltaire was a distance off, talking to Madame. " Moray," said the Seigneur quickly and quietly, " trials portend for both of us." He nodded towards Doltaire.

" But we shall come safe through," said I.

" Be of good courage, and adieu," he answered, as Doltaire turned towards us.

My last words were to Alixe. The great moment of my life was come. If I could but say one thing to her out of earshot, I would stake all on the hazard. She was standing beside a cabinet, very still, a strange glow in her eyes, a new, fine firmness at the lips. I felt I dared not look as I would; I feared there was no chance now to speak what I would. But I came slowly up the room with her mother. As we did so Doltaire exclaimed and started to the window, and the Seigneur and Madame followed. A red light was showing on the panes.

I caught Alixe's eye, and held it, coming quickly to her. All backs were on us. I took her hand and pressed it to my lips suddenly. She gave a little gasp, and I saw her bosom heave.

"I am going from prison to prison," said I, "and I leave a loved jailer behind."

She understood. "Your jailer goes also," she answered, with a sad smile.

"I love you, Alixe, I love you!" I urged.

She was very pale. "Oh, Robert!" she whispered timidly; and then, "I will be brave, I will help you, and I will not forget. God guard you."

That was all, for Doltaire turned to me and said, "They've made of La Friponne a torch to light you to the citadel, monsieur."

A moment afterwards we were outside in the keen October air, a squad of soldiers attending, our faces towards the citadel heights. I looked back, doffing my cap. The Seigneur and Madame stood at the door, but my eyes were for a window where stood Alixe. The reflection of the far-off fire bathed the glass, and her face had a glow, the eyes shining through, intense and most serious. Yet she was brave, for she lifted her handkerchief, shook it a little, and smiled.

As though the salute were meant for him, Doltaire bowed twice impressively, and then we stepped forward, the great fire over against the Heights lighting us and hurrying us on.

We scarcely spoke as we went, though Doltaire hummed

now and then the air *La Pompadour et La Friponne.*
As we came nearer I said, " Are you sure it is La Friponne,
monsieur ? "

" It is not," he said, pointing.   " See ! "

The sky was full of shaking sparks, and a smell of
burning grain came down the wind.

" One of the granaries, then," I added, " not La Friponne itself ? "

To this he nodded assent, and we pushed on.

II.

THE MASTER OF THE KING'S MAGAZINE.

" WHAT fools," said Doltaire presently, " to burn the
bread and oven too ! If only they were less honest in a
world of rogues, poor moles ! "

Coming nearer, we saw that La Friponne itself was
safe, but one warehouse was doomed and another threatened. The streets were full of people, and thousands of
excited peasants, labourers, and sailors were shouting,
" Down with the palace ! Down with Bigot ! "

We came upon the scene at the most critical moment.
None of the Governor's soldiers were in sight, but up the
Heights we could hear the steady tramp of General
Montcalm's infantry as they came on. Where were
Bigot's men ?   There was a handful—one company—
drawn up before La Friponne, idly leaning on their
muskets, seeing the great granary burn, and watching
La Friponne threatened by the mad crowd and the fire.
There was not a soldier before the Intendant's palace,
not a light in any window.

"What is this weird trick of Bigot's?" said Doltaire, musing.

The Governor, we knew, had been out of the city that day. But where was Bigot? At a word from Doltaire we pushed forward towards the palace, the soldiers keeping me in their midst. We were not a hundred feet from the great steps when two gates at the right suddenly swung open, and a carriage rolled out swiftly and dashed down into the crowd. I recognised the coachman first— Bigot's, an old one-eyed soldier of surpassing nerve, and devoted to his master. The crowd parted right and left. Suddenly the carriage stopped, and Bigot stood up, folding his arms, and glancing round with a disdainful smile without speaking a word. He carried a paper in one hand.

Here were at least two thousand armed and unarmed peasants, sick with misery and oppression, in the presence of their undefended tyrant. One shot, one blow of a stone, one stroke of a knife—to the end of a shameless pillage. But no hand was raised to do the deed. The roar of voices subsided—he waited for it—and silence was broken only by the crackle of the burning building, the tramp of Montcalm's soldiers on Palace Hill, and the tolling of the cathedral bell. I thought it strange that almost as Bigot issued forth the wild clanging gave place to a cheerful peal.

After standing for a moment, looking round him, his eye resting on Doltaire and myself (we were but a little distance from him), Bigot said in a loud voice: "What do you want with me? Do you think I may be moved by threats? Do you punish me by burning your own food, which, when the English are at our doors, is your only hope? Fools! How easily could I turn my cannon and my men upon you! You think to frighten me. Who do you think I am—a Bostonnais or an Englishman? You—revolutionists! T'sh! You are wild dogs without a leader. You want one that you can trust; you want no coward, but one who fears you not at your wildest. Well, I will be your leader. I do not fear you, and I do not love you, for how might you deserve love? By ingratitude and aspersion? Who has the King's favour? François Bigot. Who has the ear of the Grande Marquise? François Bigot. Who stands firm while others tremble lest their power pass to-morrow? François Bigot. Who else dare invite revolution, this danger "—his hand sweeping to the flames—"who but François Bigot?" He paused for a moment, and looking up to the leader of Montcalm's soldiers on the Heights, waved him back; then continued:

"And to-day, when I am ready to give you great news, you play the mad dog's game; you destroy what I had meant to give you in our hour of danger, when those English came. I made you suffer a little, that you might live then. Only to-day, because of our great and glorious victory——"

He paused again. The peal of bells became louder. Far up on the Heights we heard the calling of bugles and the beating of drums; and now I saw the whole large plan, the deep dramatic scheme. He had withheld the news of the victory that he might announce it when it would most turn to his own glory. Perhaps he had not counted on the burning of the warehouse, but this would tell now in his favour. He was not a large man, but he drew himself up with dignity, and continued in a contemptuous tone:

"Because of our splendid victory, I designed to tell you all my plans, and, pitying your trouble, divide among you at the smallest price, that all might pay, the corn which now goes to feed the stars."

At that moment some one from the Heights above called out shrilly, "What lie is in that paper, François Bigot?"

I looked up, as did the crowd. A woman stood upon a point of the great rock, a red robe hanging on her, her hair free over her shoulders, her finger pointing at the Intendant. Bigot only glanced up, then smoothed out the paper.

He said to the people in a clear but less steady voice, for I could see that the woman had disturbed him, " Go pray to be forgiven for your insolence and folly. His most Christian Majesty is triumphant upon the Ohio. The English have been killed in thousands, and their General with them. Do you not hear the joy-bells in the Church of Our Lady of the Victories? and more—listen!"

There burst from the Heights on the other side a cannon shot, and then another and another. There was a great commotion, and many ran to Bigot's carriage, reached in to touch his hand, and called down blessings on him.

"See that you save the other granaries," he urged, adding, with a sneer, "and forget not to bless La Friponne in your prayers!"

It was a clever piece of acting. Presently from the Heights above came the woman's voice again, so piercing that the crowd turned to her.

"François Bigot is a liar and a traitor!" she cried. "Beware of François Bigot! God has cast him out."

A dark look came upon Bigot's face; but presently he turned, and gave a sign to some one near the palace. The doors of the courtyard flew open, and out came squad after squad of soldiers. In a moment, they, with the people, were busy carrying water to pour upon the side of the endangered warehouse. Fortunately the wind was with them, else it and the palace also would have been burned that night.

At last Bigot beckoned to Doltaire and to me and we both came over.

"Doltaire, we looked for you at dinner," he said. "Was Captain Moray"—nodding towards me—"lost among the petticoats? He knows the trick of cup and saucer. Between the sip and click he sucked in secrets from our garrison—a spy where had been a soldier, as we thought. You once wore a sword, Captain Moray—eh?"

"If the Governor would grant me leave, I would not only wear, but use one, your excellency knows well where," said I.

"Large speaking, Captain Moray. They do that in Virginia, I am told."

"In Gascony there's quiet, your excellency."

Doltaire laughed outright, for it was said that Bigot, in his coltish days, had a shrewish Gascon wife, whom he took leave to send to heaven before her time. I saw the Intendant's mouth twitch angrily.

"Come," he said, "you have a tongue; we'll see if you have a stomach. You've languished with the girls; you shall have your chance to drink with François Bigot. Now, if you dare, when we have drunk to the first cockcrow, should you be still on your feet, you'll fight some one among us, first giving ample cause."

"I hope, your excellency," I replied, with a touch of vanity, "I have still some stomach and a wrist. I will drink to cockcrow, if you will. And if my sword prove the stronger, what?"

"There's the point," he said. "Your Englishman loves not fighting for fighting's sake, Doltaire; he must have bonbons for it. Well, see: if your sword and stomach prove the stronger, you shall go your ways to where you will. Voila!"

If I could but have seen a bare portion of the craftiness of this pair of devil's artisans! They both had ends to serve in working ill to me, and neither was content that I should be shut away in the citadel, and no more.

There was a deeper game playing. I give them their due : the trap was skilful, and in those times, with great things at stake, strategy took the place of open fighting here and there. For Bigot I was to be a weapon against another; for Doltaire, against myself.

What a gull they must have thought me ! I might have known that, with my lost papers on the way to France, they must hold me tight here till I had been tried, nor permit me to escape. But I was sick of doing nothing, thinking with horror on a long winter in the citadel, and I caught at the least straw of freedom.

" Captain Moray will like to spend a couple of hours at his lodgings before he joins us at the palace," the Intendant said, and with a nod to me he turned to his coachman. The horses wheeled, and in a moment the great doors opened, and he had passed inside to applause, though here and there among the crowd was heard a hiss, for the Scarlet Woman had made an impression. The Intendant's men essayed to trace these noises, but found no one. Looking again to the Heights, I saw that the woman had gone. Doltaire noted my glance and the inquiry in my face, and he said :

" Some bad fighting hours with the Intendant· at Château Bigot, and then a fever, bringing a kind of madness : so the story creeps about, as told by Bigot's enemies."

Just at this point I felt a man hustle me as he passed. One of the soldiers made a thrust at him, and he turned round. I caught his eye, and it flashed something to me. It was Voban the barber, who had shaved me every day for months when I first came, while my arm was stiff from a wound got fighting the French on the Ohio. It was quite a year since I had met him, and I was struck by the change in his face. It had grown much older ; its roundness was gone. We had had many

3

a talk together, he helping me with French, I listening to the tales of his early life in France, and to the later tale of a humble love, and of the home which he was fitting up for his Mathilde, a peasant girl of much beauty I was told, but whom I had never seen. I remembered at that moment, as he stood in the crowd looking at me, the piles of linen which he had bought at Ste. Anne de Beaupré, and the silver pitcher which his grandfather had got from the Duc de Valois for an act of merit. Many a time we had discussed the pitcher and the deed and fingered the linen, now talking in French, now in English ; for in France, years before, he had been a valet to an English officer at King Louis's court. But my surprise had been great when I learned that this English gentleman was no other than the best friend I ever had, next to my parents and my grandfather. Voban was bound to Sir John Godric by as strong ties of affection as I. What was more, by a secret letter I had sent to Mr. George Washington, who was then as good a Briton as myself, I had been able to have my barber's young brother, a prisoner of war, set free.

I felt that he had something to say to me now ; but he turned away and disappeared among the crowd. I might have had some clew if I had known that he had been crouched behind the Intendant's carriage while I was being bidden to the supper. I did not guess then that there was anything between him and the Scarlet Woman who railed at Bigot.

In a little while I was at my lodgings, soldiers posted at my door and one in my room. Doltaire had gone to his own quarters promising to call for me within two hours. There was little for me to do but to put in a bag the fewest necessaries, to roll up my heavy cloak, to stow safely my pipes and two goodly packets of tobacco, which were to be my chiefest solace for many a long day, and to write some letters—one to Governor Dinwiddie, one to Major Washington, one to my partner in Virginia, telling them my fresh misfortunes, and begging them to send me money, which, however useless in my captivity, would be important in my fight for life and freedom. I did not write intimately of my state, for I was not sure my letters would ever pass outside Quebec. There were only two men I could trust to do the thing. One was a fellow-countryman, Clark, a ship-carpenter, and something of a ruffian, who, to save his neck and to spare his wife and child, had turned Catholic, but who hated all Frenchmen barbarously at heart, remembering two of his bairns butchered before his eyes. The other was Voban. I knew that though Voban might not act he would not betray me. But how to reach either of them? It was clear that I must bide my chances.

One other letter I wrote, brief but vital, in which I begged the sweetest girl in the world not to have uneasiness because of me; that I trusted to my star and to my innocence to convince my judges; and begging her, if she could, to send me a line at the citadel. I told her I knew well how hard it all would be, for her mother and her father would not now look upon my love with favour. But I trusted everything to time and Providence.

I sealed my letters, put them in my pocket, and sat down to smoke and think while I waited for Doltaire. To the soldier on duty whom I did not notice at first I now offered a pipe and a glass of wine, which he accepted rather gruffly, but enjoyed, if I might judge by his devotion to them.

By-and-bye, without any relevancy at all, he said abruptly, " If a little sooner she had come—aho ! "

For a moment I could not think what he meant; but soon I saw.

" The palace would have been burned if the girl in

scarlet had come sooner—eh?" I asked. "She would have urged the people on?"

"And Bigot burnt too, maybe," he answered.

"Fire and death—eh?"

I offered him another pipeful of tobacco. He looked doubtful, but accepted.

"Aho! And that Voban, he would have had his hand in," he growled.

I began to get more light.

"She was shut up at Château Bigot—hand of iron and lock of steel—who knows the rest? But Voban was for always," he added presently.

The thing was clear. The Scarlet Woman was Mathilde. So here was the end of Voban's little romance—of the fine linen from Ste. Anne de Beaupré and the silver pitcher for the wedding wine. I saw, or felt, that in Voban I might find now a confederate, if I put my hard case on Bigot's shoulders.

"I can't see why she stayed with Bigot," I said tentatively.

"Break the dog's leg, it can't go hunting bones —*mais, non!* Holy, how stupid are you English!"

"Why doesn't the Intendant lock her up now? She's dangerous to him! You remember what she said?"

"*Tonnerre*, you shall see to-morrow," he answered; "now all the sheep go bleating with the bell. Bigot—Bigot—Bigot—there is nothing but Bigot! But, pish! Vaudreuil the Governor is the great man, and Montcalm, aho! son of Mahomet! You shall see. Now they dance to Bigot's whistling; he will lock her safe enough to-morrow, 'less some one steps in to help her. Before to-night she never spoke of him before the world—but a poor daft thing, going about all sad and wild. She missed her chance to-night—aho!"

" Why are you not with Montcalm's soldiers ? " I asked.
" You like him better."

" I was with him, but my time was out, and I left him
for Bigot.   Pish ! I left him for Bigot, for the militia ! "
He raised his thumb to his nose, and spread out his fingers.   Again light dawned on me.   He was still with the
Governor in all fact, though soldiering for Bigot—a sort
of watch upon the Intendant.

I saw my chance.   If I could but induce this fellow to
fetch me Voban !   There was yet an hour before I was to
go to the intendance.

I called up what looks of candour I could and told
him bluntly that I wished Voban to bear a letter for me
to the Seigneur Duvarney's.   At that he cocked his ear
and shook his bushy head, fiercely stroking his mustaches.

I knew that I should stake something if I said it was
a letter for Mademoiselle Duvarney, but I knew also that
if he was still the Governor's man in Bigot's pay he would
understand the Seigneur's relations with the Governor.
And a woman in the case with a soldier—that would
count for something.   So I said it was for her.   Besides,
I had no other resource but to make a friend among my
enemies if I could, while yet there was a chance.

It was like a load lifted from me when I saw his mouth
and eyes open wide in a big soundless laugh, which came
to an end with a voiceless *aho !*   I gave him another tumbler of wine.   Before he took it, he made a wide mouth
at me again, and slapped his leg.   After drinking, he
said, "*Poom*—what good ?   They're going to hang you
for a spy."

" That rope's not ready yet," I answered.   " I'll tie a
pretty knot in another string first, I trust."

" Damned if you haven't spirit ! " said he.   " That
Seigneur Duvarney, I know him ; and I know his son the
ensign—*whung*, what saltpetre is he !   And the ma'm'selle

—excellent, excellent; and a face, such a face, and a seat like leeches in the saddle. And you a British officer mewed up to kick your heels till gallows day! So droll, my dear!"

"But will you fetch Voban?" I asked.

"To trim your hair against the supper to-night—eh, like that?"

As he spoke he puffed out his red cheeks with wide boylike eyes, burst his lips in another soundless laugh, and laid a finger beside his nose. His marvellous innocence of look and his peasant openness hid, I saw, great shrewdness and intelligence—an admirable man for Vaudreuil's purpose, as admirable for mine. I knew well that if I had tried to bribe him he would have scouted me, or if I had made a motion for escape he would have shot me off-hand. But a lady—that appealed to him; and that she was the Seigneur Duvarney's daughter did the rest.

"Yes, yes," said I, "one must be well appointed in soul and body when one sups with his excellency and Monsieur Doltaire."

"Limed inside and chalked outside," he retorted gleefully. "But M'sieu' Doltaire needs no lime, for he has no soul. No, by Sainte Héloïse! The good God didn't make him. The devil laughed, and that laugh grew into M'sieu' Doltaire. But brave!—no kicking pulse is in his body."

"You will send for Voban—now?" I asked softly.

He was leaning against the door as he spoke. He reached and put the tumbler on a shelf, then turned and opened the door, his face all altered to a grimness.

"Attend here, Labrouk!" he called; and on the soldier coming, he blurted out in scorn, "Here's this English captain can't go to supper without Voban's shears to snip him. Go fetch him, for I'd rather hear a calf in a

barn-yard than this whing-whanging for ' M'sieu' Voban ! ' "

He mocked my accent in the last two words, so that
the soldier grinned, and at once started away. Then he
shut the door, and turned to me again, and said more
seriously , " How long have we before Master Devil
comes ? "—meaning Doltaire.

" At least an hour," said I.

" Good," he rejoined, and then he smoked while I sat
thinking.

It was near an hour before we heard footsteps outside ;
then came a knock, and Voban was shown in.

" Quick, m'sieu'," he said. " M'sieu' is almost at our
heels."

" This letter," said I, " to Mademoiselle Duvarney,"
and I handed four : hers, and those to Governor Dinwiddie, to Mr. Washington, and to my partner.

He quickly put them in his coat, nodding. The
soldier—I have not yet mentioned his name—Gabord,
knew not that more than one passed into Voban's
hands.

" Off with your coat, m'sieu'," said Voban, whipping
out his shears, tossing his cap aside, and rolling down his
apron. " M'sieu' is here."

I had off my coat, was in a chair in a twinkling, and
he was clipping softly at me as Doltaire's hand turned the
handle of the door.

" Beware—to-night ! " Voban whispered.

" Come to me in the prison," said I. " Remember
your brother ! "

His lips twitched. " M'sieu', I will if I can." This
he said in my ear as Doltaire entered and came forward.

" Upon my life ! " Doltaire broke out. " These English gallants ! They go to prison curled and musked by

Voban. *Voban*—a name from the court of the King, and it garnishes a barber! Who called you, Voban?"

"My mother, with the curé's help, m'sieu'."

Doltaire paused, with a pinch of snuff at his nose, and replied lazily, "I did not say 'Who called you *Voban?*' Voban, but who called you here, Voban?"

I spoke up testily then of purpose: "What would you have, monsieur? The citadel has better butchers than barbers. I sent for him."

He shrugged his shoulders and came over to Voban. "Turn round, my Voban," he said. "*Voban*—and such a figure! a knee, a back like that!"

Then, while my heart stood still, he put forth a finger and touched the barber on the chest. If he should touch the letters! I was ready to seize them—but would that save them? Twice, thrice, the finger prodded Voban's breast, as if to add an emphasis to his words. "In Quebec you are misplaced, Monsieur le Voban. Once a wasp got into a honeycomb and died."

I knew he was hinting at the barber's resentment of the poor Mathilde's fate. Something strange and devilish leaped into the man's eyes, and he broke out bitterly,

"A honey-bee got into a nest of wasps—and died."

I thought of the Scarlet Woman on the hill.

Voban looked for a moment as if he might do some wild thing. His spirit, his devilry, pleased Doltaire, and he laughed. "Who would have thought our Voban had such wit? The trade of barber is double-edged. Razors should be in fashion at Versailles."

Then he sat down, while Voban made a pretty show of touching off my person. A few minutes passed so, in which the pealing of bells, the shouting of the people, the beating of drums, and the calling of bugles came to us clearly.

A half hour afterwards, on our way to the Intendant's

palace, we heard the Benedictus chanted in the Church of the Recollets, as we passed—hundreds kneeling outside, and responding to the chant sung within:

" *That we should be saved from our enemies, and from the hands of all that hate us.*"

At the corner of a building which we passed, a little away from the crowd, I saw a solitary cloaked figure. The words of the chant, following us, I could hear distinctly:

" *That we, being delivered out of the hands of our enemies, might serve Him without fear.*"

And then, from the shadowed corner came in a high, melancholy voice the words:

" *To give light to them that sit in darkness and in the shadow of death, and to guide our feet into the way of peace.*"

Looking closer, I saw it was Mathilde.

Doltaire smiled as I turned and begged a moment's time to speak to her.

" To pray with the lost angel and sup with the Intendant, all in one night—a liberal taste, monsieur; but who shall stay the good Samaritan!"

They stood a little distance away, and I went over to her and said, " Mademoiselle—Mathilde, do you not know me?"

Her abstracted eye fired up, as there ran to her brain some little sprite out of the House of Memory and told her who I was.

" There were two lovers in the world," she said; " the Mother of God forgot them, and the devil came. I am the Scarlet Woman," she went on; " I made this red robe from the curtains of Hell——"

Poor soul! My own trouble seemed then as a speck among the stars to hers. I took her hand and held it, saying again, " Do you not know me? Think, Mathilde!"

I was not sure that she had ever seen me, to know me, but I thought it possible; for, as a hostage, I had been much noticed in Quebec, and Voban had, no doubt, pointed me out to her. Light leaped from her black eye, and then she said, putting her finger on her lips, "Tell all the lovers to hide. I have seen a hundred François Bigots."

I looked at her, saying nothing—I knew not what to say. Presently her eye steadied to mine, and her intellect rallied. "You are a prisoner, too," she said; "but they will not kill you: they will keep you till the ring of fire grows in your head, and then you will make your scarlet robe, and go out, but you will never find It—never. God hid first, and then It hides. . . . It hides, that which you lost—It hides, and you can not find It again. You go hunting, hunting, but you can not find It."

My heart was pinched with pain. I understood her. She did not know her lover now at all. If Alixe and her mother at the Manor could but care for her, I thought. But, alas! what could I do? It were useless to ask her to go to the Manor; she would not understand.

Perhaps there come to the disordered mind flashes of insight, illuminations and divinations, deeper than are given to the sane, for she suddenly said in a whisper, touching me with a nervous finger, "I will go and tell her where to hide. They shall not find her. I know the woodpath to the Manor. Hush! she shall own all I have —except the scarlet robe. She showed me where the May-apples grew. Go"—she pushed me gently away— "go to your prison, and pray to God. But you can not kill François Bigot—he is a devil." Then she thrust into my hands a little wooden cross, which she took from many others at her girdle. "If you wear that the ring of fire will not grow," she said. "I will go by the wood-path, and give her one, too. She shall live with me: I will spread the balsam branches and stir the fire. She

The Intendant's Palace.

shall be safe. Hush! Go, go softly, for their wicked eyes
are everywhere, the were-wolves!"

She put her fingers on my lips for an instant, and
then, turning, stole softly away towards the St. Charles
River.

Doltaire's mockery brought me back to myself.

"So much for the beads of the addled; now for the
bowls of sinful man," said he.

III.

THE WAGER AND THE SWORD.

As I entered the Intendant's palace with Doltaire I
had a singular feeling of elation. My spirits rose unac-
countably, and I felt as though it were a *fête* night, and
the day's duty over, the hour of play was come. I must
needs have felt ashamed of it then, and now, were I
not sure it was some unbidden operation of the senses.
Maybe a merciful Spirit sees how, left alone, we should
have stumbled and lost ourselves in our own gloom, and
so gives us a new temper fitted to our needs. I remember
that at the great door I turned back and smiled upon the
ruined granary, and sniffed the air laden with the scent
of burnt corn—the people's bread; that I saw old men
and women who could not be moved by news of victory,
shaking with cold, even beside this vast furnace, and
peevishly babbling of their hunger, and I did not say,
"Poor souls!" that for a time the power to feel my own
misfortunes seemed gone, and a hard, light indifference
came on me.

For it is true I came into the great dining-hall, and
looked upon the long loaded table, with its hundred candles, its flagons and pitchers of wine, and on the faces of

so many idle, careless gentlemen bid to a carouse, with a
manner, I believe, as reckless and jaunty as their own.
And I kept it up, though I saw it was not what they
had looked for. I did not at once know who was there,
but presently, at a distance from me, I saw the face of
Juste Duvarney, the brother of my sweet Alixe, a man
of but twenty or so, who had a name for wildness, for no
badness that I ever heard of, and for a fiery temper. He
was in the service of the Governor, an ensign. He had
been little at home since I had come to Quebec, having
been employed up to the past year in the service of the
Governor of Montreal. We bowed, but he made no motion to come to me, and the Intendant engaged me almost
at once in gossip of the town ; suddenly, however, diverg-
ing upon some questions of public tactics and civic government. He much surprised me, for though I knew him
brave and able, I had never thought of him save as the
adroit politician and servant of the King, the tyrant and
the libertine. I might have known by that very scene a
few hours before that he had a wide, deep knowledge of
human nature, and despised it ; unlike Doltaire, who had
a keener mind, was more refined even in wickedness, and,
knowing the world, laughed at it more than he despised
it, which was the sign of the greater mind. And indeed,
in spite of all the causes I had to hate Doltaire, it is but
just to say he had by nature all the large gifts—misused
and disordered as they were. He was the product of his
age ; having no real moral sense, living life wantonly,
making his own law of right or wrong. As a lad, I was
taught to think the evil person carried evil in his face, re-
pelling the healthy mind ; but long ago I found that this
was error. I had no reason to admire Doltaire, and yet
to this hour his handsome face, with its shadows and
shifting lights, haunts me, charms me. The thought
came to me as I talked with the Intendant, and I looked

round the room. Some present were of coarse calibre—
bushranging sons of seigneurs and petty nobles, dashing
and profane, and something barbarous; but most had
gifts of person and speech, and all seemed capable.

My spirits continued high. I sprang alertly to meet
wit and gossip, my mind ran nimbly here and there, I
filled the rôle of honoured guest. But when came the
table and wine, a change befell me. From the first drop
I drank, my spirits suffered a decline. On one side the
Intendant rallied me, on the other Doltaire. I ate on,
drank on; but while smiling by the force of will, I grew
graver little by little. Yet it was a gravity which had no
apparent motive, for I was not thinking of my troubles,
not even of the night's stake and the possible end of it
all; simply a sort of gray colour of the mind, a stillness
in the nerves, a general seriousness of the senses. I drank,
and the wine did not affect me, while voices got loud and
louder, and glasses rang, and spurs rattled on shuffling
heels, and a scabbard clanged on a chair. I seemed to
feel and know it all in some far-off way, but I was not
touched by the spirit of it, was not a part of it. I watched
the reddened cheeks and loose scorching mouths around
me with a sort of distant curiosity, and the ribald jests
flung right and left struck me not at all acutely. It was
as if I were reading a Book of Bacchus. I drank on even-
ly, not doggedly, and answered jest for jest without a hot
breath of drunkenness. I looked several times at Juste
Duvarney, who sat not far away, on the other side of the
table, behind a grand piece of silver filled with October
roses. He was drinking hard, and Doltaire, sitting beside
him, kept him at it. At last the silver piece was shifted,
and he and I could see each other fairly. Now and then
Doltaire spoke across to me, but somehow no word passed
between Duvarney and myself.

Suddenly, as if by magic—I know it was preconcerted

—the talk turned on the events of the evening and on the defeat of the British. Then, too, I began to be myself again, and a sense of my position grew upon me. I had been withdrawn from all real feeling and living for hours, but I believe that same suspension was my salvation. For with every man present deeply gone in liquor round me —every man save Doltaire—I was sane and steady, settling into a state of great alertness, determined on escape, if that could be, and bent on turning every chance to serve my purposes.

Now and again I caught my own name mentioned with a sneer, then with remarks of surprise, then with insolent laughter. I saw it all. Before dinner some of the revellers had been told of the new charge against me, and, by instruction, had kept it till the inflammable moment. Then the why and wherefore of my presence at this supper being in the hazard, the stake, as a wicked jest of Bigot's, was mentioned. I could see the flame grow inch by inch, fed by the Intendant and Doltaire, whose hateful final move I was yet to see. For one instant I had a sort of fear, for I was now sure they meant I should not leave the room alive; but anon I felt a river of fiery anger flow through me, rousing me, making me loathe the faces of them all. Yet not all, for in one pale face, with dark, brilliant eyes, I saw the looks of my flower of the world: the colour of her hair in his, the clearness of the brow, the poise of the head—how handsome he was !—the light, springing step, like a deer on the sod of June. I call to mind when I first saw him. He was sitting in a window of the Manor, just after he had come from Montreal, playing a violin which had once belonged to De Casson, the famous priest whose athletic power and sweet spirit endeared him to New France. His fresh cheek was bent to the brown, delicate wood, and he was playing to his sister the air of the undying chanson, " Je vais mourir pour ma belle reine." I loved the look of his face, like that of a young Apollo, open, sweet, and bold, all his body having the epic strength of life. I wished that I might have him near me as a comrade, for out of my hard experience I could teach him much, and out of his youth he could soften my blunt nature, by comradeship making flexuous the hard and ungenial.

I went on talking to the Intendant, while some of the guests rose and scattered about the rooms, at tables, to play picquet, the jesting on our cause and the scorn of myself abating not at all. I would not have it thought that anything was openly coarse or brutal; it was all by innuendo, and brow-lifting, and maddening, allusive phrases such as it is thought fit for gentlefolk to use instead of open charge. There was insult in a smile, contempt in the turn of a shoulder, challenge in the flicking of a handkerchief. With great pleasure I could have wrung their noses one by one, and afterwards have met them, tossing sword-points, in the same order. I wonder now that I did not tell them so, for I was ever hasty; but my brain was clear that night, and I held myself in due check, letting each move come from my enemies. There was no reason why I should have been at this wild feast at all, I, a prisoner charged with being a spy, save because of some plot through which fresh suffering should come to me and some one else be benefited—though how that might be I could not guess at first.

But soon I understood everything. Presently I heard a young gentleman say to Duvarney over my shoulder:

"Eating comfits and holding yarn — that was his doing at your manor when Doltaire came hunting him."

"He has dined at your table, Lancy," broke out Duvarney hotly.

"But never with our ladies," was the biting answer.

" Should prisoners make conditions ? " was the sharp, insolent retort.

The insult was conspicuous, and trouble might have followed, but that Doltaire came between them, shifting the attack.

" Prisoners, my dear Duvarney," said he, " are most delicate and exacting; they must be fed on wine and milk. It is an easy life, and hearts grow soft for them. As thus—— Indeed, it is most sad: so young and gallant; in speech, too, so confiding! And if we babble all our doings to him, think you he takes it seriously? No, no—so gay and thoughtless, there is a thoroughfare from ear to ear, and all's lost on the other side. Poor simple gentleman, he is a claimant on our courtesy, a knight without a sword, a guest without the power to leave us— he shall make conditions, he shall have his caprice. La, la! my dear Duvarney and my Lancy!"

He spoke in a clear, provoking tone, putting a hand upon the shoulder of each young gentleman as he talked, his eyes wandering over me idly, and beyond me. I saw that he was now sharpening the sickle to his office. His next words made this more plain to me:

"And if a lady gives a farewell sign to one she favours for the moment, shall not the prisoner take it as his own?" (I knew he was recalling Alixe's farewell gesture to me at the manor.) "Who shall gainsay our peacock? Shall the guinea cock? The golden crumb was thrown to the guinea cock, but that's no matter. The peacock clatters of the crumb." At that he spoke an instant in Duvarney's ear. I saw the lad's face flush, and he looked at me angrily.

Then I knew his object: to provoke a quarrel between this young gentleman and myself, which might lead to evil ends; and the Intendant's share in the conspiracy was to revenge himself upon the Seigneur for his close friendship with the Governor. If Juste Duvarney were killed in the duel which they foresaw, so far as Doltaire was concerned I was out of the counting in the young lady's sight. In any case my life was of no account, for I was sure my death was already determined on. Yet it seemed strange that Doltaire should wish me dead, for he had reasons for keeping me alive, as shall be seen.

Juste Duvarney liked me once, I knew, but still he had the Frenchman's temper, and had always to argue down his bias against my race and to cherish a good heart towards me; for he was young, and sensitive to the opinions of his comrades. I can not express what misery possessed me when I saw him leave Doltaire, and, coming to me where I stood alone, say—

"What secrets found you at our seigneury, monsieur?"

I understood the taunt—as though I were the common interrogation mark, the abominable Paul Pry. But I held my wits together.

"Monsieur," said I, "I found the secret of all good life: a noble kindness to the unfortunate."

There was a general laugh, led by Doltaire, a concerted influence on the young gentleman. I cursed myself that I had been snared to this trap.

"The insolent," responded Duvarney, "not the unfortunate."

"Insolence is no crime, at least," I rejoined quietly, "else this room were a penitentiary."

There was a moment's pause, and presently, as I kept my eye on him, he raised his handkerchief and flicked me across the face with it, saying, "Then this will be a virtue, and you may have more such virtues as often as you will."

In spite of will, my blood pounded in my veins, and a devilish anger took hold of me. To be struck across the face by a beardless Frenchman, scarce past his teens!—it

4

shook me more than now I care to own. I felt my cheek burn, my teeth clinched, and I know a kind of snarl came from me; but again, all in a moment, I caught a turn of his head, a motion of the hand, which brought back Alixe to me. Anger died away, and I saw only a youth flushed with wine, stung by suggestions, with that foolish pride the youngster feels—and he was the youngest of them all —in being as good a man as the best, and as daring as the worst. I felt how useless it would be to try the straightening of matters there, though had we two been alone a dozen words should have been enough. But to try was my duty, and I tried with all my might; almost, for Alixe's sake, with all my heart.

"Do not trouble to illustrate your meaning," said I patiently. "Your phrases are clear and to the point."

"You bolt from my words," he retorted, "like a shy mare on the curb; you take insult like a donkey on a well-wheel. What fly will the English fish rise to? Now it no more plays to my hook than an August chub."

I could not help but admire his spirit and the sharpness of his speech, though it drew me into a deeper quandary. It was clear that he would not be tempted to friendliness; for, as is often so, when men have said things fiercely, their eloquence feeds their passion and convinces them of holiness in their cause. Calmly, but with a heavy heart, I answered:

"I wish not to find offence in your words, my friend, for in some good days gone you and I had good acquaintance, and I can not forget that the last hours of a light imprisonment before I entered on a dark one were spent in the home of your father—of the brave Seigneur whose life I once saved."

I am sure I should not have mentioned this in any other situation—it seemed as if I were throwing myself on his mercy; but yet I felt it was the only thing to do

—that I must bridge this affair, if at cost of some reputation.

It was not to be. Doltaire, seeing that my words had indeed affected my opponent, said : "A double retreat! He swore to give a challenge to-night, and he cries off like a sheep from a porcupine; his courage is so slack he dares not move a step to his liberty. It was a bet, a hazard. He was to drink glass for glass with any and all of us, and fight sword for sword with any of us who gave him cause. Having drunk his courage to death, he'd now browse at the feet of those who give him chance to win his stake."

His words came slowly and bitingly, yet with an air of damnable nonchalance. I looked round me. Every man present was full-sprung with wine, and a distance away, a gentleman on either side of him, stood the Intendant, smiling detestably, a keen, houndlike look shooting out of his small round eyes.

I had had enough; I could bear no more. To be baited like a bear by these Frenchmen—it was aloes in my teeth! I was not sorry then that these words of Juste Duvarney's gave me no chance of escape from fighting; though I wished it had been any other man in the room than he. It was on my tongue to say that if some gentleman would take up his quarrel I should be glad to drive mine home, though for reasons I cared not myself to fight Duvarney. But I did not, for I knew that to carry that point farther might rouse a general thought of Alixe, and I had no wish to make matters hard for her. Everything in its own good time, and when I should be free! So, without more ado, I said to him :

"Monsieur, the quarrel was of your choosing, not mine. There was no need for strife between us, and you have more to lose than I : more friends, more years of life, more hopes. I have avoided your bait, as you call it, for your sake, not mine own. Now I take it, and you, monsieur, show us what sort of fisherman you are."

All was arranged in a moment. As we turned to pass from the room to the courtyard, I noted that Bigot was gone. When we came outside, it was just one, as I could tell by a clock striking in a chamber near. It was cold, and some of the company shivered as we stepped upon the white, frosty stones. The late October air bit the cheek, though now and then a warm, pungent current passed across the courtyard—the breath from the people's burnt corn. Even yet upon the sky was the reflection of the fire, and distant sounds of singing, shouting, and carousal came to us from the Lower Town.

We stepped to a corner of the yard and took off our coats; swords were handed us—both excellent, for we had had our choice of many. It was partial moonlight, but there were flitting clouds. That we should have light however pine torches had been brought, and these were stuck in the wall. My back was to the outer wall of the courtyard, and I saw the Intendant at a window of the palace looking down at us. Doltaire stood a little apart from the other gentlemen in the courtyard, yet where he could see Duvarney and myself at advantage.

Before we engaged, I looked intently into my opponent's face, and measured him carefully with my eye, that I might have his height and figure explicit and exact; for I know how moonlight and fire distort, how the eye may be deceived. I looked for every button; for the spot in his lean, healthy body where I could disable him, spit him, and yet not kill him—for this was the thing furthest from my wishes, God knows. Now the deadly character of the event seemed to impress him, for he was pale, and the liquor he had drunk had given him dark hollows round the eyes, and a gray shining sweat was on his cheek. But the eyes themselves were fiery and keen and there was reckless daring in every turn of his body.

I was not long in finding his quality, for he came at me violently from the start, and I had chance to know his strength and his weakness also. His hand was quick, his sight clear and sure, his knowledge to a certain point most definite and practical, his mastery of the sword delightful; but he had little imagination, he was merely a brilliant performer, he did not conceive. I saw that if I put him on the defensive I should have him at advantage, for he had not that art of the true swordsman, the prescient quality which foretells the opponent's action and stands prepared. There I had him at fatal advantage—could, I felt, give him last reward of insult at my pleasure. Yet a lust of fighting got into me, and it was difficult to hold myself in check at all, nor was it easy to meet his breathless and adroit advances.

Then, too, remarks from the bystanders worked me up to a deep sort of anger, and I could feel Doltaire looking at me with that still, cold face of his, an ironical smile at his lips. Now and then, too, a ribald jest came from some young roisterer near, and the fact that I stood alone among sneering enemies wound me up to a point where pride was more active than aught else. I began to press him a little, and I pricked him once. Then a singular feeling possessed me. I would bring this to an end when I had counted ten; I would strike home when I said " ten."

So I began, and I was not then aware that I was counting aloud. " One—two—three ! " It was weird to the onlookers, for the yard grew still, and you could hear nothing save perhaps a shifting foot or a hard breathing. " Four—five—six ! " There was a tenseness in the air, and Juste Duvarney, as if he felt a menace in the words, seemed to lose all sense of wariness, and came at me lunging, lunging with great swiftness and heat. I was incensed now, and he must take what fortune might send ; one can not guide one's sword to do least harm fighting as did we.

I had lost blood, and the game could go on no longer. " Eight ! " I pressed him sharply now. " Nine ! " I was preparing for the trick which would end the matter, when I slipped on the frosty stones, now glazed with our tramping back and forth, and trying to recover myself left my side open to his sword. It came home, though I partly diverted it. I was forced to my knees, but there, mad, unpardonable youth, he made another furious lunge at me. I threw myself back, deftly avoided the lunge, and he came plump on my upstretched sword, gave a long gasp, and sank down.

At that moment the doors of the courtyard opened, and men stepped inside, one coming quickly forward before the rest. It was the Governor, the Marquis de Vaudreuil. He spoke, but what he said I knew not, for the stark upturned face of Juste Duvarney was there before me, there was a great buzzing in my ears, and I fell back into darkness.

IV.

THE RAT IN THE TRAP.

WHEN I waked I was alone. At first nothing was clear to me ; my brain was dancing in my head, my sight was obscured, my body painful, my senses were blunted. I was in darkness, yet through an open door there showed a light, which, from the smell and flickering, I knew to be a torch. This, creeping into my senses, helped me to remember that the last thing I saw in the Intendant's courtyard was a burning torch, which suddenly multiplied to dancing hundreds and then went out. I now stretched forth a hand, and it touched a stone wall; I moved, and felt straw under me. Then I fixed my eyes steadily on the open door and the shaking light, and presently it all came to me : the events of the night, and that I was now in a cell of the citadel. Stirring, I found that the wound in my body had been bound and cared for. A loosely tied scarf round my arm showed that some one had lately left me, and would return to finish the bandaging. I raised myself with difficulty, and saw a basin of water, a sponge, bits of cloth, and a pocket-knife. Stupid and dazed though I was, the instinct of self-preservation lived, and I picked up the knife and hid it in my coat. I did it, I believe, mechanically, for a hundred things were going through my mind at the time.

All at once there rushed in on me the thought of Juste Duvarney as I saw him last—how long ago was it ? —his white face turned to the sky, his arms stretched out, his body dabbled in blood. I groaned aloud. Fool, fool ! to be trapped by these lying French ! To be tricked into playing their shameless games for them, to have a broken body, to have killed the brother of the mistress of my heart, and so cut myself off from her and ruined my life for nothing—for worse than nothing ! I had swaggered, boasted, had taken a challenge for a bout and a quarrel like any hanger-on of a tavern.

Suddenly I heard footsteps and voices outside, then one voice, louder than the other, saying, " He hasn't stirred a peg—lies like a log ! " It was Gabord.

Doltaire's voice replied, " You will not need a surgeon —no ? " His tone, as it seemed to me, was less careless than usual.

Gabord answered, " I know the trick of it all—what can a surgeon do ? This brandy will fetch him to his intellects. And by-and-bye crack'll go his spine—aho ! "

You have heard a lion growling on a bone. That is how Gabord's voice sounded to me then—a brutal rawness; but it came to my mind also that this was the man who had brought Voban to do me service!

"Come, come, Gabord, crack your jaws less, and see you fetch him on his feet again," said Doltaire. "From the seats of the mighty they have said that he must live—to die another day; and see to it, or the mighty folk will say that you must die to live another day—in a better world, my Gabord."

There was a moment in which the only sound was that of tearing linen, and I could see the shadows of the two upon the stone wall of the corridor wavering to the light of the torch; then the shadows shifted entirely, and their footsteps came on towards my door. I was lying on my back as when I came to, and, therefore, probably as Gabord had left me, and I determined to appear still in a faint. Through nearly closed eyelids however I saw Gabord enter. Doltaire stood in the doorway watching as the soldier knelt and lifted my arm to take off the bloody scarf. His manner was imperturbable as ever. Even then I wondered what his thoughts were, what pungent phrase he was suiting to the time and to me. I do not know to this day which more interested him—that very pungency of phrase, or the critical events which inspired his reflections. He had no sense of responsibility; but his mind loved talent, skill, and cleverness, and though it was scathing of all usual ethics, for the crude, honest life of the poor it had sympathy. I remember remarks of his in the market-place a year before, as he and I watched the peasant in his sabots and the good-wife in her homespun cloth.

"These are they," said he, "who will save the earth one day, for they are like it, kin to it. When they are born they lie close to it, and when they die they fall no height to reach their graves. The rest—the world—are like ourselves in dreams : we do not walk; we think we fly, over houses, over trees, over mountains; and then one blessed instant the spring breaks, or the dream gets twisted, and we go falling, falling, in a sickening fear, and, waking up, we find we are and have been on the earth all the while, and yet can make no claim upon it, and have no kin with it, and no right to ask anything of it— *quelle vie—quelle vie !* "

Sick as I was, I thought of that as he stood there, looking in at me ; and though I knew I ought to hate him I admired him in spite of all.

Presently he said to Gabord, " You'll come to me at noon to-morrow, and see you bring good news. He breathes ? "

Gabord put a hand on my chest and at my neck, and said at once, " Breath for balloons—aho ! "

Doltaire threw a cloak over his shoulder and walked away, his footsteps sounding loud in the passages. Gabord began humming to himself as he tied the bandages, and then he reached down for the knife to cut the flying strings. I could see this out of a little corner of my eye. When he did not find it, he settled back on his haunches and looked at me. I could feel his lips puffing out, and I was ready for the " *Poom !* " that came from him. Then I could feel him stooping over me, and his hot strong breath in my face. I was so near to unconsciousness at that moment by a sudden anxiety that perhaps my feigning had the look of reality. In any case, he thought me unconscious and fancied that he had taken the knife away with him ; for he tucked in the strings of the bandage. Then, lifting my head, he held the flask to my lips ; for which I was most grateful—I was dizzy and miserably faint.

I think I came to with rather more alacrity than was

wise, but he was deceived, and his first words were, " Ho, ho ! the devil's knocking ; who's for home, angels ? "

It was his way to put all things allusively, using strange figures and metaphors. Yet, when one was used to him and to them, their potency seemed greater than polished speech and ordinary phrase.

He offered me more brandy, and then, without preface, I asked him the one question which sank back on my heart like a load of ice even as I sent it forth. " Is he alive ? " I inquired. " Is Monsieur Juste Duvarney alive ? "

With exasperating coolness he winked an eye, to connect the event with what he knew of the letter I had sent to Alixe, and, cocking his head, he blew out his lips with a soundless laugh, and said :

" To whisk the brother off to heaven is to say good-bye to sister and pack yourself to Father Peter."

" For God's sake, tell me, is the boy dead ? " I asked, my voice cracking in my throat.

" He's not mounted for the journey yet," he answered, with a shrug, " but the Beast is at the door."

I plied my man with questions, and learned that they had carried Juste into the palace for dead, but found life in him, and straightway used all means to save him. A surgeon came, his father and mother were sent for, and when Doltaire had left there was hope that he would live.

I learned also that Voban had carried word to the Governor of the deed to be done that night; had for a long time failed to get admittance to him, but was at last permitted to tell his story; and Vaudreuil had gone to Bigot's palace to have me hurried to the citadel, and had come just too late.

After answering my first questions, Gabord would say nothing more, and presently he took the torch from the wall and with a gruff good-night prepared to go. When

I asked that a light be left he shook his head and said he had no orders. Whereupon he left me, the heavy door clanging to, the bolts were shot, and I was alone in darkness with my wounds and misery. My cloak had been put into the cell beside my couch, and this I now drew over me, and I lay and thought upon my condition and my prospects, which, as may be seen, were not cheering. I did not suffer great pain from my wounds—only a stiffness that troubled me not at all if I lay still. After an hour or so had passed—for it is hard to keep count of time when one's thoughts are the only timekeeper—I fell asleep.

I know not how long I slept, but I awoke refreshed. I stretched forth my uninjured arm, moving it about. In spite of will a sort of hopelessness went through me, for I could feel long blades of corn grown up about my couch, an unnatural meadow, springing from the earth floor of my dungeon. I drew the blades between my fingers, feeling towards them as if they were things of life out of place like myself. I wondered what colour they were. Surely, said I to myself, they can not be green, but rather a yellowish white, bloodless, having only fibre, the heart all pinched to death. Last night I had not noted them, yet now, looking back, I saw, as in a picture, Gabord the soldier feeling among them for the knife that I had taken. So may we see things, and yet not be conscious of them at the time, waking to their knowledge afterwards. So may we for years look upon a face without understanding, and then, suddenly, one day it comes flashing out, and we read its hidden story like a book.

I put my hand out farther, then brought it back near to my couch, feeling towards its foot mechanically, and now I touched an earthen pan. A small board lay across its top, and moving my fingers along it I found a piece

of bread. Then I felt the jar, and knew it was filled
with water. Sitting back I thought hard for a moment.
Of this I was sure : the pan and bread were not there
when I went to sleep, for this was the spot where my
eyes fell naturally while I lay in bed looking towards
Doltaire ; and I should have remembered it now, even
if I had not noted it then. My jailer had brought these
while I slept. But it was still dark. I waked again as
though out of sleep, startled : I was in a dungeon that
had no window !

Here I was, packed away in the farthest corner of
the citadel, in a deep hole that maybe had not been used
for years, to be, no doubt, denied all contact with the
outer world—I was going to say *friends*, but whom could
I name among them save that dear soul who, by last
night's madness, should her brother be dead, was forever
made dumb and blind to me ? Whom had I but her
and Voban !—and Voban was yet to be proved. The
Seigneur Duvarney had paid all debts he may have
owed me, and he now might, because of the injury to his
son, leave me to my fate. On Gabord the soldier I could
not count at all.

There I was, as Doltaire had said, like a rat in a trap.
But I would not let panic seize me. So I sat and ate the
stale but sweet bread, took a long drink of the good water
from the earthen jar, and then, stretching myself out,
drew my cloak up to my chin, and settled myself for sleep
again. And that I might keep up a kind delusion that I
was not quite alone in the bowels of the earth I reached
out my hand and affectionately drew the blades of corn
between my fingers.

Presently I drew my chin down to my shoulder, and let
myself drift out of painful consciousness almost as easily
as a sort of woman can call up tears at will. When I
waked again, it was without a start or moving, without

confusion, and I was bitterly hungry. Beside my couch, with his hands on his hips and his feet thrust out, stood Gabord, looking down at me in a quizzical and unsatisfied way. A torch was burning near him.

" Wake, my dickey-bird," said he in his rough, mocking voice, " and we'll snuggle you into the pot. You've been long hiding ; come out of the bush—aho ! "

I drew myself up painfully. " What is the hour ? " I asked, and meanwhile I looked for the earthen jar and the bread.

" Hour since when ? " said he.

" Since it was twelve o'clock last night," I answered.

" Fourteen hours since *then*," said he.

The emphasis arrested my attention. " I mean," I added, " since the fighting in the courtyard."

" Thirty-six hours and more since then, m'sieu' the dormouse," was his reply.

I had slept a day and a half since the doors of this cell closed on me. It was Friday then, now it was Sunday afternoon. Gabord had come to me three times, and seeing how sound asleep I was had not disturbed me, but had brought bread and water—my prescribed diet.

He stood there, his feet buried in the blanched corn— I could see the long yellowish-white blades—the torch throwing shadows about him, his back against the wall. I looked carefully round my dungeon. There was no sign of a window; I was to live in darkness. Yet if I were but allowed candles, or a lantern, or a torch, some books, paper, pencil, and tobacco, and the knowledge that I had not killed Juste Duvarney, I could abide the worst with some sort of calmness. How much might have happened, must have happened, in all those hours of sleep ! My letter to Alixe should have been delivered long ere this; my trial, no doubt, had been decided on. What had Voban done? Had he any word for me? Dear

Lord! here was a mass of questions tumbling one upon the other in my head, while my heart thumped behind my waistcoat like a rubber ball to a prize-fighter's fist. Misfortunes may be so great and many that one may find grim humour and grotesqueness in their impossible con-junction and multiplicity. I remembered at that moment a friend of mine in Virginia, the most unfortunate man I ever knew. Death, desertion, money losses, political de-feat, flood, came one upon the other all in two years, and coupled with this was loss of health. One day he said to me :

" Robert, I have a perforated lung, my liver is a swell-ing sponge, eating crowds my waistband like a balloon, I have a swimming in my head and a sinking at my heart, and I can not say litany for happy release from these for my knees creak with rheumatism. The devil has done his worst, Robert, for these are his—plague and pesti-lence, being final, are the will of God—and, upon my soul, it is an absurd comedy of ills! " At that he had a fit of coughing, and I gave him a glass of spirits, which eased him.

" That's better," said I cheerily to him.

" It's robbing Peter to pay Paul," he answered; " for I owed it to my head to put the *quid refert* there, and here it's gone to my lungs to hurry up my breathing. Did you ever think, Robert," he added, " that this breath-ing of ours is a labour, and that we have to work every second to keep ourselves alive? We have to pump air in and out like a blacksmith's boy." He said it so drolly, though he was deadly ill, that I laughed for half an hour at the stretch, wiping away my tears as I did it; for his pale gray face looked so sorry, with its quaint smile and that odd, dry voice of his.

As I sat there in my dungeon, with Gabord cocking his head and his eyes rolling, that scene flashed on me, and I laughed freely—so much that Gabord sulkily puffed out his lips, and flamed like bunting on a coast-guard's hut. The more he scowled and spluttered, the more I laughed, till my wounded side hurt me and my arm had twinges. But my mood changed suddenly, and I politely begged his pardon, telling him frankly then and there what had made me laugh, and how I had come to think of it. The flame passed out of his cheeks, the revolving fire of his eyes dimmed, his lips broke into a soundless laugh, and then, in his big voice, he said :

" You've got your knees to pray on yet, and crack my bones, but you'll have need to con your penitentials if tattle in the town be true."

" Before you tell of that," said I, " how is young Monsieur Duvarney ? Is—is he alive ? " I added, as I saw his look lower.

" The Beast was at door again last night, wild to be off, and foot of young Seigneur was in the stirrup, when along comes sister with drug got from an Indian squaw who nursed her when a child. She gives it him, and he drinks ; they carry him back, sleeping, and Beast must stand there tugging at the leathers yet."

" His sister—it was his sister," said I, " that brought him back to life ? "

" Like that—aho ! They said she must not come, but she will have her way. Straight she goes to the palace at night, no one knowing but—guess who ? You can't— but no ! "

A light broke in on me. " With the Scarlet Woman —with Mathilde," I said, hoping in my heart that it was so, for somehow I felt even then that she, poor vagrant, would play a part in the history of Alixe's life and mine.

" At the first shot," he said. " 'Twas the crimson one, as quiet as a baby chick, not hanging to ma'm'selle's skirts, but watching and whispering a little now and then—and she there in Bigot's palace, and he not knowing! And maids do not tell him, for they knew poor wench in better days—aho!"

I got up with effort and pain, and made to grasp his hand in gratitude, but he drew back, putting his arms behind him.

"No, no," said he, "I am your jailer. They've put you here to break your high spirits, and I'm to help the breaking."

"But I thank you just the same," I answered him; "and I promise to give you as little trouble as may be while you are my jailer—which, with all my heart, I hope may be as long as I'm a prisoner."

He waved out his hands to the dungeon walls, and lifted his shoulders as if to say that I might as well be docile, for the prison was safe enough. "*Poom!*" said he, as if in genial disdain of my suggestion.

I smiled, and then, after putting my hands on the walls here and there to see if they were, as they seemed, quite dry, I drew back to my couch and sat down. Presently I stooped to tip the earthen jar of water to my lips, for I could not lift it with one hand, but my humane jailer took it from me and held it to my mouth. When I had drunk, "Do you know," asked I as calmly as I could, "if our barber gave the letter to Mademoiselle?"

"M'sieu', you've travelled far to reach that question," said he, jangling his keys as if he enjoyed it. "And if he had—— ?"

I caught at his vague suggestion, and my heart leaped.

"A reply," said I, "a message or a letter," though I had not dared to let myself even think of that.

He whipped a tiny packet from his coat. "'Tis a sparrow's pecking—no great matter here, eh?"—he weighed it up and down on his fingers—"a little piping wren's *par pitié*."

I reached out for it. "I should read it," said he. "There must be no more of this. But new orders came *after* I'd got her dainty *à m'sieu'!* Yes, I must read it," said he—"but maybe not at first," he added, "not at first, if you'll give word of honour not to tear it."

"On my sacred honour," said I, reaching out still.

He looked it all over again provokingly, and then lifted it to his nose, for it had a delicate perfume. Then he gave a little grunt of wonder and pleasure, and handed it over.

I broke the seal, and my eyes ran swiftly through the lines, traced in a firm, delicate hand. I could see through it all the fine, sound nature, by its healthy simplicity mastering anxiety, care, and fear.

"Robert," she wrote, "by God's help my brother will live, to repent with you, I trust, of Friday night's ill work. He was near gone, yet we have held him back from that rough-rider, Death.

"You will thank God, will you not, that my brother did not die? Indeed, I feel you have. I do not blame you; I know—I need not tell you how—the heart of the affair; and even my mother can see through the wretched thing. My father says little, and he has not spoken harshly; for which I gave thanksgiving this morning in the chapel of the Ursulines. Yet you are in a dungeon, covered with wounds of my brother's making, both of you victims of others' villainy, and you are yet to bear worse things, for they are to try you for your life. But never shall I believe that they will find you guilty of dishonour. I have watched you these three years; I do not, nor ever will, doubt you, dear friend of my heart.

"You would not believe it, Robert, and you may
5

think it fanciful, but as I got up from my prayers at the chapel I looked towards a window, and it being a little open, for it is a sunny day, there sat a bird on the sill, a little brown bird that peeped and nodded. I was so won by it that I came softly over to it. It did not fly away, but hopped a little here and there. I stretched out my hand gently on the stone, and putting its head now this side, now that, at last it tripped into it, and chirped most sweetly. After I had kissed it I placed it back on the window-sill, that it might fly away again. Yet no, it would not go, but stayed there, tipping its gold-brown head at me as though it would invite me to guess why it came. Again I reached out my hand, and once more it tripped into it. I stood wondering and holding it to my bosom, when I heard a voice behind me say, ' The bird would be with thee, my child. God hath many signs.' I turned and saw the good Mère St. George looking at me, she of whom I was always afraid, so distant is she. I did not speak, but only looked at her, and she nodded kindly at me and passed on.

" And, Robert, as I write to you here in the Intendant's palace (what a great, wonderful place it is ! I fear I do not hate it and its luxury as I ought !), the bird is beside me in a cage upon the table, with a little window open, so that it may come out if it will. My brother lies in the bed asleep ; I can touch him if I but put out my hand, and I am alone save for one person. You sent two messengers : can you not guess the one that will be with me ? Poor Mathilde, she sits and gazes at me till I almost fall weeping. But she seldom speaks, she is so quiet—as if she knew that she must keep a secret. For, Robert, though I know you did not tell her, she knows —she knows that you love me, and she has given me a little wooden cross which she says will make us happy.

" My mother did not drive her away, as I half feared

she would, and at last she said that I might house her with one of our peasants. Meanwhile she is with me here. She is not so mad but that she has wisdom too, and she shall have my care and friendship.

"I bid thee to God's care, Robert. I need not tell thee to be not dismayed. Thou hast two jails, and one wherein I lock thee safe is warm and full of light. If the hours drag by, think of all thou wouldst do if thou wert free to go to thine own country—yet alas that thought!—and of what thou wouldst say if thou couldst speak to thy   ALIXE.

"*Postscript*.—I trust that they have cared for thy wounds, and that thou hast light and food and wine. Voban hath promised to discover this for me. The soldier Gabord, at the citadel, he hath a good heart. Though thou canst expect no help from him, yet he will not be rougher than his orders. He did me a good service once, and he likes me, and I him. And so fare thee well, Robert. I will not languish; I will act, and not be weary. Dost thou really love me?"

V.

THE DEVICE OF THE DORMOUSE.

WHEN I had read the letter, I handed it up to Gabord without a word. A show of trust in him was the only thing, for he had knowledge enough of our secret to ruin us, if he chose. He took the letter, turned it over, looking at it curiously, and at last, with a shrug of the shoulders, passed it back.

"'Tis a long tune on a dot of a fiddle," said he, for indeed the letter was but a small affair in bulk. "I'd need two pairs of eyes and telescope! Is it all Heart-o'-

my-heart, and Come-trip-in-dewy-grass—aho? Or is there knave at window to bear m'sieu' away?"

I took the letter from him. "Listen," said I, "to what the lady says of you." And then I read him that part of her postscript which had to do with himself.

He put his head on one side like a great wise magpie, and "H'm—ha!" said he whimsically, "aho! Gabord the soldier, Gabord, thou hast a good heart—and the birds fed the beast with plums and froth of comfits till he died, and on his sugar tombstone they carved the words, ' Gabord had a good heart.'"

"It was spoken out of a true spirit," said I petulantly, for I could not bear from a common soldier even a tone of disparagement, though I saw the exact meaning of his words. So I added, "You shall read the whole letter, or I will read it to you and you shall judge. On the honour of a gentleman, I will read all of it!"

"*Poom!*" said he, "English fire-eater! corn-cracker! Show me the ' good heart' sentence, for I'd see how it is written—how *Gabord* looks with a woman's whimsies round it."

I traced the words with my fingers, holding the letter near the torch. "' Yet he will not be rougher than his orders,'" said he after me, and "' He did me a good service once.'"

"Comfits," he continued; "well, thou shalt have comfits, too," and he fished from his pocket a parcel. It was my tobacco and my pipe.

Truly, my state might have been vastly worse. Little more was said between Gabord and myself, but he refused bluntly to carry message or letter to anybody, and bade me not vex him with petitions. But he left me the torch and a flint and steel, so I had light for a space, and I had my blessed tobacco and pipe. When the doors clanged shut and the bolts were shot I lay back on my couch.

I was not all unhappy. Thank God, they had not put chains on me, as Governor Dinwiddie had done with a French prisoner at Williamsburg, for whom I had vainly sought to be exchanged two years before, though he was my equal in all ways and importance. Doltaire was the cause of that, as you shall know. Well, there was one more item to add to his indebtedness. My face flushed and my fingers tingled at thought of him, and so I resolutely turned my meditations elsewhere, and again in a little while I seemed to think of nothing, but lay and bathed in the silence, and indulged my eyes with the good red light of the torch, inhaling its pitchy scent. I was conscious, yet for a time I had no thought: I was like something half animal, half vegetable, which feeds, yet has no mouth, nor sees, nor hears, nor has sense, but only lives. I seemed hung in space, as one feels when going from sleep to waking—a long lane of half-numb life, before the open road of full consciousness is reached.

At last I was aroused by the sudden cracking of a knot in the torch. I saw that it would last but a few hours more. I determined to put it out, for I might be allowed no more light, and even a few minutes of this torch every day would be a great boon. So I took it from its place, and was about to quench it in the moist earth at the foot of the wall, when I remembered my tobacco and my pipe. Can you think how joyfully I packed full the good brown bowl, delicately filling in every little corner, and at last held it to the flame, and saw it light? That first long whiff was like the indrawn breath of the cold, starved hunter, when, stepping into his house, he sees food, fire, and wife on his hearthstone. Presently I put out the torchlight, and then went back to my couch and sat down, the bowl shining like a star before me.

There and then a purpose came to me—something which would keep my brain from wandering, my nerves

from fretting and wearing, for a time at least. I determined to write to my dear Alixe the true history of my
life, even to the point—and after—of this thing which was
bringing me to so ill a pass. But I was in darkness, I had
no paper, pens, nor ink. After a deal of thinking I came
at last to the solution. I would compose the story, and
learn it by heart, sentence by sentence as I so composed it.

So there and then I began to run back over the
years of my life, even to my first remembrances, that I
might see it from first to last in a sort of whole and with
a kind of measurement. But when I began to dwell upon
my childhood, one little thing gave birth to another
swiftly, as you may see one flicker in the heaven multiply
and break upon the mystery of the dark, filling the night
with clusters of stars. As I thought, I kept drawing
spears of the dungeon corn between my fingers softly (they
had come to be like comrades to me), and presently there
flashed upon me the very first memory of my life. It
had never come to me before, and I knew now that it was
the beginning of conscious knowledge : for we can never
know till we can remember. When a child remembers
what it sees or feels it has begun life.

I put that recollection into the letter which I wrote
Alixe, and it shall be set down forthwith and in little
space, though it took me so very many days and weeks to
think it out, to give each word a fixed place, so that it
should go from my mind no more. Every phrase of that
story as I told it is as fixed as stone in my memory. Yet
it must not be thought I can give all here. I shall set
down only a few things, but you shall find in them the
spirit of the whole. I will come at once to the body of
the letter.

VI.

MORAY TELLS THE STORY OF HIS LIFE.

" . . . I WOULD have you know of what I am and whence I came, though I have given you glimpses in the past. That done, I will make plain why I am charged with this that puts my life in danger, which would make you blush that you ever knew me if it were true. And I will show you first a picture as it runs before me, sitting here, the corn of my dungeon garden twining in my fingers:—

" A multiplying width of green grass spotted with white flowers, an upland where sheep browsed on a carpet of purple and gold and green, a tall rock on a hill where birds perched and fluttered, a blue sky arching over all. There, sprawling in a garden, a child pulled at long blades of grass, as he watched the birds flitting about the rocks, and heard a low voice coming down the wind. Here in my dungeon I can hear the voice as I have not heard it since that day in the year 1730—that voice stilled so long ago. The air and the words come floating down (for the words I knew years afterwards) :

> ' Did ye see the white cloud in the glint o' the sun?
>   That's the brow and the eye o' my bairnie.
> Did ye ken the red bloom at the bend o' the crag ?
>   That's the rose in the cheek o' my bairnie.
> Did ye hear the gay lilt o' the lark by the burn ?
>   That's the voice of my bairnie, my dearie.
> Did ye smell the wild scent in the green o' the wood?
>   That's the breath o' my ain, o' my bairnie.
> Sae I'll gang awa' hame, to the shine o' the fire,
>   To the cot where I lie wi' my bairnie.'

" These words came crooning over the grass of that little garden at Balmore which was by my mother's home.

There I was born one day in June, though I was reared in the busy streets of Glasgow, where my father was a prosperous merchant and famous for his parts and honesty.

"I see myself, a little child of no great strength, for I was, indeed, the only one of my family who lived past infancy, and my mother feared she should never bring me up. She, too, is in that picture, tall, delicate, kind yet firm of face, but with a strong brow, under which shone grave gray eyes, and a manner so distinguished that none might dispute her kinship to the renowned Montrose, who was lifted so high in dying, though his gallows was but thirty feet, that all the world has seen him there. There was one other in that picture, standing near my mother, and looking at me, who often used to speak of our great ancestor—my grandfather, John Mitchell, the Gentleman of Balmore, as he was called, out of regard for his ancestry and his rare merits.

"I have him well in mind : his black silk breeches and white stockings and gold seals, and two eyes that twinkled with great humour when, as he stooped over me, I ran my head between his calves and held him tight. I recall how my mother said, 'I doubt that I shall ever bring him up,' and how he replied (the words seem to come through great distances to me), 'He'll live to be Montrose the second, rascal laddie ! Four seasons at the breast ? Tut, tut ! what o' that ! 'Tis but his foolery, his scampishness ! Nae, nae ! his epitaph's no for writing till you and I are tucked i' the sod, my Jeanie. Then, like Montrose's, it will be—

> 'Tull Edinburrow they led him thair,
>   And on a gallows hong ;
> They hong him high abone the rest,
>   He was so trim a boy.'

"I can hear his laugh this minute, as he gave an accent to the words by stirring me with his stick, and I caught the gold head of it and carried it off, trailing it through the garden, till I heard my mother calling, and then forced her to give me chase, as I pushed open a little gate and posted away into that wide world of green, coming quickly to the river, where I paused and stood at bay. I can see my mother's anxious face now, as she caught me to her arms; and yet I know she had a kind of pride, too, when my grandfather said, on our return, 'The rascal's at it early. Next time he'll ford the stream and skirl at ye, Jeanie, from yonner bank.'

"This is the first of my life that I remember. It may seem strange to you that I thus suddenly recall not only it, but the words then spoken too. It is strange to me, also. But here it comes to me all on a sudden in this silence, as if another self of me were speaking from far places. At first all is in patches and confused, and then it folds out—if not clearly, still so I can understand—and the words I repeat come as if filtered through many brains to mine. I do not say that it is true—it may be dreams; and yet, as I say, it is firmly in my mind.

"The next that I remember was climbing upon a chair to reach for my grandfather's musket, which hung across the chimney. I got at last upon the mantelshelf, and my hands were on the weapon, when the door opened, and my grandfather and my father entered. I was so busy I did not hear them till I was caught by the legs and swung to a shoulder, where I sat kicking. 'You see his tastes, William,' said my grandfather to my father; 'he's white o' face and slim o' body, but he'll no carry on your hopes.' And more he said to the point, though what it was I knew not. But I think it to have been suggestion (I heard him say it later) that I would bring Glasgow up to London by the sword (good doting soul!)

as my father brought it by manufactures, gaining honour thereby.

"However that may be, I would not rest till my grandfather had put the musket into my arms. I could scarcely lift it, but from the first it had a charm for me, and now and then, in spite of my mother's protests, I was let to handle it, to learn its parts, to burnish it, and by-and-bye—I could not have been more than six years old—to rest it on a rock and fire it off. It kicked my shoulder roughly in firing, but I know I did not wink as I pulled the trigger. Then I got a wild hunger to fire it at all times; so much so, indeed, that powder and shot were locked up, and the musket was put away in my grandfather's chest. But now and again it was taken out, and I made war upon the unresisting hillside, to the dismay of our neighbours in Balmore. Feeding the fever in my veins, my grandfather taught me soldiers' exercises and the handling of arms : to my dear mother's sorrow, for she ever fancied me as leading a merchant's quiet life like my father's, hugging the hearthstone, and finding joy in small civic duties, while she and my dear father sat peacefully watching me in their decline of years.

"I have told you of that river which flowed near my father's house. At this time most of my hours were spent by it in good weather, for at last my mother came to trust me alone there, having found her alert fears of little use. But she would very often come with me and watch me as I played there. I loved to fancy myself a miller, and my little mill-wheel, made by my own hands, did duty here and there on the stream, and many drives of logs did I, in fancy, saw into piles of lumber, and loads of flour sent away to the City of Desire. Then, again, I made bridges, and drove mimic armies across them; and if they were enemies, craftily let them partly cross, to tumble them in at the moment when part of the forces were on one side of the stream and part on the other, and at the mercy of my men.

" My grandfather taught me how to build forts and breastworks, and I lay in ambush for the beadle, who was my good friend, for my grandfather, and for half a dozen other village folk, who took no offence at my sport, but made believe to be bitterly afraid when I surrounded them and drove them, shackled, to my fort by the river. Little by little the fort grew, until it was a goodly pile ; for now and then a village youth helped me, or again an old man, whose heart, maybe, rejoiced to play at being child again with me.   Years after, whenever I went back to Balmore, there stood the fort, for no one ever meddled with it, or tore it down.

" And I will tell you one reason why this was, and you will think it strange that it should have played such a part in the history of the village, as in my own life. You must know that people living in secluded places are mostly superstitious.   Well, when my fort was built to such proportions that a small ladder must be used to fix new mud and mortar in place upon it, something happened.

" Once a year there came to Balmore—and he had done so for a generation—one of those beings called The Men, who are given to prayer, fasting, and prophesying, who preach the word of warning ever, calling even the ministers of the Lord sharply to account.   One day this Man came past my fort, folk with him, looking for preaching or prophecy from him.   Suddenly turning he came inside my fort, and, standing upon the ladder against the wall, spoke to them fervently.   His last words became a legend in Balmore, and spread even to Glasgow and beyond.

" ' Hear me ! ' cried he.   ' As I stand looking at ye

from this wall, calling on ye in your natural bodies to take refuge in the Fort of God, the Angel of Death is looking ower the battlements of heaven, choosing ye out, the sheep frae the goats; calling the one to burning flames, and the other into peaceable habitations. I hear the voice now,' cried he, 'and some soul among us goeth forth. Flee ye to the Fort of Refuge!' I can see him now, his pale face shining, his eyes burning, his beard blowing in the wind, his grizzled hair shaking on his forehead. I had stood within the fort watching him. At last he turned, and, seeing me intent, stooped, caught me by the arms, and lifted me upon the wall. 'See you,' said he, 'yesterday's babe a warrior to-day. Have done, have done, ye quarrelsome hearts. Ye that build forts here shall lie in darksome prisons; there is no fort but the Fort of God. The call comes frae the white ramparts. Hush!' he added solemnly, raising a finger. 'One of us goeth hence this day; are ye ready to walk i' the fearsome valley?'

"I have heard my mother speak these words over often, and they were, as I said, like an old song in Balmore and Glasgow. He set me down, and then walked away, waving the frightened people back; and there was none of them that slept that night.

"Now comes the stranger thing. In the morning The Man was found dead in my little fort, at the foot of the wall. Henceforth the spot was sacred, and I am sure it stands there as when last I saw it twelve years ago, but worn away by rains and winds.

Again and again my mother said over to me his words, 'Ye that build forts here shall lie in darksome prisons'; for always she had fear of the soldier's life, and she was moved by signs and dreams.

But this is how the thing came to shape my life:

"About a year after The Man died, there came to my

grandfather's house, my mother and I being present, a gentleman, by name Sir John Godric, and he would have my mother tell the whole story of The Man. That being done, he said that The Man was his brother, who had been bad and wild in youth, a soldier; but repenting had gone as far the other way, giving up place and property, and cutting off from all his kin.

"This gentleman took much notice of me and said that he should be glad to see more of me. And so he did, for in the years that followed he would visit at our home in Glasgow when I was at school, or at Balmore until my grandfather died.

"My father liked Sir John greatly, and they grew exceeding friendly, walking forth in the streets of Glasgow, Sir John's hand upon my father's arm. One day they came to the school in High Street, where I learned Latin and other accomplishments, together with fencing from an excellent master, Sergeant Dowie of the One Hundredth Foot. They found me with my regiment at drill; for I had got full thirty of my school-fellows under arms, and spent all leisure hours in mustering, marching, and drum-beating, and practising all manner of discipline and evolution which I had been taught by my grandfather and Sergeant Dowie.

"Those were the days soon after which came Dettingen and Fontenoy and Charles Edward the Pretender, and the ardour of arms ran high. Sir John was a follower of the Stuarts, and this was the one point at which he and my father paused in their good friendship. When Sir John saw me with my thirty lads marching in fine order, all fired with the little sport of battle—for to me it was all real, and our sham fights often saw broken heads and bruised shoulders—he stamped his cane upon the ground, and said in a big voice, 'Well done! well done! For that you shall have a hundred pounds next birthday, and as fine a suit of scarlet as you please, and a sword from London, too.'

"Then he came to me and caught me by both shoulders. 'But alack, alack! there needs some blood and flesh here, Robert Moray,' said he. 'You have more heart than muscle.'

This was true. I had ever been more eager than my strength—thank God, that day is gone!—and sometimes, after Latin and the drill of my Lightfoots, as I called them, I could have cried for weakness and weariness had I been a girl and not a proud lad. And Sir John kept his word, liking me better from that day forth, and coming now and again to see me at the school,—though he was much abroad in France—giving many a pound to my Lightfoots, who were no worse soldiers for that. His eye ran us over sharply, and his head nodded, as we marched past him; and once I heard him say, 'If they had had but ten years each on their heads, my Prince!'

"About this time my father died—that is, when I was fourteen years old. Sir John became one of the executors with my mother, and at my wish, a year afterwards, I was sent to the university, where at least fifteen of my Lightfoots went also; and there I formed a new battalion of them, though we were watched at first, and even held in suspicion, because of the known friendship of Sir John for me; and he himself had twice been under arrest for his friendship to the Stuart cause. That he helped Prince Charles was clear: his estates were mortgaged to the hilt.

"He died suddenly on that day of January when Culloden was fought, before he knew of the defeat of the Prince. I was with him at the last. After some serious business, which I shall come to by-and-bye, 'Robert,' said he, 'I wish thou hadst been with my Prince. When thou becomest a soldier, fight where thou hast heart to fight; but if thou hast conscience for it, let it be with a Stuart. I thought to leave thee a good moiety of my fortune, Robert, but little that's free is left for giving. Yet thou hast something from thy father, and down in Virginia, where my friend Dinwiddie is Governor, there's a plantation for thee, and a purse of gold, which was for me in case I should have cause to flee this troubled realm. But I need it not; I go for refuge to my Father's house. The little vineyard and the purse of gold are for thee, Robert. If thou thinkest well of it, leave this sick land for that new one. Build thyself a name in that great young country, wear thy sword honourably and bravely, use thy gifts in council and debate—for Dinwiddie will be thy friend—and think of me as one who would have been a father to thee if he could. Give thy good mother my loving farewells. . . . Forget not to wear my sword—it has come from the first King Charles himself, Robert.'

After which he raised himself upon his elbow and said, 'Life—life, is it so hard to untie the knot?' Then a twinge of agony crossed over his face, and afterwards came a great clearing and peace, and he was gone.

"King George's soldiers entered with a warrant for him even as he died and the same moment dropped their hands upon my shoulder. I was kept in durance for many days, and was not even at the funeral of my benefactor; but through the efforts of the provost of the university and some good friends who could vouch for my loyal principles I was released. But my pride had got a setback, and I listened with patience to my mother's prayers that I would not join the King's men. With the anger of a youth, I now blamed his Majesty for the acts of Sir John Godric's enemies. And though I was a good soldier of the King at heart, I would not serve him henceforth. We threshed matters back and forth, and presently it was thought I should sail to Virginia to take over my estate. My mother urged it, too, for she believed if I were weaned from my old comrades, military fame would no longer charm. So she urged me, and go I did, with a commission from some merchants of Glasgow, to give my visit to the colony more weight.

"It was great pain to leave my mother, but she bore the parting bravely, and away I set in a good ship. Arrived in Virginia, I was treated with great courtesy in Williamsburg, and the Governor gave me welcome to his home for the sake of his old friend ; and yet a little for my own, I think, for we were of one temper, though he was old and I young. We were both full of impulse and proud and given to daring hard things, and my military spirit suited him.

"In Virginia I spent a gay and busy year, and came off very well with the rough but gentlemanly cavaliers, who rode through the wide, sandy streets of the capital on excellent horses, or in English coaches, with a rusty sort of show and splendour, but always with great gallantry. The freedom of the life charmed me, and with rumours of war with the French there seemed enough to do, whether with the sword or in the House of Burgesses, where Governor Dinwiddie said his say with more force than complaisance. So taken was I with the life—my first excursion into the wide working world—that I delayed my going back to Glasgow, the more so that some matters touching my property called for action by the House of Burgesses, and I had to drive the affair to the end. Sir John had done better by me than he thought, and I thanked him over and over again for his good gifts.

"Presently I got a letter from my father's old partner to say that my dear mother was ill. I got back to Glasgow only in time—but how glad I was of that !—to hear her last words. When my mother was gone I turned towards Virginia with longing, for I could not so soon go against her wishes and join the King's army on the Continent, and less desire had I to be a Glasgow merchant. Gentlemen merchants had better times in Virginia. So there was a winding-up of the estate, not greatly to my pleasure; for it was found that by unwise ventures my father's partner had perilled the whole and lost part of the property. But as it was, I had a competence and several houses in Glasgow, and I set forth to Virginia with a goodly sum of money and a shipload of merchandise, which I should sell to merchants, if it chanced I should become a planter only. I was warmly welcomed by old friends and by the Governor and his family, and I soon set up an establishment of my own in Williamsburg, joining with a merchant there in business, while my land was worked by a neighbouring planter.

" Those were hearty days, wherein I made little money, but had much pleasure in the giving and taking of civilities, in throwing my doors open to acquaintances, and with my young friend, Mr. Washington, laying the foundation for a Virginian army, by drill and yearly duty in camp, with occasional excursions against the Indians. I saw very well what the end of our troubles with the French would be, and I waited for the time when I should put to keen use the sword Sir John Godric had given me. Life beat high then, for I was in the first flush of manhood, and the spirit of a rich new land was waking in us all, while in our vanity we held to and cherished forms and customs that one would have thought to see left behind in London streets and drawing-rooms. These things, these functions in a small place, kept us a little vain and proud, but, I also hope, it gave us some sense of civic duty.

" And now I come to that which will, comrade of my heart, bring home to your understanding what lies behind the charges against me :

6

" Trouble came between Canada and Virginia.   Major
Washington, one Captain Mackaye, and myself marched
out to the Great Meadows, where at Fort Necessity we
surrendered, after hard fighting, to a force three times our
number.   I, with one Captain Van Braam, became a hostage.   Monsieur Coulon Villiers, the French commander,
gave his bond that we should be delivered up when an
officer and two cadets, who were prisoners with us, should
be sent on.   It was a choice between Mr. Mackaye of the
Regulars and Mr. Washington, or Mr. Van Braam and
myself.   I thought of what would be best for the country ;
and besides, Monsieur Coulon Villiers pitched upon my
name at once, and held to it.   So I gave up my sword to
Charles Bedford, my lieutenant, with more regret than I
can tell, for it was sheathed in memories, charging him to
keep it safe—that he would use it worthily I knew.   And
so, sorrowfully bidding my friends good-by, away we went
upon the sorry trail of captivity, arriving in due time at
Fort Du Quesne, at the junction of the Ohio and the
Monongahela, where I was courteously treated.   There I
bettered my French and made the acquaintance of some
ladies from Quebec city, who took pains to help me with
their language.

" Now, there was one lady to whom I talked with some
freedom of my early life and of Sir John Godric.   She
was interested in all, but when I named Sir John she became at once impressed, and I told her of his great attach-
ment to Prince Charles.   More than once she returned to
the subject, begging me to tell her more ; and so I did,
still, however, saying nothing of certain papers Sir John
had placed in my care.   A few weeks after the first occa-
sion of my speaking, there was a new arrival at the fort.
It was—can you guess ?—Monsieur Doltaire.   The night
after his coming he visited me in my quarters, and after
courteous passages, of which I need not speak, he sud-

denly said, ' You have the papers of Sir John Godric—
those bearing on Prince Charles's invasion of England ? '

" I was stunned by the question, for I could not guess
his drift or purpose, though presently it dawned upon
me.—Among the papers were many letters from a great
lady in France, a growing rival with La Pompadour in
the counsels and favour of the King. She it was who
had a secret passion for Prince Charles, and these letters
to Sir John, who had been with the Pretender at Versailles, must prove her ruin if produced. I had promised
Sir John most solemnly that no one should ever have
them while I lived, except the great lady herself, that I
would give them to her some time, or destroy them. It
was Doltaire's mission to get these letters, and he had
projected a visit to Williamsburg to see me, having just
arrived in Canada, after a search for me in Scotland,
when word came from the lady gossip at Fort Du
Quesne (with whom he had been on most familiar terms
in Quebec) that I was there.

" When I said I had the papers, he asked me lightly
for ' those compromising letters,' remarking that a good
price would be paid, and adding my liberty as a pleasant
gift. I instantly refused, and told him I would not be
the weapon of La Pompadour against her rival. With
cool persistence he begged me to think again, for much
depended on my answer.

" ' See, monsieur le capitaine,' said he, ' this little
affair at Fort Necessity, at which you became a hostage,
shall or shall not be a war between England and France
as you shall dispose.' When I asked him how that was,
he said, ' First, will you swear that you will not, to aid
yourself, disclose what I tell you ? You can see that
matters will be where they were an hour ago in any case.'

" I agreed, for I could act even if I might not speak.
So I gave my word. Then he told me that if those letters

were not put into his hands, La Pompadour would be
enraged, and fretful and hesitating now would join Austria against England, since in this provincial war was
convenient cue for battle. If I gave up the letters, she
would not stir, and the disputed territory between us
should be by articles seded by the French.

"I thought much and long, during which he sat smoking and humming, and seeming to care little how my
answer went. At last I turned on him, and told him I
would not give up the letters, and if a war must hang
on a whim of malice, then, by God's help, the rightness
of our cause would be our strong weapon to bring France
to her knees.

"'That is your final answer?' asked he, rising, fin-
gering his lace, and viewing himself in a looking-glass
upon the wall.

"'I will not change it now or ever,' answered I.

"'Ever is a long time,' retorted he, as one might
speak to a wilful child. 'You shall have time to
think and space for reverie. For if you do not grant this
trifle you shall no more see your dear Virginia; and
when the time is ripe you shall go forth to a better land
as the Grande Marquise shall give you carriage.'

"'The Articles of Capitulation!' I broke out pro-
testingly.

"He waved his fingers at me. 'Ah, that,' he rejoined
—'that is a matter for conning. You are a hostage.
Well, we need not take any wastrel or nobody the English
offer in exchange for you. Indeed, why should we be
content with less than a royal duke? For you are worth
more to us just now than any prince we have ; at least so
says the Grande Marquise. Is your mind quite firm to
refuse?' he added, nodding his head in a bored sort of
way.

"'Entirely,' said I. 'I will not part with those letters.'

" ' But think once again,' he urged ; the gain of territory to Virginia, the peace between our countries!'

" ' Folly !' returned I.   ' I know well you overstate
the case.   You turn a small intrigue into a game of nations.   Yours is a schoolboy's tale, Monsieur Doltaire.'

" ' You are something of an ass,' he mused, and took
a pinch of snuff.

" ' And you—you have no name,' retorted I.

" I did not know, when I spoke, how this might strike
home in two ways or I should not have said it.   I had
not meant, of course, that he was King Louis's illegiti-
mate son.

" ' There is some truth in that,' he replied patiently,
though a red spot flamed high on his cheeks.   ' But
some men need no christening for their distinction, and
others win their names with proper weapons.   I am not
here to quarrel with you.   I am acting in a large affair
not in a small intrigue ; a century of fate may hang
on this.   Come with me,' he added.   ' You doubt my
power, maybe.'

" He opened the door of the cell, and I followed him
out, past the storehouse and the officers' apartments, to
the drawbridge.   Standing in the shadow by the gate he
took keys from his pocket.   ' Here,' said he, ' are what
will set you free.   This fort is all mine : I act for France.
Will you care to free yourself?   You shall have escort to
your own people.   You see I am most serious,' he added,
laughing lightly.   ' It is not my way to sweat or worry.
You and I hold war and peace in our hands.   Which
shall it be ?   In this trouble France or England will be
mangled.   It tires one to think of it when life can be so
easy.   Now, for the last time,' he urged, holding out the
keys.   ' Your word of honour that the letters shall be
mine—eh ? '

" ' Never,' I concluded.   ' England and France are in

greater hands than yours or mine. The God of battles
still stands beside the balances.'

"He shrugged a shoulder. 'Oh, well,' said he, 'that
ends it. It will be interesting to watch the way of the
God of battles. Meanwhile you travel to Quebec. Remember that however free you may appear you will have
watchers, that when you seem safe you will be in most
danger, that in the end we will have those letters or your
life ; that meanwhile the war will go on, that you shall
have no share in it, and that the whole power of England
will not be enough to set her hostage free. That is all
there is to say, I think. . . . Will you lift a glass of wine
with me ? ' he added courteously, waving a hand towards
the commander's quarters.

"I assented, for why, thought I, should there be a
personal quarrel between us ? We talked on many things
for an hour or more, and his I found the keenest mind
that ever I have met. There was in him a dispassionate-
ness, a breadth, which seemed most strange in a trifler of
the Court, in an exquisite—for such he was. I sometimes
think that his elegance and flippancy were deliberate, lest
he should be taking himself or life too seriously. His intelligence charmed me, held me, and, later, as we travelled
up to Quebec, I found my journey one long feast of interest. He was never dull, and his cynicism had an admirable
grace and cordiality. A born intriguer, he still was above
intrigue, justifying it on the basis that life was all sport.
In logic a leveller, praising the moles, as he called them,
the champion of the peasant, the apologist for the bourgeois—who always, he said, had civic virtues—he nevertheless held that what was was best, that it could not be
altered, and that it was all interesting. 'I never repent,'
he said to me one day. 'I have done after my nature, in
the sway and impulse of our time, and as the King has
said, After us the deluge. What a pity it is we shall see

neither the flood nor the ark! And so, when all is done, we shall miss the most interesting thing of all: ourselves dead and the gap and ruin we leave behind us. By that, from my standpoint,' he would add, 'life is a failure as a spectacle.'

"Talking in this fashion and in a hundred other ways, we came to Quebec. And you know in general what happened. I met your honoured father, whose life I had saved on the Ohio some years before, and he worked for my comfort in my bondage. You know how exchange after exchange was refused, and that for near three years I have been here, fretting my soul out, eager to be fighting in our cause, yet tied hand and foot, wasting time and losing heart, idle in an enemy's country. As Doltaire said, war was declared, but not till he had made here in Quebec last efforts to get those letters. I do not complain so bitterly of these lost years, since they have brought me the best gift of my life, your love and friendship; but my enemies here, commanded from France, have bided their time, till an accident has given them a cue to dispose of me without openly breaking the accepted law of nations. They could not decently hang a hostage, for whom they had signed articles; but they have got their chance, as they think, to try me for a spy.

"Here is the case. When I found that they were determined and had ever determined to violate their articles, that they never intended to set me free, I felt absolved from my duty as an officer on parole, and I therefore secretly sent to Mr. Washington in Virginia a plan of Fort Du Quesne and one of Quebec. I knew that I was risking my life by so doing, but that did not deter me. By my promise to Doltaire, I could not tell of the matter between us, and whatever he has done in other ways, he has preserved my life; for it would have been easy to have me dropped off by a stray bullet, or to have accidentally

drowned me in the St. Lawrence. I believe this matter of
the letters to be between myself and him and Bigot—
and perhaps not even Bigot, though surely he must know
that La Pompadour has some peculiar reason for interesting herself in a poor captain of provincials. You now can
see another motive for the duel which was brought about
between your brother and myself.

My plans and letters were given by Mr. Washington to
General Braddock, and the sequel you know: they have
fallen into the hands of my enemies, copies have gone to
France, and I am to be tried for my life. Preserving
faith with my enemy Doltaire, I can not plead the real
cause of my long detention; I can only urge that they had
not kept to their articles, and that I, therefore, was free
from the obligations of parole. I am sure they have no
intention of giving me the benefit of any doubt. My real
hope lies in escape and the intervention of England, though
my country, alas! has not concerned herself about me, as
if indeed she resented the non-delivery of those letters to
Doltaire, since they were addressed to one she looked on
as a traitor, and held by one whom she had unjustly put
under suspicion.

"So, dear Alixe, from that little fort on the banks of
the river Kelvin have come these strange twistings of my
life, and I can date this dismal fortune of a dungeon from
the day The Man made his prophecy from the wall of my
mud fort.

"Whatever comes now, if you have this record, you
will know the private history of my life. . . . I have told
all, with unpractised tongue, but with a wish to be understood, and to set forth a story of which the letter should
be as true as the spirit. Friend beyond all price to me,
some day this tale will reach your hands, and I ask you to
house it in your heart, and, whatever comes, let it be for
my remembrance. God be with you, and farewell!"

VII.

"QUOTH LITTLE GARAINE."

I HAVE given the story here as though it had been thought out and written that Sunday afternoon which brought me good news of Juste Duvarney. But it was not so. I did not choose to break the run of the tale to tell of other things and of the passing of time. The making took me many, many weeks, and in all that time I had seen no face but Gabord's, and heard no voice but his as he came twice a day to bring me bread and water. He would answer no questions concerning Juste Duvarney, or Voban, or Monsieur Doltaire, nor tell me anything of what was forward in the town. He had had his orders precise enough he said. At the end of all my hints and turnings and approaches, stretching himself up, and turning the corn about with his foot (but not crushing it, for he saw that I prized the poor little comrades), he would say :

"Snug, snug, quiet and warm! The cosiest nest in the world—aho!"

There was no coaxing him, and at last I desisted. I had no light. With resolution I set my mind to see in spite of the dark, and at the end of a month I was able to note the outlines of my dungeon ; nay, more, I was able to see my little field of corn ; and at last what joy I had when, hearing a little rustle near me, I looked closely and beheld a mouse running across the floor! I straightway began to scatter crumbs of bread, that it might, perhaps, come near me—as at last it did.

I have not spoken at all of my wounds, though they gave me many painful hours, and I had no attendance but my own and Gabord's. The wound in my side was long healing, for it was more easily disturbed as I turned in my sleep, while I could ease my arm at all times, and it came on slowly. My sufferings drew on my flesh, my blood, and my spirits, and to this was added that disease inaction, the corrosion of solitude, and the fever of suspense and uncertainty as to Alixe and Juste Duvarney. Every hour, every moment that I had ever passed in Alixe's presence, with many little incidents and scenes in which we shared, passed before me—vivid and cherished pictures of the mind. One of those incidents I will set down here.

A year or so before, soon after Juste Duvarney came from Montreal, he brought in one day from hunting a young live hawk, and put it in a cage. When I came the next morning, Alixe met me, and asked me to see what he had brought. There, beside the kitchen door, overhung with morning-glories and flanked by hollyhocks, was a large green cage, and in it the gray-brown hawk. "Poor thing, poor prisoned thing!" she said. "Look how strange and hunted it seems! See how its feathers stir! And those flashing, watchful eyes, they seem to read through you, and to say, 'Who are you? What do you want with me? Your world is not my world; your air is not my air; your homes are holes, and mine hangs high up between you and God. Who are you? Why do you pen me? You have shut me in that I may not travel not even die out in the open world. All the world is mine; yours is only a stolen field. Who are you? What do you want with me? There is a fire within my head, it eats to my eyes, and I burn away. What do you want with me?'"

She did not speak these words all at once as I have written them here, but little by little, as we stood there talking beside the cage. Yet, as she talked with me, her mind was on the bird, her fingers running up and down the cage bars soothingly, her voice now and again interjecting soft reflections and exclamations.

"Shall I set it free ? " I asked her.

She turned upon me and replied, "Ah, monsieur, I hoped you would—without my asking. You are a prisoner too," she added ; "one captive should feel for another."

"And the freeman for both," I answered meaningly, as I softly opened the cage.

She did not drop her eyes, but raised them shining honestly and frankly to mine, and said, "I wished you to think that."

Opening the cage door wide, I called the little captive to freedom. But while we stood close by it would not stir, and the look in its eyes became wilder. I moved away, and Alixe followed me. Standing beside an old well we waited and watched. Presently the hawk dropped from the perch, hopped to the door, then with a wild spring was gone, up, up, up, and was away over the maple woods beyond, lost in the sun and the good air.

I know not quite why I dwell on this scene, save that it throws some little light upon her nature, and shows how simple and yet deep she was in soul, and what was the fashion of our friendship. But I can perhaps give a clearer insight of her character if I here set down the substance of a letter written about that time, which came into my possession long afterwards. It was her custom to write her letters first in a book, and afterwards to copy them for posting. This she did that they might be an impulse to her friendships and a record of her feelings.

ALIXE DUVARNEY TO LUCIE LOTBINIÈRE.

QUEBEC CITY, *the 10th of May, 1756.*

MY DEAR LUCIE : I wish I knew how to tell you all I have been thinking since we parted at the door of the Ursulines a year ago. Then we were going to meet again in a few weeks, and now twelve months have gone ! How

have I spent them? Not wickedly, I hope, and yet sometimes I wonder if Mère St. George would quite approve
of me; for I have wild spirits now and then, and I
shout and sing in the woods and along the river as if I
were a mad youngster home from school. But indeed,
that is the way I feel at times, though again I am so quiet
that I am frightened of myself. I am a hawk to-day and
a mouse to-morrow, and fond of pleasure all the time. Ah,
what good days I have had with Juste! You remember
him before he went to Montreal? He is gay, full of
fancies, as brave as can be, and plays and sings well, but he
is very hot-headed, and likes to play the tyrant. We have
some bad encounters now and then. But we love each
other better for it; he respects me, and he does not become spoiled, as you will see when you come to us.

I have had no society yet. My mother thinks seventeen
years too few to warrant my going into the gay world. I
wonder will my wings be any stronger, will there be less
danger of scorching them at twenty-six? Years do not
make us wise; one may be as wise at twenty as at fifty.
And they do not save us from the scorching. I know
more than they guess how cruel the world may be to the
innocent as to—the other. One can not live within sight
of the Intendant's palace and the Château St. Louis without learning many things; and, for myself, though I
hunger for all the joys of life, I do not fret because my
mother holds me back from the gay doings in the town.
I have my long walks, my fishing and rowing, and sometimes shooting, with Juste and my sister Georgette, my
drawing, painting, music, needlework, and my housework.

Yet I am not entirely happy, I do not know quite
why. Do you ever feel as if there were some sorrow far
back in you, which now and then rushed in and flooded
your spirits, and then drew back, and you could not give
it a name? Well, that is the way with me. Yesterday,

as I stood in the kitchen beside our old cook Jovin, she said a kind word to me, and my eyes filled, and I ran up to my room, and burst into tears as I lay upon my bed. I could not help it. I thought at first it was because of the poor hawk that Captain Moray and I set free yesterday morning; but it could not have been that, for it was *free* when I cried, you see. You know, of course, that he saved my father's life, some years ago? That is one reason why he has been used so well in Quebec, for otherwise no one would have lessened the rigours of his captivity. But there are tales that he is too curious about our government and state, and so he may be kept close jailed, though he only came here as a hostage. He is much at our home, and sometimes walks with Juste and me and Georgette, and accompanies my mother in the streets. This is not to the liking of the Intendant who loves not my father because he is such a friend of our cousin the Governor. If their lives and characters be anything to the point the Governor must be in the right.

In truth, things are in a sad way here, for there is robbery on every hand, and who can tell what the end may be? Perhaps that we go to the English after all. Monsieur Doltaire—you do not know him, I think—says, "If the English eat us, as they swear they will, they'll die of megrims, our affairs are so indigestible." At another time he said, " Better to be English than to be damned." And when some one asked him what he meant, he said, "Is it not read from the altar, ' Cursed is he that putteth his trust in man ' ? The English trust nobody, and we trust the English." That was aimed at Captain Moray, who was present, and I felt it a cruel thing for him to say; but Captain Moray, smiling at the ladies, said, " Better to be French and damned than not to be French at all." And this pleased Monsieur Doltaire, who does not love him. I know not why, but there are vague whispers that he is acting against the Englishman for causes best known at Versailles, which have nothing to do with our affairs here. I do believe that Monsieur Doltaire would rather hear a clever thing than get ten thousand francs. At such times his face lights up, he is at once on his mettle, his eyes look almost fiendishly beautiful. He is a handsome man, but he is wicked, and I do not think he has one little sense of morals. I do not suppose he would stab a man in the back, or remove his neighbour's landmark in the night, though he'd rob him of it in open daylight, and call it " enterprise "—a usual word with him.

He is a favourite with Madame Cournal, who influences Bigot most, and one day we may see the boon companions at each other's throats; and if either falls, I hope it may be Bigot, for Monsieur Doltaire is, at least, no robber. Indeed, he is kind to the poor in a disdainful sort of way. He gives to them and scoffs at them at the same moment: a bad man, with just enough natural kindness to make him dangerous. I have not seen much of the world, but some things we know by instinct; we feel them; and I often wonder if that is not the way we know everything in the end. Sometimes when I take my long walks, or go and sit beside the Falls of Montmorenci, looking out to the great city on the Heights, to dear Isle Orleans, where we have our pretty villa (we are to go there next week for three months—happy summer months), up at the blue sky and into the deep woods, I have strange feelings, which afterwards become thoughts; and sometimes they fly away like butterflies, but oftener they stay with me, and I give them a little garden to roam in—you can guess where. Now and then I call them out of the garden and make them speak, and then I set down what they say in my journal; but I think they like their garden best. You remember the song we used to sing at school?

" ' Where do the stars grow, little Garaine?
　　The garden of moons, is it far away?
　The orchard of suns, my little Garaine,
　　Will you take us there some day?'

" ' If you shut your eyes,' quoth little Garaine,
　　'I will show you the way to go
　To the orchard of suns and the garden of moons
　　And the field where the stars do grow.

" ' But you must speak soft,' quoth little Garaine,
　　'And still must your footsteps be,
　For a great bear prowls in the field of the stars,
　　And the moons they have men to see.

" ' And the suns have the Children of Signs to guard,
　　And they have no pity at all—
　You must not stumble, you must not speak,
　　When you come to the orchard wall.

" ' The gates are locked,' quoth little Garaine,
　　'But the way I am going to tell?
　The key of your heart it will open them all:
　　And there's where the darlings dwell!' "

You may not care to read these lines again, but it
helps to show what I mean: that everything is in the
heart, and that nothing is at all if we do not feel it.
Sometimes I have spoken of these things to my mother,
but she does not see as I do. I dare not tell my father all
I think, and Juste is so much a creature of moods that I
am never sure whether he will be sensible and kind or
scoff. One can not bear to be laughed at. And as for
my sister, she never thinks; she only lives; and she looks
it—looks beautiful. But there, dear Lucie, I must not
tire you with my childish philosophy, though I feel no
longer a child. You would not know your friend. I can
not tell what has come over me. *Voilà!*

To-morrow we go to visit General Montcalm, who has

just arrived in the colony. Bigot and his gay set are not likely to be there. My mother insists that I shall never darken the doors of the Intendant's palace.

Do you still hold to your former purpose of keeping a daily journal? If so, I beg you to copy into it this epistle and your answer; and when I go up to your dear manor house at Beauce next summer, we will read over our letters and other things set down, and gossip of the changes come since we met last. Do sketch the old place for me (as will I our new villa on dear Isle Orleans), and make interest with the good *curé* to bring it to me with your letter, since there are no posts, no postmen, yet between here and Beauce. The *curé* most kindly bears this to you, and says he will gladly be our messenger. Yesterday he said to me, shaking his head in a whimsical way, " But no treason, mademoiselle, and no heresy or schism." I am not quite sure what he meant. I dare hardly think he had Captain Moray in his mind. I would not for the world so lessen my good opinion of him as to think him suspicious of me when no other dare; and so I put his words down to chance hitting, to a humorous fancy.

Be sure, dear Lucie, I shall not love you less for giving me a prompt answer. Tell me of what you are thinking and what doing. If Juste can be spared from the Governor's establishment, may I bring him with me next summer? He is a difficult, sparkling sort of fellow, but you are so steady-tempered, so full of tact, getting your own way so quietly and cleverly, that I am sure I should find plenty of straw for the bricks of my house of hope, my castle in Spain!

Do not give too much of my share of thy heart elsewhere, and continue to think me, my dear Lucie, thy friend, loyal and loving,

ALIXE DUVARNEY.

P. S.—Since the above was written we have visited the General. Both Monsieur Doltaire and Captain Moray were present, but neither took much note of me— Monsieur Doltaire not at all. Those two either hate each other lovingly, or love hatefully, I know not which, they are so biting, yet so friendly to each other's cleverness, though their style of word-play is so different: Monsieur Doltaire's like a bodkin-point, Captain Moray's like a musket-stock a-clubbing. Be not surprised to see the British at our gates any day. Though we shall beat them back I shall feel no less easy because I have a friend in the enemy's camp! You may guess who. Do not smile. *He is old enough to be my father.* He said so himself six months ago. ALIXE.

VIII.

AS VAIN AS ABSALOM.

GABORD, coming in to me one day after I had lain down to sleep, said, " See, m'sieu' the dormouse, 'tis holiday-eve; the King's sport comes to-morrow."

I sat up in bed with a start, for I knew not but that my death had been decided on without trial; and yet on second thought I was sure this could not be, for every rule of military conduct was against it.

" Whose holiday?" asked I after a moment; "and what is King's sport?"

" You're to play bear in the streets to-morrow—which is sport for the King," he retorted; "we lead you by a rope, and you dance the quickstep to please our ladies all the way to the Château, where they bring bear to drumhead."

" Who sits behind the drum?" I questioned.

7

"The Marquis de Vaudreuil," he replied, "the Intendant, Master Devil Doltaire, and the little men." By these last he meant officers of the colonial soldiery.

So, then, at last I was to be tried, to be dealt with definitely on the abominable charge. I should at least again see light and breathe fresh air, and feel about me the stir of the world. For a long year I had heard no voice but my own and Gabord's, had had no friends but my pale blades of corn and a timid mouse, day after day no light at all; and now winter was at hand again, and without fire and with poor food my body was chilled and starved. I had had no news of the world, nor of her who was dear to me, nor of Juste Duvarney, save that he lived, nor of our cause. But succeeding the thrill of delight I had at thought of seeing the open world again there came a feeling of lassitude, of indifference; I shrank from the jar of activity. But presently I got upon my feet, and with a little air of drollery straightened out my clothes and flicked a handkerchief across my gaiters. Then I twisted my head over my shoulder as if I were noting the shape of my back and the set of my clothes in a mirror, and thrust a leg out in the manner of an exquisite. I had need to do some mocking thing at the moment, or I should have given way to tears like a woman, so suddenly weak had I become.

Gabord burst out laughing.

An idea came to me. "I must be fine to-morrow," said I. "I must not shame my jailer." I rubbed my beard—I had none when I came into this dungeon first.

"Aho!" said he, his eyes wheeling.

I knew he understood me. I did not speak, but kept on running my fingers through my beard.

"As vain as Absalom," he added. "Do you think they'll hang you by the hair?"

"I'd have it off," said I, "to be clean for the sacrifice."

General Montcalm.

"You had Voban before," he rejoined; "we know what happened—a dainty bit of a letter all rose-lily scented, and comfits for the soldier. The pretty wren perches now in the Governor's house—a-cousining, a-cousining. Think you it is that she may get a glimpse of m'sieu' the dormouse as he comes to trial? But 'tis no business o' mine; and if I bring my prisoner up when called for, there's duty done!"

I saw the friendly spirit in the words.

"Voban," urged I, "Voban may come to me?"

"The Intendant said no, but the Governor yes," was the reply; "and that M'sieu' Doltaire is not yet come back from Montreal, so he had no voice. They look for him here to-morrow."

"Voban may come?" I asked again.

"At daybreak Voban—aho!" he continued. "There's milk and honey to-morrow," he added, and then, without a word, he drew forth from his coat, and hurriedly thrust into my hands, a piece of meat and a small flask of wine, and, swinging round like a schoolboy afraid of being caught in a misdemeanor, he passed through the door and the bolts clanged after him. He left the torch behind him, stuck in the cleft of the wall.

I sat down on my couch, and for a moment gazed almost vacantly at the meat and wine in my hands. I had not touched either for a year, and now I could see that my fingers, as they closed on the food nervously, were thin and bloodless, and I realized that my clothes hung loose upon my person. Here were light, meat, and wine, and there was a piece of bread on the board covering my water-jar. Luxury was spread before me, but although I had eaten little all day I was not hungry. Presently, however, I took the knife which I had hidden a year before, and cut pieces of the meat and laid them by the bread. Then I drew the cork from the bottle of

wine, and, lifting it towards that face which was always
visible to my soul I drank—drank—drank!

The rich liquor swam through my veins like glorious
fire. It wakened my brain and nerved my body. The
old spring of life came back. This wine had come from
the hands of Alixe—from the Governor's store, maybe;
for never could Gabord have got such stuff. I ate heartily
of the rich beef and bread with a new-made appetite,
and drank the rest of the wine. When I had eaten and
drunk the last I sat and looked at the glowing torch, and
felt a sort of comfort creep through me. Then there
came a delightful thought. Months ago I had put away
one last pipeful of tobacco, to save it till some day when I
should need it most. I got it now, and no man can guess
how lovingly I held it to a flying flame of the torch, saw
it light, and blew out the first whiff of smoke into the
sombre air; for November was again piercing this under-
ground house of mine, another winter was at hand! I sat
and smoked, and—can you not guess my thoughts? For
have you all not the same hearts, being British born and
bred? When I had taken the last whiff, I wrapped myself in my cloak and went to sleep. But twice or thrice
during the night I waked to see the torch still shining,
and caught the fragrance of consuming pine, and minded
not at all the smoke the burning made.

IX.

A LITTLE CONCERNING THE CHEVALIER DE LA DARANTE

I WAS wakened completely at last by the shooting of
bolts. With the opening of the door I saw the figures of
Gabord and Voban. My little friend the mouse saw them
also, and scampered from the bread it had been eating,

away among the corn, through which my footsteps had now made two rectangular paths, not disregarded by Gabord, who solicitously pulled Voban into the narrow track that he should not trespass on my harvest.

I rose, showed no particular delight at seeing Voban, but greeted him easily—though my heart was bursting to ask him of Alixe—and arranged my clothes. Presently Gabord said, "Stools for barber," and, wheeling, he left the dungeon. He was gone only an instant, but long enough for Voban to thrust a letter into my hand, which I ran into the lining of my waistcoat as I whispered, "Her brother—he is well?"

"Well, and he have go to France," he answered. "She make me say, look to the round window in the Château front."

We spoke in English—which, as I have said, Voban understood imperfectly. There was nothing more said, and if Gabord, when he returned, suspected, he showed no sign, but put down two stools, seating himself on one, as I seated myself on the other for Voban's handiwork. Presently a soldier appeared with a bowl of coffee. Gabord rose, took it from him, waved him away, and handed it to me. Never did coffee taste so sweet, and I sipped and sipped till Voban had ended his work with me. Then I drained the last drop and stood up. He handed me a mirror, and Gabord, fetching a fine white handkerchief from his pocket, said, "Here's for your tears, when they drum you to heaven, dickey-bird."

But when I saw my face in the mirror I confess I was startled. My hair, which had been black, was plentifully sprinkled with white, my face was intensely pale and thin, and the eyes were sunk in dark hollows. I should not have recognised myself. But I laughed as I handed back the glass, and said, "All flesh is grass, but a dungeon's no good meadow."

" 'Tis for the dry chaff," Gabord answered, "not for young grass—aho ! "

He rose and made ready to leave, Voban with him. " The commissariat camps here in an hour or so," he said, with a ripe chuckle.

It was clear the new state of affairs was more to his mind than the long year's rigour and silence. During all that time I never was visited by Doltaire but once, and of that event I am about to write briefly here.

It was about two months before this particular morning that he came, greeting me courteously enough.

" Close quarters here," said he, looking round as if the place were new to him and smiling to himself.

" Not so close as we all come to one day," said I.

" Dismal comparison ! " he rejoined ; " you've lost your spirits."

" Not so," I retorted ; " nothing but my liberty."

" You know the way to find it quickly," he suggested.

" The letters for La Pompadour ? " I asked.

" A dead man's waste papers," responded he ; " of no use to him or you, or to any one save the Grande Marquise."

" Valuable to me," said I.

" None but the Grande Marquise and the writer would give you a penny for them ! "

" Why should I not be my own merchant ? "

" You can—to me. If not to me to no one. You had your chance long ago, and you refused it. You must admit I dealt fairly with you. I did not move till you had set your own trap and fallen into it. Now, if you do not give me the letters—well, you will give them to none else in this world. It has been a fair game, and I am winning now. I've only used means which one gentle-man might use with another. Had you been a lesser man I should have had you spitted long ago. You understand?"

"Perfectly. But since we have played so long, do you think I'll give you the stakes now—before the end?"

"It would be wiser," he answered thoughtfully.

"I have a nation behind me," urged I.

"It has left you in a hole here to rot."

"It will take over your citadel and dig me out some day," I retorted hotly.

"What good that? Your life is more to you than Quebec to England."

"No, no," said I quickly; "I would give my life a hundred times to see your flag hauled down!"

"A freakish ambition," he replied; "mere infatuation!"

"You do not understand it, Monsieur Doltaire," I remarked ironically.

"I love not endless puzzles. There is no sport in following a maze that leads to nowhere save the grave." He yawned. "This air is heavy," he added; "you must find it trying."

"Never so trying as at this moment," I retorted.

"Come, am I so malarious?"

"You are a trickster," I answered coldly.

"Ah, you mean that night at Bigot's?" He smiled. "No, no, you were to blame—so green. You might have known we were for having you between the stones."

"But it did not come out as you wished?" hinted I.

"It served my turn," he responded; and he gave me such a smiling, malicious look that I knew he sought to convey he had his way with Alixe; and though I felt that she was true to me his cool presumption so stirred me I could have struck him in the face. I got angrily to my feet, but as I did so I shrank a little, for at times the wound in my side, not yet entirely healed, hurt me.

"You are not well," he said, with instant show of curiosity; "your wounds still trouble you? They should be healed. Gabord was ordered to see you cared for."

"Gabord has done well enough," answered I. "I have had wounds before, monsieur."

He leaned against the wall and laughed. "What braggarts you English are!" he said. "A race of swash-bucklers—even on bread and water!"

He had me at advantage, and I knew it, for he had kept his temper. I made an effort. "Both excellent," rejoined I, "and English, too."

He laughed again. "Come, that is better. That's in your old vein. I love to see you so. But how knew you our baker was English?—which he is, a prisoner like yourself."

"As easily as I could tell the water was not made by Frenchmen."

"Now I have hope of you," he broke out gaily; "you will yet redeem your nation."

At that moment Gabord came with a message from the Governor to Doltaire, and he prepared to go.

"You are set on sacrifice?" he asked. "Think—dangling from Cape Diamond!"

"I will meditate on your fate instead," I replied.

"Think!" he said again, waving off my answer with his hand. "The letters I shall no more ask for; and you will not escape death?"

"Never by that way," rejoined I.

"So. Very good. *Au plaisir*, my captain. I go to dine at the Seigneur Duvarney's."

With that last thrust he was gone, and left me wondering if the Seigneur had ever made an effort to see me, if he had forgiven the duel with his son.

That was the incident.

·   ·   *   ·   ·   ·   ·

When Gabord and Voban were gone, leaving the light behind, I went over to the torch in the wall, and drew Alixe's letter from my pocket with eager fingers. It told the whole story of her heart.

CHÂTEAU ST. LOUIS, *27th November, 1757.*

Though I write you these few words, dear Robert, I do not know that they will reach you, for as yet it is not certain they will let Voban visit you. A year, dear friend, and not a word from you, and not a word to you! I should have broken my heart if I had not heard of you one way and another. They say you are much worn in body, though you have always a cheerful air. There are stories of a visit Monsieur Doltaire paid you, and how you jested. He hates you, and yet he admires you too.

And now listen, Robert, and I beg you not to be angry—oh, do not be angry, for I am all yours; but I want to tell you that I have not repulsed Monsieur Doltaire when he has spoken flatteries to me. I have not believed them, and I have kept my spirit strong against the evil in him. I want to get you free of prison and to that end I have to work through him with the Intendant, that he will not set the Governor more against you. With the Intendant himself I will not deal at all. So I use the lesser villain, and in truth the more powerful, for he stands higher at Versailles than any here. With the Governor I have influence, for he is, as you know, a kinsman of my mother's, and of late he has shown a fondness for me. Yet you can see that I must act most warily, that I must not seem to care for you, for that would be your complete undoing. I rather seem to scoff. (Oh, how it hurts me! how my cheeks tingle when I think of it alone! and how I clench my hands, hating them all for oppressing you!)

I do not believe their slanders—that you are a spy. It is I, Robert, who have at last induced the Governor to bring you to trial. They would have put it off till next year, but I feared you would die in that awful dungeon, and I was sure that if your trial came on there would be a change, as there is to be for a time, at least. You are to be lodged in the common jail during the sitting of the court; and so that is one step gained. Yet I had to use all manner of device with the Governor.

He is sometimes so playful with me that I can pretend to sulkiness; and so one day I said that he showed no regard for our family or for me in not bringing you, who had nearly killed my brother, to justice. So he consented, and being of a stubborn nature, too, when Monsieur Doltaire and the Intendant opposed the trial, he said it should come off at once. But one thing grieves me : they are to have you marched through the streets of the town like any common criminal, and I dare show no distress nor plead, nor can my father, though he wishes to move for you in this; and I dare not urge him, for then it would seem strange the daughter asked your punishment, and the father sought to lessen it.

When you are in the common jail it will be much easier to help you. I have seen Gabord, but he is not to be bent to any purpose, though he is kind to me. I shall try once more to have him take some wine and meat to you to-night. If I fail, then I shall only pray that you may be given strength in body for your time of trouble equal to your courage.

It may be I can fix upon a point where you may look to see me as you pass on to-morrow to the Château. There must be a sign. If you will put your hand to your forehead—— But no, they may bind you, and your hands may not be free. When you see me, pause in your step for an instant, and I shall know. I will tell Voban where you shall send your glance, if he is to be let in to you, and I hope that what I plan may not fail.

And so, Robert, adieu. Time can not change me, and your misfortunes draw me closer to you. Only the dishonourable thing could make me close the doors of my heart, and I will not think you, whate'er they say, unworthy of my constant faith. Some day, maybe, we shall smile at and even cherish these sad times. In this gay house I must be flippant, for I am now of the foolish world! But under all the trivial sparkle a serious heart beats. It belongs to thee, if thou wilt have it, Robert, the heart of thy   ALIXE.

An hour after getting this good letter Gabord came again, and with him breakfast—a word which I had almost dropped from my language. True, it was only in a dungeon, on a pair of stools, by the light of a torch, but how I relished it!—a bottle of good wine, a piece of broiled fish, the half of a fowl, and some tender vegetables.

When Gabord came for me with two soldiers, an hour later—I say an hour, but I only guessed so, for I had no way of noting time—I was ready for new cares, and to see the world again. Before the others Gabord was the rough, almost brutal soldier, and soon I knew that I was to be driven out upon the St. Foye Road and on into the town. My arms were well fastened down, and I was tied about till I must have looked like a bale of living goods of no great value. Indeed, my clothes were by no means handsome, and save for my well-shaven face and clean handkerchief I was an ill-favoured spectacle; but I tried to bear my shoulders up as we marched through dark reeking corridors, and presently came suddenly into well-lighted passages.

I had to pause, for the light blinded my eyes, and they hurt me horribly, so delicate were the nerves. For some minutes I stood there, my guards stolidly waiting, Gabord muttering a little and stamping upon the floor as if in anger, though I knew he was playing a small part to deceive his comrades. The pain in my eyes grew less, and, though they kept filling with moisture from the violence of the light I soon could see without distress.

I was led into the yard of the citadel, where was drawn up a company of soldiers. Gabord bade me stand still, and advanced toward the officers' quarters. I asked him if I might not walk to the ramparts and view the scene. He gruffly assented, bidding the men watch me closely, and I walked over to a point where, standing three hundred feet above the noble river, I could look out upon its sweet expanse, across to the Levis shore with its serried legions of trees behind and its bold settlement in front upon the Heights. There, eastward, lay the well-wooded Island of Orleans, and over all the clear sun and sky, enlivened by a crisp and cheering air. Snow had fallen, but none now lay upon the ground, and I saw a rare and winning earth. I stood absorbed. I was recalling that first day of my life that I remember, when at Balmore my grandfather made prophecies upon me, and for the first time I was conscious of the world.

As I stood lost to everything about me, I heard Doltaire's voice, and presently he said over my shoulder, "To wish Captain Moray a good-morning were superfluous!"

I smiled at him: the pleasure of that scene had given me an impulse towards good nature even with my enemies.

"The best I ever had," I answered quietly.

"Contrasts are life's delights," he said. "You should thank us. You have your best day because of our worst dungeon."

"But my thanks shall not be in words; you shall have the same courtesy at our hands one day."

"I had the Bastile for a year," he rejoined, calling up a squad of men with his finger as he spoke. "I have had my best day. Two would be monotony. You think your English will take this some time?" he asked, waving a finger toward the citadel. "It will need good play to pluck that ribbon from its place." He glanced up, as he spoke, at the white flag with its golden lilies.

"So much the better sport," I answered. "We will have the ribbon and its heritage."

"You yourself shall furnish evidence to-day. Gabord here will see you temptingly disposed—the wild bull led peaceably by the nose!"

"But one day I will twist your nose, Monsieur Doltaire."

"That is fair enough, if rude," he responded. "When your turn comes you twist and I endure. You shall be nourished well like me, and I shall look a battered hulk like you. But I shall never be the fool that you are. If I had a way to slip the leash I'd slip it. You are a dolt." He was touching upon the letters again.

"I weigh it all," said I. "I am no fool—anything else you will."

"You'll be nothing soon, I fear—which is a pity."

What more he might have said I do not know, but there now appeared in the yard a tall, reverend old gentleman, in the costume of the coureur de bois, though his belt was richly chased, and he wore an order on his breast. There was something more refined than powerful in his appearance, but he had a keen, kindly eye, and a manner unmistakably superior. His dress was a little barbarous, unlike Doltaire's splendid white uniform set off with violet and gold, the lace of a fine handkerchief sticking from his belt, and a gold-handled sword at his side, but the manner of both was distinguished.

Seeing Doltaire, he came forward and they embraced.

Then he turned towards me, and as they walked off a little
distance I could see that he was curious concerning me.
Presently he raised his hand, and, as if something had
excited him, said, " No, no, no ; hang him and have done
with it, but I'll have nothing to do with it—not a thing.
'Tis enough for me to rule at——"

I could hear no further, but I was now sure that he
was some one of note who had retired from any share in
state affairs. He and Doltaire then moved on to the doors
of the citadel, and, pausing there, Doltaire turned round
and made a motion of his hand to Gabord. I was at once
surrounded by the squad of men, and the order to march
was given. A drum in front of me began to play a well-
known derisive air of the French army, The Fox and the
Wolf.

We came out on the St. Foye Road and down towards
the Château St. Louis, between crowds of shouting people
who beat drums, kettles, pans, and made all manner of
mocking noises. It was meant not only against myself,
but against the British people. The women were not
behind the men in violence ; from them all at first came
handfuls of gravel and dust which struck me in the face ;
but Gabord put a stop to that.

It was a shameful ordeal, which might have vexed me
sorely if I had not had greater trials and expected worse.
Now and again appeared a face I knew—some lady who
turned her head away, or some gentleman who watched
me curiously but made no sign.

When we came to the Château, I looked up as if casu-
ally, and there in a little round window I saw Alixe's
face—for an instant only. I stopped in my tracks, was
prodded by a soldier from behind, and then stepped on.
Entering, we were taken to the rear of the building,
where, in an open courtyard, were a company of soldiers,
some seats, and a table. On my right was the St. Law-

rence swelling on its course, hundreds of feet beneath, little boats passing hither and thither on its flood.

We were waiting for about half an hour, the noises of the clamouring crowd coming to us, as they carried me aloft in effigy, and, burning me at the cliff edge, fired guns and threw stones at me, till, rags, ashes, and flame, I was tumbled into the river far below. At last from the Château came the Marquis de Vaudreuil, Bigot, and a number of officers. The Governor looked gravely at me, but did not bow; Bigot gave me a sneering smile, eying me curiously the while, and (I could feel), remarking on my poor appearance to Cournal beside him—Cournal, who winked at his wife's dishonour for the favour of her lover, who gave him means for public robbery.

Presently the Governor was seated, and he said, looking round, " Monsieur Doltaire—he is not here?"

Bigot shook his head, and answered, "No doubt he is detained at the citadel."

"And the Seigneur Duvarney?" the Governor added.

At that moment the Governor's secretary handed him a letter. The Governor opened it. "Listen," said he. He read to the effect that the Seigneur Duvarney felt that he was ill fitted to be a judge in this case, remembering the conflict between his son and the notorious Captain Moray. And from another standpoint, though the prisoner merited any fate reserved for him, if guilty of spying, he could not forget that his life had been saved by this British captain—an obligation which, unfortunately, he could neither repay nor wipe out. After much thought, he must disobey the Governor's summons, and he prayed that his Excellency would grant his consideration thereupon.

I saw the Governor frown, but he made no remark, while Bigot said something in his ear which did not improve his humour, for he replied curtly, and turned to his

secretary. "We must have two gentlemen more," he
said.

At that moment Doltaire entered with the old noble-
man of whom I have written. The Governor instantly
brightened, and gave the stranger a warm greeting, calling him his "dear Chevalier"; and, after a deal of urging, the Chevalier de la Darante was seated as one of my
judges: which did not at all displease me, for I liked
his face.

I do not need to dwell upon the trial here. I have set
down the facts of the case before. I had no counsel and
no witnesses. There seemed no reason why the trial should
have dragged on all day, for I soon saw it was intended to
find me guilty. Yet I was surprised to see how Doltaire
brought up a point here and a question there in my favour,
which served to lengthen out the trial; and all the time
he sat near the Chevalier de la Darante, now and again
talking with him.

It was late evening before the trial came to a close.
The one point to be established was that the letters taken
from General Braddock were mine, and that I had made
the plans while a hostage. I acknowledged nothing, and
would not do so unless allowed to speak freely. This was
not permitted until just before I was sentenced.

Then Doltaire's look was fixed on me, and I knew he
waited to see if I would divulge the matter private between us. However, I stood by my compact with him.
Besides, it could not serve me to speak of it here, or use
it as an argument, and it would only hasten an end which
I felt he could prevent if he chose.

So when I was asked if I had aught to say I pleaded
only that they had not kept our Articles of War signed at
Fort Necessity, which provided that I should be free within two months and a half—that is, when prisoners in our
hands should be delivered up to them, as they were. They

had broken their bond, though we had fulfilled ours, and I held myself justified in doing what I had done for our cause and for my own life.

I was not heard patiently, though I could see that the Governor and the Chevalier were impressed; but Bigot instantly urged the case hotly against me, and the end came very soon. It was now dark; a single light had been brought and placed beside the Governor, while a soldier held a torch at a distance. Suddenly there was a silence; then, in response to a signal, the sharp ringing of a hundred bayonets as they were drawn and fastened to the muskets, and I could see them gleaming in the feeble torchlight. Presently out of the stillness the Governor's voice was heard condemning me to death by hanging, thirty days hence at sunrise. Silence fell again instantly, and then a thing occurred which sent a thrill through us all. From the dark balcony above us came a voice, weird, high, and wailing:

"Guilty! Guilty! Guilty! He is guilty, and shall die! François Bigot shall die!"

The voice was Mathilde's, and I saw Doltaire shrug a shoulder and look with malicious amusement at the Intendant. Bigot himself sat pale and furious. "Discover the intruder," he said to Gabord, who was standing near, "and have—him—jailed."

But the Governor interfered. "It is some drunken creature," he urged quietly. "Take no account of it."

8

X.

AN OFFICER OF MARINES.

WHAT was my dismay to know that I was to be taken
back again to my dungeon, and not lodged in the common
jail, as I had hoped and Alixe had hinted! When I saw
whither my footsteps were directed I said nothing, nor
did Gabord speak at all. We marched back through a
railing crowd, all silent and gloomy. I felt a chill at my
heart when the citadel loomed up again out of the November shadow, and I half paused as I entered the gates.
"Forward!" said Gabord mechanically, and I moved on
into the yard, into the prison, through the dull corridors,
the soldiers' heels clanking and resounding behind, down
into the bowels of the earth, where the air was moist and
warm, and then into my dungeon home! I stepped inside,
and Gabord ordered the ropes off my person somewhat
roughly, watched the soldiers till they were well away, and
then leaned against the wall, waiting for me to speak. I
had no impulse to smile, but I knew how I could most
touch him, and so I said lightly, "You've dickey-bird
home again."

He answered nothing and turned towards the door,
leaving the torch stuck in the wall. But he suddenly
stopped short, and thrust out to me a tiny piece of paper.

"A hand touched mine as I went through the Château,"
said he, "and when out I came, look you, this here! I
can't see to read. What does it say?" he added, with a
shrewd attempt at innocence.

I opened the little paper, held it toward the torch,
and read:

"*Because of the storm there is no sleeping. Is there
not the watcher aloft? Shall the sparrow fall unheeded?
The wicked shall be confounded.*"

It was Alixe's writing. She had hazarded this in the hands of my jailer as her only hope, and, knowing that he might not serve her, had put her message in vague sentences which I readily interpreted. I read the words aloud to him, and he laughed, and remarked, "'Tis a foolish thing that—the Scarlet Woman, most like."

"Most like," I answered quietly; "yet what should she be doing there at the Château?"

"The mad go everywhere," he answered, "even to the Intendance!"

With that he left me, going, as he said, "to fetch crumbs and wine." Exhausted with the day's business, I threw myself upon my couch, drew my cloak over me, composed myself, and in a few minutes was sound asleep. I waked to find Gabord in the dungeon, setting out food upon a board supported by two stools.

"'Tis custom to feed your dickey-bird ere you fetch him to the pot," he said, and drew the cork from a bottle of wine.

He watched me as I ate and talked, but he spoke little. When I had finished, he fetched a packet of tobacco from his pocket. I offered him money, but he refused it, and I did not press him, for he said the food and wine were not of his buying. Presently he left, and came back with pens, ink, paper, and candles, which he laid out on my couch without a word.

After a little he came again, and placed a book on the improvised table before me. It was an English Bible. Opening it, I found inscribed on the fly-leaf, *Charles Wainfleet, Chaplain to the British Army.* Gabord explained that this chaplain had been in the citadel for some weeks; had often inquired about me; had been brought from the Ohio, and had known of me, having tended the lieutenant of my Virginian infantry in his last hours. Gabord thought I should now begin to make my peace

with Heaven, and so had asked for the chaplain's Bible,
which was freely given. I bade him thank the chaplain
for me, and opening the book, I found a leaf turned down
at the words,

" *In the shadow of Thy wings will I make my refuge,
until these calamities be overpast.*"

When I was left alone, I sat down to write diligently
that history of myself which I had composed and fixed in
my memory during the year of my housing in this dungeon. The words came from my pen freely, and hour
after hour through many days, while no single word
reached me from the outside world, I wrote on; carefully
revising, but changing little from that which I had taken
so long to record in my mind. I would not even yet
think that they would hang me; and if they did, what
good could brooding do? When the last word of the
memoirs (I may call them so), addressed to Alixe, had
been written, I turned my thoughts to other friends.

The day preceding that fixed for my execution came,
yet there was no sign from friend or enemy without. At
ten o'clock of that day Chaplain Wainfleet was admitted
to me in the presence of Gabord and a soldier. I found
great pleasure in his company, brief as his visit was; and
after I had given him messages to bear for me to old friends,
if we never met again and he were set free, he left me, be-
nignly commending me to Heaven. There was the question
of my other letters. I had but one desire—Voban again,
unless at my request the Seigneur Duvarney would come,
and they would let him come. If it were certain that I
was to go to the scaffold, then I should not hesitate to tell
him my relations with his daughter, that he might comfort her when, being gone from the world myself, my
love could do her no harm. I could not think that he
would hold against me the duel with his son, and I felt
sure he would come to me if he could.

But why should I not try for both Voban and the Seigneur? So I spoke to Gabord.

"Voban! Voban!" said he. "Does dickey-bird play at peacock still? Well, thou shalt see Voban. Thou shalt go trimmed to heaven—aho!"

Presently I asked him if he would bear a message to the Governor, asking permission for the Seigneur Duvarney to visit me, if he were so inclined. At his request I wrote my petition out, and he carried it away with him, saying that I should have Voban that evening.

I waited hour after hour, but no one came. As near as I could judge it was now evening. It seemed strange to think that, twenty feet above me, the world was all white with snow; the sound of sleigh-bells and church-bells, and the cries of snowshoers ringing on the clear, sharp air. I pictured the streets of Quebec alive with people: the young Seigneur set off with furs and silken sash and sword or pistols; the long-haired, black-eyed woodsman in his embroidered moccasins and leggings with flying thrums; the peasant farmer slapping his hands cheerfully in the lighted market-place; the petty noble, with his demoiselle, hovering in the precincts of the Château St. Louis and the intendance. Up there were light, freedom, and the inspiriting frost; down here in my dungeon, the blades of corn, which, dying, yet never died, told the story of a choking air, wherein the body and soul of a man droop and take long to die. This was the night before Christmas Eve, when in England and Virginia they would be preparing for feasting and thanksgiving.

The memories of past years crowded on me. I thought of feastings and spendthrift rejoicings in Glasgow and Virginia. All at once the carnal man in me rose up and damned these lying foes of mine. Resignation went whistling down the wind. Hang me! Hang me! No, by the God that gave me breath! I sat back and laughed—laughed at my own insipid virtue, by which, to keep faith with the fanatical follower of Prince Charlie, I had refused my liberty; cut myself off from the useful services of my King; wasted good years of my life, trusting to pressure and help to come from England, which never came; twisted the rope for my own neck to keep honour with the dishonourable Doltaire, who himself had set the noose swinging; and, inexpressible misery! involved in my shame and peril a young, blithe spirit, breathing a miasma upon the health of a tender life. Every rebellious atom in my blood sprang to indignant action. I swore that if they fetched me to the gallows to celebrate their Noël, other lives than mine should go to keep me company on the dark trail. To die like a rat in a trap, oiled for the burning, and lighted by the torch of hatred! No, I would die fighting, if I must die.

I drew from its hiding-place the knife I had secreted the day I was brought into that dungeon—a little weapon, but it would serve for the first blow. At whom? Gabord? It all flashed through my mind how I might do it when he came in again: bury this blade in his neck or heart—it was long enough for the work; then, when he was dead, change my clothes for his, take his weapons, and run my chances to get free of the citadel. Free? Where should I go in the dead of winter? Who would hide me, shelter me? I could not make my way to an English settlement. Ill clad, exposed to the merciless climate, and the end death. But that was freedom—freedom! I could feel my body dilating with the thought, as I paced my dungeon like an ill-tempered beast. But kill Gabord, who had put himself in danger to serve me, who himself had kept the chains from off my ankles and body, whose own life depended upon my security—"Come, come, Robert Moray," said I, "what relish have you for that?

That's an ill game for a gentleman. Alixe Duvarney would rather see you dead than get your freedom over the body of this man."

That was an hour of storm. I am glad that I conquered the baser part of me; for, almost before I had grown calm again, the bolts of the dungeon doors shot back, and presently Gabord stepped inside, followed by a muffled figure.

"Voban the barber," said Gabord in a strange voice, and stepping again outside, he closed the door, but did not shoot the bolts.

I stood as one in a dream. Voban the barber? In spite of cap and great fur coat, I saw the outline of a figure that no barber ever had in this world. I saw two eyes shining like lights set in a rosy sky. A moment of doubt, of impossible speculation, of delicious suspense, and then the coat of Voban the barber opened, dropped away from the lithe, graceful figure of a young officer of marines, the cap flew off, and in an instant the dear head, the blushing, shining face of Alixe was on my breast.

In that moment, stolen from the calendar of hate, I ran into the haven where true hearts cast anchor and bless God that they have seen upon the heights to guide them the lights of home. The moment flashed by and was gone, but the light it made went not with it.

When I drew her blushing face up, and stood her off from me that I might look at her again, the colour flew back and forth on her cheek, as you may see the fire flutter in an uncut ruby when you turn it in the sun. Modestly drawing the cloak she wore more closely about her, she hastened to tell me how it was she came in such a guise; but I made her pause for a moment while I gave her a seat and sat down beside her. Then by the light of the flickering torch and flaring candles I watched her feelings play upon her face as the warm light of autumn shifts upon the glories of ripe fruits. Her happiness was tempered by the sadness of our position, and my heart smote me that I had made her suffer, had brought care to her young life. I could see that in the year she had grown older, yet her beauty seemed enhanced by that and by the trouble she had endured. I shall let her tell her story here unbroken by my questions and those interruptions which Gabord made, bidding her to make haste. She spoke without faltering, save here and there; but even then I could see her brave spirit quelling the riot of her emotions, shutting down the sluice-gate of her tears.

"I knew," she said, her hand clasped in mine, "that Gabord was the only person likely to be admitted to you, and so for days, living in fear lest the worst should happen, I have prepared for this chance. I have grown so in height that an old uniform of my brother's would fit me, and I had it ready—small sword and all," she added, with a sad sort of humour, touching the weapon at her side. "You must know that we have for the winter a house here upon the ramparts near the Château. It was my mother's doings, that my sister Georgette and I might have no great journeyings in the cold to the festivities hereabouts. So I, being a favourite with the Governor, ran in and out of the Château at my will; of which my mother was proud, and she allowed me much liberty, for to be a favourite of the Governor is an honour. I knew how things were going, and what the chances were of the sentence being carried out on you. Sometimes I thought my heart would burst with the anxiety of it all, but I would show that to the world. If you could but have seen me smile at the Governor and Monsieur Doltaire— nay, do not press my hand so, Robert; you know well you have no need to fear monsieur—while I learned secrets of state, among them news of you. Three nights ago Monsieur Doltaire was talking with me at a ball—ah, those feastings while you were lying in a dungeon, and I shutting up my love and your danger close in my heart, even from those who loved me best! Well, suddenly he said, ' I think I will not have our English captain shifted to a better world.'

" My heart stood still; I felt an ache across my breast so that I could hardly breathe. ' Why will you not?' said I; ' was not the sentence just?' He paused a minute, and then replied, ' All sentences are just when an enemy is dangerous.' Then said I as in surprise, ' Why, was he no spy, after all?' He sat back, and laughed a little. ' A spy according to the letter of the law, but you have heard of secret history—eh?' I tried to seem puzzled, for I had a thought there was something private between you and him which has to do with your fate. So I said, as if bewildered, ' You mean there is evidence which was not shown at the trial?' He answered slowly, ' Evidence that would bear upon the morals, not the law, of the case.' Then said I, ' Has it to do with you, monsieur?' ' It has to do with France,' he replied. ' And so you will not have his death?' I asked. ' Bigot wishes it,' he replied, ' for no other reason than that Madame Cournal has spoken nice words for the good-looking captain, and because that unsuccessful duel gave Vaudreuil an advantage over himself. Vaudreuil wishes it because he thinks it will sound well in France, and also because he really believes the man a spy. The Council do not care much ; they follow the Governor and Bigot, and both being agreed, their verdict is unanimous.' He paused, then added, ' And the Seigneur Duvarney—and his daughter—wish it because of a notable injury to one of their name.' At that I cautiously replied, ' No, my father does not wish it, for my brother gave the offence, and Captain Moray saved his life, as you know. I do not wish it, Monsieur Doltaire, because hanging is a shameful death, and he is a gentle-

man, not a ruffian. Let him be shot like a gentleman.
How will it sound at the Court of France that, on insuffi-
cient evidence, as you admit, an English gentleman was
hanged for a spy? Would not the King say (for he is a
gentleman), Why was not all this shown me before the
man's death? Is it not a matter upon which a country
would feel as gentlemen feel?'

" I knew it the right thing to say at the moment, and
it seemed the only way to aid you, though I intended, if
the worst came to the worst, to go myself to the Governor
at the last and plead for your life, at least for a reprieve.
But it had suddenly flashed upon me that a reference to
France was the thing, since the Articles of War which
you are accused of dishonouring were signed by officers
from France and England.

" Presently he turned to me with a look of curiosity,
and another sort of look also that made me tremble, and
said, 'Now, there you have put your finger on the point—
my point, the choice weapon I had reserved to prick the
little bubble of Bigot's hate and the Governor's conceit, if
I so chose, even at the last. And here is a girl, a young
girl just freed from pinafores, who teaches them the law
of nations! If it pleased me I should not speak, for Vaudreuil's and Bigot's affairs are none of mine; but, in truth,
why should you kill your enemy? It is the sport to keep
him living; you can get no change for your money from
a dead man. He has had one cheerful year; why not another, and another, and another? And so watch him
fretting to the slow-coming end, while now and again you
give him a taste of hope, to drop him back again into the
pit which has no sides for climbing.' He paused a minute, and then added, 'A year ago I thought he had touched
you, this Britisher, with his raw humour and manners;
but, my faith, how swiftly does a woman's fancy veer!'
At that I said calmly to him, ' You must remember that

then he was not thought so base.' 'Yes, yes,' he replied;
'and a woman loves to pity the captive, whatever his fault,
if he be presentable and of some notice or talent. And
Moray has gifts,' he went on. I appeared all at once to
be offended. 'Veering, indeed! a woman's fancy! I think
you might judge women better. You come from high
places, Monsieur Doltaire, and they say this and that of
your great talents and of your power at Versailles, but
what proof have we had of it? You set a girl down with
a fine patronage, and you hint at weapons to cut off my
cousin the Governor and the Intendant from their purposes; but how do we know you can use them, that you
have power with either the unnoticeable woman or the
great men?' I knew very well it was a bold move. He
suddenly turned to me, in his cruel eyes a glittering kind
of light, and said, 'I suggest no more than I can do with
those "great men"; and as for the woman, the slave can
not be patron—I am the slave. I thought not of power
before; but now that I do, I will live up to my thinking.
I seem idle, I am not; purposeless, I am not; a gamester,
I am none. I am a sportsman, and I will not leave the
field till all the hunt be over. I seem a trifler, yet I have
persistency. I am no romanticist, I have no great admiration for myself, and yet when I set out to hunt a woman
honestly, be sure I shall never back to kennel till she is
mine or I am done for utterly. Not by worth nor by de-
serving, but by unending patience and diligence—that shall
be my motto. I shall devote to the chase every art that I
have learned or known by nature. So there you have me,
mademoiselle. Since you have brought me to the point,
I will unfurl my flag. . . . I am—your—hunter,' he went
on, speaking with slow, painful emphasis, 'and I shall
make you mine. You fight against me, but it is no use.'
I got to my feet, and said with coolness, though I was
sick at heart and trembling, 'You are frank. You have

made two resolves. I shall give weight to the one as you fulfil the other'; and, smiling at him, I moved away towards my mother.

"Masterful as he is I felt that this would touch his vanity. There lay my great chance with him. If he had guessed the truth of what's between us, be sure, Robert, your life were not worth one hour beyond to-morrow's sunrise. You must know how I loathe deceitfulness, but when one weak girl is matched against powerful and evil men what can she do? My conscience does not chide me, for I know my cause is just. Robert, look me in the eyes. . . . There, like that. . . . Now tell me : You are innocent of the dishonourable thing, are you not? I believe with all my soul, but that I may say from your own lips that you are no spy, tell me so."

When I had said as she had wished, assuring her she should know all, carrying proofs away with her, and that hidden evidence of which Doltaire had spoken, she went on :

"'You put me to the test,' said monsieur. 'Doing one, it will be proof that I shall do the other.' He fixed his eyes upon me with such a look that my whole nature shrank from him, as if the next instant his hateful hands were to be placed on me. Oh, Robert, I know how perilous was the part I played, but I dared it for your sake. For a whole year I have dissembled to every one save to that poor mad soul Mathilde, who reads my heart in her wild way, to Voban, and to the rough soldier outside your dungeon. But they will not betray me. God has given us these rough but honest friends.

"Well, monsieur left me that night, and I have not seen him since, nor can I tell where he is, for no one knows, and I dare not ask too much. I did believe he would achieve his boast as to saving your life, and so, all yesterday and to-day, I have waited with most anxious

heart; but not one word! Yet there was that in all he
said which made me sure he meant to save you, and I believe he will. Yet think: if anything happened to him!
You know what wild doings go on at Bigot's château out
at Charlesbourg; or, again, in the storm of yesterday he
may have been lost. You see, there are the hundred
chances; so I determined not to trust wholly to him.
There was one other way—to seek the Governor myself,
open my heart to him, and beg for a reprieve. To-night
at nine o'clock—it is now six, Robert—we go to the Château St. Louis, my mother and my father and I, to sup
with the Governor. Oh, think what I must endure, to
face them with this awful shadow on me! If no word
come of the reprieve before that hour, I shall make my
own appeal to the Governor. It may ruin me, but it may
save you; and that done, what should I care for the rest?
Your life is more to me than all the world beside." Here
she put both hands upon my shoulders and looked me in
the eyes.

I did not answer yet, but took her hands in mine, and
she continued: "An hour past I told my mother I should
go to see my dear friend Lucie Lotbinière. Then I stole
up to my room, put on my brother's uniform, and came
down to meet Voban near the citadel, as we had arranged.
I knew he was to have an order from the Governor to
visit you. He was waiting, and to my great joy he put
the order in my hands. I took his coat and wig and cap,
a poor disguise, and came straight to the citadel, handing
the order to the soldiers at the gate. They gave it back
without a word, and passed me on. I thought this strange,
and looked at the paper by the light of the torches. What
was my surprise to see that Voban's name had been left
out! It but gave permission to the bearer. That would
serve with the common soldier, but I knew well it would
not with Gabord or with the commandant of the citadel.

All at once I saw the great risk I was running, the danger to us both. Still I would not turn back. But how good fortune serves us when we least look for it! At the commandant's very door was Gabord. I did not think to deceive him. It was my purpose from the first to throw myself upon his mercy. So there, that moment, I thrust the order into his hand. He read it, looked a moment half fiercely and half kindly, at me then turned and took the order to the commandant. Presently he came out, and said to me, 'Come, m'sieu', and see you clip the gentleman dainty fine for his sunrise travel. He'll get no care 'twixt posting-house and end of journey, m'sieu'.' This he said before two soldiers, speaking with harshness and a brutal humour. But inside the citadel he changed at once, and, taking from my head this cap and wig, he said quite gently, yet I could see he was angry, too, ' This is a mad doing, young lady.' He said no more, but led me straight to you. If I had told him I was coming, I know he would have stayed me. But at the dangerous moment he had not heart to drive me back. . . . And that is all my story, Robert."

As I have said, this tale was broken often by little questionings and exclamations, and was not told in one long narrative as I have written it here. When she had done I sat silent and overcome for a moment. There was one thing now troubling me sorely, even in the painful joy of having her here close by me. She had risked all to save my life—reputation, friends, even myself, the one solace in her possible misery. Was it not my duty to agree to Doltaire's terms, for her sake, if there was yet a chance to do so? I had made a solemn promise to Sir John Godric that those letters, if they ever left my hands, should go to the great lady who had written them; and to save my own life I would not have broken faith with my benefactor. But had I the right to add to the misery of this sweet, brave spirit? Suppose it was but for a year or two : had I the right to give her sorrow for that time, if I could prevent it, even at the cost of honour with the dead? Was it not my duty to act, and at once? Time was short.

While in a swift moment I was debating, Gabord opened the door, and said, " Come, end it, end it. Gabord has a head to save ! " I begged him for one minute more, and then giving Alixe the packet which held my story, I told her hastily the matter between Doltaire and myself, and said that now, rather than give her sorrow, I was prepared to break my word with Sir John Godric. She heard me through with flashing eyes, and I could see her bosom heave. When I had done, she looked me straight in the eyes.

" Is all that here ? " she said, holding up the packet.

" All," I answered.

" And you would not break your word to save your own life ? "

I shook my head in negation.

" Now I know that you are truly honourable," she answered, " and you shall not break your promise for me. No, no, you shall not ; you shall not stir. Tell me that you will not send word to Monsieur Doltaire—tell me ! "

When, after some struggle, I had consented, she said, " But I may act. I am not bound to secrecy. I have given no word or bond. I will go to the Governor with the tale of my love, and I do not fear the end. They will put me in a convent, and I shall see you no more, but I shall have saved you."

In vain I begged her not to do so ; her purpose was strong, and I could only get her promise that she would not act till midnight. This was hardly achieved when Gabord entered quickly, saying, " The Seigneur Duvarney ! On with your coat, wig, and cap ! Quick, mademoiselle ! "

Swiftly the disguise was put on, and I clasped her to

my breast with a joyful agony, while Gabord hastily put out the candles and torch, and drew Alixe behind the dungeon door. Then standing himself in the doorway, he loudly commended me to sleep sound and be ready for long travel in the morning. Taking the hint I threw myself upon my couch and composed myself. An instant afterwards the Seigneur appeared with a soldier. Gabord met him cheerfully, looked at the order from the Governor, and motioned the Seigneur in and the soldier away. As Duvarney stepped inside, Gabord followed, holding up a torch. I rose to meet my visitor, and as I took his hand I saw Gabord catch Alixe by the sleeve and hurry her out with a whispered word, swinging the door behind her as she passed. Then he stuck the torch in the wall, went out, shut and bolted the dungeon door, and left us two alone.

I was glad that Alixe's safety had been assured, and my greeting of her father was cordial. But he was more reserved than I had ever known him. The duel with his son, which had sent the youth to France and left him with a wound which would trouble him for many a day, weighed heavily against me. Again, I think he guessed my love for Alixe, and resented it with all his might. What Frenchman would care to have his daughter lose her heart to one accused of a wretched crime, condemned to death, an enemy of his country and a Protestant? I was sure that, should he guess at the exact relations between us, Alixe would be sent behind the tall doors of a convent, where I should knock in vain.

"You must not think, Moray," said he, "that I have been indifferent to your fate, but you can not guess how strong is the feeling against you, how obdurate is the Governor, who, if he should appear lax in dealing with you, would give a weapon into Bigot's hands which might ruin him in France one day. I have but this moment come from the Governor, and there seems no way to move him."

I saw that he was troubled greatly, and I felt his helplessness. He went on: "There is but one man who could bend the Governor, but he, alas! is no friend of yours. And what way there is to move him I know not; he has no wish, I fancy, but that you shall go to your fate."

"You mean Monsieur Doltaire?" said I quietly.

"Doltaire," he answered. "I have tried to find him, for he is the secret agent of La Pompadour, and if I had one plausible reason to weigh with him—— But I have none, unless you can give it. There are vague hints of things between you and him, and I have come to ask if you can put any fact, any argument, in my hands that would aid me with him. I would go far to serve you."

"Think not, I pray you," returned I, "that there is any debt unsatisfied between us."

He waved his hand in a melancholy way. "Indeed, I wish to serve you for the sake of past friendship between us, not only for that debt's sake."

"In spite of my quarrel with your son?" asked I.

"In spite of that, indeed," he said slowly, "though a great wedge was driven between us there."

"I am truly sorry for it," said I, with some pride. "The blame was in no sense mine. I was struck across the face; I humbled myself, remembering you, but he would have me out yes or no."

"Upon a wager!" he urged, somewhat coldly.

"With the Intendant, monsieur," I replied, "not with your son."

"I can not understand the matter," was his gloomy answer.

"I beg you not to try," I rejoined; "it is too late for explanations, and I have nothing to tell you of myself and Monsieur Doltaire. Only, whatever comes, remember I

9

have begged nothing of you, have desired nothing but justice—that only. I shall make no further move; the axe shall fall if it must. I have nothing now to do but set my house in order, and live the hours between this and sunrise with what quiet I may. I am ready for either freedom or death. Life is not so incomparable a thing that I can not give it up without pother."

He looked at me a moment steadily. "You and I are standing far off from each other," he remarked. "I will say one last thing to you, though you seem to wish me gone and your own grave closing in. I was asked by the Governor to tell you that if you would put him in the way of knowing the affairs of your provinces from the letters you have received, together with estimate of forces and plans of your forts, as you have known them, he will spare you. I only tell you this because you close all other ways to me."

"I carry," said I, with a sharp burst of anger, "the scars of wounds an insolent youth gave me. I wish now that I had killed the son of the man who dares bring me such a message."

For a moment I had forgotten Alixe, everything, in the wildness of my anger. I choked with rage; I could have struck him.

"I mean nothing against you," he urged, with great ruefulness. "I suggest nothing. I bring the Governor's message, that is all. And let me say," he added, "that I have not thought you a spy, nor ever shall think so."

I was trembling with anger still, and I was glad that at the moment Gabord opened the door and stood waiting.

"You will not part with me in peace, then?" asked the Seigneur slowly.

"I will remember the gentleman who gave a captive hospitality," I answered. "I am too near death to let a late injury outweigh an old friendship. I am ashamed, but not only for myself. Let us part in peace—ay, let us part in peace," I added with feeling, for the thought of Alixe came rushing over me, and this was her father!

"Good-by, Moray," he responded gravely. "You are a soldier, and brave. If the worst comes, I know how you will meet it. Let us waive all bitter thoughts between us. Good-by."

We shook hands then, without a word, and in a moment the dungeon door closed behind him, and I was alone. For a moment my heart was heavy beyond telling, and a terrible darkness settled on my spirit. I sat down on my couch and buried my head in my hands.

XI.

THE COMING OF DOLTAIRE.

AT last I was roused by Gabord's voice.

He sat down, and drew the leaves of faded corn between his fingers. "'Tis a poor life, this in a cage, after all—eh, dickey-bird? If a soldier can't stand in the field fighting, if a man can't rub shoulders with man, and pitch a tent of his own somewhere, why not go travelling with the Beast—aho? To have all the life sucked out like these—eh? To see the flesh melt and the hair go white, the eye to be one hour bright like a fire in a kiln, and the next like mother on working vinegar—that's not living at all—no."

The speech had evidently cost him much thinking, and when he ended, his cheeks puffed out and a soundless laugh seemed to gather, but it burst in a sort of sigh. I would have taken his hand that moment, if I had not remembered when once he drew back from such demonstrations. I did not speak, but nodded assent, and took to drawing the leaves of corn between my fingers as he was doing.

After a moment, cocking his head at me as might a surly schoolmaster in a pause of leniency, he added, " As quiet, as quiet, and never did he fly at door of cage, nor peck at jailer—aho ! "

I looked at him a minute seriously, and then, feeling in my coat, handed to him the knife which I had secreted, with the words, " Enough for pecking with, eh ? "

He looked at me so strangely, as he weighed the knife up and down in his hand, that I could not at first guess his thought; but presently I understood it, and I almost could have told what he would say. He opened the knife, felt the blade, measured it along his fingers, and then said, with a little bursting of the lips, " *Poom !* But what would ma'm'selle have thought if Gabord was found dead with a hole in his neck—behind ? Eh ? "

He had struck the very note that had sung in me when the temptation came ; but he was gay at once again, and I said to him, " What is the hour fixed ? "

" Seven o'clock," he answered, " and I will bring your breakfast first."

" Good-night, then," said I. " Coffee and a little to-bacco will be enough."

When he was gone I lay down on my bag of straw, which, never having been renewed, was now only full of worn chaff, and, gathering myself in my cloak, was soon in a dreamless sleep.

I waked to the opening of the dungeon door, to see Gabord entering with a torch and a tray that held my frugal breakfast. He had added some brandy, also, of which I was glad, for it was bitter cold outside, as I dis-covered later. He was quiet, seeming often to wish to speak, but pausing before the act, never getting beyond a stumbling *aho!* I greeted him cheerfully enough. After making a little toilette I drank my coffee with relish. At last I asked Gabord if no word had come to the citadel for me; and he said none at all, nothing save a message from the Governor, before midnight, ordering certain matters. No more was said, until, turning to the door, he told me he would return to fetch me forth in a few minutes. But when halfway out he suddenly wheeled, came back, and blurted out, "If you and I could only fight it out, m'sieu'! 'Tis ill for a gentleman and a soldier to die without thrust or parry."

"Gabord," said I, smiling at him, "you preach good sermons always, and I never saw a man I'd rather fight and be killed by than you!" Then, with an attempt at rough humour, I added, "But, as I told you once, the knot isn't at my throat, and I'll tie another one yet elsewhere if God loves honest men."

I had no hope at all, yet I felt I must say it. He nodded, but said nothing, and presently I was alone.

I sat down on my straw couch and composed myself to think; not upon my end, for my mind was made up as to that, but upon the girl who was so dear to me, whose life had crept into mine and filled it, making it of value in the world. It must not be thought that I no longer had care for our cause, for I would willingly have spent my life a hundred times for my country, as my best friends will bear witness; but there comes a time when a man has a right to set all else aside but his own personal love and welfare, and to me the world was now bounded by just so much space as my dear Alixe might move in. I fastened my thought upon her face as I had last seen it. My eyes seemed to search for it also, and to find it in the torch which stuck out, softly sputtering, from the wall. I do not pretend, even at this distance of time, after having thought much over the thing, to give any good reason

for so sudden a change as took place in me then and there.
All at once a voice appeared to say to me, "When you are
gone she will be Doltaire's. Remember what she said.
She fears him. He has a power over her."

Now, some will set it down to a low, unmanly jealousy
and suspicion. It is hard to name it, but I know that I was
seized with a misery so deep that all my past sufferings
and disappointments, and even this present horror, were
shadowy beside it. I pictured to myself Alixe in Doltaire's arms, after I had gone beyond human call. It is
strange how an idea will seize us and master us, and an
inconspicuous possibility suddenly stand out with huge
distinctness. All at once I felt in my head "the ring of
fire" of which Mathilde had warned me, a maddening
heat filled my veins, and that hateful picture grew more
vivid. Things Alixe had said the night before flashed to
my mind, and I fancied that, unknown to herself even,
he already had a substantial power over her.

He had deep determination, the gracious subtlety which
charms a woman, and she, hemmed in by his devices, overcome by his pleadings, attracted by his enviable personality,
would come at last to his will. The evening before I had
seen strong signs of the dramatic qualities of her nature.
She had the gift of imagination, the epic spirit. Even
three years previous I felt how she had seen every little incident of her daily life in a way which gave it vividness and
distinction. All things touched her with delicate emphasis—were etched upon her brain—or did not touch her
at all. She would love the picturesque in life, though her
own tastes were so simple and fine. Imagination would
beset her path with dangers; it would be to her, with her
beauty, a fatal gift, a danger to herself and others. She
would have power, and feeling it, womanlike, would use
it, dissipating her emotions, paying out the sweetness of
her soul, till one day a dramatic move, a strong pictur-

esque personality like Doltaire's, would catch her from the moorings of her truth, and the end must be tragedy to her. Doltaire! Doltaire! The name burned into my brain. Some prescient quality in me awaked, and I saw her the sacrifice of her imagination, of the dramatic beauty of her nature, my enemy her tyrant and destroyer. He would leave nothing undone to achieve his end, and do nothing that would not in the end poison her soul and turn her very glories into miseries. How could she withstand the charm of his keen knowledge of the world, the fascination of his temperament, the alluring eloquence of his frank wickedness? And I should rather a million times see her in her grave than passed through the atmosphere of his life.

This may seem madness, selfish and small; but after-events went far to justify my fears and imaginings, for behind all there was a love, an aching, absorbing solicitude. I can not think that my anxiety was all vulgar smallness then.

I called him by coarse names as I tramped up and down my dungeon; I cursed him; impotent contempt was poured out on him; in imagination I held him there before me, and choked him till his eyes burst out and his body grew limp in my arms. The ring of fire in my head scorched and narrowed till I could have shrieked in agony. My breath came short and laboured, and my heart felt as though it were in a vise and being clamped to nothing. For an instant, also, I broke out in wild bitterness against Alixe. She had said she would save me, and yet in an hour or less I should be dead. She had come to me last night—ah, true; but that was in keeping with her dramatic temperament; it was the drama of it that had appealed to her; and to-morrow she would forget me, and sink her fresh spirit in the malarial shadows of Doltaire's.

In my passion I thrust my hand into my waistcoat and

unconsciously drew out something. At first my only feeling was that my hand could clinch it, but slowly a knowledge of it travelled to my brain, as if through clouds and
vapours. Now I am no Catholic, I do not know that I
am superstitious, yet when I became conscious that the
thing I held was the wooden cross that Mathilde had given
me, a weird feeling passed through me, and there was an
arrest of the passions of mind and body; a coolness passed
over all my nerves, and my brain got clear again, the ring
of fire loosing, melting away. It was a happy, diverting
influence, which gave the mind rest for a moment, till the
better spirit, the wiser feeling, had a chance to reassert
itself; but at the time it seemed to me almost supernatural.

One can laugh when misery and danger are over, and
it would be easy to turn this matter into ridicule, but from
that hour to this the wooden cross which turned the flood
of my feelings then into a saving channel has never left
me. I keep it, not indeed for what it was, but for what
it did.

As I stood musing there came to my mind suddenly
the words of a song which I had heard some *voyageurs*
sing on the St. Lawrence as I sat on the cliff a hundred
feet above them and watched them drift down in the
twilight:

> " Brothers, we go to the Scarlet Hills:
> 　　(Little gold sun, come out of the dawn !)
> There we will meet in the cedar groves;
> 　　(Shining white dew, come down !)
> There is a bed where you sleep so sound,
> The little good folk of the hills will guard,
> Till the morning wakes and your love comes home.
> 　　(Fly away, heart, to the Scarlet Hills !)"

Something in the half-mystical, half-Arcadian spirit of the
words soothed me, lightened my thoughts, so that when,
presently, Gabord opened the door and entered with four

soldiers I was calm enough for the great shift. Gabord did not speak, but set about pinioning me himself. I asked him if he could not let me go unpinioned, for it was ignoble to go to one's death tied like a beast. At first he shook his head, but as if with a sudden impulse he cast the ropes aside, and, helping me on with my cloak, threw again over it a heavier cloak he had brought, gave me a fur cap to wear, and at last himself put on me a pair of woollen leggings, which, if they were no ornament, and to be of but transitory use (it seemed strange to me then that one should be caring for a body so soon to be cut off from all feeling), were most comforting when we came into the bitter, steely air. Gabord might easily have given these last tasks to the soldiers, but he was solicitous to perform them himself. Yet with surly brow and a rough accent he gave the word to go forward, and in a moment we were marching through the passages, up frosty steps, in the stone corridors, and on out of the citadel into the yard.

I remember that as we passed into the open air I heard the voice of a soldier singing a gay air of love and war. Presently he came in sight. He saw me, stood still for a moment looking curiously, and then, taking up the song again at the very line where he had broken off, passed round an angle of the building and was gone. To him I was no more than a moth fluttering in the candle, to drop dead a moment later.

It was just on the verge of sunrise. There was the grayish-blue light in the west, the top of a long range of forest was sharply outlined against it, and a timorous darkness was hurrying out of the zenith. In the east a sad, golden radiance was stealing up and driving back the mystery of the night and that weird loneliness of an arctic world. The city was hardly waking as yet, but straight silver columns of smoke rolled up out of many chimneys, and the golden cross on the cathedral caught the first rays of the sun. I was not interested in the city; I had now, as I thought, done with men. Besides the four soldiers who had brought me out, another squad surrounded me, commanded by a young officer whom I recognised as Captain Lancy, the rough roysterer who had insulted me at Bigot's palace over a year ago. I looked with a spirit absorbed upon the world about me, and a hundred thoughts which had to do with man's life passed through my mind. But the young officer, speaking sharply to me, ordered me on, and changed the current of my thoughts. The coarseness of the man and his insulting words were hard to bear, so that I was constrained to ask him if it were not customary to protect a condemned man from insult rather than to expose him to it. I said that I should be glad of my last moments in peace. At that he asked Gabord why I was unbound, and my jailer answered that binding was for criminals who were to be *hanged!*

I could scarcely believe my ears. I was to be shot, not hanged. I had a thrill of gratitude which I can not describe. It may seem a nice distinction, but to me there were whole seas between the two modes of death. I need not blush in advance for being shot—my friends could bear that without humiliation; but hanging would always have tainted their memory of me, try as they would against it.

"The gallows is ready, and my orders were to see him hanged," Mr. Lancy said.

"An order came at midnight that he should be shot," was Gabord's reply, producing the order and handing it over.

The officer contemptuously tossed it back, and now, a little more courteous, ordered me against the wall, and I let my cloak fall to the ground. I was placed where, looking east, I could see the Island of Orleans, on which

The Citadel.

was the summer-house of the Seigneur Duvarney. Gabord came to me and said, " M'sieu', you are a brave man "—then, all at once breaking off, he added in a low, hurried voice, " 'Tis not a long flight to heaven, m'sieu'! " I could see his face twitching as he stood looking at me. He hardly dared to turn round to his comrades, lest his emotion should be seen. But the officer roughly ordered him back. Gabord coolly drew out his watch, and made a motion to me not to take off my cloak yet.

" 'Tis not the time by six minutes," he said. " The gentleman is to be shot to the stroke—-aho ! " His voice and manner were dogged. The officer stepped forward threateningly; but Gabord said something angrily in an undertone, and the other turned on his heel and began walking up and down. This continued for a moment, in which we all were very still and bitter cold—the air cut like steel—and then my heart gave a great leap, for suddenly there stepped into the yard Doltaire. Action seemed suspended in me, but I know I listened with singular curiosity to the shrill creaking of his boots on the frosty earth, and I noticed that the fur collar of the coat he wore was all white with the frozen moisture of his breath, also that tiny icicles hung from his eyelashes. He came down the yard slowly, and presently paused and looked at Gabord and the young officer, his head laid a little to one side in a quizzical fashion, his eyelids drooping.

" What time was monsieur to be shot ? " he asked of Captain Lancy.

" At seven o'clock, monsieur," was the reply.

Doltaire took out his watch. " It wants three minutes of seven," said he. " What the devil means this business before the stroke o' the hour ? " waving a hand towards me.

" We were waiting for the minute, monsieur," was the officer's reply.

A cynical, cutting smile crossed Doltaire's face. "A charitable trick, upon my soul, to fetch a gentleman from a warm dungeon and stand him against an icy wall on a deadly morning to cool his heels as he waits for his hour to die! You'd skin your lion and shoot him afterwards —*voilà !*" All this time he held the watch in his hand.

"You, Gabord," he went on, "you are a man to obey orders—eh?"

Gabord hesitated a moment as if waiting for Lancy to speak, and then said, "I was not in command. When I was called upon I brought him forth."

"Excuses! excuses! You sweated to be rid of your charge."

Gabord's face lowered. "M'sieu' would have been in heaven by this if I hadn't stopped it," he broke out angrily.

Doltaire turned sharply on Lancy. "I thought as much," said he, "and you would have let Gabord share your misdemeanour. Yet your father was a gentleman! If you had shot monsieur before seven, you would have taken the dungeon he left. You must learn, my young provincial, that you are not to supersede France and the King. It is now seven o'clock; you will march your men back into quarters."

Then turning to me, he raised his cap. "You will find your cloak more comfortable, Captain Moray," said he, and he motioned Gabord to hand it to me, as he came forward. "May I breakfast with you?" he added courteously. He yawned a little. "I have not risen so early in years, and I am chilled to the bone. Gabord insists that it is warm in your dungeon; I have a fancy to breakfast there. It will recall my year in the Bastile."

He smiled in a quaint, elusive sort of fashion, and as I drew the cloak about me I said through chattering teeth, for I had suffered with the brutal cold, "I am glad to have the chance to offer breakfast."

"To me or any one?" he dryly suggested. "Think! by now, had I not come, you might have been in a warmer world than this—indeed, much warmer," he suddenly said, as he stooped, picked up some snow in his bare hand and clapped it to my cheek, rubbing it with force and swiftness. The cold had nipped it, and this was the way to draw out the frost. His solicitude at the moment was so natural and earnest that it was hard to think he was my enemy.

When he had rubbed awhile, he gave me his own handkerchief to dry my face; and so perfect was his courtesy, it was impossible to do otherwise than meet him as he meant and showed for the moment. He had stepped between me and death, and even an enemy who does that, no matter what the motive, deserves something at your hands.

"Gabord," he said, as we stepped inside the citadel, "we will breakfast at eight o'clock. Meanwhile I have some duties with our officers here. Till we meet in your dining-hall, then, monsieur," he added to me, and raised his cap.

"You must put up with frugal fare," I answered, bowing.

"If you but furnish locusts," he said gaily, "I will bring the wild honey. . . . What wonderful hives of bees they have at the Seigneur Duvarney's!" he continued musingly, as if with second thought; "a beautiful manor —a place for pretty birds and honey-bees!"

His eyelids drooped languidly, as was their way when he had said something a little carbolic, as this was to me because of its hateful suggestion. His words drew nothing from me, not even a look of understanding, and again bowing we went our ways.

At the door of the dungeon Gabord held the torch up
to my face.   His own had a look which came as near to
being gentle as was possible to him.   Yet he was so ugly
that it appeared almost ludicrous in him.

"*Poom!*" said he.   "A friend at court.   More comfits."

"You think Monsieur Doltaire gets comfits too?"
asked I.

He rubbed his cheek with a key.   "Aho!" mused he
—"aho!   M'sieu' Doltaire rises not early for naught."

XII.

"THE POINT ENVENOMED TOO!"

I WAS roused by the opening of the door.   Doltaire entered.   He advanced towards me with the manner of an
admired comrade, and, with no trace of what would mark
him as my foe, said, as he sniffed the air :

"Monsieur, I have been selfish.   I asked myself to
breakfast with you, yet, while I love the new experience,
I will deny myself in this.   You shall breakfast with me,
as you pass to your new lodgings.   You must not say no,"
he added, as though we were in some salon.   "I have a
sleigh here at the door, and a fellow has already gone to
fan my kitchen fires and forage for the table.   Come,"
he continued, "let me help you with your cloak."

He threw my cloak around me, and turned towards
the door.   I had not spoken a word, for what with weakness, the announcement that I was to have new lodgings,
and the sudden change in my affairs, I was like a child
walking in its sleep.   I could do no more than bow to
him and force a smile, which must have told more than
aught else of my state, for he stepped to my side and

offered me his arm. I drew back from that with thanks, for I felt a quick hatred of myself that I should take favours from the man who had moved for my destruction and to wickedly steal from me my promised wife. Yet it was my duty to live if I could, to escape if that were possible, to use every means to foil my enemies. It was all a game; why should I not accept advances at my enemy's hands, and match dissimulation with dissimulation?

When I refused his arm he smiled comically, and raised his shoulders in deprecation.

"You forget your dignity, monsieur," I said presently as we walked on, Gabord meeting us and lighting us through the passages; "you voted me a villain, a spy, at my trial!"

"Technically and publicly, you are a spy, a vulgar criminal," he replied; "privately, you are a foolish, blundering gentleman."

"A soldier also, you will admit, who keeps his compact with his enemy."

"Otherwise we should not breakfast together this morning," he answered. "What difference would it make to this government if our private matter had been dragged in? Technically you still would have been the spy. But I will say this, monsieur, to me you are a man better worth torture than death."

"Do you ever stop to think of how this may end for you?" I asked quietly.

He seemed pleased at the question. "I have thought it might be interesting," he answered; "else, as I said, you should long ago have left this naughty world. Is it in your mind that we shall cross swords one day?"

"I feel it in my bones," said I, "that I shall kill you."

At that moment we stood at the entrance to the citadel, where a good pair of horses and a sleigh awaited us. We got in, the robes were piled around us, and the horses started off at a long trot. I was muffled to the ears, but I could see how white and beautiful was the world, how the frost glistened in the trees, how the balsams were weighted down with snow, and how snug the châteaux looked with the smoke curling up from their hunched chimneys.

Presently Doltaire replied to my last remark. "Conviction is the executioner of the stupid," said he. "When a man is not great enough to let change and chance guide him he gets convictions and dies a fool."

"Conviction has made men and nations strong," I rejoined.

"Has made men and nations asses," he retorted. "The Mohammedan has conviction, so has the Christian: they die fighting each other, and the philosopher sits by and laughs. Expediency, monsieur, expediency is the real wisdom, the true master of this world. Expediency saved your life to-day; conviction would have sent you to a starry home."

As he spoke a thought came in on me. Here we were in the open world, travelling together, without a guard of any kind. Was it not possible to make a dash for freedom? The idea was put away from me, and yet it was a fresh accent of Doltaire's character that he tempted me in this way. As if he divined what I thought, he said to me —for I made no attempt to answer his question:

"Men of sense never confuse issues or choose the wrong time for their purposes. Foes may have unwritten truces."

There was the matter in a nutshell. He had done nothing carelessly; he was touching off our conflict with flashes of genius. He was the man who had roused in me last night the fiercest passions of my life, and yet this morning he had saved me from death, and though he was still my sworn enemy I was about to breakfast with him.

Already the streets of the town were filling; for it was the day before Christmas, and it would be the great market-day of the year. Few noticed us as we sped along down Palace Street, and I could not conceive whither we were going, until, passing the Hôtel Dieu, I saw in front of us the Intendance. I remembered the last time I was there and what had happened then, and a thought flashed through me that perhaps this was another trap. But I put it from me, and soon afterwards Doltaire said:

"I have now a slice of the Intendance for my own, and we shall breakfast like squirrels in a loft."

As we drove into the open space before the palace a company of soldiers standing before the great door began marching up to the road by which we came. With them was a prisoner. I saw at once that he was a British officer, but I did not recognise his face. I asked his name of Doltaire and found it was one Lieutenant Stevenson, of Rogers's Rangers, those brave New-Englanders. After an interview with Bigot he was being taken to the common jail. To my request that I might speak with him Doltaire assented, and at a sign from my companion the soldiers stopped. Stevenson's eyes were fixed on me with a puzzled, disturbed expression. He was well built, of intrepid bearing, with a fine openness of manner joined to handsome features. But there was a recklessness in his eye which seemed to me to come nearer the swashbuckling character of a young French seigneur than the wariness of a British soldier.

I spoke his name and introduced myself. His surprise and pleasure were pronounced, for he had thought (as he said) that by this time I should be dead. There was an instant's flash of his eye, as if a suspicion of my loyalty had crossed his mind; but it was gone on the instant, and

10

immediately Doltaire, who also had interpreted the look, smiled, and said he had carried me off to breakfast while the furniture of my former prison was being shifted to my new one. After a word or two more, with Stevenson's assurance that the British had recovered from Braddock's defeat and would presently be knocking at the portals of the Château St. Louis, we parted, and soon Doltaire and I got out at the high stone steps of the palace.

Standing there for a moment I looked round. In this space surrounding the Intendance was gathered the history of New France. This palace, large enough for the king of a European country with a population of a million, was the official residence of the commercial ruler of a province. It was the house of the miller, and across the way was the King's storehouse, La Friponne, where poor folk were ground between the stones. The great square was already filling with people who had come to trade. Here were barrels of malt being unloaded; there, great sacks of grain, bags of dried fruits, bales of home-made cloth, and loads of fine-sawn boards and timber. Moving about among the peasants were the regular soldiers in their white uniforms faced with blue, red, yellow, or violet, with black three-cornered hats, and black gaiters from foot to knee, and the militia in coats of white with black facings. Behind a great collar of dogskin a pair of jet-black eyes flashed out from under a pretty forehead; and presently one saw these same eyes grown sorrowful or dull under heavy knotted brows, which told of a life too vexed by care and labour to keep alive a spark of youth's romance. Now the bell in the tower above us rang a short peal, the signal for the opening of La Friponne, and the bustling crowd moved towards its doors. As I stood there on the great steps, I chanced to look along the plain, bare front of the palace to an annex at the end, and standing in a doorway opening on a pair of steps was Voban. I

was amazed that he should be there—the man whose life
had been spoiled by Bigot. At the same moment Doltaire
motioned to him to return inside; which he did.

Doltaire laughed at my surprise, and, as he showed me
inside the palace, said: "There is no barber in the world
like Voban. Interesting! interesting! I love to watch
his eye when he draws the razor down my throat. It
would be so easy to fetch it across; but Voban, as you see,
is not a man of absolute conviction. It will be sport, some
day, to put Bigot's valet to bed with a broken leg or a fit
of spleen, and send Voban to shave him."

"Where is Mathilde?" I asked, as though I knew
naught of her whereabouts.

"Mathilde is where none may touch her, monsieur:
even under the protection of the daintiest lady of New
France. It is her whim; and when a lady is charming,
an Intendant, even, must not trouble her caprice."

He did not need to speak more plainly. It was he
who had prevented Bigot from taking Mathilde away
from Alixe and locking her up, or worse. I said nothing, however, and soon we were in a large room sumptu-
ously furnished, looking out on the great square. The
morning sun stared in, some snowbirds twittered on the
window-sill, and inside, a canary, in an alcove hung with
plants and flowers, sang as if it were the heart of summer.
All was warm and comfortable, and it was like a dream
that I had just come from the dismal chance of a miserable death. My cloak and cap and leggings had been taken
from me when I entered, as courteously as though I had
been King Louis himself, and a great chair was drawn
solicitously to the fire. All this was done by the servant,
after one quick look from Doltaire. The man seemed
to understand his master perfectly, to read one look as
though it were a volume—

"The constant service of the antique world."

Such was Doltaire's influence. The closer you came to him, the more compelling was he—a devilish attraction, notably selfish, yet capable of benevolence. Two years before this time I saw him lift a load from the back of a peasant woman and carry it home for her, putting into her hand a gold piece on leaving. At another time, an old man had died of a foul disease in a miserable upper room of a warehouse. Doltaire was passing at the moment when the body should be carried to burial. The stricken widow of the dead man stood below, waiting, but no one would fetch forth the corpse. Doltaire stopped and questioned her kindly, and in another minute he was driving the carter and another upstairs at the point of his sword. Together they brought the body down, and Doltaire followed it to the burying-ground, keeping the gravedigger at his task when he would have run away, and saying the responses to the priest in the short service read above the grave.

I said to him then, " You rail at the world and scoff at men and many decencies, and yet you do these things ! "

To this he replied—he was in my own lodgings at the time—" The brain may call all men liars and fools, but the senses feel the shock of misery which we do not ourselves inflict. Inflicting, we are prone to cruelty, as you have seen a schoolmaster begin punishment with tears, grow angry at the shrinking back under his cane, and give way to a sudden lust of torture. I have little pity for those who can help themselves—let them fight or eat the leek ; but the child and the helpless and the sick it is a pleasure to aid. I love the poor as much as I love anything. I could live their life, if I were put to it. As a gentleman, I hate squalor and the puddles of wretchedness : but I could have worked at the plough or the anvil ; I could have dug in the earth till my knuckles grew big and my shoulders hardened to a roundness, have eaten my beans and pork and pea-soup, and have been a healthy ox, munching the bread of industry and trailing the puissant pike, an obedient serf. I have no ethics, and yet I am on the side of the just when they do not put thorns in my bed to keep me awake at night!"

Upon the walls hung suits of armour, swords of beautiful make, spears, belts of wonderful workmanship, a tattered banner, sashes knit by ladies' fingers, pouches, bandoleers, and many agreeable sketches of scenes that I knew well. Now and then a woman's head in oils or pencil peeped out from the abundant ornaments. I recalled then another thing he said at that time of which I write:

"I have never juggled with my conscience—never 'made believe' with it. My will was always stronger than my wish for anything, always stronger than temptation. I have chosen this way or that deliberately. I am ever ready to face consequences, and I never cry out. It is the ass undeserving of either reward or punishment who says that something carried him away, and, being weak, he fell. That is a poor man who is no stronger than his passions. I can understand the devil fighting God, and taking the long punishment without repentance, like a powerful prince as he was. I could understand a peasant killing King Louis in the palace, and being ready, if he had a hundred lives, to give them all, having done the deed he set out to do. If a man must have convictions of that sort, he can escape everlasting laughter—the final hell—only by facing the rebound of his wild deeds."

These were strange sentiments in the mouth of a man who was ever the mannered courtier, and as I sat there alone, while he was gone elsewhere for some minutes, many such things he had said came back to me, suggested, no doubt, by this new, inexplicable attitude towards myself. I could trace some of his sentiments, perhaps vaguely, to the fact that—as I had come to know through the Seigneur Duvarney—his mother was of peasant blood, the beautiful daughter of a farmer of Poictiers, who had died soon after giving birth to Doltaire. His peculiar nature had shown itself in his refusal to accept a title. It was his whim to be the plain "Monsieur"; behind which was, perhaps, some native arrogancy that made him prefer this to being a noble whose origin, well known, must ever interfere with his ambitions. Then, too, maybe, the peasant in him—never in his face or form, which were patrician altogether—spoke for more truth and manliness than he was capable of, and so he chose to be the cynical, irresponsible courtier, while many of his instincts had urged him to the peasant's integrity. He had undisturbed however one instinct of the peasant —a good directness, evident mostly in the clearness of his thoughts.

As these things hurried through my mind, my body sunk in a kind of restfulness before the great fire, Doltaire came back.

"I will not keep you from breakfast," said he. "Voban must wait, if you will pass by untidiness."

A thought flashed through my mind. Perhaps Voban had some word for me from Alixe! So I said instantly, "I am not hungry. Perhaps you will let me wait yonder while Voban tends you. As you said, it should be interesting."

"You will not mind the disorder of my dressing-room? Well, then, this way, and we can talk while Voban plays with temptation."

So saying, he courteously led the way into another chamber where Voban stood waiting. I spoke to him, and he bowed but did not speak; and then Doltaire said:

"You see, Voban, your labour on monsieur was wasted

so far as concerns the world to come. You trimmed him
for the glorious company of the apostles, and see, he
breakfasts with Monsieur Doltaire—in the Intendance,
too, my Voban, which, as you know, is wicked—a very
nest of wasps!"

I never saw more hate than shot out of Voban's eyes
at that moment; but the lids drooped over them at once,
and he made ready for his work, as Doltaire, putting aside
his coat, seated himself, laughing. There was no little
daring, as there was cruelty, in thus torturing a man
whose life had been broken by Doltaire's associate. I
wondered now and then if Doltaire were not really putting acid on the barber's bare nerves for some other purpose than mere general cruelty. Even as he would have
understood the peasant's murder of King Louis, so he
would have seen a logical end to a terrible game in Bigot's
death at the hand of Voban. Possibly he wondered that
Voban did not strike, and he himself took delight in
showing him his own wrongs occasionally. Then, again,
Doltaire might wish for Bigot's death, to succeed him
in his place! But this I put by as improbable, for the
Intendant's post was not his ambition, or, favourite of La
Pompadour as he was, he would, desiring, have long ago
achieved that end. Moreover, every evidence showed that
he would gladly return to France, for his clear brain foresaw the final ruin of the colony and the triumph of the
British. He had once said in my hearing:

"Those swaggering Englishmen will keep coming on.
They are too stupid to turn back. The eternal sameness
of it all will so distress us we shall awake one morning,
find them at our bedsides, give a kick, and die from sheer
ennui. They'll use our banners to boil their fat puddings
in, they'll roast oxen in the highways, and after our
girls have married them they'll turn them into kitchen
wenches with frowsy skirts and ankles like beeves!"

But, indeed, beneath his dangerous irony there was a strain of impishness, and he would, if need be, laugh at his own troubles, and torture himself as he had tortured others. This morning he was full of a carbolic humour. As the razor came to his neck he said :

"Voban, a barber must have patience. It is a sad thing to mistake friend for enemy. What is a friend? Is it one who says sweet words?"

There was a pause, in which the shaving went on, and then he continued :

"Is it he who says, I have eaten Voban's bread, and Voban shall therefore go to prison or be hurried to Walhalla? Or is it he who stays the iron hand, who puts nettles in Voban's cold, cold bed, that he may rise early and go forth among the heroes?"

I do not think Voban understood that, through some freak of purpose, Doltaire was telling him thus obliquely he had saved him from Bigot's cruelty, from prison or death. Once or twice he glanced at me, but not meaningly, for Doltaire was seated opposite a mirror, and could see each motion made by either of us. Presently Doltaire said to me idly :

"I dine to-day at the Seigneur Duvarney's. You will be glad to hear that mademoiselle bids fair to rival the charming Madame Cournal. Her followers are as many, so they say, and all in one short year she has suddenly thrown out a thousand new faculties and charms. Doubtless you remember she was gifted, but who would have thought she could have blossomed so! She was all light and softness and air; she is now all fire and skill as well. Matchless! matchless! Every day sees her with some new capacity, some fresh and delicate aplomb. She has set the town admiring, and jealous mothers prophesy trist ending for her. Her swift mastery of the social arts is weird, they say. La! la! The social arts! A good brain, a gift of penetration, a manner—which is a grand necessity, and it must be with birth—and no heart to speak of, and the rest is easy. No heart—there is the thing; with a good brain and senses all warm with life—to feel, but never to have the arrow strike home. You must never think to love and be loved, and be wise too. The emotions blind the judgment. Be heartless, be perfect with heavenly artifice, and, if you are a woman, have no vitriol on your tongue—and you may rule at Versailles or Quebec. But with this difference: in Quebec you may be virtuous; at Versailles you must not. It is a pity that you may not meet Mademoiselle Duvarney. She would astound you. She was a simple ballad a year ago; to-morrow she may be an epic."

He nodded at me reflectively, and went on:

"'Mademoiselle,' said the Chevalier de la Darante to her at dinner, some weeks ago, 'if I were young, I should adore you.' 'Monsieur,' she answered, 'you use that "if" to shirk the responsibility.' That put him on his mettle. 'Then, by the gods, I adore you now!' he answered. 'If I were young, I should blush to hear you say so,' was her reply. 'I empty out my heart, and away trips the disdainful nymph with a laugh,' he rejoined gaily, the rusty old courtier; 'there's nothing left but to fall upon my sword!' 'Disdainful nymphs are the better scabbards for distinguished swords,' she said, with charming courtesy. Then, laughing softly, 'There is an Egyptian proverb which runs thus: "If thou, Dol, son of Hoshti, hast emptied out thy heart, and it bring no fruit in exchange, curse not thy gods and die, but build a pyramid in the vineyard where thy love was spent, and write upon it, *Pride hath no conqueror.*"' It is a mind for a palace, is it not?"

I could see in the mirror facing him the provoking devilry of his eyes. I knew that he was trying how much he could stir me. He guessed my love for her, but I could see he was sure that she no longer—if she ever had—thought of me. Besides, with a lover's understanding, I saw also that he liked to talk of her. His eyes, in the mirror, did not meet mine, but were fixed, as on some distant and pleasing prospect, though there was, as always, a slight disdain at his mouth. But the eyes were clear, resolute, and strong, never wavering—and I never saw them waver—yet in them something distant and inscrutable. It was a candid eye, and he was candid in his evil; he made no pretence; and though the means to his ends were wicked, they were never low. Presently, glancing round the room, I saw an easel on which was a canvas. He caught my glance.

"Silly work for a soldier and a gentleman," he said, "but silliness is a great privilege. It needs as much skill to carry folly well as to be an ambassador. Now, you are often much too serious, Captain Moray."

At that he rose, and, after putting on his coat, came over to the easel and threw up the cloth, exposing a portrait of Alixe! It had been painted in by a few bold strokes, full of force and life, yet giving her face more of that look which comes to women bitterly wise in the ways of this world than I cared to see. The treatment was daring, and it cut me like a knife that the whole painting had a red glow: the dress was red, the light falling on the hair was red, the shine of the eyes was red also. It was fascinating, but weird, and, to me, distressful. There flashed through my mind the remembrance of Mathilde in her scarlet robe as she stood on the Heights that momentous night of my arrest. I looked at the picture in silence. He kept gazing at it with a curious, half-quizzical smile, as if he were unconscious of my presence. At last he said, with a slight knitting of his brows:

"It is strange—strange. I sketched that in two nights ago, by the light of the fire, after I had come from the Château St. Louis—from memory, as you see. It never struck me where the effect was taken from, that singular glow over all the face and figure. But now I see it; it returns: it is the impression of colour in the senses, left from the night that lady-bug Mathilde flashed out on the Heights! A fine—a fine effect! H'm! for another such one might give another such Mathilde!"

At that moment we were both startled by a sound behind us, and, wheeling, we saw Voban, a look of rage in his face, in the act of throwing at Doltaire a short spear which he had caught up from a corner. The spear flew from his hand even as Doltaire sprang aside, drawing his sword with great swiftness. I thought he must have been killed, but the rapidity of his action saved him, for the spear passed his shoulder so close that it tore away a shred of his coat and stuck in the wall behind him. In another instant Doltaire had his sword-point at Voban's throat. The man did not cringe, did not speak a word, but his hands clinched and the muscles of his face worked painfully. At first there was a fury in Doltaire's face and a metallic hardness in his eyes, and I was sure he meant to pass his sword through the other's body; but after standing for a moment, death hanging on his sword-point, he quietly lowered his weapon, and, sitting on a chair-arm, looked curiously at Voban, as one might sit and watch a mad animal within a cage. Voban did not stir, but stood rooted to the spot, his eyes never moving from Doltaire. It was clear that he had looked for death, and now expected punishment and prison. Doltaire took out his handkerchief and wiped a sweat from his cheeks. He turned to me soon, and said, in a singularly impersonal way, as though he were speaking of some animal:

"He had great provocation. The Duchess de Valois

had a young panther once which she had brought up
from the milk. She was inquisitive, and used to try its
temper. It was good sport, but one day she took away
its food, gave it to the cat, and pointed her finger at
monsieur the panther. The Duchess de Valois never
bared her breast thereafter to an admiring world—a panther's claws leave scars." He paused, and presently continued : " You remember it, Voban ; you were the Duke's
valet then—you see I recall you ! Well, the panther lost
his head, both figuratively and in fact. The panther did
not mean to kill, maybe, but to kill the lady's beauty was
death to her. . . . Voban, yonder spear was poisoned ! "

He wiped his face, and said to me, " I think you saw
that at the dangerous moment I had no fear; yet now
when the game is in my own hands my cheek runs with
cold sweat. How easy to be charged with cowardice !
Like evaporation, the hot breath of peril passing suddenly into the cold air of safety leaves this ! "—he wiped
his cheek again.

He rose, moved slowly to Voban, and, pricking him
with his sword, said, " You are a bungler, barber. Now
listen. I never wronged you ; I have only been your blis-
ter. I prick your sores at home. Tut ! tut ! they prick
them openly in the market-place. I gave you life a minute ago ; I give you freedom now. Some day I may ask
that life for a day's use, and then, Voban, then will you
give it ? "

There was a moment's pause, and the barber answered, " M'sieu', I owe you nothing. I would have
killed you then ; you may kill me, if you will."

Doltaire nodded musingly. Something was passing
through his mind. I judged he was thinking that here
was a man who, as a servant, would be invaluable.

" Well, well, we can discuss the thing at leisure,
Voban," he said at last. " Meanwhile you may wait here

till Captain Moray has breakfasted, and then you shall be at his service; and I would have a word with you, also."

Turning with a polite gesture to me, he led the way into the breakfast-room, and at once, half famished, I was seated at the table, drinking a glass of good wine, and busy with a broiled whitefish of delicate quality. We were silent for a time, and the bird in the alcove kept singing as though it were in Eden, while chiming in between the rhythms there came the silvery sound of sleigh-bells from the world without. I was in a sort of dream, and I felt there must be a rude awakening soon. After a while, Doltaire, who seemed thinking keenly, ordered the servant to take in a glass of wine to Voban.

He looked up at me after a little, as if he had come back from a long distance, and said, " It is my fate to have as foes the men I would have as friends, and as friends the men I would have as foes. The cause of my friends is often bad; the cause of my enemies is sometimes good. It is droll. I love directness, yet I have ever been the slave of complication. I delight in following my reason, yet I have been of the motes that stumble in the sunlight. I have enough cruelty in me, enough selfishness and will, to be a ruler, and yet I have never held an office in my life. I love true diplomacy, yet I have been comrade to the official liar and am the captain of intrigue—la! la! "

" You have never had an enthusiasm, a purpose?" said I.

He laughed, a dry, ironical laugh. " I have both an enthusiasm and a purpose," he answered, " or you would by now be snug in bed forever."

I knew what he meant, though he could not guess I understood. He was referring to Alixe and the challenge she had given him. I did not feel that I had anything to get by playing a part of friendliness, and besides, he was a man to whom the boldest speaking was always palatable, even when most against himself.

"I am sure neither would bear daylight," said I.

"Why, I almost blush to say that they are both honest—would at this moment endure a moral microscope. The experience, I confess, is new, and has the glamour of originality."

"It will not stay honest," I retorted. "Honesty is a new toy with you. You will break it on the first rock that shows."

"I wonder," he answered, "I wonder, . . . and yet I suppose you are right. Some devilish incident will twist things out of gear, and then the old Adam must improvise for safety and success. Yes, I suppose my one beautiful virtue will get a twist."

What he had said showed me his mind as in a mirror. He had no idea that I had the key to his enigmas. I felt as had Voban in the other room. I could see that he had set his mind on Alixe, and that she had roused in him what was perhaps the first honest passion of his life.

What further talk we might have had I can not tell, but while we were smoking and drinking coffee the door opened suddenly, and the servant said:

"His Excellency the Marquis de Vaudreuil!"

Doltaire got to his feet, a look of annoyance crossing his face; but he courteously met the Governor, and placed a chair for him. The Governor, however, said frostily, "Monsieur Doltaire, it must seem difficult for Captain Moray to know who is Governor in Canada, since he has so many masters. I am not sure who needs assurance most upon the point, you or he. This is the second time he has been feasted at the Intendance when he should have been in prison. I came too late that other time; now it seems I am opportune."

Doltaire's reply was smooth: "Your Excellency will

pardon the liberty. The Intendance was a sort of half-way house between the citadel and the jail."

"There is news from France," the Governor said, "brought from Gaspé. We meet in council at the Château in an hour. A guard is without to take Captain Moray to the common jail."

In a moment more, after a courteous good-by from Doltaire, and a remark from the Governor to the effect that I had spoiled his night's sleep to no purpose, I was soon on my way to the common jail, where arriving, what was my pleased surprise to see Gabord! He had been told off to be my especial guard, his services at the citadel having been deemed so efficient. He was outwardly surly —as rough as he ever was before the world, and, without speaking a word to me, he had a soldier lock me in a cell.

XIII.

"A LITTLE BOAST."

My new abode was more cheerful than the one I had quitted in the citadel. It was not large, but it had a window, well barred, through which came the good strong light of the northern sky. A wooden bench for my bed stood in one corner, and, what cheered me much, there was a small iron stove. Apart from warmth, its fire would be companionable, and to tend it a means of passing the time. Almost the first thing I did was to examine it. It was round, and shaped like a small bulging keg on end. It had a lid on top and in the side a small door with bars for draught, suggesting to me in little the delight of a fireplace. A small pipe carried away the smoke into a chimney in the wall. It seemed to me luxurious, and my spirits came back apace.

There was no fire yet, and it was bitter cold, so that I took to walking up and down to keep warmth in me. I was ill nourished, and I felt the cold intensely. But I trotted up and down, plans of escape already running through my head. I was as far off as you can imagine from that event of the early morning when I stood wait-ing, half frozen, to be shot by Lancy's men.

After I had been walking swiftly up and down for an hour or more, slapping my hands against my sides to keep them warm—for it was so cold I ached and felt a nausea —I was glad to see Gabord enter with a soldier carrying wood and shavings. I do not think I could much longer have borne the chilling air—a dampness, too, had risen from the floor, which had been washed that morning—for my clothes were very light in texture and much worn. I had had but the one suit since I entered the dungeon in the citadel, for my other suit, which was by no means smart, had been taken from me when I was imprisoned the year before. As if many good things had been des-tined to come at once, soon afterwards another soldier entered with a knapsack, which he laid down on the bench. It held my other poor suit of clothes, together with a rough set of woollens, a few handkerchiefs, two pairs of stockings, and a wool cap for night wear.

Gabord did not speak to me at all, but roughly hur-ried the soldier at his task of fire-lighting, and ordered the other to fetch a pair of stools and a jar of water. Meanwhile I stood near, watching, and stretched out my skinny hands to the grateful heat as soon as the fire was lighted. I had a boy's delight in noting how the draught pumped the fire into violence, shaking the stove till it puffed and roared. I was so filled, that moment, with the domestic spirit that I thought a steaming kettle on the little stove would give me a tabby-like com-fort.

"Why not a kettle on the hob?" said I gaily to Gabord.

"Why not a cat before the fire, a bit of bacon on the coals, a pot of mulled wine at elbow, and wench's chin to chuck, baby-bumbo!" said Gabord in a mocking voice, which made the soldiers laugh at my expense. "And a spinet, too, for ducky dear, Scarrat; a piece of cake and cherry wine, and a soul to go to heaven! Tonnerre!" he added, with an oath, "these English prisoners want the world for a sou, and they'd owe that till judgment day."

I saw at once the meaning of his words, for he turned his back on me, and, going to the window, tried the stanchions, seeming much concerned about them, and muttering to himself. I drew from my pocket two gold pieces, and gave them to the soldier Scarrat; and the other soldier coming in just then, I did the same with him; and I could see that their respect for me mightily increased. Gabord, still muttering, turned to us again, and began to berate the soldiers for their laziness. As the two men turned to go, Scarrat, evidently feeling that something was due for the gold I had given, said to Gabord, "Shall m'sieu' have the kettle?"

Gabord took a step forward as if to strike the soldier, but stopped short, blew out his cheeks, and laughed in a loud, mocking way.

"Ay, ay, fetch m'sieu' the kettle, and fetch him flax to spin, and a pinch of snuff, and hot flannels for his stomach, and every night at sundown you shall feed him with pretty biscuits soaked in milk. Ah, go to the devil and fetch the kettle, fool!" he added roughly again, and quickly the place was empty save for him and myself.

"Those two fellows are to sit outside your cage door, dickey-bird, and two are to march beneath your window
11

yonder, so you shall not lack care if you seek to go abroad.
Those are the new orders."

"And you, Gabord," said I, "are you not to be my
jailer?" I said it sorrowfully, for I had a genuine feeling for him, and I could not keep that from my voice.

When I had spoken so feelingly, he stood for a moment, flushing and puffing, as if confused by the compliment in the tone, and then he answered, "I'm to keep
you safe till word comes from the King what's to be done
with you."

Then he suddenly became surly again, standing with
legs apart and keys dangling; for Scarrat entered with
the kettle and put it on the stove. "You will bring
blankets for m'sieu'," he added, "and there's an order
on my table for tobacco, which you will send your comrade for."

In a moment we were left alone.

"You'll live like a stuffed pig here," he said, "though
'twill be cold o' nights."

After another pass or two of words he left me, and I
hastened to make a better toilet than I had done for a
year. My old rusty suit which I exchanged for the one I
had worn seemed almost sumptuous, and the woollen wear
comforted my weakened body. Within an hour my cell
looked snug, and I sat cosily by the fire, feeding it lazily.

It must have been about four o'clock when there was
a turning of keys and a shooting of bolts, the door opened,
and who should step inside but Gabord, followed by Alixe!
I saw Alixe's lips frame my name thrice, though no word
came forth, and my heart was bursting to cry out and clasp
her to my breast. But still, with a sweet, serious look cast
on me, she put out her hand and stayed me.

Gabord, looking not at us at all, went straight to the
window, and, standing on a stool, busied himself with the
stanchions and began to whistle. I took Alixe's hands

and held them, and spoke her name softly, and she smiled up at me with so perfect a grace that I thought there never was aught like it in the world.

She was the first to break the good spell. I placed a seat for her, and sat down by her. She held out her fingers to the fire, and then, after a moment, she told me the story of last night's affair. First she made me tell her briefly of the events of the morning, of which she knew, but not fully. This done, she began. I will set down her story as a whole, and you must understand as you read that it was told as women tell a story, with all little graces and diversions, and those small details with which even momentous things are enveloped in their eyes. I loved her all the more because of these, and I saw, as Doltaire had said, how admirably poised was her intellect, how acute her wit, how delicate and astute a diplomatist she was becoming; and yet, through all, preserving a simplicity of character almost impossible of belief. Such qualities, in her directed to good ends, in lesser women have mostly made them infamous. Once that day Alixe said to me, breaking off as her story went on, " Oh, Robert, when I see what power I have to dissimulate— for it is that, call it by what name you will—when I see how I enjoy accomplishing against all difficulty, how I can blind even so skilled a diplomatist as Monsieur Doltaire, I almost tremble. I see how, if God had not given me something here "—she placed her hand upon her heart—" that saves me, I might be like Madame Cournal, and far worse, far worse than she. For I love power— I do love it; I can see that ! "

She did not realize that it was her strict honesty with herself which was her true safeguard.

Here is the story she told me :

" When I left you last night, I went at once to my home, and was glad to get in without being seen. At nine o'clock we were to be at the Château, and while my sister Georgette was helping me with my toilette—oh, how I wished she would go and leave me quite alone!—my head was in a whirl, and now and then I could feel my heart draw and shake like a half-choked pump, and there was a strange pain behind my eyes. Georgette is of such a warm disposition, so kind always to me, whom she would yield to in everything, so simple in her affections, that I seemed standing there by her like an intrigante, as one who had got wisdom at the price of a good something lost. But do not think, Robert, that for one instant I was sorry I played a part, and have done so for a long year and more. I would do it again, and more, if it were for you.

"Georgette could not understand why it was I stopped all at once and caught her head to my breast, as she sat by me where I stood arranging my gown. I do not know quite why I did it, but perhaps it was from my yearning that never should she have a lover in such sorrow and danger as mine, and that never should she have to learn to mask her heart as I have done. Ah, sometimes I fear, Robert, that when all is over, and you are free, and you see what the world and all this playing at hide-and-seek have made me, you will feel that such as Georgette, who have never looked inside the hearts of wicked people, and read the tales therein for knowledge to defeat wickedness—that such as she were better fitted for your life and love. No, no, please do not take my hand—not till you have heard all I am going to tell."

She continued quietly; yet her eye flashed, and now and then something in her thoughts as to how she, a weak, powerless girl, had got her ends against astute evil men, sent a little laugh to her lips; for she had by nature as merry a heart as serious.

"At nine o'clock we came to the Château St. Louis

from Ste. Anne Street, where our winter home is—yet how much do I prefer the Manor House! There were but few guests to supper, and Monsieur Doltaire was not among them. I affected a genial surprise, and asked the Governor if one of the two vacant chairs at the table was for monsieur; and looking a little as though he would reprove me—for he does not like to think of me as interested in monsieur—he said it was, but that monsieur was somewhere out of town, and there was no surety that he would come. The other chair was for the Chevalier de la Darante, one of the oldest and best of our nobility, who pretends great roughness and barbarism, but is a kind and honourable gentleman, though odd. He was one of your judges, Robert; and though he condemned you, he said that you had some reason on your side. I will show you how he stood for you last night.

"I need not tell you how the supper passed, while I was planning—planning to reach the Governor if monsieur did not come; and if he did come, how to play my part so he should suspect nothing but a vain girl's caprice, and maybe heartlessness. Moment after moment went by, and he came not. I almost despaired. Presently the Chevalier de la Darante entered, and he took the vacant chair beside me. I was glad of this. I had gone in upon the arm of a rusty gentleman of the Court, who is over here to get his health again, and does so by gaming and drinking at the Château Bigot. The Chevalier began at once to talk to me, and he spoke of you, saying that he had heard of your duel with my brother, and that formerly you had been much a guest at our house. I answered him with what carefulness I could, and brought round the question of your death, by hint and allusion getting him to speak of the mode of execution.

"Upon this point he spoke his mind strongly, saying that it was a case where the penalty should be the musket, not the rope. It was no subject for the supper table, and the Governor felt this, and I feared he would show displeasure; but other gentlemen took up the matter, and he could not easily change the talk at the moment. The feeling was strong against you. My father stayed silent, but I could see he watched the effect upon the Governor. I knew that he himself had tried to have the mode of execution changed, but the Governor had been immovable. The Chevalier spoke most strongly, for he is afraid of no one, and he gave the other gentlemen raps upon the knuckles.

"'I swear,' he said at last, 'I am sorry now I gave in to his death at all, for it seems to me that there is much cruelty and hatred behind the case against him. He seemed to me a gentleman of force and fearlessness, and what he said had weight. Why was the gentleman not exchanged long ago? He was here three years before he was tried on this charge. Ay, there's the point! Other prisoners were exchanged—why not he? If the gentleman is not given a decent death, after these years of captivity, I swear I will not leave Kamaraska again to set foot in Quebec.'

"At that the Governor gravely said, 'These are matters for our Council, dear Chevalier.' To this the Chevalier replied, 'I meant no reflection on your Excellency, but you are good enough to let the opinions of gentlemen not so wise as you weigh with you in your efforts to be just; and I have ever held that one wise autocrat was worth a score of juries.' There was an instant's pause, and then my father said quietly, 'If his Excellency had always councillors and colleagues like the Chevalier de la Darante, his path would be easier, and Canada happier and richer.' This settled the matter, for the Governor, looking at them both for a moment, suddenly said, 'Gentlemen, you shall have your way, and I thank you for your confidence.—If the ladies will pardon a sort of council of state here!' he added. The Governor called a servant, and ordered pen, ink, and paper; and there before us all he wrote an order to Gabord, your jailer, to be delivered before midnight.

"He had begun to read it aloud to us, when the curtains of the entrance-door parted, and Monsieur Doltaire stepped inside. The Governor did not hear him, and monsieur stood for a moment listening. When the reading was finished he gave a dry little laugh, and came down to the Governor, apologizing for his lateness, and bowing to the rest of us. He did not look at me at all, but once he glanced keenly at my father, and I felt sure that he had heard my father's words to the Governor.

"'Have the ladies been made councillors?' he asked lightly, and took his seat, which was opposite to mine. 'Have they all conspired to give a criminal one less episode in his life for which to blush? . . . May I not join the conspiracy?' he added, glancing round, and lifting a glass of wine. Not even yet had he looked at me. Then he waved his glass the circuit of the table and said, 'I drink to the councillors and applaud the conspirators,' and as he raised his glass to his lips his eyes came abruptly to mine and stayed, and he bowed profoundly and with an air of suggestion. He drank, still looking, and then turned again to the Governor. I felt my heart stand still. Did he suspect my love for you, Robert? Had he discovered something? Was Gabord a traitor to us? Had I been watched, detected? I could have shrieked at the suspense. I was like one suddenly faced with a dreadful accusation, with which was a great fear. But I held myself still—oh, so still, so still!—and as in a dream I heard the Governor say pleasantly, 'I would I had such conspirators always by me. I am sure you would wish them to take more responsibility than you will now as-

sume in Canada.' Doltaire bowed and smiled, and the
Governor went on : ' I am sure you will approve of Captain Moray being shot instead of hanged. But indeed it
has been my good friend the Chevalier here who has
given me the best council I have held in many a day.'

" To this Monsieur Doltaire replied : ' A council unknown to statute, but approved of those who stand for
etiquette with one's foes at any cost. For myself, it is
so unpleasant to think of the rope ' " (here Alixe hid her
face in her hands for a moment) " ' that I should eat no
breakfast to-morrow if the gentleman from Virginia were
to hang.' It was impossible to tell from his tone what
was in his mind, and I dared not think of his failure to
interfere as he had promised me. As yet he had done
nothing, I could see, and in eight or nine hours more you
were to die. He did not look at me again for some time,
but talked to my mother and my father and the Chevalier, commenting on affairs in France and the war between our countries, but saying nothing of where he had
been during the past week. He seemed paler and thinner
than when I last saw him, and I felt that something had
happened to him. You shall hear soon what it was.

" At last he turned from the Chevalier to me, and said,
' When did you hear from your brother, mademoiselle ? '
I told him ; and he added, ' I have had a letter since, and
after supper, if you will permit me, I will tell you of it.'
Turning to my father and my mother, he assured them
of Juste's well-being, and afterwards engaged in talk with
the Governor, to whom he seemed to defer. When we all
rose to go to the *salon*, he offered my mother his arm,
and I went in upon the arm of the good Chevalier. A
few moments afterwards he came to me, and remarked
cheerfully, ' In this farther corner, where the spinet
sounds most, we can talk best ' ; and we went near to the
spinet, where Madame Lotbinière was playing. ' It is

true,' he began, ' that I have had a letter from your
brother. He begs me to use influence for his advancement. You see, he writes to me instead of to the Governor. You can guess how I stand in France. Well, we
shall see what I may do. . . . Have you not wondered
concerning me this week?' he asked. I said to him, ' I
scarce expected you till after to-morrow, when you would
plead some accident as cause for not fulfilling your pretty
little boast.' He looked at me sharply for a minute and
then said : ' A pretty *little* boast, is it? H'm! you touch
great things with light fingers.' I nodded. ' Yes,' said I,
' when I have no great faith.' ' You have marvellous coldness for a girl that promised warmth in her youth,' he
answered. ' Even I, who am old in these matters, can
not think of this Moray's death without a twinge, for it
is not like an affair of battle ; but you seem to think of it
in its relation to my " little boast," as you call it. Is it
not so?'

" ' No, no,' said I, with apparent indignation, ' you
must not make me out so cruel. I am not so hard-hearted
as you think. My brother is well—I have no feeling
against Captain Moray on his account ; and as for spying
—well, it is only a painful epithet for what is done here
and everywhere all the time.' ' Dear me, dear me,' he
remarked lightly, ' what a mind you have for argument !—
a born casuist ; and yet, like all women, you would let
your sympathy rule you in matters of state. But come,'
he added, ' where do you think I have been?' It was
hard to answer him gaily, and yet it must be done, and so
I said, ' You have probably put yourself in prison, that
you should not keep your tiny boast.' ' I have been in
prison,' he answered, ' and I was on the wrong side, with
no key—even locked in a chest-room of the Intendance,'
he explained, ' but as yet I do not know by whom, nor am
I sure why. After two days without food or drink I man-

aged to get out through the barred window. I spent three days in my own room, ill, and here I am. You must not speak of this—you will not?' he asked me. 'To no one,' I answered gaily, 'but my other self.' 'Where is your other self?' he asked. 'In here,' said I, touching my bosom. I did not mean to turn my head away when I said it, but indeed I felt I could not look him in the eyes at the moment, for I was thinking of you.

"He mistook me; he thought I was coquetting with him, and he leaned forward to speak in my ear, so that I could feel his breath on my cheek. I turned faint, for I saw how terrible was this game I was playing; but oh, Robert, Robert"—her hands fluttered towards me, then drew back—"it was for your sake, for your sake, that I let his hand rest on mine an instant, as he said: 'I shall go hunting *there* to find your other self. Shall I know the face if I see it?' I drew my hand away, for it was torture to me, but I only said, a little scornfully, 'You do not stand by your words. You said'—here I laughed disdainfully—'that you would meet the first test to prove your right to follow the second boast.'

"He got to his feet, and said in a low, firm voice: 'Your memory is excellent, your aplomb perfect. You are young to know it all so well. But you bring your own punishment,' he added, with a wicked smile, 'and you shall pay hereafter. I am going to the Governor. Bigot has arrived, and is with Madame Cournal yonder. You shall have proof in half an hour.'

"Then he left me. An idea occurred to me. If he succeeded in staying your execution, you would in all likelihood be placed in the common jail. I would try to get an order from the Governor to visit the jail to distribute gifts to the prisoners, as my mother and I had done before on the day before Christmas. So, while Monsieur Doltaire was passing with Bigot and the Chevalier de la

Darante into another room, I made my request of the Governor; and that very moment, at my wish, he had his secretary write the order, which he countersigned and handed me, with a gift of gold for the prisoners. As he left my mother and myself, Monsieur Doltaire came back with Bigot, and, approaching the Governor, they led him away, engaging at once in serious talk. One thing I noticed: as monsieur and Bigot came up, I could see monsieur eying the Intendant askance, as though he would read treachery; for I feel sure that it was Bigot who contrived to have monsieur shut up in the chestroom. I can not quite guess the reason, unless it be true what gossips say, that Bigot is jealous of the notice Madame Cournal has given Doltaire, who visits much at her house.

"Well, they asked me to sing, and so I did; and can you guess what it was? Even the *voyageurs'* song—

'Brothers, we go to the Scarlet Hills,
(Little gold sun, come out of the dawn!)'

I know not how I sang it, for my heart, my thoughts, were far away in a whirl of clouds and mist, as you may see a flock of wild ducks in the haze upon a river, flying they know not whither, save that they follow the sound of the stream. I was just ending the song when Monsieur Doltaire leaned over me, and said in my ear, 'To-morrow I shall invite Captain Moray from the scaffold to my breakfast-table—or, better still, invite myself to his own.' His hand caught mine, as I gave a little cry; for when I felt sure of your reprieve, I could not, Robert, I could not keep it back. He thought I was startled at his hand-pressure, and did not guess the real cause.

"'I have met one challenge, and I shall meet the other,' he said quickly. 'It is not so much a matter of power, either; it is that engine opportunity. You and I should go far in this wicked world,' he added. 'We think together, we see through ladders. I admire you, mademoiselle. Some men will say they love you; and they should, or they have no taste; and the more they love you, the better pleased am I—if you are best pleased with me. But it is possible for men to love and not to admire. It is a foolish thing to say that reverence must go with love. I know men who have lost their heads and their souls for women whom they knew infamous. But when one admires where one loves, then in the ebb and flow of passion the heart is safe, for admiration holds when the sense is cold.'

"You know well, Robert, how clever he is; how, listening to him, you must admit his talent and his power. But oh, believe that, though I am full of wonder at his cleverness, I can not bear him very near me."

She paused. I looked most gravely at her, as well one might who saw so sweet a maid employing her heart thus, and the danger that faced her. She misread my look a little, maybe, for she said at once:

"I must be honest with you, and so I tell you all—all, else the part I play were not possible to me. To you I can speak plainly, pour out my soul. Do not fear for me. I see a battle coming between that man and me, but I shall fight it stoutly, worthily, so that in this, at least, I shall never have to blush for you that you loved me. Be patient, Robert, and never doubt me; for that would make me close the doors of my heart, though I should never cease to aid you, never weary in labour for your wellbeing. If these things, and fighting all these wicked men, to make Monsieur Doltaire help me to save you, have schooled to action some worse parts of me, there is yet in me that which shall never be brought low, never be dragged to the level of Versailles or the Château Bigot —never!"

She looked at me with such dignity and pride that my eyes filled with tears, and, not to be stayed, I reached out and took her hands, and would have clasped her to my breast, but she held back from me.

"You believe in me, Robert?" she said most earnestly. "You will never doubt me? You know that I am true and loyal."

"I believe in God, and in you," I answered reverently, and I took her in my arms and kissed her. I did not care at all whether or no Gabord saw; but indeed he did not, as Alixe told me afterwards, for, womanlike, even in this sweet crisis she had an eye for such details.

"What more did he say?" I asked, my heart beating hard in the joy of that embrace.

"No more, or little more, for my mother came that instant and brought me to talk with the Chevalier de la Darante, who wished to ask me for next summer to Kamaraska or Isle aux Coudres, where he has manorhouses. Before I left Monsieur Doltaire, he said to me, 'I never made a promise but I wished to break it. This one shall balance all I've broken, for I'll never unwish it.'

"My mother heard this, and so I summoned all my will, and said gaily, 'Poor broken crockery! You stand a tower among the ruins.' This pleased him, and he answered, 'On the tower base is written, This crockery outserves all others.' My mother looked sharply at me, but said nothing, for she has come to think that I am heartless and cold to men and to the world, selfish in many things."

At this moment Gabord turned round, saying, "'Tis time to be done. Madame comes."

"It is my mother," said Alixe, standing up, and hastily placing her hands in mine. "I must be gone. Good-bye, good-bye."

There was no chance for further adieu, and I saw her

pass out with Gabord; but she turned at the last, and said in English, for she spoke it fairly now, " Believe and remember."

XIV.

ARGAND COURNAL.

The most meagre intelligence came to me from the outer world. I no longer saw Gabord; he had suddenly been withdrawn and a new jailer substituted, and the sentinels outside my door and beneath the window of my cell refused all information. For months I had no news whatever of Alixe or of those affairs nearest my heart. I heard nothing of Doltaire, little of Bigot, and there was no sign of Voban.

Sometimes I could see my new jailer studying me, as if my plans were a puzzle to his brain. At first he used regularly to try the bars of the window, and search the wall as though he thought my devices might be found there.

Scarrat and Flavelle, the guards at my door, set too high a price on their favours, and they talked seldom, and then with brutal jests and ribaldry of matters in the town which were not vital to me. Yet once or twice, from things they said, I came to know that all was not well between Bigot and Doltaire on one hand, and Doltaire and the Governor on the other. Doltaire had set the Governor and the Intendant scheming against him because of his adherence to the cause of neither, and his power to render the plans of either of no avail when he chose, as in my case. Vaudreuil's vanity was injured, and, besides, he counted Doltaire too strong a friend of Bigot. Bigot, I doubted not, found in Madame Cournal's liking for Doltaire all sorts of things of which he never would have dreamed ; for there is no such potent devilry in this world as the jealousy of such a sort of man over a woman whose vanity and cupidity are the springs of her affections. Doltaire's imprisonment in a room of the Intendance was not so mysterious as suggestive. I foresaw a strife, a complication of intrigues, and internal enmities which would be (as they were) the ruin of New France. I saw, in imagination, the English army at the gates of Quebec, and those who sat in the seats of the mighty, sworn to personal enmities—Vaudreuil through vanity, Bigot through cupidity, Doltaire by the innate malice of his nature—sacrificing the country ; the scarlet body of British power moving down upon a dishonoured city, never to take its foot from that sword of France which fell there on the soil of the New World.

But there was another factor in the situation on which I have not before dwelt. Over a year earlier, when war was being carried into Prussia by Austria and France, and against England, the ally of Prussia, the French Minister of War, D'Argenson, had, by the grace of La Pompadour, sent General the Marquis de Montcalm to Canada, to protect the colony with a small army. From the first, Montcalm, fiery, impetuous, and honourable, was at variance with Vaudreuil, who, though honest himself, had never dared to make open stand against Bigot. When Montcalm came, practically taking the military command out of the hands of the Governor, Vaudreuil developed a singular jealous spirit against the General. It began to express itself about the time I was thrown into the citadel dungeon, and I knew from what Alixe had told me, and from the gossip of the soldiers that there was a more open show of disagreement now.

The Governor, seeing how ill it was to be at variance with both Montcalm and Bigot, presently began to covet a reconciliation with the latter. To this Bigot was by no

means averse, for his own position had danger. His followers and confederates, Cournal, Marin, Cadet, and Rigaud, were robbing the King with a daring and effrontery
which must ultimately bring disaster. This he knew, but it
was his plan to hold on for a time longer, and then to retire before the axe fell with an immense fortune. Therefore, about the time set for my execution, he began to close
with the overtures of the Governor, and presently the two
formed a confederacy against the Marquis de Montcalm.
Into it they tried to draw Doltaire, and were surprised to
find that he stood them off as to anything more than outward show of friendliness.

Truth was, Doltaire, who had no sordid feeling in him,
loathed alike the cupidity of Bigot and the incompetency
of the Governor, and respected Montcalm for his honour
and reproached him for his rashness. From first to last
he was, without show of it, the best friend Montcalm had
in the province ; and though he held aloof from bringing
punishment to Bigot, he despised him and his friends,
and was not slow to make that plain. D'Argenson made
inquiry of Doltaire when Montcalm's honest criticisms
were sent to France in cipher, and Doltaire returned the
reply that Bigot was the only man who could serve Canada efficiently in this crisis ; that he had abounding fer-
tility of resource, a clear head, a strong will, and great ad-
ministrative faculty. This was all he would say, save that
when the war was over other matters might be conned.
Meanwhile France must pay liberally for the Intendant's
services !

Through a friend in France, Bigot came to know that
his affairs were moving to a crisis, and saw that it would
be wise to retire ; but he loved the very air of crisis, and
Madame Cournal, anxious to keep him in Canada, en-
couraged him in his natural feeling to stand or fall with
the colony. He never showed aught but a bold and con-

fident face to the public, and was in all regards the most conspicuous figure in New France. When, two years before, Montcalm took Oswego from the English, Bigot threw open his palace to the populace for two days' feasting, and every night during the war he entertained lavishly, though the people went hungry, and their own corn, bought for the King, was sold back to them at famine prices.

As the Governor and the Intendant grew together in friendship, Vaudreuil sinking past disapproval in present selfish necessity, they quietly combined against Doltaire as against Montcalm. Yet at this very time Doltaire was living in the Intendance, and, as he had told Alixe, not without some personal danger. He had before been offered chambers at the Château St. Louis; but these he would not take, for he could not bear to be within touch of the Governor's vanity and timidity. He would of preference have stayed in the Intendance had he known that pitfalls and traps were at every footstep. Danger gave a piquancy to his existence. Perhaps he did not greatly value Madame Cournal's admiration of himself; but when it drove Bigot to retaliation, his imagination got an impulse, and he entered upon a conflict which ran parallel with the war, and with that delicate antagonism which Alixe waged against him, long undiscovered by himself.

At my wits' ends for news, at last I begged my jailer to convey a message for me to the Governor, asking that the barber be let come to me. The next day an answer arrived in the person of Voban himself, accompanied by the jailer. For a time there was little speech between us, but as he tended me we talked. We could do so with safety, for Voban knew English; and though he spoke it brokenly, he had freedom in it, and the jailer knew no word of it. At first the fellow blustered, but I waved him off. He was a man of better education than Gabord, but of inferior judgment and shrewdness. He made no

12

trial thereafter to interrupt our talk, but sat and drummed upon a stool with his keys, or loitered at the window, or now and again thrust his hand into my pockets, as if to see if weapons were concealed in them.

"Voban," said I, "what has happened since I saw you at the Intendance? Tell me first of mademoiselle. You have nothing from her for me?"

"Nothing," he answered. "There is no time. A soldier come an hour ago with an order from the Governor, and I must go all at once. So I come as you see. But as for the ma'm'selle, she is well. *Voilà*, there is no one like her in New France. I do not know all, as you can guess, but they say she can do what she will at the Château. It is a wonder to see her drive. A month ago a droll thing come to pass. She is driving on the ice with Ma'm'selle Lotbinière and her brother Charles. M'sieu' Charles, he has the reins. Soon, ver' quick, the horses start with all their might. M'sieu' saw and pull, but they go the faster. Like that for a mile or so; then ma'm'selle remember there is a great crack in the ice a mile farther on, and beyond, the ice is weak and rotten, for there the curren' is ver' strongest. She sees that M'sieu' Charles, he can do nothing, so she reach and take the reins. The horses go on; it make no diff'rence at first. But she begin to talk to them so sof', and to pull ver' steady, and at last she get them shaping to the shore. She have the reins wound on her hands, and people on the shore, they watch. Little on little the horses pull up, and stop at last not a hunder' feet from the great crack and the rotten ice. Then she turn them round and drive them home.

"You should hear the people cheer as she drive up Mountain Street. The bishop stand at the window of his palace and smile at her as she pass, and m'sieu' "— he looked at the jailer and paused—"m'sieu' the gen-

tleman we do not love, he stand in the street with his
cap off for two minutes as she come, and after she go
by, and say a grand compliment to her so that her face
go pale. He get froze ears for his pains—that was a
cold day. Well, at night there was a grand dinner at
the Intendance, and afterwards a ball in the splendid
room which that man" (he meant Bigot: I shall use
names when quoting him further, that he may be better understood) "built for the poor people of the land for
to dance down their sorrows. So you can guess I would
be there—happy. Ah yes, so happy! I go and stand in
the great gallery above the hall of dance, with crowd of
people, and look down at the grand folk.

"One man come to me and say, 'Ah, Voban, is it you
here? Who would think it!'—like that. Another, he
come and say, 'Voban, he can not keep away from the Intendance. Who does he come to look for? But no, *she*
is not here—no.' And again, another, 'Why should not
Voban be here? One man has not enough bread to eat,
and Bigot steals his corn. Another hungers for a wife to
sit by his fire, and Bigot takes the maid, and Voban stuffs
his mouth with humble pie like the rest. Chut! shall
not Bigot have his fill?' And yet another, and, *voilà*,
she was a woman, she say, 'Look at the Intendant down
there with madame. And M'sieu' Cournal, he also is
there. What does M'sieu' Cournal care? No, not at all.
The rich man, what he care, if he has gold? Virtue!
ha, ha! what is that in your wife if you have gold for it?
Nothing. See his hand at the Intendant's arm. See how
M'sieu' Doltaire look at them, and then up here at us.
What is it in his mind, you think? Eh? You think he
say to himself, A wife all to himself is the poor man's one
luxury? Eh? Ah, M'sieu' Doltaire, you are right, you
are right. You catch up my child from its basket in the
market-place one day, and you shake it ver' soft, an' you

say, 'Madame, I will stake the last year of my life that I can put my finger on the father of this child.' And when I laugh in his face, he say again, 'And if he thought he wasn't its father, he would cut out the liver of the other —eh?' And I laugh, and say, 'My Jacques would follow him to hell to do it.' Then he say, Voban, he say to me, 'That is the difference between you and us. We only kill men who meddle with our mistresses!' Ah, that M'sieu' Doltaire, he put a louis in the hand of my babe, and he not even kiss me on the cheek. Pshaw! Jacques would sell him fifty kisses for fifty louis. But sell me, or a child of me? Well, Voban, you can guess! Pah, barber, if you do not care what he did to the poor Mathilde, there are other maids in St. Roch.'"

Voban paused a moment, then added quietly, "How do you think I bear it all? With a smile? No, I hear with my ears open and my heart close tight. Do they think they can teach me? Do they guess I sit down and hear all without a cry from my throat or a will in my body? Ah, m'sieu' le Capitaine, it is you who know. You saw what I would have go to do with M'sieu' Doltaire before the day of the Great Birth. You saw if I am a coward— if I not take the sword when it was at my throat without a whine. No, m'sieu', I can wait. There is a time for everything. At first I am all in a muddle, I not know what to do; but by-and-bye it all come to me, and you shall see one day what I wait for. Yes, you shall see. I look down on that people dancing there, quiet and still, and I hear some laugh at me, and now and then some one say a good word to me that make me shut my hands tight, so the tears not come to my eyes. But I felt alone—so much alone. The world does not want a sad man. In my shop I try to laugh as of old, and I am not sour or heavy, but I can see men do not say droll things to me as once back time. No, I am not as I was. What am I to do? There is but one way. What is great to one man is not to another. What kills the one does not kill the other. Take away from some people one thing, and they will not care; from others that same, and there is nothing to live for, except just to live, and because a man does not like death."

He paused. "You are right, Voban," said I. "Go on."

He was silent again for a time, and then he moved his hand in a helpless sort of way across his forehead. It had become deeply lined and wrinkled all in a couple of years. His temples were sunken, his cheeks hollow, and his face was full of those shadows which lend a sort of tragedy to even the humblest and least distinguished countenance. His eyes had a restlessness, anon an intense steadiness almost uncanny, and his thin, long fingers had a stealthiness of motion, a soft swiftness, which struck me strangely. I never saw a man so changed. He was like a vessel wrested from its moorings; like some craft, filled with explosives, set loose along a shore lined with fishing-smacks, which might come foul of one, and blow the company of men and boats into the air. As he stood there, his face half turned to me for a moment, this came to my mind, and I said to him, "Voban, you look like some wicked gun which would blow us all to pieces."

He wheeled, and came to me so swiftly that I shrank back in my chair with alarm, his action was so sudden, and, peering into my face, he said, glancing, as I thought, anxiously at the jailer, "Blow—blow—how blow us all to pieces, m'sieu'?" He eyed me with suspicion, and I could see that he felt like some hurt animal among its captors, ready to fight, yet not knowing from what point danger would come. Something pregnant in what I said had struck home, yet I could not guess then what it was, though afterwards it came to me with great force and vividness.

"I meant nothing, Voban," answered I, "save that you look dangerous."

I half put out my hand to touch his arm in a friendly way, but I saw that the jailer was watching, and I did not. Voban felt what I was about to do, and his face instantly softened, and his blood-shot eyes gave me a look of gratitude. Then he said :

"I will tell you what happen next. I know the palace very well, and when I see the Intendant and M'sieu' Doltaire and others leave the ballroom I knew that they go to the chamber which they call 'la Chambre de la Joie,' to play at cards. So I steal away out of the crowd into a passage which, as it seem, go nowhere, and come quick, all at once, to a bare wall. But I know the way. In one corner of the passage I press a spring, and a little panel open. I crawl through and close it behin'. Then I feel my way along the dark corner till I come to another panel. This I open, and I see light. You ask how I can do this ? Well, I tell you. There is the valet of Bigot, he is my friend. You not guess who it is ? No ? It is a man whose crime in France I know. He was afraid when he saw me here, but I say to him, 'No, I will not speak— never'; and he is all my friend just when I most need. Eh, *voilà*, I see light, as I said, and I push aside heavy curtains ver' little, and there is the Chamber of the Joy below. There they all are, the Intendant and the rest, sitting down to the tables. There was Capitaine Lancy, M'sieu' Cadet, M'sieu' Cournal, M'sieu' le Chevalier de Levis, and M'sieu' le Générale, le Marquis de Montcalm. I am astonish to see him there, the great General, in his grand coat of blue and gold and red, and laces *très beau* at his throat, with a fine jewel. Ah, he is not ver' high on his feet, but he has an eye all fire, and a laugh come quick to his lips, and he speak ver' *galant*, but he never let them, Messieurs Cadet, Marin, Lancy, and the rest, be thick friends with him. They do not clap their hands on his shoulder *comme le bon camarade—non!*

"Well, they sit down to play, and soon there is much noise and laughing, and then sometimes a silence, and then again the noise, and you can see one snuff a candle with the points of two rapiers, or hear a sword jangle at a chair, or listen to some one sing ver' soft a song as he hold a good hand of cards, or the ring of louis on the table, or the sound of glass as it break on the floor. And once a young gentleman—alas! he is so young—he got up from his chair, and cry out, 'All is lost! I go to die!' He raise a pistol to his head; but M'sieu' Doltaire catch his hand, and say quite soft and gentle, 'No, no, *mon enfant*, enough of making fun of us. Here is the hunder' louis I borrow of you yesterday. Take your revenge.' The lad sit down slow, looking ver' strange at M'sieu' Doltaire. And it is true: he take his revenge out of M'sieu' Cadet, for he win—I saw it—three hunder' louis. Then M'sieu' Doltaire lean over to him and say, 'M'sieu', you will carry for me a message to the citadel for M'sieu' Ramesay, the commandant.' Ah, it was a sight to see M'sieu' Cadet's face, going this way and that. But it was no use: the young gentleman pocket his louis, and go away with a letter from M'sieu' Doltaire. But M'sieu' Doltaire, he laugh in the face of M'sieu' Cadet, and say ver' pleasant, 'That is a servant of the King, m'sieu', who live by his sword alone. Why should civilians be so greedy? Come, play, m'sieu' Cadet. If M'sieu' the General will play with me, we two will see what we can do with you and his Excellency the Intendant.'

"They sit just beneath me, and I hear all what is said, I see all the looks of them, every card that is played. M'sieu' the General have not play yet, but watch M'sieu' Doltaire and the Intendant at the cards. With a smile he now sit down. Then M'sieu' Doltaire, he say, 'M'sieu''

Cadet, let us have no mistake—let us be commercial.'
He take out his watch. ' I have two hours to spare; are
you dispose to play for that time only? To the moment
we will rise, and there shall be no question of satisfaction,
no discontent anywhere—eh, shall it be so, if m'sieu' the
General can spare the time also?' It is agree that the
General play for one hour and go, and that M'sieu' Doltaire and the Intendant play for the rest of the time.

" They begin, and I hide there and watch. The time
go ver' fast, and my breath catch in my throat to see how
great the stakes they play for. I hear M'sieu' Doltaire
say at last, with a smile, taking out his watch, ' M'sieu'
the General, your time is up, and you take with you twenty
thousan' francs.'

" The General, he smile and wave his hand, as if sorry
to take so much from M'sieu' Cadet and the Intendant.
M'sieu Cadet sit dark, and speak nothing at first, but at
last he get up and turn on his heel and walk away, leaving what he lose on the table. M'sieu' the General bow
also, and go from the room. Then M'sieu' Doltaire and
the Intendant play. One by one the other players stop,
and come and watch these. Something get into the two
gentlemen, for both are pale, and the face of the Intendant all of spots, and his little round eyes like specks of
red fire; but M'sieu' Doltaire's face, it is still, and his
brows bend over, and now and then he make a little laughing out of his lips. All at once I hear him say, ' Double
the stakes, your Excellency!' The Intendant look up
sharp and say, ' What! Two hunder' thousan' francs!'
—as if M'sieu' Doltaire could not pay such a sum like
that. M'sieu' Doltaire smile ver' wicked, and answer,
' Make it three hunder' thousan' francs, your Excellency.'
It is so still in the Chamber of the Joy that all you hear
for a minute was the fat Monsieur Varin breathe like a hog,
and the rattle of a spur as some one slide a foot on the floor.

" The Intendant look blank; then he nod his head for answer, and each write on a piece of paper. As they begin, M'sieu' Doltaire take out his watch and lay it on the table, and the Intendant do the same, and they both look at the time. The watch of the Intendant is all jewels. ' Will you not add the watches to the stake?' say M'sieu' Doltaire. The Intendant look, and shrug a shoulder, and shake his head for no, and M'sieu' Doltaire smile in a sly way, so that the Intendant's teeth show at his lips and his eyes almost close, he is so angry.

" Just this minute I hear a low noise behind me, and then some one give a little cry. I turn quick and see Madame Cournal. She stretch her hand, and touch my lips, and motion me not to stir. I look down again, and I see that M'sieu' Doltaire look up to the place where I am, for he hear that sound, I think—I not know sure. But he say once more, ' The watch, the watch, your Excellency! I have a fancy for yours!' I feel madame breathe hard beside me, but I not like to look at her. I am not afraid of men, but a woman that way—ah, it make me shiver! She will betray me, I think. All at once I feel her hand at my belt, then at my pocket, to see if I have a weapon; for the thought come to her that I am there to kill Bigot. But I raise my hands and say ' No,' ver' quiet, and she nod her head all right.

" The Intendant wave his hand at M'sieu' Doltaire to say he would not stake the watch, for I know it is one madame give him; and then they begin to play. No one stir. The cards go out *flip*, *flip*, on the table, and with a little soft scrape in the hands, and I hear Bigot's hound munch a bone. All at once M'sieu' Doltaire throw down his cards, and say, ' Mine, Bigot! Three hunder' thousan' francs, and the time is up!' The other get from his chair, and say, ' How would you have pay if you had lost, Doltaire?' And m'sieu' answer, ' From the coffers of the

King, like you, Bigot.' His tone is odd. I feel madame's breath go hard. Bigot turn round and say to the others, ' Will you take your way to the great hall, messieurs, and M'sieu' Doltaire and I will follow. We have some private conf'rence.' They all turn away, all but M'sieu' Cournal, and leave the room, whispering. ' I will join you soon, Cournal,' say his Excellency. M'sieu' Cournal not go, for he have been drinking, and something stubborn get into him. But the Intendant order him rough, and he go. I can hear madame gnash her teeth sof' beside me.

" When the door close, the Intendant turn to M'sieu' Doltaire and say, ' What is the end for which you play ? ' M'sieu' Doltaire make a little motion of his hand, and answer, ' For three hunder' thousan' francs.' ' And to pay, m'sieu', how to pay if you had lost ? ' M'sieu' Doltaire lay his hand on his sword sof'. ' From the King's coffers, as I say; he owes me more than he has paid. But not like you, Bigot. I have earned, this way and that, all that I might ever get from the King's coffers— even this three hunder' thousan' francs, ten times told. But you, Bigot—tush ! why should we make bubbles of words ? ' The Intendant get white in the face, but there are spots on it like on a late apple of an old tree. ' You go too far, Doltaire,' he say. ' You have hint before my officers and my friends that I make free with the King's coffers.' M'sieu' answer, ' You should see no such hints, if your palms were not musty.' ' How know you,' ask the Intendant, ' that my hands are musty from the King's coffers ? ' M'sieu' arrange his laces, and say light, ' As easy from the must as I tell how time passes in your nights by the ticking of this trinket here.' He raise his sword and touch the Intendant's watch on the table.

" I never hear such silence as there is for a minute, and then the Intendant say, ' You have gone one step too far. The must on my hands, seen through your eyes, is

no matter, but when you must the name of a lady there is
but one end. You understan', m'sieu', there is but one
end.' M'sieu' laugh. 'The sword, you mean? Eh?
No, no, I will not fight with you. I am not here to rid
the King of so excellent an officer, however large fee he
force for his services.' 'And I tell you,' say the Intendant, 'that I will not have you cast a slight upon a lady.'
Madame beside me start up, and whisper to me, 'If you
betray me, you shall die. If you be still, I too will say
nothing.' But then a thing happen. Another voice
sound from below, and there, coming from behind a great
screen of oak wood, is M'sieu' Cournal, his face all red
with wine, his hand on his sword. 'Bah!' he say, coming forward—'bah! I will speak for madame. I will
speak. I have been silent long enough.' He come between the two, and, raising his sword, he strike the time-
piece and smash it. 'Ha! ha!' he say, wild with drink,
'I have you both here alone.' He snap his finger under
the Intendant's nose. 'It is time I protect my wife's
name from you, and, by God, I will do it!' At that
M'sieu' Doltaire laugh, and Cournal turn to him and say,
'Bâtard!' The Intendant have out his sword, and he
roar in a hoarse voice, 'Dog, you shall die!' But M'sieu'
Doltaire strike up his sword, and face the drunken man.
'No, leave that to me. The King's cause goes shipwreck;
we can't change helmsman now. Think—scandal and
your disgrace!' Then he make a pass at M'sieu' Cournal, who parry quick. Another, and he prick his shoulder. Another, and then madame beside me, as I spring
back, throw aside the curtains, and cry out, 'No, m'sieu'!
no! For shame!'

"I kneel in a corner behind the curtains, and wait and
listen. There is not a sound for a moment; then I hear
a laugh from M'sieu' Cournal, such a laugh as make me
sick—loud, and full of what you call not care and the

devil. Madame speak down at them. 'Ah,' she say, 'it
is so fine a sport to drag a woman's name in the mire!'
Her voice is full of spirit, and she look beautiful—beautiful. I never guess how a woman like that look; so full
of pride, and to speak like you could think knives sing as
they strike steel—sharp and cold. 'I came to see how
gentlemen look at play, and they end in brawling over a
lady!'

"M'sieu' Doltaire speak to her, and they all put up
their swords, and M'sieu' Cournal sit down at a table, and
he stare and stare up at the balcony, and make a motion
now and then with his hand. M'sieu' Doltaire say to her,
'Madame, you must excuse our entertainment; we did
not know we had an audience so distinguished.' She reply, 'As scene-shifter and prompter, M'sieu' Doltaire, you
have a gift. Your Excellency,' she say to the Intendant,
'I will wait for you at the top of the great staircase, if
you will be so good as to take me to the ballroom.' The
Intendant and M'sieu' Doltaire bow, and turn to the door,
and M'sieu' Cournal scowl, and make as if to follow; but
madame speak down at him, 'M'sieu'—Argand'—like
that! and he turn back, and sit down. I think she forget me, I keep so still. The others bow and scrape, and
leave the room, and the two are alone—alone, for what
am I? What if a dog hear great people speak? No, it
is no matter!

"There is all still for a little while, and I watch her
face as she lean over the rail and look down at him; it is
like stone that aches, and her eyes stare and stare at
him. He look up at her and scowl; then he laugh,
with a toss of the finger, and sit down. All at once he
put his hand on his sword, and gnash his teeth.

"Then she speak down to him, her voice ver' quiet.
'Argand,' she say, 'you are more a man drunk than sober.
Argand,' she go on, 'years ago, they said you were a brave

man; you fight well, you do good work for the King, your name goes with a sweet sound to Versailles. You had only your sword and my poor fortune and me then— that is all; but you were a man. You had ambition, so had I. What can a woman do? You had your sword, your country, the King's service. I had beauty; I wanted power—ah yes, power, that was the thing! But I was young and a fool; you were older. You talked fine things then, but you had a base heart, so much baser than mine. . . . I might have been a good woman. I was a fool, and weak, and vain, but you were base—so base— coward and betrayer, you!'

"At that m'sieu' start up and snatch at his sword, and speak out between his teeth, 'By God, I will kill you to-night!' She smile cold and hard, and say, 'No, no, you will not; it is too late for killing; that should have been done before. You sold your right to kill long ago, Argand Cournal. You have been close friends with the man who gave me power, and you gold.' Then she get fierce. 'Who gave you gold before he gave me power, traitor?' Like that she speak. 'Do you never think of what you have lost?' Then she break out in a laugh. 'Pah! Listen: if there must be killing, why not be the great Roman—drunk!'

"Then she laugh so hard a laugh, and turn away, and go quick by me and not see me. She step into the dark, and he sit down in a chair, and look straight in front of him. I do not stir, and after a minute she come back sof', and peep down, her face all differen'. 'Argand! Argand!' she say ver' tender and low, 'if—if—if '—like that. But just then he see the broken watch on the floor, and he stoop, with a laugh, and pick up the pieces; then he get a candle and look on the floor everywhere for the jewels, and he pick them up, and put them away one by one in his purse like a miser. He keep on looking, and once the fire of the candle burn his beard, and he swear, and she stare and stare at him. He sit down at the table, and look at the jewels and laugh to himself. Then she draw herself up, and shake, and put her hands to her eyes, and, ' *C'est fini! c'est fini!* ' she whisper, and that is all.

"When she is gone, after a little time he change—ah, he change much. He go to a table and pour out a great bowl of wine, and then another, and he drink them both, and he begin to walk up and down the floor. He sway now and then, but he keep on for a long time. Once a servant come, but he wave him away, and he scowl and talk to himself, and shut the doors and lock them. Then he walk on and on. At last he sit down, and he face me. In front of him are candles, and he stare between them, and stare and stare. I sit and watch, and I feel a pity. I hear him say, ' Antoinette! Antoinette! My dear Antoinette! We are lost forever, my Antoinette! ' Then he take the purse from his pocket, and throw it up to the balcony where I am. ' Pretty sins,' he say, 'follow the sinner! ' It lie there, and it have sprung open, and I can see the jewels shine, but I not touch it—no. Well, he sit there long—long, and his face get gray and his cheeks all hollow.

"I hear the clock strike *one! two! three! four!* Once some one come and try the door, but go away again, and he never stir ; he is like a dead man. At last I fall asleep. When I wake up, he still sit there, but his head lie in his arms. I look round. Ah, it is not a fine sight —no. The candles burn so low, and there is a smell of wick, and the grease runs here and there down the great candlesticks. Upon the floor, this place and that, is a card, and pieces of paper, and a scarf, and a broken glass, and something that shine by a small table. This is a picture in a little gold frame. On all the tables stand glasses, some full and some empty, of wine. And just as the dawn come in through the tall windows, a cat crawl out from somewhere, all ver' thin and shy, and walk across the floor; it makes the room look so much alone. At last it come and move against m'sieu's legs, and he lift his head and look down at it, and nod, and say something which I not hear. After that he get up, and pull himself together with a shake, and walk down the room. Then he see the little gold picture on the floor which some drunk young officer drop, and he pick it up and look at it, and walk again. 'Poor fool!' he say, and look at the picture again. 'Poor fool! Will he curse her some day—a child with a face like that? Ah!' And he throw the picture down. Then he walk away to the doors, unlock them, and go out. Soon I steal away through the panels, and out of the palace ver' quiet, and go home. But I can see that room in my mind."

Again the jailer hurried Voban. There was no excuse for him to remain longer; so I gave him a message to Alixe, and slipped into his hand a transcript from my journal. Then he left me, and I sat and thought upon the strange events of the evening which he had described to me. That he was bent on mischief I felt sure, but how it would come, what were his plans, I could not guess. Then suddenly there flashed into my mind my words to him, " blow us all to pieces," and his consternation and strange eagerness. It came to me suddenly : he meant to blow up the Intendance. When? And how? It seemed absurd to think of it. Yet—yet—— The grim humour of the thing possessed me, and I sat back and laughed heartily.

In the midst of my mirth the cell door opened and let in Doltaire.

XV.

IN THE CHAMBER OF TORTURE.

I STARTED from my seat; we bowed, and, stretching out a hand to the fire, Doltaire said, "Ah, my captain, we meet too seldom. Let me see: five months—ah yes, nearly five months. Believe me, I have not breakfasted so heartily since. You are looking older—older. Solitude to the active mind is not to be endured alone—no."

"Monsieur Doltaire is the surgeon to my solitude," said I.

"H'm!" he answered, "a jail surgeon merely. And that brings me to a point, monsieur. I have had letters from France. The Grande Marquise—I may as well be frank with you—womanlike, yearns violently for those silly letters which you hold. She would sell our France for them. There is a chance for you who would serve your country so. Serve it, and yourself—and me. We have no news yet as to your doom, but be sure it is certain. La Pompadour knows all, and if you are stubborn, twenty deaths were too few. I can save you little longer, even were it my will so to do. For myself, the great lady girds at me for being so poor an agent. You, monsieur" —he smiled whimsically—"will agree that I have been persistent—and intelligent."

"So much so," rejoined I, "as to be intrusive."

He smiled again. "If La Pompadour could hear you, she would understand why I prefer the live amusing lion to the dead dog. When you are gone, I shall be inconsolable. I am a born inquisitor."

"You were born for better things than this," I answered.

He took a seat and mused for a moment. "For larger things, you mean," was his reply. "Perhaps—perhaps.

I have one gift of the strong man—I am inexorable when I make for my end. As a general, I would pour men into the maw of death as corn into the hopper, if that would build a bridge to my end. You call to mind how those Spaniards conquered the Mexique city which was all canals like Venice? They filled the waterways with shattered houses and the bodies of their enemies, as they fought their way to Montezuma's palace. So I would know not pity if I had a great cause. In anything vital I would have success at all cost, and to get, destroy as I went—if I were a great man."

I thought with horror of his pursuit of my dear Alixe. "I am your hunter," had been his words to her, and I knew not what had happened in all these months.

"If you were a great man, you should have the best prerogative of greatness," I remarked quietly.

"And what is that? Some excellent moral, I doubt not," was the rejoinder.

"Mercy," I replied.

"Tush!" he retorted, "mercy is for the fireside, not for the throne. In great causes, what is a screw of tyranny here, a bolt of oppression there, or a few thousand lives!" He suddenly got to his feet, and, looking into the distance, made a swift motion of his hand, his eyes half closed, his brows brooding and firm. "I should look beyond the moment, the year, or the generation. Why fret because the hour of death comes sooner than we looked for? In the movement of the ponderous car some honest folk must be crushed by the wicked wheels. No, no, in large affairs there must be no thought of the detail of misery, else what should be done in the world! He who is the strongest shall survive, and he alone. It is all conflict— all. For when conflict ceases, and those who could and should be great spend their time chasing butterflies among the fountains, there comes miasma and their doom. Mercy?

13

Mercy? No, no: for none but the poor and sick and over-ridden, in time of peace; in time of war, mercy for none, pity nowhere, till the joybells ring the great man home."

"But mercy to women always," said I, "in war or peace."

He withdrew his eyes as if from a distant prospect, and they dropped to the stove, where I had corn parching. He nodded, as if amused, but did not answer at once, and taking from my hand the feather with which I stirred the corn, softly whisked some off for himself, and smiled at the remaining kernels as they danced upon the hot iron. After a little while he said, "Women? Women should have all that men can give them. Beautiful things should adorn them; no man should set his hand in cruelty on a woman—after she is his. Before—before? Woman is wilful, and sometimes we wring her heart that we may afterwards comfort it."

"Your views have somewhat changed," I answered. "I mind when you talked less sweetly."

He shrugged a shoulder. "That man is lost who keeps one mind concerning woman. I will trust the chastity of no woman, yet I will trust her virtue—if I have her heart. They are a foolish tribe, and all are vulnerable in their vanity. They are of consequence to man, but of no consequence in state matters. When they meddle there we have La Pompadour and war with England, and Captain Moray in the Bastile of New France."

"You come from a court, monsieur, which believes in nothing, not even in itself."

"I come from a court," he rejoined, "which has made a gospel of artifice, of frivolity a creed; buying the toys for folly with the savings of the poor. His most Christian Majesty has set the fashion of continual silliness and universal love. He begets children in the peasant's oven and in the chamber of Charlemagne alike. And we are all good subjects of the King.   We are brilliant, exquisite, brave, and naughty; and for us there is no to-morrow."

"Nor for France," I suggested.

He laughed, as he rolled a kernel of parched corn on his tongue.   "Tut, tut! that is another thing.   We are the fashion of an hour, but France is a fact as stubborn as the natures of you English; for beyond stubbornness and your Shakespeare you have little.   Down among the moles, in the peasants' huts, the spirit of France never changes—it is always the same; it is for all time.   You English, nor all others, you can not blow out that candle which is the spirit of France.   I remember the Abbé Bobon preaching once upon the words, 'The spirit of man is the candle of the Lord'; well, the spirit of France is the candle of Europe, and you English will be its screen against the blowing out, though in spasms of stupidity you flaunt the extinguisher.   You—you have no imagination, no passion, no temperament, no poetry.   Yet I am wrong.   The one thing you have——"

He broke off, nodding his head in amusement.   "Yes, you have, but it is a secret.   You English are the true lovers, we French the true poets; and I will tell you why. You are a race of comrades, the French, of gentlemen; you cleave to a thing, we to an idea; you love a woman best when she is near, we when she is away; you make a romance of marriage, we of intrigue; you feed upon yourselves, we upon the world; you have fever in your blood, we in our brains; you believe the world was made in seven days, we have no God; you would fight for the seven days, we would fight for the danseuse on a bonbon box.   The world will say 'fie!' at us and love us; it will respect you and hate you.   That is the law and the gospel," he added, smiling.

"Perfect respect casteth out love," said I ironically.

He waved his fingers in approval.   "By the Lord, but you are pungent now and then!" he answered; "cabined

here you are less material. By the time you are chastened
unto heaven you will be too companionable to lose."

"When is that hour of completed chastening?" I
asked.

"Never," he said, "if you will oblige me with those
letters."

"For a man of genius you discern but slowly," retorted I.

"Discern your amazing stubbornness?" he asked.
"Why should you play at martyr, when your talent is
commercial? You have no gifts for martyrdom but
wooden tenacity. Pshaw! the leech has that. You mistake your calling."

"And you yours," I answered. "This is a poor game
you play, and losing it you lose all. La Pompadour will
pay according to the goods you bring."

He answered with an amusing candor: "Why, yes,
you are partly in the right. But when La Pompadour
and I come to our final reckoning, when it is a question
who can topple ruins round the King quickest, his mistress or his 'cousin,' there will be tales to tell."

He got up, and walked to and fro in the cell, musing,
and his face grew darker and darker. "Your Monmouth
was a fool," he said. "He struck from the boundaries;
the blow should fall in the very chambers of the King."
He put a finger musingly upon his lip. "I see—I see
how it could be done. Full of danger, but brilliant, brilliant and bold! Yes, yes . . . yes!" Then all at once
he seemed to come out of a dream, and laughed ironically.
"There it is," he said; "there is my case. I have the
idea, but I will not strike; it is not worth the doing unless I'm driven to it. We are brave enough, we idlers,"
he went on; "we die with an air—all artifice, artifice!
. . . Yet of late I have had dreams. Now that is not
well. It is foolish to dream, and I had long since ceased

to do so. But somehow all the mad fancies of my youth come back. This dream will go, it will not last; it is— my fate, my doom," he added lightly, " or what you will ! "

I knew, alas, too well where his thoughts were hanging, and I loathed him anew; for, as he hinted, his was a passion, not a deep, abiding love. His will was not stronger than the general turpitude of his nature. As if he had divined my thought, he said, " My will is stronger than any passion that I have; I can never plead weakness in the day of my judgment. I am deliberate. When I choose evil it is because I love it. I could be an anchorite; I am, as I said—what you will."

" You are a conscienceless villain, monsieur."

" Who salves not his soul," he added, with a dry smile, " who will play his game out as he began; who repents nor ever will repent of anything; who sees for him and you some interesting moments yet. Let me make one now," and he drew from his pocket a packet. He smiled hatefully as he handed it to me, and said, " Some books which monsieur once lent Mademoiselle Duvarney—poems, I believe. Mademoiselle found them yesterday, and desired me to fetch them to you; and I obliged her. I had the pleasure of glancing through the books before she rolled them up. She bade me say that monsieur might find them useful in his captivity. She has a tender heart— even to the worst of criminals."

I felt a strange churning in my throat, but with composure I took the books, and said, " Mademoiselle Duvarney chooses distinguished messengers."

" It is a distinction to aid her in her charities," he replied.

I could not at all conceive what was meant. The packet hung in my hands like lead. There was a mystery I could not solve. I would not for an instant think what he meant to convey by a look—that her choice of him to carry back my gift to her was a final repulse of past advances I had made to her, a corrective to my romantic memories. I would not believe that, not for one fleeting second. Perhaps, I said to myself, it was a ruse of this scoundrel. But again, I put that from me, for I did not think he would stoop to little meannesses, no matter how vile he was in great things. I assumed indifference to the matter, laying the packet down upon my couch, and saying to him, "You will convey my thanks to Mademoiselle Duvarney for these books, whose chief value lies in the honourable housing they have had."

He smiled provokingly; no doubt he was thinking that my studied compliment smelt of the oil of solitude. "And add—shall I—your compliments that they should have their airing at the hands of Monsieur Doltaire?"

"I shall pay those compliments to Monsieur Doltaire himself one day," I replied.

He waved his fingers. "The sentiments of one of the poems were commendable, fanciful. I remember it"—he put a finger to his lip—"let me see." He stepped towards the packet, but I made a sign of interference—how grateful was I of this afterwards!—and he drew back courteously. "Ah well," he said, "I have a fair memory; I can, I think, recall the morsel. It impressed me. I could not think the author an Englishman. It runs thus," and with admirable grace he recited the words:

"O flower of all the world, O flower of all!
   The garden where thou dwellest is so fair,
Thou art so goodly, and so queenly tall,
   Thy sweetness scatters sweetness everywhere,
      O flower of all!

"O flower of all the years, O flower of all!
   A day beside thee is a day of days;
Thy voice is softer than the throstle's call,

There is not song enough to sing thy praise,
    O flower of all!

" O flower of all the years, O flower of all!
    I seek thee in thy garden, and I dare
To love thee; and though my deserts be small,
    Thou art the only flower I would wear,
        O flower of all!"

"Now that," he said, "is the romantic, almost the Arcadian, spirit. We have lost it, but it lingers like some good scent in the folds of lace. It is also but artifice, yet so is the lingering perfume. When it hung in the flower it was lost after a day's life, but when gathered and distilled into an essence it becomes, through artifice, an abiding sweetness. So with your song there. It is the spirit of devotion, gathered, it may be, from a thousand flowers, and made into an essence, which is offered to one only. It is not the worship of this one, but the worship of a thousand distilled at last to one delicate liturgy. So much for sentiment," he continued. "Upon my soul, Captain Moray, you are a boon. I love to have you caged. I shall watch your distressed career to its close with deep scrutiny. You and I are wholly different, but you are interesting. You never could be great. Pardon the egotism, but it is truth. Your brain works heavily, you are too tenacious of your conscience, you are a blunderer. You will always sow, and others will reap."

I waved my hand in deprecation, for I was in no mood for further talk, and I made no answer. He smiled at me, and said, "Well, since you doubt my theories, let us come, as your Shakespeare says, to Hecuba. . . . If you will accompany me," he added, as he opened my cell door and motioned me courteously to go outside. I drew back, and he said, "There is no need to hesitate; I go to show you only what will interest you."

We passed in silence through the corridors, two sentinels attending, and at last came into a large square room, wherein stood three men with hands tied over their heads against the wall, their faces twitching with pain. I drew back in astonishment, for, standing before them, were Gabord and another soldier. Doltaire ordered from the room the soldier and my two sentinels, and motioned me to one of two chairs set in the middle of the floor.

Presently his face became hard and cruel, and he said to the tortured prisoners, " You will need to speak the truth, and promptly. I have an order to do with you what I will. Hear me. Three nights ago, as Mademoiselle Duvarney was returning from the house of a friend beside the Intendance, she was set upon by you. A cloak was thrown over her head, she was carried to a carriage, where two of you got inside with her. Some gentlemen and myself were coming that way. We heard the lady's cries, and two gave chase to the carriage, while one followed the others. By the help of soldier Gabord here you all were captured. You have hung where you are for two days, and now I shall have you whipped. When that is done, you shall tell your story. If you do not speak truth, you shall be whipped again, and then hung. Ladies shall have safety from rogues like you."

Alixe's danger told in these concise words made me, I am sure, turn pale ; but Doltaire did not see it, he was engaged with the prisoners. As I thought and wondered four soldiers were brought in, and the men were made ready for the lash. In vain they pleaded they would tell their story at once. Doltaire would not listen ; the whipping first, and their story after. Soon their backs were bared, their faces were turned to the wall, and, as Gabord with harsh voice counted, the lashes were mercilessly laid on. There was a horrible fascination in watching the skin corrugate under the cords, rippling away in red and purple blotches, the grooves in the flesh crossing and recrossing, the raw misery spreading from the hips to the shoulders. Now and again Doltaire drew out a box and took a pinch of snuff, and once, coolly and curiously, he walked up to the most stalwart prisoner and felt his pulse, then to the weakest, whose limbs and body had stiffened as though dead. "*Ninety-seven! Ninety-eight! Ninety-nine!*" growled Gabord, and then came Doltaire's voice:

"Stop! Now fetch some brandy."

The prisoners were loosened, and Doltaire spoke sharply to a soldier who was roughly pulling one man's shirt over the excoriated back. Brandy was given by Gabord, and the prisoners stood, a most pitiful sight, the weakest livid.

"Now tell your story," said Doltaire to this last.

The man, with broken voice and breath catching, said that they had erred. They had been hired to kidnap Madame Cournal, not Mademoiselle Duvarney.

Doltaire's eyes flashed. "I see, I see," he said aside to me. "The wretch speaks truth."

"Who was your master?" he asked of the sturdiest of the villains; and he was told that Monsieur Cournal had engaged them. To the question what was to be done with Madame Cournal, another answered that she was to be waylaid as she was coming from the Intendance, kidnapped, and hurried to a nunnery, there to be imprisoned for life.

Doltaire sat for a moment, looking at the men in silence. "You are not to hang," he said at last; "but ten days hence, when you have had one hundred lashes more, you shall go free. Fifty for you," he continued to the weakest, who had first told the story.

"Not fifty, nor one!" was the shrill reply, and, being unbound, the prisoner snatched something from a bench near, there was a flash of steel, and he came huddling in a heap on the floor, muttering a malediction on the world.

" There was some bravery in that," said Doltaire, looking at the dead man. " If he has friends, hand over the
body to them. This matter must not be spoken of—at
your peril," he added sternly. " Give them food and
brandy."

Then he accompanied me to my cell, and opened the
door. I passed in, and he was about going without a word,
when on a sudden his old nonchalance came back, and he
said :

" I promised you a matter of interest. You have had
it. Gather philosophy from this : you may with impunity
buy anything from a knave and fool except his nuptial
bed. He throws the money in your face some day."

So saying he plunged in thought again, and left me.

XVI.

BE SAINT OR IMP.

IMMEDIATELY I opened the packet. As Doltaire had
said, the two books of poems I had lent Alixe were there,
and between the pages of one lay a letter addressed to
me. It was, indeed, a daring thing to make Doltaire
her messenger. But she trusted to his habits of courtesy; he had no small meannesses—he was no spy or
thief.

DEAR ROBERT (the letter ran) : I know not if this
will ever reach you, for I am about to try a perilous thing,
even to make Monsieur Doltaire my letter-carrier. Bold
as it is, I hope to bring it through safely.

You must know that my mother now makes Monsieur
Doltaire welcome to our home, for his great talents and
persuasion have so worked upon her that she believes him

not so black as he is painted. My father, too, is not un-
moved by his amazing address and complaisance. I do
not think he often cares to use his arts—he is too indo-
lent; but with my father, my mother, and my sister he
has set in motion all his resources.

Robert, all Versailles is here. This Monsieur Doltaire
speaks for it. I know not if every court in the world is
the same, but if so, I am at heart no courtier; though
I love the sparkle, the sharp play of wit and word, the
very touch-and-go of weapons. I am in love with life,
and I wish to live to be old, very old, that I will have
known it all, from helplessness to helplessness again, miss-
ing nothing, even though much be sad to feel and bear.
Robert, I should have gone on many years, seeing little,
knowing little, I think, if it had not been for you and for
your troubles, which are mine, and for this love of ours,
cherished in the midst of sorrows. Georgette is now as
old as when I first came to love you, and you were thrown
into the citadel, and yet, in feeling and experience, I am
ten years older than she; and necessity has made me
wiser. Ah, if necessity would but make me happy too,
by giving you your liberty, that on these many miseries
endured we might set up a sure home! I wonder if you
think—if you think of that: a little home away from all
these wars, aloof from vexing things.

But there! all too plainly I am showing you my heart.
Yet it is so good a comfort to speak on paper to you, in
this silence here. Can you guess where is that *here*, Robert? It is not the Château St. Louis—no. It is not the
manor. It is the château, dear Château Alixe—my
father has called it that—on the island of Orleans. Three
days ago I was sick at heart, tired of all the junketings
and feastings, and I begged my mother to fetch me here,
though it is yet but early spring, and snow is on the
ground.

First, you must know that this new château is built upon, and is joined to, the ruins of an old one, owned long years ago by the Baron of Beaugard, whose strange history you must learn some day, out of the papers we have found here. I begged my father not to tear the old portions of the manor down, but, using the first foundations, put up a house half castle and half manor. Pictures of the old manor were found, and so we have a place that is no patchwork, but a renewal. I made my father give me the old surviving part of the building for my own, and so it is.

It is all set on high ground abutting on the water almost at the point where I am, and I have the river in my sight all day. Now, think yourself in the new building. You come out of a dining-hall, hung all about with horns and weapons and shields and such bravery, go through a dark, narrow passage, and then down a step or two. You open a door, bright light breaks on your eyes, then two steps lower, and you are here with me. You might have gone outside the dining-hall upon a stone terrace, and so have come along to the deep window where I sit so often. You may think of me hiding in the curtains, watching you, though you knew it not till you touched the window and I came out quietly, startling you, so that your heart would beat beyond counting!

As I look up towards the window, the thing first in sight is the cage, with the little bird which came to me in the cathedral the morning my brother got lease of life again : you *do* remember—is it not so ? It never goes from my room, and though I have come here but for a week I muffled the cage well and brought it over ; and there the bird swings and sings the long day through. I have heaped the window-seats with soft furs, and one of these I prize most rarely. It was a gift—and whose, think you ? Even a poor soldier's. You see I have not all friends among the great folk. I often lie upon that soft robe of sable—ay, sable, Master Robert—and think of him who gave it to me. Now I know you are jealous, and I can see your eyes flash up. But you shall at once be soothed. It is no other than Gabord's gift. He is now of the Governor's body-guard, and I think is by no means happy, and would prefer service with the Marquis de Montcalm, who goes not comfortably with the Intendant and the Governor.

One day Gabord came to our house on the ramparts, and, asking for me, blundered out, "Aho, what shall a soldier do with sables? They are for gentles and for wrens to snuggle in. Here comes a Russian count oversea, and goes mad in tavern. Here comes Gabord, and saves count from ruddy crest for kissing the wrong wench. Then count falls on Gabord's neck, and kisses both his ears, and gives him sables, and crosses oversea again; and so good-bye to count and his foolery. And sables shall be ma'm'selle's, if she will have them." He might have sold the thing for many louis, and yet he brought it to me; and he would not go till he had seen me sitting on it, muffling my hands and face in the soft fur.

Just now, as I am writing, I glance at the table where I sit—a small brown table of oak, carved with the name of Félise, Baroness of Beaugard. She sat here; and some day, when you hear her story, you will know why I begged Madame Lotbinière to give it to me in exchange for another, once the King's. Carved, too, beneath her name, are the words, "*O tarry thou the Lord's leisure.*"

And now you shall laugh with me at a droll thing Georgette has given me to wipe my pen upon. There are three little circles of deerskin and one of ruby velvet, stitched together in the centre. Then, standing on the velvet is a yellow wooden chick, with little eyes of beads, and a little wooden bill stuck in most quaintly, and a head that twists like a weathercock. It has such a piquant silliness of look that I laugh at it most heartily, and I have an almost elfish fun in smearing its downy feathers. I am sure you did not think I could be amused so easily. You shall see this silly chick one day, humorously ugly and all daubed with ink.

There is a low couch in one corner of the room, and just above hangs a picture of my mother. In another corner is a little shelf of books, among them two which I have studied constantly since you were put in prison— your great Shakespeare, and the writings of one Mr. Addison. I had few means of studying at first, so difficult it seemed, and all the words sounded hard; but there is here, as you know, your countryman, one Lieutenant Stevens of Rogers's Rangers, a prisoner, and he has helped me, and is ready to help you when the time comes for stirring. I teach him French; and though I do not talk of you, he tells me in what esteem you are held in Virginia and in England, and is not slow to praise you on his own account, which makes me more forgiving when he would come to sentiment!

In another corner is my spinning-wheel, and there stands a harpsichord, just where the soft sun sends in a ribbon of light; and I will presently play for you a pretty song. I wonder if you can hear it? Where I shall sit at the harpsichord the belt of sunlight will fall across my shoulder, and, looking through the window, I shall see your prison there on the Heights; the silver flag with its gold lilies on the Château St. Louis; the great guns of the citadel; and far off at Beauport the Manor House and garden which you and I know so well, and the Falls of Montmorenci, falling like white flowing hair from the tall cliff.

You will care to know of how these months have been spent, and what news of note there is of the fighting be-

The Manor-House at Beauport.

tween our countries. No matters of great consequence have come to our ears, save that it is thought your navy may descend on Louisburg; that Ticonderoga is also to be set upon, and Quebec to be besieged in the coming summer. From France the news is various. Now, Frederick of Prussia and England defeat the allies, France, Russia, and Austria; now, they, as Monsieur Doltaire says, " send the great Prussian to verses and the megrims." For my own part, I am ever glad to hear that our cause is victorious, and letters that my brother writes me rouse all my ardour for my country. Juste has grown in place and favour, and in his latest letter he says that Monsieur Doltaire's voice has got him much advancement. He also remarks that Monsieur Doltaire has reputation for being one of the most reckless, clever, and cynical men in France. Things that he has said are quoted at ball and rout. Yet the King is angry with him, and La Pompadour's caprice may send him again to the Bastile. These things Juste heard from D'Argenson, Minister of War, through his secretary, with whom he is friendly.

I will now do what I never thought to do: I will send you here some extracts from my journal, which will disclose to you the secrets of a girl's troubled heart. Some folk might say that I am unmaidenly in this. But I care not, I fear not.

———

December 24. I was with Robert to-day. I let him see what trials I had had with Monsieur Doltaire, and what were like to come. It hurt me to tell him, yet it would have hurt me more to withhold them. I am hurt whichever way it goes. Monsieur Doltaire rouses the worst parts of me. On the one hand I detest him for his hatred of Robert, and for his evil life, yet on the other I must needs admire him for his many graces—why are not the graces of the wicked horrible?—for his singular abili-

ties, and because, gamester though he may be, he is no
public robber.   Then, too, the melancholy of his birth and
history claim some sympathy.   Sometimes when I listen
to him speak, hear the almost piquant sadness of his words,
watch the spirit of isolation which, by design or otherwise, shows in him, for the moment I am conscious of a
pity or an interest which I flout in wiser hours.   This is
his art, the deep danger of his personality.

To-night he came, and with many fine phrases wished
us a happy day to-morrow, and most deftly worked upon
my mother and Georgette by looking round and speaking
with a quaint sort of raillery—half pensive, it was—of the
peace of this home-life of ours; and, indeed, he did it so
inimitably that I was not sure how much was false and
how much true.   I tried to avoid him to-day, but my
mother constantly made private speech between us easy.
At last he had his way, and then I was not sorry; for
Georgette was listening to him with more colour than she
is wont to wear.   I would rather see her in her grave than
with her hand in his, her sweet life in his power.   She is
unschooled in the ways of the world, and she never will
know it as I now do.   How am I sounding all the depths !
Can a woman walk the dance with evil, and be no worse
for it by-and-bye?   Yet for a cause, for a cause !   What
can I do?   I can not say, " Monsieur Doltaire, you must
not speak with me, or talk with me ; you are a plague-
spot."   No, I must even follow this path, so it but lead at
last to Robert and his safety.

Monsieur, having me alone at last, said to me, " I have
kept my word as to the little boast : this Captain Moray
still lives."

" You are not greater than I thought," said I.

He professed to see but one meaning in my words, and
answered, " It was, then, mere whim to see me do this
thing, a lady's curious mind, eh ?   My faith, I think your

sex are the true scientists: you try experiment for no
other reason than to see effect."

"You forget my deep interest in Captain Moray," said
I, with airy boldness.

He laughed. He was disarmed. How could he think
I meant it! "My imagination halts," he rejoined. "Mil-
lenium comes when you are interested. And yet," he
continued, "it is my one ambition to interest you, and I
will do it, or I will say my prayers no more."

> "But how can that be done no more,
> Which ne'er was done before?"

I retorted, railing at him, for I feared to take him seriously.

"There you wrong me," he said. "I am devout; I
am a lover of the Scriptures—their beauty haunts me; I
go to mass—its dignity affects me; and I have prayed, as
in my youth I wrote verses. It is not a matter of morality, but of temperament. A man may be religious and
yet be evil. Satan fell, but he believed and he admired,
as the English Milton wisely shows it."

I was most glad that my father came between us at
that moment; but before monsieur left, he said to me,
"You have challenged me. Beware: I have begun this
chase. Yet I would rather be your follower, rather have
your arrow in me, than be your hunter." He said it with
a sort of warmth, which I knew was a glow in his senses
merely; he was heated with his own eloquence.

"Wait," returned I. "You have heard the story of
King Artus?"

He thought a moment. "No, no. I never was a child
as other children. I was always comrade to the imps."

"King Artus," said I, "was most fond of hunting."
(It is but a legend with its moral, as you know.) "It was
forbidden by the priests to hunt while mass was being said.

14

One day, at the lifting of the host, the King, hearing a
hound bay, rushed out, and gathered his pack together;
but as they went, a whirlwind caught them up into the
air, where they continue to this day, following a lonely
trail, never resting, and all the game they get is one fly
every seventh year. And now, when all on a sudden at
night you hear the trees and leaves and the sleepy birds
and crickets stir, it is the old King hunting—for the fox
he never gets."

Monsieur looked at me with curious intentness. " You
have a great gift," he said ; " you make your point by allusion. I follow you. But see : *when I am blown into the
air I shall not ride alone.* Happiness is the fox we ride
to cover, you and I, though we find but a firefly in the
end."

"A poor reply," I remarked easily ; " not worthy of
you."

"As worthy as I am of you," he rejoined ; then he
kissed my hand. " I will see you at mass to-morrow."

Unconsciously, I rubbed the hand he kissed with my
handkerchief.

" I am not to be provoked," he said. " It is much to
have you treat my kiss with consequence."

March 25. No news of Robert all this month. Gabord has been away in Montreal. I see Voban only now
and then, and he is strange in manner, and can do nothing. Mathilde is better—so still and desolate, yet not
wild ; but her memory is all gone, save for that "François Bigot is a devil." My father has taken anew a strong
dislike to Monsieur Doltaire, because of talk that is
abroad concerning him and Madame Cournal. I once
thought she was much sinned against, but now I am sure
she is not to be defended. She is most defiant, though
people dare not shut their doors against her. A change

seemed to come over her all at once, and over her husband
also.   He is now gloomy and taciturn, now foolishly gay,
yet he is little seen with the Intendant, as before.   However it be, Monsieur Doltaire and Bigot are no longer in-
timate.   What should I care for that, if Monsieur Doltaire had no power, if he were not the door between Robert
and me ?   What care I, indeed, how vile he is, so he but
serve my purpose ?   Let him try my heart and soul and
senses as he will ; I will one day purify myself of his presence and all this soiling, and find my peace in Robert's
arms—or in the quiet of a nunnery.

This morning I got up at sunrise, it being the Annun-
ciation of the Virgin, and prepared to go to mass in the
chapel of the Ursulines.   How peaceful was the world !
So still, so still.   The smoke came curling up here and
there through the sweet air of spring, a snowbird tripped
along the white coverlet of the earth, and before a Calvary I saw a peasant kneel and say an Ave as he went to
market.   There was springtime in the sun, in the smell
of the air ; springtime everywhere but in my heart, which
was all winter.   I seemed alone—alone—alone.   I felt the
tears start.   But that was for a moment only, I am glad
to say, for I got my courage again, as I did the night before when Monsieur Doltaire placed his arm at my waist,
and poured into my ears a torrent of protestations !

I did not move at first.   But I could feel my cheeks
grow cold, and something clamp my heart.   Yet had ever
man such hateful eloquence !   There is that in him—oh,
shame ! oh, shame !—which goes far with a woman.   He
has the music of passion, and though it is lower than
love, it is the poetry of the senses.   I spoke to him calmly, I think, begging him place his merits where they
would have better entertainment ; but I said hard, cold
things at last, when other means availed not ; which presently made him turn upon me in another fashion.

His words dropped slowly, with a consummate careful-ness, his manner was pointedly courteous, yet there was an underpressure of force, of will, which made me see the danger of my position. He said that I was quite right; that he would wish no privilege of a woman which was not given with a frank eagerness; that to him no woman was worth the having who did not throw her whole nature into the giving. Constancy—that was another matter. But a perfect gift while there was giving at all—that was the way.

"There is something behind all this," he said. "I am not so vain as to think any merits of mine would influence you. But my devotion, my admiration of you, the very force of my passion, should move you. Be you ever so set against me—and I do not think you are—you should not be so strong to resist the shock of feeling. I do not know the cause, but I will find it out; and when I do, I shall remove it or be myself removed." He touched my arm with his fingers. "When I touch you like that," he said, "summer riots in my veins. I will not think that this which rouses me so is but power upon one side, and effect upon the other. Something in you called me to you, some-thing in me will wake you yet. *Mon Dieu*, I could wait a score of years for my touch to thrill you as yours does me! And I will—I will."

"You think it suits your honour to force my affec-tions?" I asked; for I dared not say all I wished.

"What is there in this reflecting on my honour?" he answered. "At Versailles, believe me, they would say I strive here for a canonizing. No, no; think me so gal-lant that I follow you to serve you, to convince you that the way I go is the way your hopes will lie. Honour? To fetch you to the point where you and I should start to-gether on the Appian Way, I would traffic with that, even, and say I did so, and would do so a thousand times, if in the end it put your hand in mine. Who, who can give you what I offer, can offer? See: I have given myself to a hundred women in my time—but what of me? That which was a candle in a wind, and the light went out. There was no depth, no life, in that; only the shadow of a man was there those hundred times. But here, now, the whole man plunges into this sea, and he will reach the lighthouse on the shore, or be broken on the reefs. Look in my eyes, and see the furnace there, and tell me if you think that fire is for cool corners in the gardens at Neuilly or for the Hills of—— " He suddenly broke off, and a singular smile followed. " There, there," he said, " I have said enough. It came to me all at once how droll my speech would sound to our people at Versailles. It is an elaborate irony that the occasional virtues of certain men turn and mock them. That is the penalty of being inconsistent. Be saint or imp; it is the only way. But this imp that mocks me relieves you of reply. Yet I have spoken truth, and again and again I will tell it you, till you believe according to my gospel."

How glad I was that he himself lightened the situation! I had been driven to despair, but this strange twist in his mood made all smooth for me. " That 'again and again' sounds dreary," said I. " It might almost appear I must sometime accept your gospel, to cure you of preaching it, and save me from eternal drowsiness."

We were then most fortunately interrupted. He made his adieus, and I went to my room, brooded till my head ached, then fell a-weeping, and wished myself out of the world, I was so sick and weary. Now and again a hot shudder of shame and misery ran through me, as I thought of monsieur's words to me. Put them how he would, they sound an insult now, though as he spoke I felt the power of his passion. " If you had lived a thousand years ago, you would have loved a thousand times," he said to

me one day.   Sometimes I think he spoke truly; I have
a nature that responds to all eloquence in life.

Robert, I have bared my heart to thee.   I have hidden nothing.   In a few days I shall go back to the city
with my mother, and when I can I will send news; and
do thou send me news also, if thou canst devise a safe
way.   Meanwhile I have written my brother Juste to be
magnanimous, and to try for thy freedom.   He will not
betray me, and he may help us.   I have begged him to
write to thee a letter of reconcilement.

And now, comrade of my heart, do thou have courage.
I also shall be strong as I am ardent.   Having written
thee, I am cheerful once more; and when again I may, I
will open the doors of my heart that thou mayst come in.
That heart is thine, Robert.   Thy

ALIXE,

who loves thee all her days.

P. S.—I have found the names and places of the men
who keep the guard beneath thy window.   If there is
chance for freedom that way, fix the day some time ahead,
and I will see what may be done.   Voban fears nothing;
he will act secretly for me.

The next day I arranged for my escape, which had
been long in planning.

XVII.

THROUGH THE BARS OF THE CAGE.

I SHOULD have tried escape earlier but that it was
little use to venture forth in the harsh winter in a hostile
country.   But now April had come, and I was keen to
make a trial of my fortune.   I had been saving food for
a long time, little by little, and hiding it in the old knap-

sack which had held my second suit of clothes. I had used the little stove for parching my food—Indian corn, for which I had professed a fondness to my jailer, and liberally paid for out of funds which had been sent me by Mr. George Washington in answer to my letter, and other moneys to a goodly amount in a letter from Governor Dinwiddie. These letters had been carefully written, and the Marquis de Vaudreuil, into whose hands they had first come, was gallant enough not to withhold them—though he read them first.

Besides Indian corn, the parching of which amused me, I had dried ham and tongue, and bread and cheese, enough, by frugal use, to last me a month at least. I knew it would be a journey of six weeks or more to the nearest English settlement, but if I could get that month's start I should forage for the rest, or take my fate as I found it: I was used to all the turns of fortune now. My knapsack gradually filled, and meanwhile I slowly worked my passage into the open world. There was the chance that my jailer would explore the knapsack; but after a time I lost that fear, for it lay untouched with a blanket in a corner, and I cared for my cell with my own hands.

The real point of danger was the window. There lay my way. It was stoutly barred with iron up and down, and the bars were set in the solid limestone. Soon after I entered this prison I saw that I must cut a groove in the stone from stanchion to stanchion, and then, by drawing one to the other, make an opening large enough to let my body through. For tools I had only a miserable knife with which I cut my victuals, and the smaller but stouter one which Gabord had not taken from me. There could be no pounding, no chiselling, but only rubbing of the hard stone. So hour after hour I rubbed away, in constant danger of discovery however. My jailer had a trick of sudden entrance which would have been grotesque had it not been so serious to me. To provide against the flurried inquisition of his eye I kept near me bread well chewed, with which I filled the hole, covering it with the sand I had rubbed or the ashes of my pipe. I lived in dread of these entrances, but at last I found that they chanced only within certain hours, and I arranged my times of work accordingly. Once or twice, however, being impatient, I scratched the stone with some asperity and noise, and was rewarded by hearing my fellow stumbling in the hall; for he had as uncertain limbs as ever I saw. He stumbled upon nothing, as you have seen a child trip itself up by tangling of its feet.

The first time that he came, roused by the grating noise as he sat below, he stumbled in the very centre of the cell, and fell upon his knees. I would have laughed if I had dared, but I yawned over the book I had hastily snatched up, and puffed great whiffs from my pipe. I dreaded lest he should go to the window. He started for it, but suddenly made for my couch, and dragged it away, as if looking to find a hole dug beneath it. Still I did not laugh at him, but gravely watched him; and presently he went away. At another time I was foolishly harsh with my tools; but I knew now the time required by him to come upstairs, and I swiftly filled the groove with bread, strewed ashes and sand over it, rubbed all smooth, and was plunged in my copy of Montaigne when he entered. This time he went straight to the window, looked at it, tried the stanchions, and then, with an amused attempt at being cunning and hiding his own vigilance, he asked me, with laborious hypocrisy, if I had seen Captain Lancy pass the window. And so for weeks and weeks we played hide-and-seek with each other.

At last I had nothing to do but sit and wait, for the groove was cut, the bar had room to play. I could not bend it, for it was fast at the top; but when my hour of adventure was come, I would tie a handkerchief round the two bars and twist it with the piece of hickory used for stirring the fire. Here was my engine of escape, and I waited till April should wind to its close, when I should, in the softer weather, try my fortune outside these walls.

So time went on until one eventful day, even the 30th of April of that year 1758. It was raining and blowing when I waked, and it ceased not all the day, coming to a hailstorm towards night. I felt sure that my guards without would relax their vigilance. In the evening I listened, and heard no voices nor any sound of feet, only the pelting rain and the whistling wind. Yet I did not stir till midnight. Then I slung the knapsack in front of me, so that I could force it through the window first, and tying my handkerchief round the iron bars, I screwed it up with my stick. Presently the bars came together, and my way was open. I got my body through by dint of squeezing, and let myself go plump into the mire below. Then I stood still a minute, and listened again.

A light was shining not far away. Drawing near, I saw that it came from a small hut or lean-to. Looking through the cracks, I observed my two gentlemen drowsing in the corner. I was eager for their weapons, but I dared not make the attempt to get them, for they were laid between their legs, the barrels resting against their shoulders. I drew back, and for a moment paused to get my bearings. Then I made for a corner of the yard where the wall was lowest, and, taking a run at it, caught the top, with difficulty scrambled up, and speedily was over and floundering in the mud. I knew well where I was, and at once started off in a northwesterly direction, toward the St. Charles River, making for a certain farm-house above the town. Yet I took care, though it was dangerous, to travel a street in which was Voban's house.

There was no light in the street nor in his house, nor had I seen any one abroad as I came, not even a sentinel.

I knew where was the window of the barber's bed-room, and I tapped upon it softly. Instantly I heard a stir; then there came the sound of flint and steel, then a light, and presently a hand at the window, and a voice asking who was there.

I gave a quick reply; the light was put out, the window opened, and there was Voban staring at me.

"This letter," said I, "to Mademoiselle Duvarney," and I slipped ten louis into his hand also.

The coins he quickly handed back. "M'sieu'," said he, "if I take it I would seem to myself a traitor—no, no. But I will give the letter to ma'm'selle."

Then he asked me in; but I would not, yet begged him, if he could, to have a canoe at my disposal at a point below the Falls of Montmorenci two nights hence.

"M'sieu'," said he, "I will do so if I can, but I am watched. I would not pay a sou for my life—no. Yet I will serve you, if there is a way."

Then I told him what I meant to do, and bade him repeat it exactly to Alixe. This he swore to do, and I cordially grasped the good wretch's shoulder, and thanked him with all my heart. I got from him a weapon, also, and again I put gold louis into his hand, and bade him keep them, for I might need his kind offices to spend it for me. To this he consented, and I plunged into the dark again. I had not gone far when I heard footsteps coming, and I drew aside into the corner of a porch. A moment, then the light flashed full upon me. I had my hand upon the hanger I had got from Voban, and I was ready to strike if there were need, when Gabord's voice broke on my ear, and his hand caught at the short sword by his side.

"'Tis dickey-bird, aho!" cried he. There was exul-

tation in his eye and voice. Here was a chance for him
to prove himself against me; he had proved himself for
me more than once.

"Here was I," added he, "making for M'sieu' Voban,
that he might come and bleed a sick soldier, when who
should come running but our English captain! Come
forth, aho!"

"No, Gabord," said I, "I'm bound for freedom." I
stepped forth. His sword was poised against me. I was
intent to make a desperate fight.

"March on," returned he, gruffly, and I could feel the
iron in his voice.

"But not with you, Gabord. My way lies towards Virginia."

I did not care to strike the first blow, and I made to
go past him. His lantern came down, and he made a
catch at my shoulder. I swung back, threw off my cloak
and up my weapon.

Then we fought. My knapsack troubled me, for it
was loose, and kept shifting. Gabord made stroke after
stroke, watchful, heavy, offensive, muttering to himself as
he struck and parried. There was no hatred in his eyes,
but he had the lust of fighting on him, and he was breathing easily and could have kept this up for hours. As
we fought I heard a clock strike one in a house near.
Then a cock crowed. I had received two slight wounds,
and I had not touched my enemy. But I was swifter,
and I came at him suddenly with a rush, and struck for
his left shoulder when I saw my chance. I felt the steel
strike the bone. As I did so he caught my wrist and
lunged most fiercely at me, dragging me to him. The
blow struck straight at my side, but it went through the
knapsack, which had swung loose, and so saved my life;
for another instant and I had tripped him up, and he lay
bleeding badly.

"Aho! 'twas a fair fight," said he. "Now get you gone. I call for help."

"I can not leave you so, Gabord," said I. I stooped and lifted up his head.

"Then you shall go to citadel," said he, feeling for his small trumpet.

"No, no," I answered; "I'll go fetch Voban."

"To bleed me more!" quoth he whimsically; and I knew well he was pleased I did not leave him. "Nay, kick against yonder door. It is Captain Lancy's."

At that moment a window opened, and Lancy's voice was heard. Without a word I seized the soldier's lantern and my cloak, and made away as hard as I could go.

"I'll have a wing of you for lantern there!" roared Gabord, swearing roundly as I ran off with it.

With all my might I hurried, and was soon outside the town, and coming fast to the farmhouse about two miles beyond. Nearing it, I hid the lantern beneath my cloak and made for an outhouse. The door was not locked, and I passed in. There was a loft nearly full of hay, and I crawled up and dug a hole far down against the side of the building, and climbed in, bringing with me for drink a nest of hen's eggs which I found in the corner. The warmth of the dry hay was comforting, and after caring for my wounds, which I found were but scratches, I had somewhat to eat from my knapsack, drank up two eggs, and then coiled myself for sleep. It was my purpose, if not discovered, to stay where I was two days, and then to make for the point below the Falls of Montmorenci where I hoped to find a canoe of Voban's placing.

When I waked it must have been near noon, so I lay still for a time, listening to the cheerful noise of fowls and cattle in the yard without, and to the clacking of a hen above me. The air smelt very sweet. I also heard my unknowing host, at whose table I had once sat, two years before, talking with his son, who had just come over from Quebec, bringing news of my escape, together with a wonderful story of the fight between Gabord and myself. It had, by his calendar, lasted some three hours, and both of us, in the end, fought as we lay upon the ground. "But presently along comes a cloaked figure, with horses, and he lifts m'sieu' the Englishman upon one, and away they ride like the devil towards St. Charles River and Beauport. Gabord was taken to the hospital, and he swore that Englishman would not have got away if stranger had not fetched him a crack with a pistol-butt which sent him dumb and dizzy. And there M'sieu' Lancy sleep snug through all until the horses ride away!"

The farmer and his son laughed heartily, with many a "By Gar!" their sole English oath. Then came the news that six thousand livres were offered for me, dead or living, the drums beating far and near to tell the people so.

The farmer gave a long whistle, and in a great bustle set to calling all his family to arm themselves and join with him in this treasure-hunting. I am sure at least a dozen were at the task, searching all about; nor did they neglect the loft where I lay. But I had dug far down, drawing the hay over me as I went, so that they must needs have been keen to smell me out. After about three hours' poking about over all the farm, they met again outside this building, and I could hear their gabble plainly. The smallest among them, the piping chore-boy, he was for spitting me without mercy; and the milking-lass would toast me with a hay-fork, that she would, and six thousand livres should set her up forever.

In the midst of their rattling came two soldiers, who ordered them about, and with much blustering began searching here and there, and chucking the maids under the chins, as I could tell by their little bursts of laughter and the "La m'sieu's!" which trickled through the hay.

I am sure that one such little episode saved me; for I heard a soldier just above me poking and tossing hay with uncomfortable vigour. But presently the amorous hunter turned his thoughts elsewhere, and I was left to myself, and to a late breakfast of parched beans, and bread, and raw eggs, after which I lay and thought; and the sum of the thinking was that I would stay where I was till the first wave of the hunt had passed.

Near midnight of the second day I came out secretly from my lurking-place, and faced straight for the St. Charles River. Finding it at high water, I plunged in, with my knapsack and cloak on my head, and made my way across, reaching the opposite shore safely. After going two miles or so, I discovered friendly covert in the woods, where, in spite of my cloak and dry cedar boughs wrapped round, I shivered as I lay until the morning. When the sun came up, I drew out; and after I was dry again I crawled back into my nest and fell into a broken sleep. Many times during the day I heard the horns of my hunters, and voices near me more than once. But I had crawled into the hollow of a half-uprooted stump, and the cedar branches, which had been cut off a day or two before, were a screen. I could see soldiers here and there, armed and swaggering, and faces of peasants and shop-keepers whom I knew.

A function was being made of my escape; it was a hunting-feast, in which women were as eager as their husbands and their brothers. There was something devilish in it, when you come to think of it: a whole town roused and abroad to hunt down one poor fugitive, whose only sin was, in themselves, a virtue—loyalty to his country. I saw women armed with sickles and iron forks, and lads bearing axes and hickory poles cut to a point like a spear, while blunderbusses were in plenty. Now and again a weapon was fired, and, to watch their motions and peepings, it might have been thought I was a dragon, or that they all were hunting La Jongleuse, their fabled witch, whose villainies, are they not told at every fireside?

Often I shivered violently, and anon I was burning hot; my adventure had given me a chill and fever. Late in the evening of this day, my hunters having drawn off with as little sense as they had hunted me, I edged cautiously down past Beauport and on to the Montmorenci Falls. I came along in safety, and reached a spot near the point where Voban was to hide the boat. The highway ran between. I looked out cautiously. I could hear and see nothing, and so I ran out, crossed the road, and pushed for the woods on the banks of the river. I had scarcely got across when I heard a shout, and looking round I saw three horsemen, who instantly spurred towards me. I sprang through the underbrush, and came down roughly into a sort of quarry, spraining my ankle on a pile of stones. I got up quickly; but my ankle hurt me sorely, and I turned sick and dizzy. Limping a little way, I set my back against a tree and drew my hanger. As I did so, the three gentlemen burst in upon me. They were General Montcalm, a gentleman of the Governor's household, and Doltaire!

"It is no use, dear captain," said Doltaire. "Yield up your weapon."

General Montcalm eyed me curiously, as the other gentleman talked in low, excited tones; and presently he made a gesture of courtesy, for he saw that I was hurt. Doltaire's face wore a malicious smile; but when he noted how sick I was, he came and offered me his arm, and was constant in courtesy till I was set upon a horse; and with him and the General riding beside me I came to my new imprisonment. They both forbore to torture me with words, for I was suffering greatly; but they fetched me to the Château St. Louis, followed by a crowd, who hooted at me. Doltaire turned on them at last, and stopped them.

The Governor, whose petty vanity was roused, showed a foolish fury at seeing me, and straightway ordered me to the citadel again.

"It's useless kicking 'gainst the pricks," said Doltaire to me cynically, as I passed out limping between two soldiers; but I did not reply. In another half hour of bitter journeying I found myself in my dungeon. I sank upon the old couch of straw, untouched since I had left it; and when the door shut upon me, desponding, aching in all my body, now feverish and now shivering, my ankle in great pain, I could bear up no longer, and I bowed my head and fell a-weeping like a woman.

XVIII.

THE STEEP PATH OF CONQUEST.

Now I am come to a period on which I shall not dwell, nor repeat a tale of suffering greater than that I had yet endured. All the first night of this new imprisonment I tossed on my wretched bed in pain and misery. A strange and surly soldier came and went, bringing bread and water; but when I asked that a physician be sent me, he replied, with a vile oath, that the devil should be my only surgeon. Soon he came again, accompanied by another soldier, and put irons on me. With what quietness I could I asked him by whose orders this was done; but he vouchsafed no reply save that I was to "go bound to fires of hell."

"There is no journeying there," I answered; "here is the place itself."

Then a chain was roughly put round my injured

ankle, and it gave me such agony that I turned sick, but I kept back groaning, for I would not have these varlets catch me quaking.

"I'll have you grilled for this one day," said I. "You are no men, but butchers. Can you not see my ankle has been sorely hurt?"

"You are for killing," was the gruff reply, "and here's a taste of it."

With that he drew the chain with a jerk round the hurt member, so that it drove me to madness. I caught him by the throat and hurled him back against the wall, and, snatching a pistol from his comrade's belt, aimed it at his head. I was beside myself with pain, and if he had been further violent I should straightway have shot him. His fellow dared not stir in his defence, for the pistol was trained on him too surely; and so at last the wretch, promising better treatment, crawled to his feet, and made motion for the pistol to be given him. But I would not yield it, telling him it should be a guarantee of truce. Presently the door closed behind them, and I sank back upon the half-fettered chains.

I must have sat for more than an hour, when there was a noise without, and there entered the commandant, the Marquis de Montcalm, and the Seigneur Duvarney. The pistol was in my hand, and I did not put it down, but struggled to my feet, and waited for them to speak.

For a moment there was silence, and then the commandant said, "Your guards have brought me word, Monsieur le Capitaine, that you are violent. You have resisted them, and have threatened them with their own pistols"

"With one pistol, monsieur le commandant," answered I. Then, in bitter words, I told them of my treatment by those rascals, and I showed them how my ankle had been tortured. "I have no fear of death," said I,

15

"but I will not lie and let dogs bite me with ' I thank you.'
Death should come but once; it is a damned brutality to
make one die a hundred and yet live—the work of Turks,
not Christians! If you want my life, why, take it and
have done."

The Marquis de Montcalm whispered to the commandant. The Seigneur Duvarney, to whom I had not yet
spoken, nor he to me, stood leaning against the wall, gazing at me seriously and kindly.

Presently Ramesay, the Commandant, spoke, not un-
kindly: "It was ordered you should wear chains, but not
that you should be maltreated. A surgeon shall be sent
to you, and this chain shall be taken from your ankle.
Meanwhile, your guards shall be changed."

I held out the pistol, and he took it. "I can not hope
for justice here," said I, "but men are men, and not dogs,
and I ask for humane usage till my hour comes and my
country is your jailer."

The Marquis smiled, and his gay eyes sparkled.
"Some find comfort in daily bread, and some in prophe-
cy," he rejoined. "One should envy your spirit, Captain
Moray."

"Permit me, your Excellency," replied I; "all Englishmen must envy the spirit of the Marquis de Montcalm,
though none is envious of his cause."

He bowed gravely. "Causes are good or bad as they
are ours or our neighbours'. The lion has a good cause
when it goes hunting for its young; the deer has a good
cause when it resists the lion's leap upon its fawn."

I did not reply, for I felt a faintness coming; and at
that moment the Seigneur Duvarney came to me and
put his arm through mine. A dizziness seized me, my
head sank upon his shoulder, and I felt myself floating
away into darkness, while from a great distance came a
voice:

"It had been kinder to have ended it last year."

"He nearly killed your son, Duvarney." This was the voice of the Marquis in a tone of surprise.

"He saved my life, Marquis," was the sorrowful reply. "I have not paid back those forty pistoles, nor ever can, in spite of all."

"Ah, pardon me, seigneur," was the courteous rejoinder of the General.

That was all I heard, for I had entered the land of complete darkness. When I came to, I found that my foot had been bandaged, there was a torch in the wall, and by my side something in a jug, of which I drank, according to directions in a surgeon's hand on a paper beside it.

I was easier in all my body, yet miserably sick still, and I remained so, now shivering and now burning, a racking pain in my chest. My couch was filled with fresh straw, but in no other wise was my condition altered from the first time I had entered this place. My new jailer was a man of no feeling that I could see, yet of no violence or cruelty; one whose life was like a wheel, doing the eternal round. He did no more nor less than his orders, and I made no complaint nor asked any favour. No one came to me, no message found its way.

Full three months went by in this fashion, and then, one day, who should step into my dungeon, torch in hand, but Gabord! He raised the light above his head, and looked down at me quizzically.

"Upon my soul—Gabord!" said I. "I did not kill you, then?"

"Upon your soul and upon your body, you killed not Gabord."

"And what now, quarrelsome Gabord?" I questioned cheerfully.

He shook some keys. "Back again to dickey-bird's

cage. 'Look you,' quoth Governor, 'who will guard and bait this prisoner like the man he mauled?' 'No one,' quoth a lady who stands by Governor's chair. And she it was who had Governor send me here—even Ma'm'selle Duvarney. And she it was who made Governor loose off these chains."

He began to free me from the chains. I was in a vile condition. The irons had made sores upon my wrists and legs, my limbs now trembled so beneath me that I could scarcely walk, and my head was very light and dizzy at times. Presently Gabord ordered a new bed of straw brought in; and from that hour we returned to our old relations, as if there had not been between us a fight to the death. Of what was going on abroad he would not tell me, and soon I found myself in as ill a state as before. No Voban came to me, no Doltaire, no one at all. I sank into a deep silence, dropped out of a busy world, a morsel of earth slowly coming to Mother Earth again.

A strange apathy began to settle on me. All those resources of my first year's imprisonment had gone, and I was alone: my mouse was dead; there was no history of my life to write, no incident to break the pitiful monotony. There seemed only one hope: that our army under Amherst would invest Quebec and take it. I had no news of any movement, winter again was here, and it must be five or six months before any action could successfully be taken; for the St. Lawrence was frozen over in winter, and if the city was to be seized it must be from the water, with simultaneous action by land.

I knew the way, the only way, to take the city. At Sillery, west of the town, there was a hollow in the cliffs, up which men, secretly conveyed above the town by water, could climb. At the top was a plateau, smooth and fine as a parade-ground, where battle could be given, or move be made upon the city and citadel, which lay on ground no higher. Then, with the guns playing on the town from the fleet, and from the Levis shore with forces on the Beauport side, attacking the lower town where was the Intendant's palace, the great fortress might be taken and Canada be ours.

This passage up the cliff side at Sillery I had discovered three years before.

When winter set well in Gabord brought me a blanket, and though last year I had not needed it, now it was most grateful. I had been fed for months on bread and water, as in my first imprisonment, but at last—whether by orders or not, I never knew—he brought me a little meat every day, and some wine also. Yet I did not care for them, and often left them untasted. A hacking cough had never left me since my attempt at escape, and I was miserably thin and so weak that I could hardly drag myself about my dungeon. So, many weeks of the winter went on, and at last I was not able to rise from my bed of straw, and could do little more than lift a cup of water to my lips and nibble at some bread. I felt that my hours were numbered.

At last, one day I heard commotion at my dungeon door; it opened, and Gabord entered and closed it after him. He came and stood over me, as with difficulty I lifted myself upon my elbow.

"Come, try your wings," said he.

"It is the end, Gabord?" asked I.

"Not paradise yet!" said he.

"Then I am free?" I asked.

"Free from this dungeon," he answered cheerily.

I raised myself and tried to stand upon my feet, but fell back. He helped me to rise, and I rested an arm on his shoulder.

I tried to walk, but a faintness came over me, and I sank back. Then Gabord laid me down, went to the

door, and called in two soldiers with a mattress. I was
wrapped in my cloak and blankets, laid thereon, and so
was borne forth, all covered even to my weak eyes. I
was placed in a sleigh, and as the horses sprang away,
the clear sleigh bells rang out, and a gun from the ramparts was fired to give the noon hour, I sank into unconsciousness.

XIX.

A DANSEUSE AND THE BASTILE.

RECOVERING, I found myself lying on a couch, in a
large, well-lighted room hung about with pictures and
adorned with trophies of the hunt. A wide window faced
the foot of the bed where I lay, and through it I could
see—though the light hurt my eyes greatly—the Levis
shore, on the opposite side of the St. Lawrence. I lay
and thought, trying to discover where I was. It came to
me at last that I was in a room of the Château St. Louis.
Presently I heard breathing near me, and, looking over, I
saw a soldier sitting just inside the door.

Then from another corner of the room came a surgeon
with some cordial in a tumbler, and, handing it to me, he
bade me drink. He felt my pulse; then stopped and put
his ear to my chest, and listened long.

" Is there great danger?" asked I.

"The trouble would pass," said he, "if you were
stronger. Your life is worth fighting for, but it will be a
struggle. That dungeon was slow poison. You must
have a barber," added he; "you are a ghost like this."

I put my hand up, and I found my hair and beard
were very long and almost white. Held against the light,
my hands seemed transparent. "What means my coming
here?" asked I.

He shook his head. "I am but a surgeon," he answered shortly, meanwhile writing with a flourish on a piece of paper. When he had finished, he handed the paper to the soldier with an order. Then he turned to go, politely bowing to me, but came again and said, "I would not, were I you, trouble to plan escape these months yet. This is a comfortable prison, but it is easier coming in than going out. Your mind and body need quiet. You have, we know, a taste for adventure "—he smiled—" but is it wise to fight a burning powder magazine?"

"Thank you, monsieur," said I, "I am myself laying the fuse to that magazine. It fights for me by-and-bye."

He shrugged a shoulder. "Drink," said he, with a professional air which almost set me laughing, "good milk and brandy, and think of nothing but that you are a lucky man to have this sort of prison."

He bustled out in an important way, shaking his head and talking to himself. Tapping the chest of a bulky soldier who stood outside, he said brusquely, "Too fat, too fat; you'll come to apoplexy. Go fight the English, lazy ruffian!"

The soldier gave a grunt, made a mocking gesture, and the door closed on me and my attendant. This fellow would not speak at all, and I did not urge him, but lay and watched the day decline and night come down. I was taken to a small alcove which adjoined the room, where I slept soundly.

Early the next morning I waked, and there was Voban sitting just outside the alcove, looking at me. I sat up in bed and spoke to him, and he greeted me in an absent sort of way. He was changed as much as I; he moved as one in a dream; yet there was the ceaseless activity of the eye, the swift, stealthy motion of the hand. He began to attend me, and I questioned him; but he said he had orders from mademoiselle that he was to tell nothing—that she, as soon as she could, would visit me.

About three hours after this, as I lay upon the couch in the large room, clean and well shaven, the door opened, and some one entered, saying to my guard, "You will remain outside. I have the Governor's order."

I knew the voice; an instant, and I saw the face shining with expectancy, the eyes eager, yet timid, a small white hand pressed to a pulsing breast—my one true friend, the jailer of my heart!

For a moment she was all trembling and excited, her hand softly clutching at my shoulder, tears dripping from her eyes and falling on my cheek, as hers lay pressed to mine; but presently she grew calm, and her face was lifted with a smile, and, brushing back some flying locks of hair, she said in a tone most quaint and touching too, "Poor gentleman! poor English prisoner! poor hidden lover! I ought not, I ought not," she added, "show my feelings thus, nor excite you so." My hand was trembling on hers, for in truth I was very weak. "It was my purpose," she continued, "to come most quietly to you, but there are times when one must cry out or the heart will burst."

I spoke then as a man may who has been delivered from bondage into the arms of love. She became very quiet, looking at me in her grave, sweet way, her deep eyes shining with sincerity.

"Honest, honest eyes," said I—"eyes that never deceive and never were deceived."

"All this in spite of what you do not know," she answered. For an instant a look elfish and childlike came into her eyes, and she drew back from me, stood in the middle of the floor, and caught her skirts in her fingers.

"See," she said, "is there no deceit here?"

Then she began to dance softly, her feet seeming hardly

to touch the ground, her body swaying like a tall flower in the wind, her face all light and fire. I was charmed, fascinated. I felt my sleepy blood stirring to the delicate rise and fall of her bosom, the light of her eyes flashing a dozen colours. There was scarce a sound; her steps could not be heard across the room.

All at once she broke off from this, and stood still.

" Did my eyes seem all honest then?" she asked, with a strange, wistful expression. Then she came to the couch where I was.

" Robert," said she, " can you, do you, trust me even when you see me at such witchery?"

" I trust you always," answered I. " Such witcheries are no evils that I can see."

She put her finger upon my lips, with a kind of bashfulness. " Hush, till I tell you where and when I danced like that, and then, and then——"

She settled down in a low chair. " I have at least an hour," she continued. " The Governor is busy with my father and General Montcalm, and they will not be free for a long time. For your soldiers, I have been bribing them to my service these weeks past, and they are safe enough for to-day. Now I will tell you of that dancing.

" One night last autumn there was a grand dinner at the Intendance. Such gentlemen as my father were not asked; only the roisterers and hard drinkers, and gambling friends of the Intendant. You would know the sort of upspring it would be. Well, I was sitting in my window, looking down into the garden, for the moon was shining. Presently I saw a man appear below, glance up towards me, and beckon. It was Voban. I hurried down to him, and he told me that there had been a wild carousing at the palace, and that ten gentlemen had determined, for a wicked sport, to mask themselves, go to the citadel at midnight, fetch you forth, and make you run the gant-

let in the yard of the Intendance, and afterwards set you
fighting for your life with another prisoner, a common
criminal. To this, Bigot, heated with wine, had made no
objection. Monsieur Doltaire was not present; he had, it
was said, taken a secret journey into the English country.
The Governor was in Montreal, where he had gone to discuss matters of war with the Council.

"There was but one thing to do—get word to General Montcalm. He was staying at the moment with the
Seigneur Pipon at his manor by the Montmorenci Falls.
He must needs be sought there: he would never allow this
shameless thing. So I bade Voban go thither at once,
getting a horse from any quarter, and to ride as though
for his life. He promised, and left me, and I returned
to my room to think. Voban had told me that his news
came from Bigot's valet, who is his close friend. This I
knew, and I knew the valet too, for I had seen something
of him when my brother lay wounded at the palace. Under the best circumstances General Montcalm could not
arrive within two hours. Meanwhile, these miserable men
might go on their dreadful expedition. Something must
be done to gain time. I racked my brain for minutes, till
the blood pounded at my temples. Presently a plan came
to me.

"There is in Quebec one Madame Jamond, a great
Parisian dancer, who, for reasons which none knows, save
perhaps Monsieur Doltaire, has been banished from France.
Since she came to Canada, some nine months ago, she has
lived quietly and religiously, though many trials have been
made to bring her talents into service; and the Intendant has made many efforts to have her dance in the palace
for his guests. But she would not.

"Madame Lotbinière had come to know Jamond, and
she arranged, after much persuasion, for lessons in dancing to be given to Lucy, myself, and Georgette. To me

the dancing was a keen delight, a passion. As I danced I saw and felt a thousand things, I can not tell you how. Now my feet appeared light as air, like thistledown, my body to float. I was as a lost soul flying home, flocks of birds singing me to come with them into a pleasant land.

" Then all that changed, and I was passing through a bitter land, with harsh shadows and tall, cold mountains. From clefts and hollows figures flew out and caught at me with filmy hands. These melancholy things pursued me as I flew, till my wings drooped, and I felt that I must drop into the dull marsh far beneath, round which travelled a lonely mist.

" But this, too, passed, and I came through a land all fire, so that, as I flew swiftly, my wings were scorched, and I was blinded often, and often missed my way, and must change my course of flight. It was all scarlet, all that land—scarlet sky and scarlet sun and scarlet flowers, and the rivers running red, and men and women in long red robes, with eyes of flame, and voices that kept crying, ' The world is mad, and all life is a fever ! ' "

She paused for a moment, seeming to come out of a dream, and then she laughed a little. " Will you not go on ? " I asked gently.

" Sometimes, too," she said, " I fancied I was before a king and his court, dancing for my life or for another's. Oh, how I scanned the faces of my judges, as they sat there watching me ; some meanwhile throwing crumbs to fluttering birds that whirled round me, some stroking the ears of hounds that gaped at me, while the king's fool at first made mock at me, and the face of a man behind the king's chair smiled like Satan—or Monsieur Doltaire ! Ah, Robert, I know you think me fanciful and foolish, as indeed I am ; but you must bear with me.

" I danced constantly, practising hour upon hour with Jamond, who came to be my good friend ; and you shall

hear from me some day her history—a sad one indeed;
a woman sinned against, not sinning. But these lessons
went on secretly, for I was sure, if people knew how
warmly I followed this recreation, they would set it down
to wilful desire to be singular—or worse. It gave me new
interest in lonely days. So the weeks went on.

"Well, that wicked night I sent Voban to General
Montcalm, and, as I said, a thought came to me: I would
find Jamond, beg her to mask herself, go to the Intendance and dance before the gentlemen there, keeping
them amused until the General came, as I was sure he
would at my suggestion, for he is a just man and a generous. All my people, even Georgette, were abroad at a
soirée, and would not be home till late. So I sought Mathilde, and she hurried with me, my poor daft protector,
to Jamond's, whose house is very near the bishop's palace.

"We were at once admitted to Jamond, who was lying
upon a couch. I hurriedly told her what I wished her to
do, what was at stake, everything but that I loved you;
laying my interest upon humanity and to your having
saved my father's life. She looked troubled at once, and
then took my face in her hands. 'Dear child,' she said,
'I understand. You have sorrow too young—too young.'
'But you will do this for me?' I cried. She shook her
head sadly. 'I can not. I am lame these two days,' she
answered. 'I have had a sprain.' I sank on the floor beside her, sick and dazed. She put her hand pitifully on
my head, then lifted up my chin. Looking into her eyes,
I read a thought there, and I got to my feet with a spring.
'I myself will go,' said I; 'I will dance there till the General comes.' She put out her hand in protest. 'You
must not,' she urged. 'Think: you may be discovered,
and then the ruin that must come!'

"'I shall put my trust in God,' said I. 'I have no
fear. I will do this thing.' She caught me to her breast.

'Then God be with you, child,' was her answer; 'you shall do it.' In ten minutes I was dressed in a gown of hers, which last had been worn when she danced before King Louis. It fitted me well, and with the wig the colour of her hair, brought quickly from her boxes, and use of paints which actors use, I was transformed. Indeed, I could scarce recognize myself without the mask, and with it on my mother would not have known me. 'I will go with you,' she said to me, and she hurriedly put on an old woman's wig and a long cloak, quickly lined her face, and we were ready. She walked lame, and must use a stick, and we issued forth towards the Intendance, Mathilde remaining behind.

"When we got to the palace, and were admitted, I asked for the Intendant's valet, and we stood waiting in the cold hall until he was brought. 'We come from Voban the barber,' I whispered to him, for there were servants near; and he led us at once to his private room. He did not recognize me, but looked at us with sidelong curiosity. 'I am,' said I, throwing back my cloak, 'a dancer, and I have come to dance before the Intendant and his guests.' 'His Excellency does not expect you?' he asked. 'His Excellency has many times asked Madame Jamond to dance before him,' I replied. He was at once all complaisance, but his face was troubled. 'You come from Monsieur Voban?' he inquired. 'From Monsieur Voban,' answered I. 'He has gone to General Montcalm.' His face fell, and a kind of fear passed over it. 'There is no peril to any one save the English gentleman,' I urged. A light dawned on him. 'You dance until the General comes?' he asked, pleased at his own penetration. 'You will take me at once to the dining-hall,' said I, nodding. 'They are in the Chambre de la Joie,' he rejoined. 'Then the Chamber de la Joie,' said I; and he led the way. When we came near to the chamber I said to him, 'You

will tell the Intendant that a lady of some gifts in dancing would entertain his guests; but she must come and
go without exchange of individual courtesies and at her
own will.

"He opened the door of the chamber, and we followed
him; for just inside there was a large oak screen, and
from its shadow we could see the room and all therein.
At the first glance I shrank back, for, apart from the
noise and the clattering of tongues, such a riot of carousal
I have never seen. I was shocked to note gentlemen
whom I had met in society, with the show of decorum
about them, loosed now from all restraint, and swaggering like woodsmen at a fair. I felt a sudden fear, and
drew back sick; but that was for an instant, for even as
the valet came to the Intendant's chair a dozen or more
men, who were sitting together in noisy yet half-secret
conference, rose to their feet, each with a mask in his
hand, and started towards the door. I felt the blood fly
back and forth in my heart with great violence, and I
leaned against the oak screen for support. 'Courage!'
said the voice of Jamond in my ear, and I ruled myself
to quietness.

"Just then the Intendant's voice stopped the men in
their movement towards the great entrance door, and
drew the attention of the whole company. 'Messieurs,'
said he, 'a lady has come to dance for us. She makes
conditions which must be respected. She must be let to
come and go without individual courtesies. Messieurs,'
he added, 'I grant her request in your name and my
own.'

"There was a murmur of 'Jamond! Jamond!' and
every man stood looking towards the great entrance door.
The Intendant, however, was gazing towards the door
where I was, and I saw he was about to come, as if to welcome me. Welcome from François Bigot to a dancing-

woman! I slipped off the cloak, looked at Jamond, who murmured once again, ' Courage ! ' and then I stepped out swiftly, and made for a low, large dais at one side of the room. I was so nervous that I knew not how I went. The faces and forms of the company were blurred before me, and the lights shook and multiplied distractedly. The room shone brilliantly, yet just under the great canopy, over the dais, there were shadows, and they seemed to me, as I stepped under the red velvet, a relief, a sort of hiding-place from innumerable candles and hot, unnatural eyes.

" Once there I was changed. I did not think of the applause that greeted me, the murmurs of surprise, approbation, questioning, rising round me. Suddenly as I paused and faced them all, nervousness passed out of me, and I saw nothing—nothing but a sort of far-off picture. My mind was caught away into that world which I had created for myself when I danced, and these rude gentlemen were but visions. All sense of indignity passed from me. I was only a woman fighting for a life and for her own and another's happiness.

" As I danced I did not know how time passed—only that I must keep those men where they were till General Montcalm came. After a while, when the first dazed feeling had passed, I could see their faces plainly through my mask, and I knew that I could hold them ; for they ceased to lift their glasses, and stood watching me, sometimes so silent that I could hear their breathing only, sometimes making a great applause, which passed into silence again quickly. Once, as I wheeled, I caught the eyes of Jamond watching me closely. The Intendant never stirred from his seat, and scarcely moved, but kept his eyes fixed on me. Nor did he applaud. There was something painful in his immovability.

" I saw it all as in a dream, yet I did see it, and I was

resolute to triumph over the wicked designs of base and abandoned men. I feared that my power to hold them might stop before help came. Once, in a slight pause, when a great noise of their hands and a rattling of scabbards on the table gave me a short respite, some one— Captain Lancy, I think—snatched up a glass, and called on all to drink my health.

"'Jamond! Jamond!' was the cry, and they drank, the Intendant himself standing up, and touching the glass to his lips, then sitting down again, silent and immovable as before. One gentleman, a nephew of the Chevalier de la Darante, came swaying towards me with a glass of wine, begging me in a flippant courtesy to drink; but I waved him back, and the Intendant said most curtly, 'Monsieur de la Darante will remember my injunction.'

"Again I danced, and I can not tell you with what anxiety and desperation!—for there must be an end to it before long, and your peril, Robert, come again, unless these rough fellows changed their minds. Moment after moment went, and though I had danced beyond reasonable limits, I still seemed to get new strength, as I have heard men say, in fighting, they 'come to their second wind.' At last, at the end of the most famous step that Jamond had taught me, I stood still for a moment to renewed applause; and I must have wound these men up to excitement beyond all sense, for they would not be dissuaded, but swarmed towards the dais where I was, and some called on me to remove my mask.

"Then the Intendant came down among them, bidding them stand back, and himself moved towards me. I felt affrighted, for I liked not the look in his eyes, and so, without a word, I stepped down from the dais—I did not dare to speak, lest they should recognize my voice—and made for the door with as much dignity as I might. But the Intendant came quickly to me with a mannered courtesy, and said in my ear, ' Madame, you have won all our hearts; will you not accept some hospitality—a glass of wine and a wing of partridge, in a room where none shall disturb you?' I shuddered, and passed on. ' Nay, nay, madame, not even myself with you, unless you would have it otherwise,' he added.

"Still I did not speak, but put out my hand in protest, and moved on towards the screen, we two alone, for the others had fallen back with whisperings and side-speeches. Oh, how I longed to take the mask from my face and spurn them! The hand that I put out in protest the Intendant caught within his own, and would have held it, but that I drew it back with indignation, and kept on towards the screen. Then I realized that a new-comer had seen the matter, and I stopped short, dumfounded—for it was Monsieur Doltaire! He was standing beside the screen, just within the room, and he sent at the Intendant and myself a keen, piercing glance.

"Now he came forward quickly, for the Intendant also half stopped at sight of him, and a malignant look shot from his eyes; hatred showed in the profane word that was chopped off at his teeth. When Monsieur Doltaire reached us, he said, his eyes resting on me with intense scrutiny, ' His Excellency will present me to his distinguished entertainer?' He seemed to read behind my mask. I knew he had discovered me, and my heart stood still. But I raised my eyes and met his gaze steadily. The worst had come. Well, I would face it now. I could endure defeat with courage. He paused an instant, a strange look passed over his face, his eyes got hard and very brilliant, and he continued (oh, what suspense that was!) : 'Ah yes, I see—Jamond, the perfect and wonderful Jamond, who set us all a-kneeling at Versailles. If madame will permit me?' He made to take my hand. Here the Intendant interposed, putting out his hand

16

also. 'I have promised to protect madame from individual courtesy while here,' he said. Monsieur Doltaire
looked at him keenly. 'Then your Excellency must build
stone walls about yourself,' he rejoined, with cold emphasis. 'Sometimes great men are foolish. To-night your
Excellency would have let'—here he raised his voice so
that all could hear—'your Excellency would have let a
dozen cowardly gentlemen drag a dying prisoner from his
prison, forcing back his Majesty's officers at the dungeon
doors, and, after baiting, have matched him against a
common criminal. That was unseemly in a great man
and a King's chief officer, the trick of a low law-breaker.
Your Excellency promised a lady to protect her from
individual courtesy, if she gave pleasure—a pleasure beyond price—to you and your guests, and you would have
broken your word without remorse. General Montcalm
has sent a company of men to set your Excellency right
in one direction, and I am come to set you right in the
other.'

"The Intendant was white with rage. He muttered
something between his teeth, then said aloud, 'Presently
we will talk more of this, monsieur. You measure
strength with François Bigot: we will see which proves
the stronger in the end.' 'In the end the unjust steward
kneels for mercy to his master,' was Monsieur Doltaire's
quiet answer; and then he made a courteous gesture
towards the door, and I went to it with him slowly, wondering what the end would be. Once at the other side of
the screen, he peered into Jamond's face for an instant,
then he gave a low whistle. 'You have an apt pupil, Jamond, one who might be your rival one day,' said he.
Still there was a puzzled look on his face, which did not
leave it till he saw Jamond walking. 'Ah yes,' he added,
'I see now. You are lame. This was a desperate yet successful expedient.'

"He did not speak to me, but led the way to where, at the great door, was the Intendant's valet standing with my cloak. Taking it from him, he put it round my shoulders. 'The sleigh by which I came is at the door,' he said, 'and I will take you home.' I knew not what to do, for I feared some desperate act on his part to possess me. I determined that I would not leave Jamond, in any case, and I felt for a weapon which I had hidden in my dress. We had not, however, gone a half dozen paces in the entrance hall when there were quick steps behind, and four soldiers came towards us, with an officer at their head—an officer whom I had seen in the chamber, but did not recognize.

"'Monsieur Doltaire,' the officer said; and monsieur stopped. Then he cried in surprise, 'Legrand, you here!' To this the officer replied by handing monsieur a paper. Monsieur's hand dropped to his sword, but in a moment he gave a short, sharp laugh, and opened up the packet. 'H'm,' he said, 'the Bastile! The Grande Marquise is fretful—eh, Legrand? You will permit me some moments with these ladies?' he added. 'A moment only,' answered the officer. 'In another room?' monsieur again asked. 'A moment where you are, monsieur,' was the reply. Making a polite gesture for me to step aside, Monsieur Doltaire said, in a voice which was perfectly controlled and courteous, though I could hear behind all a deadly emphasis, 'I know everything now. You have foiled me, blindfolded me and all others these three years past. You have intrigued against the captains of intrigue, you have matched yourself against practised astuteness. On one side I resent being made a fool and tool of; on the other, I am lost in admiration of your talent. But henceforth there is no such thing as quarter between us. Your lover shall die, and I will come again. This whim of the Grande Marquise will last but till I see her; then I will return to you—forever. Your lover shall die, your love's labour for him shall be lost. I shall reap where I did not sow—his harvest and my own. I am as ice to you, mademoiselle, at this moment; I have murder in my heart. Yet warmth will come again. I admire you so much that I will have you for my own, or die. You are the high priestess of diplomacy; your brain is a statesman's, your heart is a vagrant; it goes covertly from the sweet meaddow of France to the marshes of England, a taste unworthy of you. You shall be redeemed from that by Tinoir Doltaire. Now thank me for all I have done for you, and let me say adieu.' He stooped and kissed my hand. 'I can not thank you for what I myself achieved,' I said. 'We are, as in the past, to be at war, you threaten, and I have no gratitude.' 'Well, well, adieu and *au revoir*, sweetheart,' he answered. 'If I should go to the Bastile, I shall have food for thought; and I am your hunter to the end! In this good orchard I pick sweet fruit one day.' His look fell on me in such a way that shame and anger were at equal height in me. Then he bowed again to me and to Jamond, and, with a sedate gesture, walked away with the soldiers and the officer.

"You can guess what were my feelings. You were safe for the moment—that was the great thing. The terror I had felt when I saw Monsieur Doltaire in the Chambre de la Joie had passed, for I felt he would not betray me. He is your foe, and he would kill you; but I was sure he would not put me in danger while he was absent in France—if he expected to return—by making public my love for you and my adventure at the palace. There is something of the noble fighter in him, after all, though he is so evil a man. A prisoner himself now, he would have no immediate means to hasten your death. But I can never forget his searching, cruel look when he recognized me! Of Jamond I was sure. Her own past had been full of sorrow, and her life was now so secluded and religious that I could not doubt her. Indeed, we have been blessed with good, true friends, Robert, though they are not of those who are powerful, save in their loyalty."

Alixe then told me that the officer Legrand had arrived from France but two days before the eventful night of which I have just written, armed with an order from the Grande Marquise for Doltaire's arrest and transportation. He had landed at Gaspé, and had come on to Quebec overland. Arriving at the Intendance, he had awaited Doltaire's coming. Doltaire had stopped to visit General Montcalm at Montmorenci Falls, on his way back from an expedition to the English country, and had thus himself brought my protection and hurried to his own undoing. I was thankful for his downfall, though I believed it was but for a moment.

I was curious to know how it chanced I was set free of my dungeon, and I had the story from Alixe's lips; but not till after I had urged her, for she was sure her tale had wearied me, and she was eager to do little offices of comfort about me; telling me gaily, while she shaded the light, freshened my pillow, and gave me a cordial to drink, that she would secretly convey me wines and preserves and jellies and such kickshaws, that I should better get my strength.

"For you must know," she said, "that though this gray hair and transparency of flesh become you, making your eyes look like two jets of flame and your face to have shadows most theatrical, a ruddy cheek and a stout hand are more suited to a soldier. When you are young again in body these gray hairs shall render you distinguished."

Then she sat down beside me, and clasped my hand, now looking out into the clear light of afternoon to the farther shores of Levis, showing green here and there from a sudden March rain, the boundless forests beyond, and the ample St. Lawrence still covered with its vast bridge of ice; anon into my face, while I gazed into those deeps of her blue eyes that I had drowned my heart in. I loved to watch her, for with me she was ever her own absolute self, free from all artifice, lost in her perfect naturalness: a healthy, quiet soundness, a primitive simplicity beneath the artifice of usual life. She had a beautiful hand, long, warm, and firm, and the fingers, when they clasped, seemed to possess and inclose your own—the tenderness of the maidenly, the protectiveness of the maternal. She carried with her a wholesome fragrance and beauty, as of an orchard, and while she sat there I thought of the engaging words:

"*Thou art to me like a basket of summer fruit, and I seek thee in thy cottage by the vineyard, fenced about with good commendable trees.*"

Of my release she spoke thus: "Monsieur Doltaire is to be conveyed overland to the coast *en route* for France, and he has sent me by his valet a small arrow studded with emeralds and pearls, and a skull all polished, with a message that the arrow was for myself, and the skull for another—remembrances of the past, and earnests of the future—truly an insolent and wicked man. When he was gone I went to the Governor, and, with show of interest in many things pertaining to the government (for he has been flattered by my attentions—me, poor little bee in the buzzing hive!), came to the question of the English prisoner. I told him it was I that prevented the disgrace to his good government by sending to General Montcalm to ask for your protection.

"He was impressed, and opened out his vain heart about the state in divers ways. But I may not tell you of these—only what concerns yourself; the rest belongs to his honour. When he was in his most pliable mood, I

grew serious and told him there was a danger which perhaps he did not see. Here was his English prisoner, who,
they said abroad in the town, was dying. There was
no doubt that the King would approve the sentence of
death, and if it were duly and with some display enforced,
it would but add to the Governor's reputation in France.
But should the prisoner die in captivity, or should he go
an invalid to the scaffold, there would only be pity excited
in the world for him. For his own honour, it were better
the Governor should hang a robust prisoner, who in full
blood should expiate his sins upon the scaffold. The ad-
vice went down like wine; and when he knew not what
to do, I urged your being brought here, put under guard,
and fed and nourished for your end. And so it was.

"The Governor's counsellor in the matter will remain
a secret, for by now he will be sure that he himself had
the sparkling inspiration. There, dear Robert, is the
present climax to many months of suspense and perse-
cution, the like of which I hope I may never see again.
Some time I will tell you all: those meetings with Monsieur Doltaire, his designs and approaches, his pleadings
and veiled threats, his numberless small seductions of
words, manners, and deeds, his singular changes of mood,
when I was uncertain what would happen next; the part
I had to play to know all that was going on in the Château
St. Louis, in the Intendance, and with General Montcalm;
the difficulties with my own people; the despair of my
poor father, who does not know that it is I who have kept
him from trouble by my influence with the Governor.
For since the Governor and the Intendant are reconciled,
he takes sides with General Montcalm, the one sound
gentleman in office in this poor country—alas!"

Soon afterwards we parted. As she passed out she told
me I might at any hour expect a visit from the Governor.

XX.

UPON THE RAMPARTS.

THE Governor visited me. His attitude was marked by nothing so much as a supercilious courtesy, a manner which said, You must see I am not to be trifled with; and though I have you here in my château, it is that I may make a fine scorching of you in the end. He would make of me an example to amaze and instruct the nations— when I was robust enough to die.

I might easily have flattered myself on being an object of interest to the eyes of nations. I almost pitied him. He appeared so lost in self-admiration that he would never see disaster when it came.

"There is but one master here in Canada," he said, "and I am he. If things go wrong it is because my orders are not obeyed. Your people have taken Louisburg; had I been there, it should never have been given up. Drucour was hasty—he listened to the women. I should allow no woman to move me. I should be inflexible. They might send two Amhersts and two Wolfes against me, I would hold my fortress."

"They will never send two, your Excellency," said I.

He did not see the irony, and he prattled on: "That Wolfe, they tell me, is bandy-legged; is no better than a girl at sea, and never well ashore. I am always in raw health—the strong mind in the potent body. Had I been at Louisburg, I should have held it as I held Ticonderoga last July, and drove the English back with monstrous slaughter."

Here was news. I had had no information in many months, and all at once two great facts were brought to me.

"Your Excellency, then, was at Ticonderoga?" said I.

" I sent Montcalm to defend it," he replied pompously.
" I told him how he must act; I was explicit, and it came
out as I had said : we were victorious. Yet he would
have done better had he obeyed me in everything. If I
had been at Louisburg——"

I could not at first bring myself to flatter the vice-regal
peacock ; for it had been my mind to fight these Frenchmen always ; to yield in nothing ; to defeat them like a
soldier, not like a juggler. But I brought myself to say,
half ironically, " If all great men had capable instruments,
they would seldom fail."

" You have touched the heart of the matter," said he,
credulously. " It is a pity," he added, with complacent
severity, " that you have been so misguided and criminal ; you have, in some things, more sense than folly."

I bowed, as to a compliment from a great man. Then,
all at once, I spoke to him with an air of apparent frank-
ness, and said that if I must die, I cared to do so like a
gentleman, with some sort of health, and not like an invalid. He must admit that at least I was no coward. He
might fence me about with what guards he chose, but I
prayed him to let me walk upon the ramparts, when I was
strong enough to be abroad under all due espionage. I
had already suffered many deaths, I said, and I would go
to the final one looking like a man, and not like an out-
cast of humanity.

" Ah, I have heard this before," said he. " Monsieur
Doltaire, who is in prison here, and is to fare on to the
Bastile, was insolent enough to send me a message yesterday that I should keep you close in your dungeon. But
I had had enough of Monsieur Doltaire ; and, indeed, it
was through me that the Grande Marquise had him called
to durance. He was a muddler here. They must not
interfere with me ; I am not to be cajoled or crossed in
my plans. We shall see, we shall see about the ramparts,"

he continued. " Meanwhile prepare to die." This he said with such importance that I almost laughed in his face. But I bowed with a sort of awed submission, and he turned and left the room.

I grew stronger slowly day by day, but it was quite a month before Alixe came again. Sometimes I saw her walking on the banks of the river, and I was sure she was there that I might see her, though she made no sign towards me, nor ever seemed to look towards my window.

Spring was now fully come. The snow had gone from the ground, the tender grass was springing, the air was soft and kind. One fine day, at the beginning of May, I heard the booming of cannons and a great shouting, and, looking out, I could see crowds of people upon the banks, and many boats in the river, where yet the ice had not entirely broken up. By stretching from my window, through the bars of which I could get my head, but not my body, I noted a squadron sailing round the point of the Island of Orleans. I took it to be a fleet from France bearing re-enforcements and supplies—as indeed afterwards I found was so ; but the re-enforcements were so small and the supplies so limited that it is said Montcalm, when he knew, cried out, " Now is all lost ! Nothing remains but to fight and die. I shall see my beloved Candiac no more."

For the first time all the English colonies had combined against Canada. Vaudreuil and Montcalm were at variance, and Vaudreuil had, through his personal hatred and envy of Montcalm, signed the death-warrant of the colony by writing to the colonial minister that Montcalm's agents, going for succour, were not to be trusted. Yet at that moment I did not know these things, and the sight made me grave, though it made me sure also that this year would find the British battering this same Château.

General Wolfe.

Presently there came word from the Governor that I might walk upon the ramparts, and I was taken forth for several hours each day; always, however, under strict surveillance, my guards, well armed, attending, while the ramparts were, as usual, patrolled by soldiers. I could see that ample preparations were being made against a siege, and every day the excitement increased. I got to know more definitely of what was going on, when, under vigilance, I was allowed to speak to Lieutenant Stevens, who also was permitted some such freedom as I had enjoyed when I first came to Quebec. He had private information that General Wolfe or General Amherst was likely to proceed against Quebec from Louisburg, and he was determined to join the expedition.

For months he had been maturing plans for escape. There was one Clark, a ship-carpenter (of whom I have before written), and two other bold spirits, who were sick of captivity, and it was intended to fare forth one night and make a run for freedom. Clark had had a notable plan. A wreck of several transports had occurred at Belle Isle, and it was intended by the authorities to send him down the river with a sloop to bring back the crew, and break up the wreck. It was his purpose to arm his sloop with Mr. Stevens and some English prisoners the night before she was to sail, and steal away with her down the river. But whether or not the authorities suspected him, the command was at the last given to another.

It was proposed, however, to get away on a dark night to some point on the river, where a boat should be stationed—though that was a difficult matter, for the river was well patrolled and boats were scarce—and drift quietly down the stream, till a good distance below the city. Mr. Stevens said he had delayed the attempt on the faint hope of fetching me along. Money, he said, was needed, for

Clark and all were very poor, and common necessaries were now at exorbitant prices in the country. Tyranny and robbery had made corn and clothing luxuries. All the old tricks of Bigot and his La Friponne, which, after the outbreak the night of my arrest at the Seigneur Duvarney's, had been somewhat repressed, were in full swing again, and robbery in the name of providing for defence was the only habit.

I managed to convey to Mr. Stevens a good sum of money, and begged him to meet me every day upon the ramparts, until I also should see my way to making a dart for freedom. I advised him in many ways, for he was more bold than shrewd, and I made him promise that he would not tell Clark or the others that I was to make trial to go with them. I feared the accident of disclosure, and any new failure on my part to get away would, I knew, mean my instant death, consent of King or no consent.

One evening, a soldier entered my room, whom in the half-darkness I did not recognize, till a voice said, " There's orders new ! Not dungeon now, but this room Governor bespeaks for gentlemen from France."

" And where am I to go, Gabord ? "

" Where you will have fighting," he answered.

" With whom ? "

" Yourself, aho ! " A queer smile crossed his lips, and was followed by a sort of sternness. There was something graver in his manner than I had ever seen. I could not guess his meaning. At last he added, pulling roughly at his mustache, " And when that's done, if not well done, to answer to Gabord the soldier ; for, God take my soul without bed-going, but I will call you to account ! That Seigneur's home is no place for you."

" You speak in riddles," said I. Then all at once the

matter burst upon me. "The Governor quarters me at the Seigneur Duvarney's?" I asked.

"No other," answered he. "In three days to go."

I understood him now. He had had a struggle, knowing of the relations between Alixe and myself, to avoid telling the Governor all. And now, if I involved her, used her to effect my escape from her father's house! Even his peasant brain saw my difficulty, the danger to my honour—and hers. In spite of the joy I felt at being near her, seeing her, I shrank from the situation. If I escaped from the Seigneur Duvarney's, it would throw suspicion upon him, upon Alixe, and that made me stand abashed. Inside the Seigneur Duvarney's house I should feel bound to certain calls of honour concerning his daughter and himself. I stood long, thinking, Gabord watching me.

Finally, "Gabord," said I, "I give you my word of honour that I will not put Mademoiselle or Monsieur Duvarney in peril."

"You will not try to escape?"

"Not to use them for escape. To elude my guards, to fight my way to liberty—yes—yes—yes!"

"But that mends not. Who's to know the lady did not help you?"

"You. You are to be my jailer again there?"

He nodded, and fell to pulling his mustache. "'Tis not enough," he said decisively.

"Come, then," said I, "I will strike a bargain with you. If you will grant me one thing, I will give my word of honour not to escape from the seigneur's house."

"Say on."

"You tell me I am not to go to the seigneur's for three days yet. Arrange that mademoiselle may come to me to-morrow at dusk—at six o'clock, when all the world

dines—and I will give my word. No more do I ask you
—only that."

"Done," said he. "It shall be so."

"You will fetch her yourself ? " I asked.

"On the stroke of six. Guard changes then."

Here our talk ended. He went, and I plunged deep
into my great plan ; for all at once, as we had talked,
came a thing to me which I shall make clear ere long.
I set my wits to work. Once since my coming to the
château I had been visited by the English chaplain,
who had been a prisoner at the citadel the year before.
He was now on parole, and had freedom to come and go
in the town. The Governor had said he might visit me
on a certain day every week, at a fixed hour, and the
next day at five o'clock was the time appointed for his
second visit. Gabord had promised to bring Alixe to
me at six.

The following morning I met Mr. Stevens on the
ramparts. I told him it was my purpose to escape the
next night, if possible. If not, I must go to the Seigneur Duvarney's, where I should be on parole—to Gabord. I bade him fulfil my wishes to the letter, for
on his boldness and my own, and the courage of his
men, I depended for escape. He declared himself ready
to risk all, and die in the attempt, if need be, for he
was sick of idleness. He could, he said, mature his plans
that day, if he had more money. I gave him secretly
a small bag of gold, and then I made explicit note of
what I required of him : that he should tie up in a
loose but safe bundle a sheet, a woman's skirt, some
river grasses and reeds, some phosphorus, a pistol and
a knife, and some saltpetre and other chemicals. That
evening, about nine o'clock, which was the hour the
guard changed, he was to tie this bundle to a string I
should let down from my window and I would draw

it up. Then, the night following, the others must steal away to that place near Sillery—the west side of the town was always ill guarded—and wait there with a boat. He should see me at a certain part on the ramparts, and, well armed, we also would make our way to Sillery, and from the spot called the Anse du Foulon drift down the river in the dead of night.

He promised to do all as I wished.

The rest of the day I spent in my room fashioning strange toys out of willow rods. I had got these rods from my guards, to make whistles for their children, and they had carried away many of them. But now, with pieces of a silk handkerchief tied to the whistle and filled with air, I made a toy which, when squeezed, sent out a weird lament. Once, when my guard came in, I pressed one of these things in my pocket, and it gave forth a sort of smothered cry, like a sick child. At this he started, and looked round the room in trepidation; for, of all peoples, these Canadian Frenchmen are the most superstitious, and may be worked on without limit. The cry had seemed to come from a distance. I looked around also, and appeared serious, and he asked me if I had heard the thing before.

"Once or twice," said I.

"Then you are a dead man," said he; "'tis a warning, that!"

"Maybe it is not I, but one of you," I answered. Then, with a sort of hush, "Is't like the cry of La Jongleuse?" I added. (La Jongleuse was their fabled witch, or spirit of disaster.)

He nodded his head, crossed himself, mumbled a prayer, and turned to go, but came back. "I'll fetch a crucifix," he said. "You are a heathen, and you bring her here. She is the devil's dam."

He left with a scared face, and I laughed to myself

quietly, for I saw success ahead of me. True to his word he brought a crucifix and put it up—not where he wished, but, at my request, opposite the door, upon the wall. He crossed himself before it, and was most devout.

It looked singular to see this big, rough soldier, who was in most things a swaggerer, so childlike in all that touched his religion. With this you could fetch him to his knees; with it I would cow him that I might myself escape.

At half past five the chaplain came, having been delayed by the guard to have his order indorsed by Captain Lancy of the Governor's household. To him I told my plans so far as I thought he should know them, and then I explained what I wished him to do. He was grave and thoughtful for some minutes, but at last consented. He was a pious man, and of as honest a heart as I have known, albeit narrow and confined, which sprang perhaps from his provincial practice and his theological cutting and trimming. We were in the midst of a serious talk, wherein I urged him upon matters which shall presently be set forth, when we heard a noise outside. I begged him to retire to the alcove where my bed was, and draw the curtain for a few moments, nor come forth until I called. He did so, yet I thought it hurt his sense of dignity to be shifted to a bedroom.

As he disappeared the door opened, and Gabord and Alixe entered. "One half hour," said Gabord, and went out again.

Presently Alixe told me her story.

"I have not been idle, Robert, but I could not act, for my father and mother suspect my love for you. I have come but little to the château without them, and I was closely watched. I knew not how the thing would end, but I kept up my workings with the Governor, which is easier now Monsieur Doltaire is gone, and I got you the freedom to walk upon the ramparts. Well, once, before my father suspected me, I said that if his Excellency disliked your being in the Château, you could be as well guarded in my father's house with sentinels always there, until you could, in better health, be taken to the common jail again. What was my surprise when yesterday came word to my father that he should make ready to receive you as a prisoner; being sure that he, his Excellency's cousin, the father of the man you had injured, and the most loyal of Frenchmen, would guard you diligently; he now needed all extra room in the Château for the entertainment of gentlemen and officers lately come from France.

"When my father got the news, he was thrown into dismay. He knew not what to do. On what ground could he refuse the Governor? Yet when he thought of me he felt it his duty to do so. Again, on what ground could he refuse this boon to you, to whom we all owe the blessing of his life? On my brother's account? But my brother has written to my father justifying you, and magnanimously praising you as a man, while hating you as an English soldier. On my account? But he could not give this reason to the Governor. As for me, I was silent, I waited—and I wait; I know not what will be the end. Meanwhile preparations go on to receive you."

I could see that Alixe's mood was more tranquil since Doltaire was gone. A certain restlessness had vanished. Her manner had much dignity, and every movement a peculiar grace and elegance. She was dressed in a soft cloth of a gray tone, touched off with red and slashed with gold, and a cloak of gray, trimmed with fur, with bright silver buckles, hung loosely on her, thrown off at one shoulder. There was a sweet disorder in her hair, which indeed was prettiest when freest.

17

When she had finished speaking she looked at me, as I thought, with a little anxiety.

"Alixe," I said, "we have come to the cross-roads, and the way we choose now is for all time."

She looked up, startled, yet governing herself, and her hand sought mine and nestled there. "I feel that, too," she replied. "What is it, Robert?"

"I can not in honour escape from your father's house. I can not steal his daughter, and his safety too——"

"You must escape," she interrupted firmly.

"From here, from the citadel, from anywhere but your house; and so I will not go to it."

"You will not go to it?" she repeated slowly and strangely. "How may you not? You are a prisoner. If they make my father your jailer——" She laughed.

"I owe that jailer and that jailer's daughter——"

"You owe them your safety and your freedom. Oh, Robert, I know, I know what you mean. But what care I what the world may think by-and-bye, or to-morrow, or to-day? My conscience is clear."

"Your father——" I persisted.

She nodded. "Yes, yes, you speak truth, alas! And yet you must be freed. And "—here she got to her feet, and with flashing eyes spoke out—"and you shall be set free. Let come what will, I owe my first duty to you, though all the world chatter; and I will not stir from that. As soon as I can make it possible, you shall escape."

"You shall have the right to set me free," said I, "if I must go to your father's house. And if I do not go there, but out to my own country, you shall still have the right before all the world to follow, or to wait till I come to fetch you."

"I do not understand you, Robert," said she. "I do not——" Here she broke off, looking, looking at me wistfully, and trembling a little.

Then I stooped and whispered softly in her ear. She gave a little cry, and drew back from me; yet instantly her hand came out and caught my arm.

"Robert, Robert! I can not, I dare not!" she cried softly. "No, no, it may not be," she added in a whisper of fear.

I went to the alcove, drew back the curtain, and asked Mr. Wainfleet to step forth.

"Sir," said I, picking up my Prayer Book and putting it in his hands, "I beg you to marry this lady and myself."

He paused, dazed. "Marry you—here—now?" he asked shakingly.

"Before ten minutes go round, this lady must be my wife," said I.

"Mademoiselle Duvarney, you——" he began.

"Be pleased, dear sir, to open the book at '*Wilt thou have*,'" said I. "The lady is a Catholic; she has not the consent of her people; but when she is my wife, made so by you, whose consent need we ask? Can you not tie us fast enough, a man and woman of sense sufficient, but you must pause here? Is the knot you tie safe against picking and stealing?"

I had touched his vanity and his ecclesiasticism. "Married by me," he replied, "once chaplain to the Bishop of London, you have a knot that no sword can cut. I am in full orders. My parish is in Boston itself."

"You will hand a certificate to my wife to-morrow, and you will uphold this marriage against all gossip?" asked I.

"Against all France and all England," he answered, roused now.

"Then come," I urged.

"But I must have a witness," he interposed, opening the book.

"You shall have one in due time," said I. "Go on. When the marriage is performed, and at the point where you shall proclaim us man and wife, I will have a witness."

I turned to Alixe, and found her pale and troubled. "Oh, Robert, Robert!" she cried, "it cannot be. Now, now I am afraid, for the first time in my life, dear, the first time!"

"Dearest lass in the world," I said, "it must be. I shall not go to your father's. To-morrow night I make my great stroke for freedom, and when I am free I shall return to fetch my wife."

"You will try to escape from here to-morrow?" she asked, her face flushing finely.

"I will escape or die," I answered; "but I shall not think of death. Come—come and say with me that we shall part no more—in spirit no more; that, whatever comes, you and I have fulfilled our great hope, though under the shadow of the sword."

At that she put her hand in mine with pride and sweetness, and said, "I am ready, Robert. I give my heart, my life, and my honour to you—forever."

Then, with simplicity and solemnity she turned to the clergyman: "Sir, my honour is also in your hands. If you have mother or sister, or true care of souls upon you, I pray you, in the future act as becomes good men."

"Mademoiselle," he said earnestly, "I am risking my freedom, maybe my life, in this; do you think——"

Here she took his hand and pressed it. "Ah, I ask your pardon. I am of a different faith from you, and I have known how men forget when they should remember." She smiled at him so perfectly that he drew himself up with pride.

"Make haste, sir," said I. "Jailers are curious folk."

The room was not yet lighted, the evening shadows were creeping in, and up out of the town came the ringing of the vesper bell from the church of the Recollets. For a moment there was stillness in the room and all around us, and then the chaplain began in a low voice: "*I require and charge you both*——" and so on. In a few moments I had made the great vow, and had put on Alixe's finger a ring which the clergyman drew from his own hand. Then we knelt down, and I know we both prayed most fervently with the good man that we might "ever remain in perfect love and perfect peace together."

Rising, he paused, and I went to the door and knocked upon it. It was opened by Gabord. "Come in, Gabord," said I. "There is a thing that you must hear."

He stepped back and got a light, and then entered, holding it up and shutting the door. A strange look came upon his face when he saw the chaplain, and dismay followed when, stepping beside Alixe, I took her hand, and Mr. Wainfleet declared us man and wife. He stood like one dumbfounded, and he did not stir, as Alixe, turning to me, let me kiss her on the lips, and then went to the crucifix on the wall and embraced the feet of it, and stood for a moment praying. Nor did he move or make a sign till she came back and stood beside me.

"A pretty scene!" he burst forth then with anger. "But, by God! no marriage is it!"

Alixe's hand tightened on my arm, and she drew close to me.

"A marriage that will stand at Judgment Day, Gabord," said I.

"But not in France or here. 'Tis mating wild, with end of doom."

"It is a marriage our great Archbishop at Lambeth Palace will uphold against a hundred popes and kings," said the chaplain with importance.

"You are no priest, but holy peddler!" cried Gabord roughly. "This is not mating as Christians, and fires of hell shall burn—aho! I will see you all go down, and hand of mine shall not be lifted for you!"

He puffed out his cheeks, and his great eyes rolled like fire-wheels.

"You are a witness to this ceremony," said the chaplain. "And you shall answer to your God, but you must speak the truth for this man and wife."

"Man and wife?" laughed Gabord wildly. "May I die and be damned to——"

Like a flash Alixe was beside him, and put to his lips swiftly the little wooden cross that Mathilde had given her.

"Gabord, Gabord," she said in a sad voice, "when you may come to die, a girl's prayers will be waiting at God's feet for you."

He stopped, and stared at her. Her hand lay on his arm, and she continued : "No night gives me sleep, Gabord, but I pray for the jailer who has been kind to an ill-treated gentleman."

"A juggling gentleman, that cheats Gabord before his eyes, and smuggles in mongrel priest!" he blustered.

I waved my hand at the chaplain, or I think he would have put his Prayer Book to rougher use than was its wont, and I was about to answer, but Alixe spoke instead, and to greater purpose than I could have done. Her whole mood changed, her face grew still and proud, her eyes flashed bravely.

"Gabord," she said, "vanity speaks in you there, not honesty. No gentleman here is a juggler. No kindness you may have done warrants insolence. You have the power to bring great misery on us, and you may have the will, but, by God's help, both my husband and myself shall be delivered from cruel hands. At any moment I may stand alone in the world, friends, people, the Church, and all the land against me : if you desire to hasten that time, to bring me to disaster, because you would injure my husband "—how sweet the name sounded on her lips ! —" then act, but do not insult us. But no, no," she broke off softly, " you spoke in temper, you meant it not, you were but vexed with us for the moment. Dear Gabord," she added, " did we not know that if we had asked you first, you would have refused us ? You care so much for me, you would have feared my linking life and fate with one——"

" With one the death-man has in hand, to pay price for wicked deed," he interrupted.

" With one innocent of all dishonour, a gentleman wronged every way. Gabord, you know it is so, for you have guarded him and fought with him, and you are an honourable gentleman," she added gently.

" No gentleman I," he burst forth, " but jailer base, and soldier born upon a truss of hay. But honour is an apple any man may eat since Adam walked in garden. . . . 'Tis honest foe, here," he continued magnanimously, and nodded towards me.

" We would have told you all," she said, " but how dare we involve you, or how dare we tempt you, or how dare we risk your refusal ? It was love and truth drove us to this ; and God will bless this mating as the birds mate, even as He gives honour to Gabord who was born upon a truss of hay."

" Poom ! " said Gabord, puffing out his cheeks, and smiling on her with a look half sour, and yet with a dog-like fondness, " Gabord's mouth is shut till 's head is off, and then to tell the tale to Twelve Apostles ! "

Through his wayward, illusive speech we found his meaning. He would keep faith with us, and be best proof of this marriage, at risk of his head even.

As we spoke, the chaplain was writing in the blank fore-pages of the Prayer Book. Presently he said to me, handing me the pen, which he had picked from a table, "Inscribe your names here. It is a rough record of the ceremony, but it will suffice before all men, when to-morrow I have given Mistress Moray another record."

We wrote our names, and then the pen was handed to Gabord. He took it, and at last, with many flourishes and *ahos*, and by dint of puffings and rolling eyes, he wrote his name so large that it filled as much space as the other names and all the writing, and was indeed like a huge indorsement across the record.

When this was done, Alixe held out her hand to him. "Will you kiss me, Gabord?" she said.

The great soldier was all taken back. He flushed like a schoolboy, yet a big humour and pride looked out of his eyes.

"I owe you for the sables, too," she said. "But kiss me—not on my ears, as the Russian count kissed Gabord, but on my cheek."

This won him to our cause utterly, and I never think of Gabord, as I saw him last in the sway and carnage of battle, fighting with wild uproar and covered with wounds, but the memory of that moment, when he kissed my young wife, comes back to me.

At that he turned to leave. "I'll hold the door for ten minutes," he added; and bowed to the chaplain, who blessed us then with tears in his eyes, and smiled a little to my thanks and praises and purse of gold, and to Alixe's gratitude. With lifting chin—good honest gentleman, who afterwards proved his fidelity and truth—he said that he would die to uphold this sacred ceremony. And so he made a little speech, as if he had a pulpit round him, and he wound up with a benediction which sent my dear girl to tears and soft trembling:

"*The Lord bless you and keep you: the Lord make his face to shine upon you; the Lord lift up his countenance upon you, and give you peace, now and for evermore.*"

A moment afterwards the door closed, and for ten minutes I looked into my dear wife's face, and told her my plans for escape. When Gabord opened the door upon us, we had passed through years of understanding and resolve. Our parting was brave—a bravery on her side that I do not think any other woman could match. She was quivering with the new life come upon her, yet she was self-controlled; she moved as in a dream, yet I knew her mind was alert, vigilant, and strong; she was aching with thought of this separation, with the peril that faced us both, yet she carried a quiet joy in her face, a tranquil gravity of bearing.

"Whom God hath joined——" said I gravely at the last.

"Let no man put asunder," she answered softly and solemnly.

"Aho!" said Gabord, and turned his head away.

Then the door shut upon me, and, though I am no Catholic, I have no shame in saying that I kissed the feet on the crucifix which her lips had blessed.

XXI.

LA JONGLEUSE.

AT nine o'clock I was waiting by the window, and even as a bugle sounded "lights out" in the barracks and change of guard, I let the string down. Mr. Stevens shot round the corner of the château, just as the departing sentinel disappeared, attached a bundle to the string, and I drew it up.

"Is all well?" I called softly down.

"All well," said Mr. Stevens, and, hugging the wall of the château, he sped away. In another moment a new sentinel began pacing up and down, and I shut the window and untied my bundle. All that I had asked for was there. I hid the things away in the alcove and went to bed at once, for I knew that I should have no sleep on the following night.

I did not leave my bed till the morning was well advanced. Once or twice during the day I brought my guards in with fear on their faces, the large fat man more distorted than his fellow, by the lamentable sounds I made with my willow toys. They crossed themselves again and again, and I myself appeared devout and troubled. When we walked abroad during the afternoon, I chose to loiter by the river rather than walk, for I wished to conserve my strength, which was now vastly increased, though, to mislead my watchers and the authorities, I assumed the delicacy of an invalid, and appeared unfit for any enterprise—no hard task, for I was still very thin and worn.

So I sat upon a favourite seat on the cliff, set against a solitary tree, fixed in the rocks. I gazed long on the river, and my guards, stoutly armed, stood near, watching me, and talking in low tones. Eager to hear their gossip I appeared to sleep. They came nearer, and, facing me, sat upon a large stone, and gossipped freely concerning the strange sounds heard in my room at the château.

"See you, my Bamboir," said the lean to the fat soldier, "the British captain, he is to be carried off in burning flames by that La Jongleuse. We shall come in one morning, find a smell of sulphur only, and a circle of red on the floor where the imps danced before La Jongleuse said to them, 'Up with him, darlings, and away!'"

At this Bamboir shook his head, and answered, "To-morrow I'll go to the Governor and tell him what's coming. My wife, she falls upon my neck this morning. 'Argose,' she says, ''twill need the bishop and his college to drive La Jongleuse out of the grand château.'"

"No less," replied the other. "A deacon and sacred palm and sprinkle of holy water would do for a cottage, or even for a little manor house, with twelve candles burning, and a hymn to the Virgin. But in a king's house——"

"It's not the King's house."

"But yes, it is the King's house, though his Most Christian Majesty lives in France. The Marquis de Vaudreuil stands for the King, and we are sentinels in the King's house. But, my faith, I'd rather be fighting against Frederick, the Prussian boar, than watching this mad Englishman."

"But see you, my brother, that Englishman's a devil. Else how has he not been hanged long ago? He has vile arts to blind all, or he'd not be sitting there. It is well known that M'sieu' Doltaire, even the King's son—his mother worked in the fields like your Nanette, Bamboir——"

"Or your Lablanche, my friend. She has hard hands, with warts, and red knuckles therefrom——"

"Or your Nanette, Bamboir, with nose that blisters in the summer, as she goes swingeing flax, and swelling feet that sweat in sabots, and chin thrust out from carrying pails upon her head——"

"Ay, like Nanette and like Lablanche, this peasant mother of M'sieu' Doltaire, and maybe no such firm breasts like Nanette——"

"Nor such an eye as has Lablanche. Well, M'sieu' Doltaire, who could override them all, he could not kill this barbarian. And Gabord—you know well how they fought, and the black horse and his rider came and carried him away. Why, the young M'sieu' Duvarney had him on his knees, the blade at his throat, and a sword flash out from the dark—they say it was the devil's—and took him in the ribs and well-nigh killed him."

"But what say you to Ma'm'selle Duvarney coming to him that day, and again yesterday with Gabord?"

"Well, well, who knows, Bamboir? This morning I say to Nanette, 'Why is't, all in one moment, you send me to the devil, and pray to meet me in Abraham's bosom too?' What think you she answer me? Why, this, my Bamboir: 'Why is't Adam loved his wife and swore her down before the Lord also, all in one moment?' Why Ma'm'selle Duvarney does this or that is not for muddy brains like ours. It is some whimsy. They say that women are more curious about the devil than about St. Jean Baptiste. Perhaps she got of him a magic book."

"No, no! If he had the magic Petit Albert, he would have turned us into dogs long ago. But I do not like him. He is but thirty years, they say, and yet his hair is white as a pigeon's wing. It is not natural. Nor did he ever, says Gabord, do aught but laugh at everything they did to him. The chains they put would not stay, and when he was set against the wall to be shot, the watches stopped—the minute of his shooting passed. Then M'sieu' Doltaire come, and say a man that could do a trick like that should live to do another. And he did it, for M'sieu' Doltaire is gone to the Bastile. *Voyez*, this Englishman is a damned heretic, and has the wicked arts."

"But see, Bamboir, do you think he can cast spells?"

"What mean those sounds from his room!"

"So, so. Yet if he be a friend of the devil, La Jongleuse would not come for him, but——"

Startled and excited, they grasped each other's arms. "But for us—for us!"

"It would be a work of God to send him to the devil,"

said Bamboir in a loud whisper. "He has given us trouble enough. Who can tell what comes next? Those damned noises in his room, eh—eh?"

Then they whispered together, and presently I caught a fragment, by which I understood that, as we walked near the edge of the cliff, I should be pushed over, and they would make it appear that I had drowned myself.

They talked in low tones again, but soon got louder, and presently I knew that they were speaking of La Jongleuse; and Bamboir—the fat Bamboir, who the surgeon had said would some day die of apoplexy—was rash enough to say that he had seen her. He described her accurately, with the spirit of the born *raconteur*:

"Hair so black as the feather in the Governor's hat, and green eyes that flash fire, and a brown face with skin all scales. Oh, my saints of heaven, when she pass I hide my head, and I go cold like stone. She is all covered with long reeds and lilies about her head and shoulders, and blue-red sparks fly up at every step. Flames go round her, and she burns not her robe—not at all. And as she go I hear cries that make me sick, for it is, I said, some poor man in torture, and I think perhaps it is Jacques Villon, perhaps Jean Rivas, perhaps Angèle Damgoche. But no, it is a young priest of St. Clair, for he is never seen again—never!"

In my mind I commended this fat Bamboir as an excellent story-teller, and thanked him for his true picture of La Jongleuse, whom, to my regret, I had never seen. I would not forget his stirring description, as he should see. I gave point to the tale by squeezing an inflated toy in my pocket, with my arm, while my hands remained folded in front of me; and it was as good as a play to see the faces of these soldiers as they sprang to their feet, staring round in dismay. I myself seemed to wake with a start, and, rising to my feet, I asked what meant the noise and their amazement. We were in a spot where we could not easily be seen from any distance, and no one was in sight, nor were we to be remarked from the fort. They exchanged looks, as I started back towards the château, walking very near the edge of the cliff. A spirit of bravado came on me, and I said musingly to them as we walked :

"It would be easy to throw you both over the cliff, but I love you too well. I have proved that by making toys for your children."

It was as cordial to me to watch their faces. They both drew away from the cliff, and grasped their fire-arms apprehensively.

"My God," said Bamboir, "those toys shall be burned to-night! Alphonse has the smallpox and Susanne the croup—damned devil!" he added · furiously, stepping forward to me with gun raised, "I'll——"

I believe he would have shot me, but that I said quickly, "If you did harm to me you'd come to the rope. The Governor would rather lose a hand than my life."

I pushed his musket down. "Why should you fret? I am leaving the château to-morrow for another prison. You fools, d'ye think I'd harm the children? I know as little of the devil or La Jongleuse as do you. We'll solve the witcheries of these sounds, you and I, to-night. If they come, we'll say the Lord's Prayer, and make the sacred gesture, and if it goes not, we'll have a priest to drive out the whining spirit."

This quieted them, and I was glad of it, for they had looked bloodthirsty enough, and though I had a weapon on me, there was little use in seeking fighting or flight till the auspicious moment. They were not satisfied, however, and they watched me diligently as we came on to the château.

I could not bear that they should be frightened about their children, so I said:

"Make for me a sacred oath, and I will swear by it that those toys will do your children no harm."

I drew out the little wooden cross that Mathilde had given me, and held it up. They looked at me astonished. What should I, a heretic and a Protestant, do with this sacred emblem? "This never leaves me," said I; "it was a pious gift."

I raised the cross to my lips and kissed it.

"That's well," said Bamboir to his comrade. "If otherwise, he'd have been struck down by the Avenging Angel."

We got back to the Château without more talk, and I was locked in, while my guards retired. As soon as they had gone I got to work, for my great enterprise was at hand.

At ten o'clock I was ready for the venture. When the critical moment came, I was so arrayed that my dearest friend would not have known me. My object was to come out upon my guards as La Jongleuse, and, in the fright and confusion which should follow, make my escape through the corridors and to the entrance doors, past the sentinels, and so on out. It may be seen now why I got the woman's garb, the sheet, the horsehair, the phosphorus, the reeds, and such things; why I secured the knife and pistol may be conned likewise. Upon the lid of a small stove in the room I placed my saltpetre, and I rubbed the horsehair on my head with phosphorus, also on my hands, and face, and feet, and on many objects in the room. The knife and pistol were at my hand, and as soon as the clock had struck ten I set my toys wailing.

Then I knocked upon the door with solemn taps, hurried back to the stove, and waited for the door to

open before I applied the match. I heard a fumbling
at the lock, then the door was thrown wide open. All
was darkness in the hall without, save for a spluttering
candle which Bamboir held over his head, as he and his
fellow, deadly pale, peered into the chamber. Suddenly
they gave a cry, for I threw the sheet from my face and
shoulders, and to their excited imagination La Jongleuse
stood before them, all in flames. As I started down on
them, the coloured fire flew up, making the room all blue
and scarlet for a moment, in which I must have looked
devilish indeed, with staring eyes and outstretched chalky
hands, and wailing cries coming from my robe.

I moved swiftly, and Bamboir, without a cry, dropped
like a log (poor fellow, he never rose again ! the apoplexy
which the surgeon promised had come), his comrade gave
a cry, and sank in a heap in a corner, mumbling a
prayer and making the sign of the cross, his face stark
with terror.

I passed him, came along the corridor and down one
staircase, without seeing any one ; then two soldiers appeared in the half-lighted hallway. Presently a door
opened behind me, and some one came out. By now the
phosphorus light had diminished a little, but still I was
a villainous picture, for in one hand I held a small cup,
from which suddenly sprang red and blue fires. The
men fell back, and I sailed past them, but I had not
gone far down the lower staircase when a shot rang
after me and a bullet passed by my head. Now I came
rapidly to the outer door, where two more sentinels
stood. They shrank back, and suddenly one threw
down his musket and ran ; the other, terrified, stood
stock-still. I passed him, opened the door, and came out
upon the Intendant, who was just alighting from his
carriage.

The horses sprang away, frightened at sight of me,

and nearly threw Bigot to the ground. I tossed the tin cup with its chemical fires full in his face, as he made a dash for me. He called out, and drew his sword. I wished not to fight, and I sprang aside; but he made a pass at me, and I drew my pistol and was about to fire, when another shot came from the hallway and struck him. He fell almost at my feet, and I dashed away into the darkness. Fifty feet ahead I cast one glance back and saw Monsieur Cournal standing in the doorway. I was sure that his second shot had not been meant for me, but for the Intendant—wild attempt at a revenge long delayed, for the worst of wrongs.

I ran on, and presently came full upon five soldiers, two of whom drew their pistols, fired, and missed. Their comrades ran away howling. They barred my path, and now I fired too, and brought one down; then came a shot from behind them, and another fell. The last one took to his heels, and a moment later I had my hand in that of Mr. Stevens. It was he who had fired the opportune shot that rid me of one foe. We came quickly along the river brink, and, skirting the citadel, got clear of it without discovery, though we could see soldiers hurrying past, roused by the firing at the château.

In about half an hour of steady running, with a few bad stumbles and falls, we reached the old windmill above the Anse du Foulon at Sillery, and came plump upon our waiting comrades. I had stripped myself of my disguise, and rubbed the phosphorus from my person as we came along, but enough remained to make me an uncanny figure. It had been kept secret from these people that I was to go with them, and they sullenly kept their muskets raised; but when Mr. Stevens told them who I was they were agreeably surprised. I at once took command of the enterprise, saying firmly at the same time that I would shoot the first man who disobeyed my orders.

18

I was sure that I could bring them to safety, but my will must be law. They took my terms like men, and swore to stand by me.

XXII.

THE LORD OF KAMARASKA.

WE were five altogether—Mr. Stevens, Clark, the two Boston soldiers, and myself; and presently we came down the steep passage in the cliff to where our craft lay, secured by my dear wife—a birch canoe, well laden with necessaries. Our craft was none too large for our party, but she must do; and safely in, we pushed out upon the current, which was in our favour, for the tide was going out. My object was to cross the river softly, skirt the Levis shore, pass the Isle of Orleans, and so steal down the river. There was excitement in the town, as we could tell from the lights flashing along the shore, and boats soon began to patrol the banks, going swiftly up and down, and extending a line round to the St. Charles River towards Beauport.

It was well for us the night was dark, else we had never run that gantlet. But we were lucky enough, by hard paddling, to get past the town on the Levis side. Never were better boatmen. The paddles dropped with agreeable precision, and no boatswain's rattan was needed to keep my fellows to their task. I, whose sight was long trained to darkness, could see a great distance round us, and so could prevent a trap, though once or twice we let our canoe drift with the tide, lest our paddles should be heard. I could not paddle long, I had so little strength. After the Isle of Orleans was passed I drew a breath of relief, and played the part of captain and boatswain merely.

Yet when I looked back at the town on those strong

heights, and saw the bonfires burn to warn the settlers of our escape, saw the lights sparkling in many homes, and even fancied I could make out the light shining in my dear wife's window, I had a strange feeling of loneliness. There, in the shadow of my prison walls, was the dearest thing on earth to me. Ought she not to be with me? She had begged to come, to share with me these dangers and hardships; but that I could not, would not grant. She would be safer with her people. As for us desperate men bent on escape, we must face hourly peril.

Thank God, there was work to do. Hour after hour the swing and dip of the paddles went on. No one showed weariness, and when dawn broke slow and soft over the eastern hills I motioned my good boatmen towards the shore, and we landed safely. Lifting our frigate up, we carried her into a thicket, there to rest with us till night, when we would sally forth again into the friendly darkness. We were in no distress all that day, for the weather was fine, and we had enough to eat; and in this case were we for ten days and nights, though indeed some of the nights were dreary and very cold, for it was yet but the beginning of May.

It might thus seem that we were leaving danger well behind, after having travelled so many heavy leagues, but it was yet several hundred miles to Louisburg, our destination, and we had escaped only immediate danger. We passed Isle aux Coudres and the Isles of Kamaraska, and now we ventured by day to ramble the woods in search of game, which was most plentiful. In this good outdoor life my health came slowly back, and I should soon be able to bear equal tasks with any of my comrades. Never man led better friends, though I have seen adventurous service near and far since that time. Even the genial ruffian Clark was amenable, and took sharp reprimand without revolt.

On the eleventh night, after our escape our first real trial came. We were keeping the middle of the great river, as safest from detection, and when the tide was with us we could thus move more rapidly. We had had a constant favouring breeze, but now suddenly, though we were running with the tide, the wind turned easterly and blew up the river against the ebb. Soon it became a gale, to which was added snow and sleet, and a rough, choppy sea followed.

I saw it would be no easy task to fetch our craft to the land. The waves broke in upon us, and presently, while half of us were paddling with laboured and desperate stroke, the other half were bailing. Lifted on a crest, our canoe, heavily laden, dropped at both ends; and again, sinking into the hollows between the short, brutal waves, her gunwales yielded outward, and her waist gaped in a dismal way. We looked to see her with a broken back at any moment. To add to our ill fortune, a violent current set in from the shore, and it was vain to attempt a landing. Spirits and bodies flagged, and it needed all my cheerfulness to keep my fellows to their tasks.

At last, the ebb of tide being almost spent, the waves began to fall, the wind shifted a little to the northward, and a piercing cold instantly froze our drenched clothes on our backs. But with the current changed there was a good chance of reaching the shore. As daylight came we passed into a little sheltered cove, and sank with exhaustion on the shore. Our frozen clothes rattled like tin, and we could scarce lift a leg. But we gathered a fine heap of wood, flint and steel were ready, and the tinder was sought; which, when found, was soaking. Not a dry stitch or stick could we find anywhere, till at last, within a leather belt, Mr. Stevens found a handkerchief, which was, indeed, as he told me afterwards, the gift and pledge of a lady to him ; and his returning to her without it nearly lost him another and better gift and pledge, for this went to light our fire. We had had enough danger and work in one night to give us relish for some days of rest, and we piously took them.

The evening of the second day we set off again and had a good night's run, and in the dawn, spying a snug little bay, we stood in and went ashore. I sent my two Provincials foraging with their guns, and we who remained set about to fix our camp for the day and prepare breakfast. A few minutes only passed, and my hunters came running back with rueful faces to say they had seen two Indians near, armed with muskets and knives. My plans were made at once. We needed their muskets, and the Indians must pay the price of their presence here, for our safety should be had at any cost.

I urged my men to utter no word at all, for none but Clark could speak French, and he but poorly. For myself, my accent would pass, after these six years of practice. We came to a little river, beyond which we could observe the Indians standing on guard. We could only cross by wading, which we did ; but one of my Provincials came down, wetting his musket and himself thoroughly. Reaching the shore, we marched together, I singing the refrain of an old French song as we went, so attracting the attention of the Indians. The better to deceive, we all were now dressed in the costume of the French peasant—I had taken pains to have Mr. Stevens secure these for us before starting ; a pair of homespun trousers, a coarse brown jacket, with thrums like waving tassels, a silk handkerchief about the neck, and a strong, thick worsted wig on the head ; no smart toupet, nor buckle ; nor combed, nor powdered ; and all crowned by a dull black cap. I myself was, as became my purpose, most like a small captain of militia, doing wood service, in the braver costume of the *coureur de bois*.

I signalled to the Indians, and, coming near, addressed them in French. They were deceived, and presently, abreast of them, in the midst of apparent ceremony, their firelocks were seized, and Mr. Stevens and Clark had them safe. I told them we must be satisfied as to who they were, for English prisoners escaped from Quebec were abroad, and no man could go unchallenged. They must at once lead me to their camp. So they did, and at their bark wigwam they said they had seen no English-men. They were guardians of the fire; that is, it was their duty to light a fire on the shore when a hostile fleet should appear; and from another point farther up, other guardians, seeing, would do the same, until beacons would be shining even to Quebec, three hundred leagues away.

While I was questioning them, Clark rifled the wig-wam; and presently, the excitable fellow, finding some excellent stores of skins, tea, maple sugar, coffee, and other things, broke out into English expletives. Instantly the Indians saw they had been trapped, and he whom Mr. Stevens held made a great spring from him, caught up a gun, and gave a wild yell which echoed far and near. Mr. Stevens, with great rapidity, levelled his pistol and shot him in the heart, while I, in a close struggle with my captive, was glad—for I was not yet strong—that Clark finished my assailant: and so both lay there dead, two foes less of our King.

Not far from where we stood was a pool of water, and we sank the bodies there; but I did not know till long afterwards that Clark, with a barbarous and dis-gusting spirit, carried away their scalps to sell them in New York, where they would bring, as he confided to one of the Provincials, twelve pounds each. Before we left, we shot a poor howling dog that mourned for his masters, and sank him also in the dark pool.

We had but got back to our camp, when, looking out,

we saw a well-manned four-oared boat making for the shore. My men were in dismay until I told them that, having begun the game of war, I would carry it on to the ripe end. This boat and all therein should be mine. Safely hidden, we watched the rowers draw in to shore with brisk strokes, singing a quaint farewell song of the *voyageurs*, called La Pauvre Mère, of which the refrain is:

> " And his mother says, ' My dear,
>   For your absence I shall grieve ;
>   Come you home within the year.' "

They had evidently been upon a long journey, and by their toiling we could see their boat was deep loaded ; but they drove on, like a horse that, at the close of day, sees ahead the inn where he is to bait and refresh, and, rousing to the spur, comes cheerily home. The figure of a reverend old man was in the stern, and he sent them in to shore with brisk words. Bump came the big shallop on the beach, and at that moment I ordered my men to fire, but to aim wide, for I had another end in view than killing.

We were exactly matched as to numbers, so that a fight would have been fair enough, but I hoped for peaceful conquest. As we fired I stepped out of the thicket, and behind me could be seen the barrels of our threatening muskets. The old gentleman stood up while his men cried for quarter. He waved them down with an impatient gesture, and stepped out on the beach. Then I recognized him. It was the Chevalier de la Darante. I stepped towards him, my sword drawn.

" Monsieur the Chevalier de la Darante, you are my prisoner," said I.

He started, then recognized me. " Now, by the blood of man ! now, by the blood of man ! " he said, and paused, dumfounded.

" You forget me, monsieur ? " asked I.

" Forget you, monsieur ? " said he. " As soon forget the devil at mass ! But I thought you dead by now, and——"

" If you are disappointed," said I, " there is a way " ; and I waved towards his men, then to Mr. Stevens and my own ambushed fellows.

He smiled an acid smile, and took a pinch of snuff. " It is not so fiery-edged as that," he answered ; " I can endure it."

" You shall have time, too, for reverie," answered I.

He looked puzzled. " What is't you wish ? " he asked.

" Your surrender first," said I, " and then your company at breakfast."

" The latter has meaning and compliment," he responded, " the former is beyond me. What would you do with me ? "

" Detain you and your shallop for the services of my master, the King of England, soon to be the master of your master, if the signs are right."

" All signs fail with the blind, monsieur."

" Monsieur," he added, with great, almost too great dignity, " I am of the family of the Duc de Mirepoix. The whole Kamaraska Isles are mine, and the best gentlemen in this province do me vassalage. I make war on none, I have stepped aside from all affairs of state, I am a simple gentleman. I have been a great way down this river, at large expense and toil, to purchase wheat, for all the corn of these counties above goes to Quebec to store the King's magazine, the adored La Friponne. I know not your purposes, but I trust you will not push your advantage "—he waved towards our muskets—" against a private gentleman."

" You forget, Chevalier," said I, " that you gave verdict for my death."

"Upon the evidence," he replied. "And I have no doubt you deserve hanging a thousand times."

I almost loved him for his boldness. I remembered also that he had no wish to be one of my judges, and that he spoke for me in the presence of the Governor. But he was not the man to make a point of that.

"Chevalier," said I, "I have been foully used in yonder town; by the fortune of war you shall help me to compensation. We have come a long, hard journey; we are all much overworked; we need rest, a better boat, and good sailors. You and your men, Chevalier, shall row us to Louisburg. When we are attacked, you shall be in the van; when we are at peace, you shall industriously serve under King George's flag. Now will you give up your men, and join me at breakfast?"

For a moment the excellent gentleman was mute, and my heart almost fell before his venerable white hair and his proud bearing; but something a little overdone in his pride, a little ludicrous in the situation, set me smiling; there came back on me the remembrance of all I had suffered, and I let no sentiment stand between me and my purposes.

"I am the Chevalier de la——" he began.

"If you were King Louis himself, and every man in your boat a peer of his realm, you should row a British subject now," said I; "or, if you choose, you shall have fighting instead." I meant there should be nothing uncertain in my words.

"I surrender," said he; "and if you are bent on shaming me, let us have it over soon."

"You shall have better treatment than I had in Quebec," answered I.

A moment afterwards his men were duly surrendered, disarmed, and guarded, and the Chevalier breakfasted with me, now and again asking me news of Quebec. He was amazed to hear that Bigot had been shot, and distressed that I could not say whether fatally or not.

I fixed on a new plan. We would now proceed by day as well as by night, for the shallop could not leave the river, and, besides, I did not care to trust my prisoners on shore. I threw from the shallop into the stream enough wheat to lighten her, and now, well stored and trimmed, we pushed away upon our course, the Chevalier and his men rowing, while my men rested and tended the sail, which was now set. I was much loath to cut our good canoe adrift, but she stopped the shallop's way, and she was left behind.

After a time our prisoners were in part relieved, and I made the Chevalier rest also, for he had taken his task in good part, and had ordered his men to submit cheerfully. In the late afternoon, after an excellent journey, we saw a high and shaggy point of land, far ahead, which shut off our view. I was anxious to see beyond it, for ships of war might appear at any moment. A good breeze brought up this land, and when we were abreast of it a lofty frigate was disclosed to view—a convoy (so the Chevalier said) to a fleet of transports which that morning had gone up the river. I resolved instantly, since fight was useless, to make a run for it. Seating myself at the tiller, I declared solemnly that I would shoot the first man who dared to stop the shallop's way, to make sign, or speak a word. So, as the frigate stood across the river, I had all sail set, roused the men at the oars, and we came running by her stern. Our prisoners were keen enough to get past in safety, for they were between two fires, and the excellent Chevalier was as alert and laborious as the rest. They signalled us from the frigate by a shot to bring to, but we came on gallantly. Another shot whizzed by at a distance, but we did not change our course, and then balls came flying over our heads, dropping round us, cooling their hot protests in the river. But none struck us, and presently all fell short.

We durst not slacken pace that night, and by morning, much exhausted, we deemed ourselves safe, and rested for a while, making a hearty breakfast, though a sombre shadow had settled on the face of the good Chevalier. Once more he ventured to protest, but I told him my resolution was fixed, and that I would, at all costs, secure escape from my six years' misery. He must abide the fortune of this war.

For several days we fared on, without more mishap. At last, one morning, as we hugged the shore, I saw a large boat lying on the beach. On landing we found the boat of excellent size and made for swift going, and presently Clark discovered the oars. Then I turned to the Chevalier, who was watching me curiously, yet hiding anxiety, for he had upheld his dignity with some accent since he had come into my service:

"Chevalier," said I, "you shall find me more humane than my persecutors at Quebec. I will not hinder your going, if you will engage on your honour—as would, for instance, the Duc de Mirepoix!"—he bowed to my veiled irony—"that you will not divulge what brought you back thus far, till you shall reach your Kamaraska Isles; and you must undertake the same for your fellows here."

He consented, and I admired the fine, vain old man, and lamented that I had had to use him so.

"Then," said I, "you may depart with your shallop. Your mast and sail, however, must be ours; and for these I will pay. I will also pay for the wheat which was thrown into the river, and you shall have a share of our provisions, got from the Indians."

"Monsieur," said he, "I shall remember with pride that I have dealt with so fair a foe. I can not regret the pleasure of your acquaintance, even at the price. And see, monsieur, I do not think you the criminal they have made you out, and so I will tell a lady——"

I raised my hand at him, for I saw that he knew something, and Mr. Stevens was near us at the time.

" Chevalier," said I, drawing him aside, " if, as you say, I have used you honourably, then, if trouble falls upon my wife before I see her again, I beg you to stand her friend. In the sad fortunes of war and hate of me, she may need a friend—even against her own people, on her own hearthstone."

I never saw a man so amazed. To his rapid questionings I gave the one reply, that Alixe was my wife. His lip trembled.

" Poor child ! poor child ! " said he ; " they will put her in a nunnery. You did wrong, monsieur."

" Chevalier," said I, " did you ever love a woman ? "

He made a motion of the hand, as if I had touched upon a tender point, and said, " So young ! so young ! "

" But you will stand by her," I urged, " by the memory of some good woman you have known ! "

He put out his hand again with a chafing sort of motion. " There, there," said he, " the poor child shall never want a friend. If I can help it, she shall not be made the victim of the Church or of the State, nor yet of family pride—good God, no ! "

Presently we parted, and soon we lost our grateful foes in the distance. All night we jogged along with easy sail, but just at dawn, in a sudden opening of the land, we saw a sloop at anchor near a wooded point, her pennant flying. We pushed along, unheeding her fiery signal to bring to ; and declining, she let fly a swivel loaded with grape, and again another, riddling our sail ; but we were travelling with wind and tide, and we soon left the indignant patrol behind. Towards evening came a freshening wind and a cobbling sea, and I thought it best to make for shore. So, easing the sail, we brought our shallop before the wind. It was very dark, and there was a heavy surf running; but we had to take our fortune as it came, and we let drive for the unknown shore, for it was all alike to us. Presently, as we ran close in, our boat came hard upon a rock, which bulged her bows open. Taking what provisions we could, we left our poor craft upon the rocks, and fought our way to safety.

We had little joy that night in thinking of our shallop breaking on the reefs, and we discussed the chances of crossing overland to Louisburg; but we soon gave up that wild dream : this river was the only way. When daylight came, we found our boat, though badly wrecked, still held together. Now Clark rose to the great necessity, and said that he would patch her up to carry us on, or never lift a hammer more. With labour past reckoning we dragged her to shore and got her on the stocks, and then set about to find materials to mend her. Tools were all too few—a hammer, a saw, and an adze were all we had. A piece of board or a nail was a treasure then, and when the timbers of the craft were covered, for oakum we had to resort to tree-gum. For caulking, one spared a handkerchief, another a stocking, and another a piece of shirt, till she was stuffed in all her fissures. In this labour we passed eight days, and then were ready for the launch again.

On the very afternoon fixed for starting, we saw two sails standing down the river and edging towards our shore. One of them let anchor go right off the place where our patched boat lay. We had prudently carried on our work behind rocks and trees, so that we could not be seen, unless our foes came ashore. Our case seemed desperate enough, but all at once I determined on a daring enterprise.

The two vessels—convoys, I felt sure—had anchored some distance from each other, and from their mean ap-

pearance I did not think that they would have a large
freight of men and arms; for they seemed not ships from
France, but vessels of the country. If I could divide the
force of either vessel, and quietly, under cover of night,
steal on her by surprise, then I would trust our desperate
courage, and open the war which soon General Wolfe and
Admiral Saunders were to wage up and down this river.

I had brave fellows with me, and if we got our will it
would be a thing worth remembrance. So I disclosed my
plan to Mr. Stevens and the others, and, as I looked for,
they had a fine relish for the enterprise. I agreed upon a
signal with them, bade them to lie close along the ground,
picked out the nearer (which was the smaller) ship for my
purpose, and at sunset, tying a white handkerchief to a
stick, came marching out of the woods, upon the shore,
firing a gun at the same time. Presently a boat was put
out from the sloop, and two men and a boy came rowing
towards me. Standing off a little distance from the shore,
they asked what was wanted.

"The King's errand," was my reply in French, and
I must be carried down the river by them, for which I
would pay generously. Then, with idle gesture, I said
that if they wished some drink, there was a bottle of rum
near my fire, above me, to which they were welcome; also
some game, which they might take as a gift to their captain and his crew.

This drew them like a magnet, and, as I lit my pipe,
their boat scraped the sand, and, getting out, they hauled
her up and came towards me. I met them, and, pointing
towards my fire, as it might appear, led them up behind
the rocks, when, at a sign, my men sprang up, the fellows
were seized, and were forbidden to cry out on peril of
their lives. I compelled them to tell what hands and
what arms were left on board. The sloop from which
they came, and the schooner, its consort, were bound for

ADMIRAL SAUNDERS.

Gaspé, to bring provisions for a thousand Indians assembled at Miramichi and Aristiguish, who were to go by these same vessels to re-enforce the garrison of Quebec.

The sloop, they said, had six guns and a crew of twenty men ; but the schooner, which was much larger, carried no arms save muskets, but had a crew and a guard of thirty men.

In this country there is no twilight, and with sunset came instantly the dusk. Already silence and dark inclosed the sloop. I had the men bound to a tree, and gagged also, engaging to return and bring them away safe and unhurt when our task was over. I chose for pilot the boy, and presently, with great care, launching our patched shallop from the stocks—for the ship-boat was too small to carry six safely—we got quietly away. Rowing with silent stroke we came alongside the sloop. No light burned save that in the binnacle, and all hands, except the watch, were below at supper and at cards.

I could see the watch pacing forward as we dropped silently alongside the stern. My object was to catch this fellow as he came by. This I would trust to no one but myself ; for now, grown stronger, I had the old spring in my blood, and I had also a good wish that my plans should not go wrong through the bungling of others. I motioned my men to sit silent, and then, when the fellow's back was toward me, coming softly up the side, I slid over quietly and drew into the shadow of a boat that hung near.

He came on lazily, and when just past me I suddenly threw my arms about him, clapping my hand upon his mouth. He was stoutly built, and he began at once to struggle. He was no coward, and feeling for his knife, drew it, and would have had it in me but that I was quicker, and, with a desperate wrench, my hand still over his mouth, half swung him round and drove my dagger home.

He sank in my arms with a heaving sigh, and I laid him down, still and dead, upon the deck. Then I whispered up my comrades, the boy leading. As the last man came over, his pistol, stuck in his belt, caught the ratlings of the shrouds, and it dropped upon the deck. This gave the alarm, but I was at the companion-door on the instant, as the master came bounding up, sword showing, and calling to his men, who swarmed after him. I fired; the bullet travelled along his spine, and he fell back stunned.

A dozen others came on. Some reached the deck and grappled with my men. I never shall forget with what fiendish joy Clark fought that night—those five terrible minutes. He was like some mad devil, and by his imprecations I knew that he was avenging the brutal death of his infant daughter some years before. He was armed with a long knife, and I saw four men fall beneath it, while he himself got but one bad cut. Of the Provincials, one fell wounded, and the other brought down his man. Mr. Stevens and myself held the companion-way, driving the crew back, not without hurt, for my wrist was slashed by a cutlass, and Mr. Stevens had a bullet in his thigh. But presently we had the joy of having those below cry quarter.

We were masters of the sloop. Quickly battening down the prisoners, I had the sails spread, the windlass going, the anchor apeak quickly, and we soon were moving down upon the schooner, which was now all confusion, commands ringing out on the quiet air. But when, laying alongside, we gave her a dose, and then another, from all our swivels at once, sweeping her decks, the timid fellows cried quarter, and we boarded her. With my men's muskets cocked, I ordered her crew and soldiers below, till they were all, save two lusty youths, stowed away. Then I had everything of value brought from the sloop, together with the swivels, which we fastened to the schooner's side ; and when all was done, we set fire to the sloop, and I stood and watched her burn with a proud—too proud—spirit.

Having brought our prisoners from the shore, we placed them with the rest below. At dawn I called a council with Mr. Stevens and the others—our one wounded Provincial was not omitted—and we all agreed that some of our captives should be sent off in the long boat, and that a portion of the rest should be used to work the ship. So we had half the fellows up, and giving them fishing-lines, rum, and provisions, with a couple of muskets and ammunition, we sent them off to shift for themselves, and, raising anchor, we got on our way down the broad river, in perfect weather.

The days that followed are like a good dream to me, for we came on all the way without challenge and with no adventure, even round Gaspé, to Louisburg, thirty-eight days after my escape from the fortress.

XXIII.

WITH WOLFE AT MONTMORENCI.

At Louisburg we found that Admiral Saunders and General Wolfe were gone to Quebec. They had passed us as we came down, for we had sailed inside some islands of the coast, getting shelter and better passage, and the fleet had, no doubt, passed outside. This was a blow to me, for I had hoped to be in time to join General Wolfe and proceed with him to Quebec, where my knowledge of the place should be of service to him. It was, however, no time for lament, and I set about to find my way back again. Our prisoners I handed over to the authorities.

19

The two Provincials decided to remain and take service under General Amherst; Mr. Stevens would join his own Rangers at once, but Clark would go back with me to have his hour with his hated foes.

I paid Mr. Stevens and the two Provincials for their shares in the schooner, and Clark and I manned her afresh, and prepared to return instantly to Quebec. From General Amherst I received correspondence to carry to General Wolfe and Admiral Saunders. Before I started back, I sent letters to Governor Dinwiddie and to Mr. (now Colonel) George Washington, but I had no sooner done so than I received others from them through General Amherst. They had been sent to him to convey to General Wolfe at Quebec, who was, in turn, to hand them to me, when, as was hoped, I should be released from captivity, if not already beyond the power of men to free me.

The letters from these friends almost atoned for my past sufferings, and I was ashamed that ever I had thought my countrymen forgot me in my misery; for this was the first matter I saw when I opened the Governor's letter:

By the House of Burgesses.

Resolved, That the sum of three hundred pounds be paid to Captain Robert Moray, in consideration of his services to the country and his singular sufferings in his confinement, as a hostage, in Quebec.

This, I learned, was one of three such resolutions.

But there were other matters in his letter which much amazed me. An attempt, the Governor said, had been made one dark night upon his strong-room, which would have succeeded but for the great bravery and loyalty of an old retainer. Two men were engaged in the attempt, one of whom was a Frenchman. Both men were masked, and, when set upon, fought with consummate bravery, and escaped. It was found the next day that the safe of my partner had also been rifled and all my papers stolen. There was no doubt in my mind what this meant. Doltaire, with some renegade Virginian who knew Williamsburg and myself, had made essay to get my papers. But they had failed in their designs, for all my valuable documents—and those desired by Doltaire among them—remained safe in the Governor's strong-room.

I got away again for Quebec five days after reaching Louisburg. We came along with good winds, having no check, though twice we sighted French sloops, which, however, seemed most concerned to leave us to ourselves. At last, with colours flying, we sighted Kamaraska Isles, which I saluted, remembering the Chevalier de la Darante; then Isle aux Coudres, below which we poor fugitives came so near disaster. Here we all felt new fervour, for the British flag flew from a staff on a lofty point, tents were pitched thereon in a pretty cluster, and, rounding a point, we came plump upon Admiral Durell's little fleet, which was here to bar the advance of French ships and to waylay stragglers.

On a blithe summer day we sighted, far off, the Isle of Orleans and the tall masts of two patrol ships of war, which in due time we passed, saluting, and ran abreast of the island in the North Channel. Coming up this passage, I could see on an eminence, far distant, the tower of the Château Alixe!

Presently there opened on our sight the great bluff at the Falls of Montmorenci, and, crowning it with tents and batteries, the camp of General Wolfe himself, and the good ship Centurion standing off like a sentinel at a point where the Basin, the river Montmorenci, and the North Channel seem to meet. To our left, across the shoals, was

Major Hardy's post, on the extreme eastern point of the Isle of Orleans; and again beyond that, in a straight line, Point Levis on the south shore, where Brigadier-General Monckton's camp was pitched; and farther on his batteries, from which shell and shot were poured into the town. How all had changed in the two months since I left there! Around the Seigneur Duvarney's manor, in the sweet village of Beauport, was encamped the French army, and redoubts and batteries were ranged where Alixe and I and her brother Juste had many a time walked in a sylvan quiet. Here, as it were, round the bent and broken sides of a bowl, war raged, and the centre was like some caldron, out of which imps of ships sprang to hand up fires of hell to the battalions on the ledges. Here swung Admiral Saunders's and Admiral Holmes's divisions, out of reach of the French batteries, yet able to menace and destroy and to feed the British camps with men and munitions. There were no French ships in sight—only two old hulks with guns in the mouth of the St. Charles River, to protect the road to the palace gate—that is, the gate at the Intendance.

It was all there before me, the investment of Quebec, for which I had prayed and waited seven long years.

All at once, on a lull in the fighting which had lasted twenty-four hours, the heavy batteries from the Levis shore opened upon the town, emptying therein the fatal fuel. Mixed feelings possessed me. I had at first listened to Clark's delighted imprecations and devilish praises with a feeling of brag almost akin to his own—that was the soldier and the Briton in me. But all at once the man, the lover, and the husband spoke: my wife was in that beleaguered town under that monstrous shower! She had said that she would never leave it till I came to fetch her. Yet might she not be dead—or, if living, immured in a convent? For I knew well that our marriage must be-

A PLAN of the RIVER St LAWRENCE, from the Falls of Montmorenci to Sillery; with the Operations of the SIEGE of QUEBEC.

Charleb...

R. St Charles or the little River

Larrey R.

N.D. de Anges

les Isleis

Place of Arms to Defend the Head of the Bridge

FRENCH ENCAMPMEN...

Hospital General

New Batt. of 3 Guns each

The Place where a Feint was made by the Boats of y. Fleet in the night whilst y. Troops landed at Sillery

3 Guns

Floating Batt of 12 Guns

3 Guns

Bridge

Batt. of 5 Guns to play against the Town

A SHOA'L Dry at Lo...

Sillery

1 Gun & 1 Battery 1 Mortar

UPPER TOWN

THE BAS...

Adml Sau...

French Wreck

LOWER TOWN

Rafts of Fire Ships

Admiral Holmes's Division

C. Diamond

Rafts of Fire

RIVER St LAWRENCE

Frigates

Pt Ley...

Redoubt

Road from St Nicholas

2 Guns

St Joseph...

Brigr. Genl. Monckton's Camp

References
1 Small Vessels with Artillery Stores _____
2 Sea Horse ----------
3 Leostoff . ----------
4 Squirrel . ----------
5 Transports with Troops ready for Landing, after the First Batallion had gained the Heights
6 Buoys that deceived the Enemy, and to which the Boats moor'd that protected the Fleet from y. Rafts of Fire

British Miles

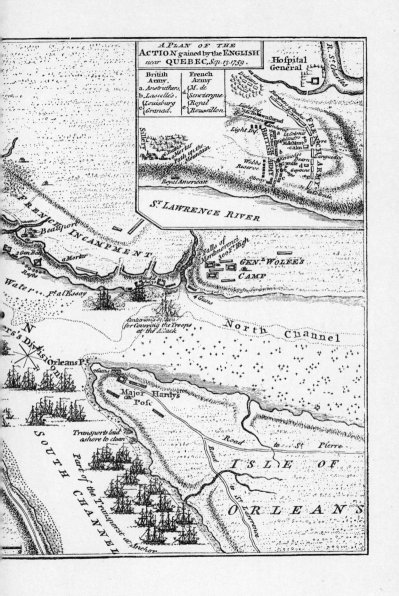

A PLAN OF THE
ACTION gained by the ENGLISH
near QUEBEC, Sep. 13. 1759.

British   French
Army   Army
a. Anstruthers.   M. de
b. Lascelle's.   d. Sentzergue
    Louisburg   Royal
c. Granad.   e. Roussillon

Hospital
General

R. St Charles

FRENCH ARMY

Light Inf.
Light Inf.
Light Bt.
BRITISH ARMY
Webb's
Reserve
Royal American

La Colonie
Montcalm
Kneelled
Bearn
Wolfe
Laguna

Hore
Languedoc
La Serie

Mortar Path on the Mountain
Sillery

St LAWRENCE RIVER

FRENCH INCAMPMENT

Beauport

3 Gun Bat.
a Mortar

Reft

Water··· Pt al Essay

Falls of Montmorenci
300 Feet High

GEN.L WOLFE'S CAMP

4 Guns

North Channel

···s's Division

N

Orleans Pt.

Centorions's Boat
for Covering the Troops
at the Attack

Major Hardy's
Post

Gun

Transports laid
ashore to clean

Road   to St Pierre

Road

ISLE OF

SOUTH CHANNEL

Part of the Transports at Anchor

ORLEANS

come known after I had escaped ; that she would not, for
her own good pride and womanhood, keep it secret then ;
that it would be proclaimed while yet Gabord and the
excellent chaplain were alive to attest all.

Summoned by the Centurion, we were passed on beyond
the eastern point of the Isle of Orleans to the admiral's
ship, which lay in the channel off the point, with battle-
ships in front and rear, and a line of frigates curving
towards the rocky peninsula of Quebec. Then came a
line of buoys beyond these, with manned boats moored
alongside to protect the fleet from fire rafts, which once
already the enemy had unavailingly sent down to ruin and
burn our fleet.

Admiral Saunders received me with great cordiality,
thanked me for the dispatches, heard with applause of my
adventures with the convoy, and at once, with dry humour,
said he would be glad, if General Wolfe consented, to
make my captured schooner one of his fleet. Later, when
her history and doings became known in the fleet, she was
at once called the Terror of France ; for she did a wild
thing or two before Quebec fell, though from first to last
she had but her six swivel guns, which I had taken from
the burned sloop. Clark had command of her.

From Admiral Saunders I learned that Bigot had recovered from his hurt, which had not been severe, and of
the death of Monsieur Cournal, who had ridden his horse
over the cliff in the dark. From the admiral I came to
General Wolfe at Montmorenci.

I shall never forget my first look at my hero, that
flaming, exhaustless spirit, in a body so *gauche* and so un-
shapely. When I was brought to him, he was standing
on a knoll alone, looking through a glass towards the batteries of Levis. The first thing that struck me, as he
lowered the glass and leaned against a gun, was the melancholy in the line of his figure. I never forget that, for

it seemed to me even then that, whatever glory there was for British arms ahead, there was tragedy for him. Yet, as he turned at the sound of our footsteps, I almost laughed; for his straight red hair, his face defying all regularity, with the nose thrust out like a wedge and the chin falling back from an affectionate sort of mouth, his tall, straggling frame and far from athletic shoulders, all challenged contrast with the compact, handsome, graciously shaped Montcalm. In Montcalm was all manner of things to charm—all save that which presently filled me with awe, and showed me wherein this sallow-featured, pain-racked Briton was greater than his rival beyond measure : in that searching, burning eye, which carried all the distinction and greatness denied him elsewhere. There resolution, courage, endurance, deep design, clear vision, dogged will, and heroism lived : a bright furnace of daring resolves, which gave England her sound desire.

An officer of his staff presented me. The General looked at me with piercing intelligence, and then, presently, his long hand made a swift motion of knowledge and greeting, and he said :

"Yes, yes, and you are welcome, Captain Moray. I have heard of you, of much to your credit. You were for years in durance there."

He pointed towards the town, where we could see the dome of the cathedral shine, and the leaping smoke and flame of the roaring batteries.

"Six years, your Excellency," said I.

"Papers of yours fell into General Braddock's hands, and they tried you for a spy—a curious case—a curious case ! Wherein were they wrong and you justified, and why was all exchange refused ?"

I told him the main, the bare facts, and how, to force certain papers from me, I had been hounded to the edge of the grave. He nodded, and seemed lost in study of the mud-flats at the Beauport shore, and presently took to beating his foot upon the ground. After a minute, as if he had come back from a distance, he said: "Yes, yes, broken articles. Few women have a sense of national honour, such as La Pompadour none! An interesting matter."

Then, after a moment: "You shall talk with our chief engineer; you know the town; you should be useful to me, Captain Moray. What do you suggest concerning this siege of ours?"

"Has any attack been made from above the town, your Excellency?"

He lifted his eyebrows. "Is it vulnerable from there? From Cap Rouge, you mean?"

"They have you at advantage everywhere, sir," I said. "A thousand men could keep the town, so long as this river, those mud-flats, and those high cliffs are there."

"But above the town——"

"Above the citadel there is a way—the only way: a feint from the basin here, a sham menace and attack, and the real action at the other door of the town."

"They will, of course, throw fresh strength and vigilance above, if our fleet run their batteries and attack there; the river at Cap Rouge is like this Montmorenci for defence." He shook his head. "There is no way, I fear."

"General," said I, "if you will take me into your service, and then give me leave to handle my little schooner in this basin and in the river above, I will prove that you may take your army into Quebec, by entering it myself, and returning with that as precious to me as the taking of Quebec to you."

He looked at me piercingly for a minute, then a sour sort of smile played at his lips. "A woman!" he said.

"Well, it were not the first time the love of a wench opened the gates to a nation's victory."

"Love of a wife, sir, should carry a man farther."

He turned on me a commanding look. "Speak plainly," said he. "If we are to use you, let us know you in all."

He waved farther back the officers with him.

"I have no other wish, your Excellency," I answered him. Then I told him briefly of the Seigneur Duvarney, of Alixe, and of Doltaire.

"Duvarney! Duvarney!" he said, and a light came into his look. Then he called an officer. "Was it not one Seigneur Duvarney who this morning prayed protection for his château on the Isle of Orleans?" he asked.

"Even so, your Excellency," was the reply; "and he said that if Captain Moray was with us, he would surely speak for the humanity and kindness he and his household had shown to British prisoners."

"You speak, then, for this gentleman?" he asked, with a dry sort of smile.

"With all my heart," I answered. "But why does he ask protection at this late day?"

"New orders are issued to lay waste the country; hitherto all property was safe," was the General's reply. 'See that the Seigneur Duvarney's suit is granted," he, added to his officer, "and say that it is by Captain Moray's intervention.—There is another matter of this kind to be arranged this noon," he continued: "an exchange of prisoners, among whom are some ladies of birth and breeding, captured but two days ago. A gentleman comes from General Montcalm directly upon the point. You might be useful herein," he added, "if you will come to my tent in an hour." He turned to go.

"And my ship, and permission to enter the town, your Excellency?" I asked.

"What do you call your—ship?" he asked a little grimly.

I told him how the sailors had already christened her. He smiled. "Then let her prove her title to Terror of France," he said, "by being pilot to the rest of our fleet up the river, and you, Captain Moray, be guide to a footing on those heights"—he pointed to the town. "Then this army and its General, and all England, please God, will thank you. Your craft shall have commission as a rover —but if she gets into trouble?"

"She will do as her owner has done these six years, your Excellency : she will fight her way out alone."

He gazed long at the town and at the Levis shore. "From above, then, there is a way?"

"For proof, if I come back alive——"

"For proof that you have been——" he answered meaningly, with an amused flash of his eyes, though at the very moment a spasm of pain crossed his face, for he was suffering from an incurable disease, and went about his great task in daily misery, yet cheerful and inspiring.

"For proof, my wife, sir!" said I.

He nodded, but his thoughts were diverted instantly, and he went from me at once abstracted. But again he came back. "If you return," said he, "you shall serve upon my staff. You will care to view our operations," he added, motioning towards the intrenchments at the river. Then he stepped quickly away, and I was taken by an officer to the river, and though my heart warmed within me to hear that an attack was presently to be made from the shore, not far distant from the falls, I felt that the attempt could not succeed : the French were too well intrenched.

At the close of an hour I returned to the General's tent. It was luncheon-time, and they were about to sit as I was announced. The General motioned me to a seat, and then again, as if on second thought, made as though to introduce me to some one who stood beside him. My amazement was unbounded when I saw, smiling cynically at me, Monsieur Doltaire!

He was the envoy from Quebec. I looked him in the eyes steadily for a moment, into malicious, unswerving eyes, as maliciously and unswervingly myself; and then we both bowed.

"Captain Moray and I have sat at meat together before," he said, with mannered coolness. "We have played host and guest also: but that was ere he won our hearts by bold, romantic feats. Still, I dared scarcely hope to meet him at this table."

"Which is sacred to good manners," said I, meaningly and coolly, for my anger and surprise were too deep for excitement.

I saw the General look at both of us keenly, then his marvellous eyes flashed intelligence, and a grim smile played at his lips a moment. After a little general conversation Doltaire addressed me:

"We are not yet so overwhelmed with war but your being here again will give a fillip to our gossip. It must seem sad to you—you were so long with us—you have broken bread with so many of us—to see us pelted so. Sometimes a dinner-table is disordered by a riotous shell."

He was bent on torturing me. It was not hard to do that, for how knew I what had happened! How was it he came back so soon from the Bastile? It was incredible. Perhaps he had never gone, in spite of all. After luncheon, the matter of exchange of prisoners was gone into, and one by one the names of the French prisoners in our hands—ladies and gentlemen apprehended at the château—were ticked off, and I knew them all save two. The General deferred to me several times as to the persons and positions of the captives, and asked my sugges-

tions.   Immediately I proposed Mr. Wainfleet, the chaplain, in exchange for a prisoner, though his name was not
on the list, but Doltaire shook his head in a blank sort
of way.

"Mr. Wainfleet!   Mr. Wainfleet!   There was no
such prisoner in the town," he said.

I insisted, but he stared at me inscrutably, and said
that he had no record of the man.   Then I spoke most
forcibly to the General, and said that Mr. Wainfleet should
be produced, or an account of him be given by the French
Governor.   Doltaire then said :

"I am only responsible for these names recorded.   Our
General trusts to your honour, and you to ours, Monsieur le Générale."

There was nothing more to say, and presently the ex-
changes were arranged, and, after compliments, Doltaire
took his leave.   I left the Governor also, and followed
Doltaire.   He turned to meet me.

"Captain Moray and I," he remarked to the officers
near, "are old—enemies; and there is a sad sweetness in
meetings like these.   May I——"

The officers drew away at a little distance before the
suggestion was really made, and we were left alone.   I
was in a white heat, but yet in fair control.

"You are surprised to see me here," he said.   "Did
you think the Bastile was for me?   Tut!   I had not got
out of the country when a packet came, bearing fresh
commands.   La Pompadour forgave me, and in the
King's name bade me return to New France, and in her
own she bade me get your papers, or hang you straight.
And—you will think it singular—if need be, I was to
relieve the Governor, and Bigot also, and work to save
New France with the excellent Marquis de Montcalm."
He laughed.   "You can see how absurd that is.   I have
held my peace, and I keep my commission in my pocket."

I looked at him amazed that he should tell me this. He read my look, and said :

"Yes, you are my confidant in this. I do not fear you. Your enemy is bound in honour, your friend may seek to serve himself." Again he laughed. "As if I, Tinoir Doltaire—note the agreeable combination of peasant and gentleman in my name—who held his hand from ambition for large things in France, should stake a lifetime on this foolish hazard ! When I play, Captain Moray, it is for things large and vital. Else I remain the idler, the courtier—the son of the King."

"Yet you lend your vast talent, the genius of those unknown possibilities, to this, monsieur—this little business of exchange of prisoners," I retorted ironically.

"That is my whim—a social courtesy."

"You said you knew nothing of the chaplain," I broke out.

"Not so. I said he was on no record given me. Officially I know nothing of him."

"Come," said I, "you know well how I am concerned for him. You quibble ; you lied to our General."

A wicked light shone in his eyes. "I choose to pass that by, for the moment," said he. "I am sorry you forget yourself ; it were better for you and me to be courteous till our hour of reckoning. Shall we not meet to purpose some day ? " he said, with a sweet hatred in his tone.

"With all my heart."

"But where ? "

"In yonder town," said I, pointing.

He laughed provokingly. "You are melodramatic," he rejoined. "I could hold that town with one thousand men against all your army and five times your fleet."

"You have ever talked and nothing done," said I. "Will you tell me the truth concerning the chaplain ? "

" Yes, in private the truth you shall hear," he said. " The man is dead."

" If you speak true, he was murdered," I broke out. " You know well why ! "

" No, no," he answered. " He was put in prison, escaped, made for the river, was pursued, fought, and was killed. So much he got for serving you ! "

" Will you answer me one question ? " said I. " Is my wife well ? Is she safe ? She is there set among villainies."

" Your wife ? " he answered, sneering. " If you mean Mademoiselle Duvarney, she is not there." Then he added solemnly and slowly : " She is in no fear of your batteries now—she is beyond them. When she was there, she was not child enough to think that foolish game with the vanished chaplain was a marriage. Did you think to gull a lady so beyond the minute's wildness ? She is not there," he added again in a low voice.

" She is dead ? " I gasped. " My wife is dead ? "

" Enough of that," he answered with cold fierceness. " The lady saw the folly of it all, before she had done with the world. You—you, monsieur ! It was but the pity of her gentle heart, of a romantic nature. You— you blundering alien, spy, and seducer ! "

With a gasp of anger I struck him in the face, and whipped out my sword. But the officers near came instantly between us, and I could see that they thought me gross and ill-mannered, to do this thing before the General's tent, and to an envoy.

Doltaire stood still a moment. Then presently he wiped a little blood from his mouth, and said :

" Messieurs, Captain Moray's anger was justified ; and for the blow, he will justify that in some happier time— for me. He said that I had lied, and I proved him wrong. I called him a spy and a seducer—he sought

to shame, he covered with sorrow, one of the noblest
families of New France—and he has yet to prove me
wrong. As envoy I may not fight him now, but I may
tell you that I have every cue to send him to hell one
day. He will do me the credit to say that it is not
cowardice that stays me."

"If no coward in the way of fighting, coward in all
other things," I retorted instantly.

"Well, well, as you may think." He turned to go.
"We will meet there, then?" he said, pointing to the
town. "And when?"

"To-morrow," said I.

He shrugged his shoulder as to a boyish petulance,
for he thought it an idle boast. "To-morrow? Then
come and pray with me in the cathedral, and after that
we will cast up accounts—to-morrow," he said, with a
poignant and exultant malice. A moment afterwards he
was gone, and I was left alone.

Presently I saw a boat shoot out from the shore below, and he was in it. Seeing me, he waved a hand in
an ironical way. I paced up and down, sick and distracted, for half an hour or more. I knew not whether
he lied concerning Alixe, but my heart was wrung with
misery, for indeed he spoke with an air of truth.

Dead! dead! dead! "In no fear of your batteries
now," he had said. "Done with the world!" he had
said. What else could it mean? Yet, the more I
thought, there came a feeling that somehow I had been
tricked. "Done with the world!" Ay, a nunnery—was
that it? But then, "In no fear of your batteries now"—
that, what did that mean but death?

At this distressful moment a message came from the
General, and I went to his tent, trying to calm myself,
but overcome with apprehension. I was kept another
half hour waiting, and then, coming in to him, he ques-

tioned me closely for a little time about Doltaire, and I told him the whole story briefly. Presently his secretary brought me the commission for my appointment to special service on the General's own staff.

"Your first duty," said his Excellency, "will be to—reconnoitre ; and if you come back safe, we will talk further."

While he was speaking I kept looking at the list or prisoners which still lay upon his table. It ran thus :

> Monsieur and Madame Joubert.
> Monsieur and Madame Carçanal.
> Madame Rousillon.
> Madame Champigny.
> Monsieur Pipon.
> Mademoiselle La Rose.
> L'Abbé Durand.
> Monsieur Halboir.
> La Sœur Angélique.
> La Sœur Séraphine.

I know not why it was, but the last three names held my eyes. Each of the other names I knew, and their owners also. When I looked close, I saw that where "La Sœur Angélique" now was another name had been written and then erased. I saw also that the writing was recent. Again, where "Halboir" was written there had been another name, and the same process of erasure and substitution had been made. It was not so with "La Sœur Séraphine." I said to the General at once, "Your Excellency, it is possible you have been tricked." I pointed out what I had noted. He nodded.

"Will you let me go, sir ?" said I. "Will you let me see this exchange ?"

"I fear you will be too late," he answered. "It is not a vital matter, I fancy."

"Perhaps to me most vital," said I, and I explained my fears.

"Then go, go," he said kindly. He quickly gave directions to have me carried to Admiral Saunders's ship, where the exchange was to be effected, and at the same time I was handed a general passport.

In a few moments we were hard on our way. Now the batteries were silent. By the General's orders, the bombardment ceased while the exchange was being effected, and the French batteries also stopped firing. A sudden quietness seemed to settle on land and sea, and there was only heard, now and then, the note of a bugle from a ship of war. The water in the basin was moveless, and the air was calm and quiet. This heraldry of war was all unnatural in the golden weather and sweet-smelling land.

I urged the rowers to their task, and we flew on. We passed another boat loaded with men, singing boisterously a disorderly sort of song, called "Hot Stuff," set to the air "Lilies of France." It was out of touch with the general quiet :

> "When the gay Forty-Seventh is dashing ashore,
>   While bullets are whistling and cannons do roar,
>   Says Montcalm, ' Those are Shirleys—I know the lapels.'
>   ' You lie,' says Ned Botwood, ' we swipe for Lascelles !
>   Though our clothing is changed, and we scout powder-puff,
>   Here's at you, ye swabs—here's give you Hot Stuff !' "

While yet we were about two miles away, I saw a boat put out from the admiral's ship, then, at the same moment, one from the Lower Town, and they drew towards each other. I urged my men to their task, and as we were passing some of Admiral Saunders's ships, their sailors cheered us. Then came a silence, and it seemed to me that all our army and fleet, and that at Beauport, and the garrison of Quebec, were watching us; for the ramparts and shore were crowded. We drove on at an angle, to intercept the boat that left the admiral's ship before it reached the town.

War leaned upon its arms and watched a strange duel. There was no authority in any one's hands save my own to stop the boat, and the two armies must avoid firing, for the people of both nations were here in this space between—ladies and gentlemen in the French boat going to the town, Englishmen and a poor woman or two coming to our own fleet.

My men strained every muscle, but the pace was impossible—it could not last; and the rowers in the French boat hung over their oars also with enthusiasm. With the glass of the officer near me—Kingdon of Anstruther's Regiment—I could now see Doltaire standing erect in the boat, urging the boatmen on.

All round that basin, on shore and cliff and mountains, thousands of veteran fighters—Fraser's, Otway's, Townsend's, Murray's; and on the other side the splendid soldiers of La Sarre, Languedoc, Béarn, and Guienne —watched in silence. Well they might, for in this *entr'acte* was the little weapon forged which opened the door of New France to England's glory. So may the little talent or opportunity make possible the genius of the great.

The pain of this suspense grew so, that I longed for some sound to break the stillness; but there was nothing for minute after minute. Then, at last, on the halcyon air of the summer day floated the Angelus from the cathedral tower. Only a moment, in which one could feel, and see also, the French army praying, then came from the ramparts the sharp, inspiring roll of a drum, and presently all was still again. Nearer and nearer the boat of prisoners approached the stone steps of the landing, and we were several hundred yards behind.

I motioned to Doltaire to stop, but he made no sign. I saw the cloaked figures of the nuns near him, and I strained my eyes, but I could not note their faces. My

20

men worked on ardently, and presently we gained. But
I saw that it was impossible to reach them before they set
foot on shore. Now their boat came to the steps, and one
by one they hastily got out. Then I called to Doltaire to
stop. The air was still, and my voice carried distinctly.
Suddenly one of the cloaked figures sprang towards the
steps with arms outstretched, calling aloud, " Robert!
Robert!" After a moment, " Robert, my husband!"
rang out again, and then a young officer and the other
nun took her by the arm to force her away. At the sharp
instigation of Doltaire, some companies of marines filed
in upon the place where they had stood, leveled their muskets on us, and hid my beloved wife from my view. I
recognized the young officer who had put a hand upon
Alixe. It was her brother Juste.

" Alixe! Alixe!" I called, as my boat still came on.

" Save me, Robert!" came the anguished reply, a faint
but searching sound, and then no more.

Misery and mystery were in my heart all at once. Doltaire had tricked me. " Those batteries can not harm her
now!" Yes, yes, they could not while she was a prisoner
in our camp. " Done with the world!" Truly, when
wearing the garb of the Sister Angélique. But why
that garb? I swore that I would be within that town
by the morrow, that I would fetch my wife into safety,
out from the damnable arts and devices of Master Devil
Doltaire, as Gabord had called him.

The captain of the marines warned us that another
boat's length would fetch upon us the fire of his men.
There was nothing to do but to turn back, while from the
shore I was reviled by soldiers and by the rabble. My
marriage with Alixe had been made a national matter—
of race and religion. So, as my men rowed back towards
our fleet, I faced my enemies, and looked towards them
without moving. I was grim enough that moment, God

knows; I felt turned to stone. I did not stir when—ineffaceable brutality—the batteries on the heights began to play upon us, the shot falling round us, and passing over our heads, and musket-firing followed.

"Damned villains! Faithless brutes!" cried Kingdon beside me. I did not speak a word, but stood there defiant, as when we first had turned back. Now, sharply, angrily, from all our batteries, there came reply to the French; and as we came on, with only one man wounded and one oar broken, our whole fleet cheered us. I steered straight for the Terror of France, and there Clark and I, he swearing violently, laid plans.

XXIV.

THE SACRED COUNTERSIGN.

THAT night, at nine o'clock, the Terror of France, catching the flow of the tide, with one sail set and a gentle wind, left the fleet and came slowly up the river, under the batteries of the town. In the gloom we passed lazily on with the flow of the tide, unquestioned, soon leaving the citadel behind, and ere long arrived safely at that point called Anse du Foulon, above which Sillery stood. The shore could not be seen distinctly, but I knew by a perfect instinct the cleft in the hillside where was the path leading up the mountain. I bade Clark come up the river again two nights hence to watch for my signal, which was there agreed upon. If I did not come, then, with General Wolfe's consent, he must show the General this path up the mountain. He swore that all should be as I wished; and indeed you would have thought that he and his Terror of France were to level Quebec to the water's edge.

I stole softly to the shore in a boat, which I drew up among the bushes, hiding it as well as I could in the dark, and then, feeling for my pistols and my knife, I crept upward, coming presently to the passage in the mountain. I toiled on to the summit without a sound of alarm from above. Pushing forward, a light flashed from the windmill, and a man, and then two men, appeared in the open door. One of them was Captain Lancy, whom I had very good reason to remember. The last time I saw him was that famous morning when he would have had me shot five minutes before the appointed hour, rather than endure the cold and be kept from his breakfast. I itched to call him to account then and there, but that would have been foolish play. I was outside the belt of light falling from the door, and stealing round I came near to the windmill on the town side. I was not surprised to see such poor watch kept. Above the town, up to this time, the guard was of a perfunctory sort, for the great cliffs were thought impregnable; and even if surmounted, there was still the walled town to take, surrounded by the St. Lawrence, the St. Charles, and these massive bulwarks.

Presently Lancy stepped out into the light, and said, with a hoarse laugh, " Blood of Peter, it was a sight to-day! She has a constant fancy for the English filibuster. ' Robert! my husband !' she bleated like a pretty lamb, and Doltaire grinned at her."

" But Doltaire will have her yet."

" He has her pinched like a mouse in a weasel's teeth."

" My faith, mademoiselle has no sweet road to travel since her mother died," was the careless reply.

I almost cried out. Here was a blow which staggered me. Her mother dead !

Presently the scoffer continued : " The Duvarneys would remain in the city, and on that very night, as they

The Old Gates of Quebec.

sit at dinner, a shell disturbs them, a splinter strikes madame, and two days later she is carried to her grave."

They linked arms and walked on.

It was a dangerous business I was set on, for I was sure that I would be hung without shrift if captured. As I discovered afterwards, I had been proclaimed, and it was enjoined on all Frenchmen and true Catholics to kill me if the chance showed.

Only two things could I depend on : Voban, and my disguise, which was very good. From the Terror of France I had got a peasant's dress, and by rubbing my hands and face with the stain of butternut, cutting again my new-grown beard, and wearing a wig, I was well guarded against discovery.

How to get into the city was the question. By the St. Charles River and the Palace Gate, and by the St. Louis Gate, not far from the citadel, were the only ways, and both were difficult. I had, however, two or three plans, and these I chewed as I travelled across Maître Abraham's fields, and came to the main road from Sillery to the town.

Soon I heard the noise of clattering hoofs, and jointly with this I saw a figure rise up not far ahead of me, as if waiting for the coming horseman. I drew back. The horseman passed me, and, as he came on slowly, I saw the figure spring suddenly from the roadside and make a stroke at the horseman. In a moment they were a rolling mass upon the ground, while the horse trotted down the road a little and stood still. I never knew the cause of that encounter—robbery, or private hate, or paid assault ; but there was scarcely a sound as the two men struggled. Presently there was groaning, and both lay still. I hurried to them, and found one dead, and the other dying, and dagger wounds in both ; for the assault had been at such close quarters that the horseman had had no chance to use a pistol.

My plans were changed on the instant. I drew the military coat, boots, and cap off the horseman, and put them on myself; and thrusting my hand into his waist-coat—for he looked like a courier—I found a packet. This I put into my pocket, and then, making for the horse which stood quiet in the road, I mounted it and rode on towards the town. Striking a light, I found that the packet was addressed to the Governor. A serious thought disturbed me: I could not get into the town through the gates without the countersign. I rode on, anxious and perplexed.

Presently a thought pulled me up. The courier was insensible when I left him, and he was the only person who could help me in this. I reproached myself for leaving him while he was still alive. "Poor devil," thought I to myself, "there is some one whom his death will hurt. He must not die alone. He was no enemy of mine." I went back, and, getting from the horse, stooped to him, lifted up his head, and found that he was not dead. I spoke in his ear. He moaned, and his eyes opened.

"What is your name?" said I.

"Jean—Labrouk," he whispered.

Now I remembered him. He was the soldier whom Gabord had sent as messenger to Voban the night I was first taken to the citadel.

"Shall I carry word for you to any one?" asked I.

There was a slight pause; then he said, "Tell my—Babette—Jacques Dobrotte owes me ten francs—and—a leg—of mutton. Tell—my Babette—to give my coat of beaver fur to Gabord the soldier. Tell " . . . he sank back, but raised himself, and continued: "Tell my Babette I weep with her. . . . Ah, *mon grand homme de Calvaire—bon soir!*" He sank back again, but I roused him with one question more, vital to me. I must have the countersign.

"Labrouk! Labrouk!" said I sharply.

He opened his dull, glazed eyes.

" *Qui va là?* " said I, and I waited anxiously.

Thought seemed to rally in him, and, staring—alas! how helpless and how sad: that look of a man brought back for an instant from the Shadows!—his lips moved.

"France," was the whispered reply.

"Advance and give the countersign!" I urged.

"Jésu——" he murmured faintly. I drew from my breast the cross that Mathilde had given me, and pressed it to his lips. He sighed softly, lifted his hand to it, and then fell back, never to speak again.

After covering his face and decently laying the body out, I mounted the horse again. Glancing up, I saw that this bad business had befallen not twenty feet from a high Calvary at the roadside.

I was in a painful quandary. Did Labrouk mean that the countersign was " *Jésu,*" or was that word the broken prayer of his soul as it hurried forth? So strange a countersign I had never heard, and yet it might be used in this Catholic country. This day might be some great feast of the Church—possibly that of the naming of Christ (which was the case, as I afterwards knew). I rode on, tossed about in my mind. So much hung on this. If I could not give the countersign, I should have to fight my way back again the road I came. But I must try my luck. So I went on, beating up my heart to confidence; and now I came to the St. Louis Gate. A tiny fire was burning near, and two sentinels stepped forward as I rode boldly on the entrance.

" *Qui va là?* " was the sharp call.

"France," was my reply, in a voice as like a peasant's as possible.

"Advance and give the countersign," came the demand.

Another voice called from the darkness of the wall: "Come and drink, comrade; I've a brother with Bougainville."

"*Jésu*," said I to the sentinel, answering his demand for the countersign, and I spurred on my horse idly, though my heart was thumping hard, for there were several sturdy fellows lying beyond the dull handful of fire.

Instantly the sentinel's hand came to my bridle-rein. "*Halt!*" roared he.

Surely some good spirit was with me then to prompt me, for, with a careless laugh, as though I had not before finished the countersign, "*Christ*," I added—"*Jésu Christ!*"

With an oath the soldier let go the bridle-rein, the other opened the gates, and I passed through. I heard the first fellow swearing roundly to the others that he would "send yon courier to fires of hell if he played with him again so."

The gates closed behind me, and I was in the town which had seen the worst days and best moments of my life. I rode along at a trot, and once again beyond the citadel was summoned by a sentinel. Safely passed on, I came down towards the Château St. Louis. I rode boldly up to the great entrance door, and handed the packet to the sentinel.

"From whom?" he asked.

"Look in the corner," said I. "And what business is't of yours?"

"There is no word in the corner," answered he doggedly. "Is't from Monsieur le Générale at Cap Rouge?"

"Bah! Did you think it was from an English wolf?" I asked.

His dull face broke a little. "Is Jean Labrouk with Bougainville yet?"

"He's done with Bougainville; he's dead," I answered.

"Dead! dead!" said he, a sort of grin playing on his face.

I made a shot at a venture. "But you're to pay his wife Babette the ten francs and the leg of mutton in twenty-four hours, or his ghost will follow you. Swallow that, pudding-head! And see you pay it, or every man in our company swears to break a score of shingles on your bare back."

"I'll pay, I'll pay," he said, and he began to tremble.

"Where shall I find Babette?" asked I. "I come from the Isle aux Coudres; I know not this rambling town."

"A little house hugging the cathedral rear," he answered. "Babette sweeps out the vestry, and fetches water for the priests."

"Good," said I. "Take that to the Governor at once, and send the corporal of the guard to have this horse fed and cared for, as he's to carry back the Governor's messenger. I've further business for the General in the town. And tell your captain of the guard to send and pick up two dead men in the highway, just against the first Calvary beyond the town."

He did my bidding, and I dismounted, and was about to get away, when I saw the Chevalier de la Darante and the Intendant appear at the door. They paused upon the steps. The Chevalier was speaking most earnestly:

"To a nunnery—a piteous shame! it should not be, your Excellency."

"To decline upon Monsieur Doltaire, then?" asked Bigot, with a sneer.

"Your Excellency believes in no woman," responded the Chevalier stiffly.

"Ah yes, in one!" was the cynical reply.

"Is it possible? And she remains a friend of your Excellency!" came back in irony.

"The very best; she finds me unendurable."

"Philosophy shirks the solving of that problem, your Excellency," was the cold reply.

"No, it is easy. The woman to be trusted is she who never trusts."

"The paragon—or prodigy—who is she?"

"Even Madame Jamond."

"She danced for you once, your Excellency, they tell me."

"She was a devil that night; she drove us mad."

So Doltaire had not given up the secret of that affair! There was silence for a moment, and then the Chevalier said, "Her father will not let her go to a nunnery—no, no. Why should he yield to the Church in this?"

Bigot shrugged a shoulder. "Not even to hide—shame?"

"Liar—ruffian!" said I through my teeth. The Chevalier answered for me:

"I would stake my life on her truth and purity."

"You forget the mock marriage, dear Chevalier."

"It was after the manner of his creed and people."

"It was after a manner we all have used at times."

"Speak for yourself, your Excellency," was the austere reply. Nevertheless, I could see that the Chevalier was much troubled.

"She forgot race, religion, people—all, to spend still hours with a foreign spy in prison," urged Bigot, with damnable point and suggestion.

"Hush, sir!" said the Chevalier. "She is a girl once much beloved and ever admired among us. Let not your rancour against the man be spent upon the maid. Nay, more, why should you hate the man so? It is said, your Excellency, that this Moray did not fire the shot that wounded you, but one who has less reason to love you."

Bigot smiled wickedly, but said nothing.

The Chevalier laid a hand on Bigot's arm. "Will you not oppose the Governor and the bishop? Her fate is sad enough."

" I will not lift a finger. There are weightier matters. Let Doltaire, the idler, the Don Amato, the hunter of that fawn, save her from the holy ambush. Tut, tut, Chevalier. Let her go. Your nephew is to marry her sister; let her be swallowed up—a shame behind the veil, the sweet litany of the cloister."

The Chevalier's voice set hard as he said in quick reply, " My family honour, François Bigot, needs no screen. And if you doubt that, I will give you argument at your pleasure." So saying, he turned and went back into the château.

Thus the honest Chevalier kept his word, given to me when I released him from serving me on the St. Lawrence.

Bigot came down the steps, smiling detestably, and passed me with no more than a quick look. I made my way cautiously through the streets towards the cathedral, for I owed a duty to the poor soldier who had died in my arms, through whose death I had been able to enter the town.

Disarray and ruin met my sight at every hand. Shot and shell had made wicked havoc. Houses where, as a hostage, I had dined, were battered and broken; public buildings were shapeless masses, and dogs and thieves prowled among the ruins. Drunken soldiers staggered past me; hags begged for sous or bread at corners; and devoted priests and long-robed Recollet monks, cowled and alert, hurried past, silent, and worn with labours, watchings, and prayers. A number of officers in white uniforms rode by, going towards the château, and a company of *coureurs de bois* came up from Mountain Street, singing :

> " *Giron, giran ! le canon grand—*
> *Commencez-vous, commencez-vous ! "*

Here and there were fires lighted in the streets, though it was not cold, and beside them peasants and soldiers drank, and quarrelled over food—for starvation was abroad in the land.

By one of these fires, in a secluded street—for I had come a roundabout way—were a number of soldiers of Languedoc's regiment (I knew them by their trick of headgear and their stoutness), and with them reckless girls, who, in their abandonment, seemed to me like those revellers in Herculaneum who danced their way into the Cimmerian darkness. I had no thought of staying there to moralize upon the theme ; but, as I looked, a figure came out of the dusk ahead and moved swiftly towards me.

It was Mathilde. She seemed bent on some errand, but the revellers at the fire caught her attention, and she suddenly swerved towards them and came into the dull glow, her great black eyes shining with bewildered brilliancy and vague keenness, her long fingers reaching out with a sort of chafing motion. She did not speak till she was among them. I drew into the shade of a broken wall, and watched. She looked all round the circle, and then, without a word, took an iron crucifix which hung upon her breast and silently lifted it above their heads for a moment. I myself felt a kind of thrill go through me, for her wild beauty was almost tragical. Her madness was not grotesque, but solemn and dramatic. There was something terribly deliberate in her strangeness ; it was full of awe to the beholder, more searching and pitiful than melancholy.

Coarse hands fell away from wanton waists; ribaldry hesitated; hot faces drew apart; and all at once a girl with a crackling laugh threw a tin cup of liquor into the fire. Even as she did it, a wretched dwarf sprang into the circle without a word, and, snatching the cup out of the flames, jumped back again into the darkness, peering into it with a hollow laugh. A soldier raised a heavy stick to throw at him; but the girl caught him by the arms, and said, with a hoarse pathos, "My God, no, Alphonse! It is my brother!"

Here Mathilde, still holding out the cross, said in a loud whisper, "'Sh, 'sh! My children, go not to the palace, for there is François Bigot, and he has a devil. But if you have no cottage, I will give you a home. I know the way to it up in the hills. Poor children, see, I will make you happy."

She took a dozen little wooden crosses from her girdle, and, stepping round the circle, gave each person one. No soldier refused, save a young militiaman; and when, with a sneering laugh, he threw his into the fire, she stooped over him and said, "Poor boy! poor boy!"

She put her fingers on her lips and whispered, "*Beati immaculati—miserere mei, Deus*," stray phrases gathered from the liturgy, pregnant to her brain, order and truth flashing out of wandering and fantasy. No one of the girls refused, but sat there, some laughing nervously, some silent; for this mad maid had come to be surrounded with a superstitious reverence in the eyes of the common people. It was said she had a home in the hills somewhere, to which she disappeared for days and weeks, and came back hung about the girdle with crosses; and it was also said that her red robe never became frayed, shabby, or disordered.

Suddenly she turned and left them. I let her pass unchecked, and went on towards the cathedral, humming an old French chanson. I did this because now and then I met soldiers and patrols, and my free and careless manner disarmed notice. Once or twice drunken soldiers stopped me and threw their arms about me, saluting me on the cheeks *à la mode*, asking themselves to drink with me. Getting free of them, I came on my way, and was glad to reach the cathedral unchallenged. Here and there a broken buttress or a splintered wall told where our guns had played upon it, but inside I could hear an organ playing and a *Miserere* being chanted. I went round to its rear, and there I saw the little house described by the sentinel at the château. Coming to the door, I knocked, and it was opened at once by a warm-faced woman of thirty or so, who instantly brightened on seeing me. "Ah, you come from Cap Rouge, m'sieu'," she said, looking at my clothes—her own husband's, though she knew it not.

"I come from Jean," said I, and stepped inside.

She shut the door, and then I saw sitting in a corner, by a lighted table, an old man, bowed and shrunken, white hair and white beard falling all about him, and nothing of his features to be seen save high cheek-bones and two hawklike eyes which peered up at me.

"So, so, from Jean," he said in a high, piping voice. "Jean's a pretty boy—ay, ay, Jean's like his father, but neither with a foot like mine—a foot for the court, said Frontenac to me—yes, yes, I knew the great Frontenac——"

The wife interrupted his gossip. "What news from Jean?" said she. "He hoped to come one day this week."

"He says," responded I gently, "that Jacques Dobrotte owes you ten francs and a leg of mutton, and that you are to give his great beaver coat to Gabord the soldier."

" Ay, ay, Gabord the soldier, he that the English spy near sent to heaven," quavered the old man.

The bitter truth was slowly dawning upon the wife. She was repeating my words in a whisper, as if to grasp their full meaning.

" He said also," I continued, " ' Tell Babette I weep with her.' "

She was very still and dazed ; her fingers went to her white lips, and stayed there for a moment. I never saw such a numb misery in any face.

" And, last of all, he said, ' *Ah, mon grand homme de Calvaire—bon soir!* ' "

She turned round and went and sat down beside the old man, looked into his face for a minute silently, and then said, " Grandfather, Jean is dead ; our Jean is dead ! "

The old man peered at her for a moment, then broke into a strange laugh, which had in it the reflection of a distant misery, and said, " Our little Jean, our little Jean Labrouk ! Ha! ha! There was Villon, Marmon, Gabriel, and Gouloir, and all their sons ; and they all said the same at the last, ' *Mon grand homme—de Calvaire— bon soir!* ' Then there was little Jean, the pretty little Jean. He could not row a boat, but he could ride a horse, and he had an eye like me. Ha! ha! I have seen them all say good-night. Good-morning, my children, I will say one day, and I will give them all the news, and I well tell them all I have done these hundred years. Ha, ha, ha !——"

The wife put her fingers on his lips, and, turning to me, said with a peculiar sorrow, " Will they fetch him to me ? "

I assured her that they would.

The old man fixed his eyes on me most strangely, and then, stretching out his finger and leaning forward, he said, with a voice of senile wildness, " Ah, ah, the coat of our little Jean ! "

I stood there like any criminal caught in his shameful act. Though I had not forgotten that I wore the dead man's clothes, I could not think that they would be recognized, for they seemed like others of the French army —white, with violet facings. I can not tell to this day what it was that enabled them to detect the coat; but there I stood condemned before them.

The wife sprang to her feet, came to me with a set face, and stared stonily at the coat for an instant. Then, with a cry of alarm, she made for the door ; but I stepped quickly before her, and bade her wait till she heard what I had to say. Like lightning it all went through my brain. I was ruined if she gave an alarm : all Quebec would be at my heels, and my purposes would be defeated. There was but one thing to do—tell her the whole truth, and trust her ; for I had at least done fairly by her and by the dead man.

So I told them how Jean Labrouk had met his death ; told them who I was and why I was in Quebec—how Jean died in my arms ; and, taking from my breast the cross that Mathilde had given me, I swore by it that every word which I said was true. The wife scarcely stirred while I spoke, but with wide dry eyes, and hands clasping and unclasping, heard me through. I told her how I might have left Jean to die without a sign or message to them, how I had put the cross to his lips as he went forth, and how by coming here at all I placed my safety in her hands, and now, by telling my story, my life itself.

It was a daring and a difficult task. When I had finished, both sat silent for a moment, and then the old man said, " Ay, ay, Jean's father and his uncle Marmon were killed a-horseback, and by the knife. Ay, ay, it is our way. Jean was good company—none better, mass over on a Sunday. Come, we will light candles for Jean, and comb his hair back sweet, and masses shall be said, and——"

Again the woman interrupted, quieting him. Then she turned to me, and I awaited her words with a desperate sort of courage.

"I believe you," she said. "I remember you now. My sister was the wife of your keeper at the common jail. You shall be safe. Alas! my Jean might have died without a word to me—all alone in the night. *Merci mille fois, monsieur!*" Then she rocked a little to and fro, and the old man looked at her like a curious child. At last, "I must go to him," she said. "My poor Jean must be brought home."

I told her I had already left word concerning the body at headquarters. She thanked me again. Overcome as she was, she went and brought me a peasant's hat and coat. Such trust and kindness touched me. Trembling, she took from me the coat and hat I had worn, and she put her hands before her eyes when she saw a little spot of blood upon the flap of a pocket. The old man reached out his hands, and, taking them, he held them on his knees, whispering to himself.

"You will be safe here," the wife said to me. "The loft above is small, but it will hide you, if you have no better place."

I was thankful that I had told her all the truth. I should be snug here, awaiting the affair in the cathedral on the morrow. There was Voban, but I knew not of him, or whether he was open to aid or shelter me. His own safety had been long in peril; he might be dead, for all I knew. I thanked the poor woman warmly, and then asked her if the old man might not betray me to strangers. She bade me leave all that to her—that I should be safe for a while, at least.

21

Soon afterwards I went abroad, and made my way by
a devious route to Voban's house. As I passed, I could
see the lights of our fleet in the Basin, and the camp-fires
of our army on the Levis shore, on the Isle of Orleans,
and even at Montmorenci, and the myriad lights in the
French encampment at Beauport. How impossible it all
looked—to unseat from this high rock the Empire of
France! And how hard it would be to get out of this
same city with Alixe!

Voban's house stood amid a mass of ruins, itself
broken a little, but still sound enough to live in. There
was no light. I clambered over the *débris*, made my way
to his bedroom window, and tapped on the shutter.
There was no response. I tried to open it, but it would
not stir. So I thrust beneath it, on the chance of his
finding it if he opened the casement in the morning, a
little piece of paper, with one word upon it—the name of
his brother. He knew my handwriting, and he would
guess where to-morrow would find me, for I had also
hastily drawn upon the paper the entrance of the cathedral.

I went back to the little house by the cathedral, and
was admitted by the stricken wife. The old man was
abed. I climbed up to the small loft, and lay wide-awake
for hours. At last came the sounds that I had waited
for, and presently I knew by the tramp beneath, and by
low laments coming through the floor, that a wife was
mourning over the dead body of her husband. I lay long
and listened to the varying sounds, but at last all became
still, and I fell asleep.

XXV.

IN THE CATHEDRAL.

I AWOKE with the dawn, and, dressing, looked out of the window, seeing the brindled light spread over the battered roofs and ruins of the Lower Town. A bell was calling to prayers in the battered Jesuit College not far away, and bugle-calls told of the stirring garrison. Soldiers and stragglers passed down the streets near by and a few starved peasants crept about the cathedral with downcast eyes, eager for crumbs that a well-fed soldier might cast aside. Yet I knew that in the Intendant's palace and among the officers of the army there was abundance, with revelry and dissipation.

Presently I drew to the trap-door of my loft, and, raising it gently, came down the ladder to the little hallway, and softly opened the door of the room where Labrouk's body lay. Candles were burning at his head and his feet, and two peasants sat dozing in chairs near by. I could see Labrouk's face plainly in the flickering light : a rough, wholesome face it was, refined by death, yet unshaven and unkempt, too. Here was work for Voban's shears and razor. Presently there was a footstep behind me, and, turning, I saw in the half-light the widowed wife.

" Madame," said I in a whisper, " I too weep with you. I pray for as true an end for myself."

" He was of the true faith, thank the good God," she said sincerely. She passed into the room, and the two watchers, after taking refreshment, left the house. Suddenly she hastened to the door, called one back, and, pointing to the body, whispered something. The peasant nodded and turned away. She came back into the room, stood looking at the face of the dead man for a moment, and bent over and kissed the crucifix clasped in the cold hands. Then she stepped about the room, moving a chair and sweeping up a speck of dust in a mechanical way. Presently, as if she again remembered me, she asked me to enter the room. Then she bolted the outer door of the house. I stood looking at the body of her husband, and said, " Were it not well to have Voban the barber ? "

" I have sent for him and for Gabord," she replied. " Gabord was Jean's good friend. He is with General Montcalm. The Governor put him in prison because of the marriage of Mademoiselle Duvarney, but Monsieur Doltaire set him free, and now he serves General Montcalm.

" I have work in the cathedral," continued the poor woman, " and I shall go to it this morning as I have always gone. There is a little unused closet in a gallery where you may hide, and still see all that happens. It is your last look at the lady, and I will give it to you, as you gave me to know of my Jean."

" My last look ? " I asked eagerly.

" She goes into the nunnery to-morrow, they say," was the reply. " Her marriage is to be set aside by the bishop to-day—in the cathedral. This is her last night to live as such as I—but no, she will be happier so."

" Madame," said I, " I am a heretic, but I listened when your husband said, ' *Mon grand homme de Calvaire, bon soir!* ' Was the cross less a cross because a heretic put it to his lips ? Is a marriage less a marriage because a heretic is the husband ? Madame, you loved your Jean ; if he were living now, what would you do to keep him ? Think, madame, is not love more than all ? "

She turned to the dead body. " *Mon petit* Jean ! " she murmured, but made no reply to me, and for many minutes the room was silent. At last she turned, and

The Cathedral, with Market in the rear.

said, " You must come at once, for soon the priests will be at the church. A little later I will bring you some breakfast, and you must not stir from there till I come to fetch you—no."

" I wish to see Voban," said I.

She thought a moment. " I will try to fetch him to you by-and-bye," she said. She did not speak further, but finished the sentence by pointing to the body.

Presently, hearing footsteps, she drew me into another little room. " It is the grandfather," she said. " He has forgotten you already, and he must not see you again."

We saw the old man hobble into the room we had left, carrying in one arm Jean's coat and hat. He stood still, and bowed to the body and mumbled to himself; then he went over and touched the hands and forehead, nodding wisely ; after which he came to his armchair, and, sitting down, spread the coat over his knees, put the cap on it, and gossipped with himself.

> " In eild our idle fancies all return,
> The mind's eye cradled by the open grave."

A moment later, the woman passed from the rear of the house to the vestry door of the cathedral. After a minute, seeing no one near, I followed, came to the front door, entered, and passed up a side aisle towards the choir. There was no one to be seen, but soon the woman came out of the vestry and beckoned to me nervously. I followed her quick movements, and was presently in a narrow stairway, coming, after fifty steps or so, to a sort of cloister, from which we went into a little cubiculum, or cell, with a wooden lattice door which opened on a small gallery. Through the lattices the nave and choir could be viewed distinctly.

Without a word the woman turned and left me, and

I sat down on a little stone bench and waited. I saw
the acolytes come and go, and priests move back and
forth before the altar; I smelt the grateful incense as it
rose when mass was said, and watched the people gather
in little clusters at the different shrines, or seek the
confessional, or kneel to receive the blessed sacrament.
Many who came were familiar—among them Mademoiselle Lucie Lotbinière. Lucie prayed long before a
shrine of the Virgin, and when she rose at last her
face bore signs of weeping. Also I noticed her suddenly start as she moved down the aisle, for a figure
came forward from seclusion and touched her arm. As
he half turned I saw that it was Juste Duvarney. The
girl drew back from him, raising her hand as if in protest, and it struck me that her grief and her repulse of
him had to do with putting Alixe away into a nunnery.

I sat hungry and thirsty for quite three hours, and then
the church became empty, and only an old verger kept
his seat by the door, half asleep, though the artillery of
both armies was at work, and the air was laden with the
smell of powder. (Until this time our batteries had
avoided firing on the churches.) At last I heard footsteps
near me in the dark stairway, and I felt for my pistols,
for the feet were not those of Labrouk's wife. I waited
anxiously, and was overjoyed to see Voban enter my hiding-place, bearing some food. I greeted him warmly, but
he made little demonstration. He was like one who, occupied with some great matter, passed through the usual
affairs of life with a distant eye. Immediately he handed
me a letter, saying :

"M'sieu', I give my word to hand you this—in a day
or a year, as I am able. I get your message to me this
morning, and then I come to care for Jean Labrouk, and
so I find you here, and I give the letter. It come to me
last night."

The letter was from Alixe. I opened it with haste, and in the dim light read :

My beloved Husband : Oh, was there no power in earth or heaven to bring me to your arms to-day ?

To-morrow they come to see my marriage annulled by the Church. And every one will say it is annulled—every one but me. I, in God's name, will say no, though it break my heart to oppose myself to them all.

Why did my brother come back? He has been hard —O Robert, he has been hard upon me, and yet I was ever kind to him ! My father, too, he listens to the Church, and, though he likes not Monsieur Doltaire, he works for him in a hundred ways without seeing it. I, alas ! see it too well, and my brother is as wax in monsieur's hands. Juste loves Lucie Lotbinière—that should make him kind. She, sweet friend, does not desert me, but is kept from me. She says she will not yield to Juste's suit until he yields to me. If—oh, if Madame Jamond had not gone to Montreal !

. . . As I was writing the foregoing sentence, my father asked to see me, and we have had a talk—ah, a most bitter talk !

"Alixe," said he, " this is our last evening together, and I would have it peaceful."

" My father," said I, " it is not my will that this evening be our last; and for peace, I long for it with all my heart."

He frowned, and answered, " You have brought me trouble and sorrow. Mother of God ! was it not possible for you to be as your sister Georgette ? I gave her less love, yet she honours me more."

" She honours you, my father, by a sweet, good life, and by marriage into an honourable family, and at your word she gives her hand to Monsieur Auguste de la Darante. She marries to your pleasure, therefore she has peace and your love. I marry a man of my own choosing, a bitterly wronged gentleman, and you treat me as some wicked thing. Is that like a father who loves his child?"

"The wronged gentleman, as you call him, invaded that which is the pride of every honest gentleman," he said.

"And what is that?" asked I quietly, though I felt the blood beating at my temples.

"My family honour, the good name and virtue of my daughter."

I got to my feet, and looked my father in the eyes with an anger and a coldness that hurt me now when I think of it, and I said, "I will not let you speak so to me. Friendless though I be, you shall not. You have the power to oppress me, but you shall not slander me to my face. Can not you leave insults to my enemies?"

"I will never leave you to the insults of this mock marriage," answered he, angrily also. "Two days hence I take command of five hundred burghers, and your brother Juste serves with General Montcalm. There is to be last fighting soon between us and the English. I do not doubt of the result, but I may fall, and your brother also, and, should the English win, I will not leave you to him you call your husband. Therefore you shall be kept safe where no alien hands may reach you. The Church will hold you close."

I calmed myself again while listening to him, and I asked, "Is there no other way?"

He shook his head.

"Is there no Monsieur Doltaire?" said I. "He has a king's blood in his veins!"

He looked sharply at me. "You are mocking," he

replied. "No, no, that is no way, either. Monsieur Doltaire must never mate with daughter of mine. I will take
care of that; the Church is a perfect if gentle jailer."

I could bear it no longer. I knelt to him. I begged
him to have pity on me. I pleaded with him; I recalled
the days when, as a child, I sat upon his knee and listened
to the wonderful tales he told; I begged him, by the memory of all the years when he and I were such true friends
to be kind to me now, to be merciful—even though he
thought I had done wrong—to be merciful. I asked him
to remember that I was a motherless girl, and that if I
had missed the way to happiness he ought not to make
my path bitter to the end. I begged him to give me back
his love and confidence, and, if I must for evermore be
parted from you, to let me be with him, not to put me
away into a convent.

"Oh, how my heart leaped when I saw his face soften!
"Well, well," he said, "if I live, you shall be taken from
the convent; but for the present, till this fighting is over,
it is the only safe place. There, too, you shall be safe
from Monsieur Doltaire."

It was poor comfort. "But should you be killed, and
the English take Quebec?" said I.

"When I am dead," he answered, "when I am dead,
then there is your brother."

"And if he speaks for Monsieur Doltaire?" asked I.

"There is the Church and God always," he answered.

"And my own husband, the man who saved your life,
my father," I urged gently; and when he would have
spoken I threw myself into his arms—the first time in
such long, long weeks!—and stopping his lips with my
fingers, burst into tears on his breast. I think much of
his anger against me passed, yet before he left he said he
could not now prevent the annulment of the marriage,

even if he would, for other powers were at work; which powers I supposed to be the Governor, for certain reasons of enmity to my father and me—alas! how changed is he, the vain old man!—and Monsieur Doltaire, whose ends I knew so well. So they will unwed us to-morrow, Robert; but be sure that I shall never be unwed in my own eyes, and that I will wait till I die, hoping you will come and take me—oh, Robert, my husband—take me home!

If I had one hundred men I would fight my way out of this city, and to you; but, dear, I have none, not even Gabord, who is not let come near me. There is but Voban. Yet he will bear you this, if it be possible, for he comes to-night to adorn my fashionable brother. The poor Mathilde I have not seen of late. She has vanished. When they began to keep me close, and carried me off at last into the country, where we were captured by the English, I could not see her, and my heart aches for her.

God bless you, Robert, and farewell. How we shall smile when all this misery is done! Oh, say we shall, say we shall smile, and all this misery cease! Will you not take me home? Do you still love thy wife, thy

ALIXE?

I bade Voban come to me at the little house behind the church that night at ten o'clock, and by then I should have arranged some plan of action. I knew not whether to trust Gabord or not. I was sorry now that I had not tried to bring Clark with me. He was fearless, and he knew the town well; but he lacked discretion, and that was vital.

Two hours of waiting, then came a scene which is burned into my brain. I looked down upon a mass of people, soldiers, couriers of the woods, beggars, priests,

camp followers, and anxious gentlefolk, come from seclusion, or hiding, or vigils of war, to see a host of powers
torture a young girl who through suffering had been made
a woman long before her time. Out in the streets was
the tramping of armed men, together with the call of
bugles and the sharp rattle of drums. Presently I heard
the hoofs of many horses, and soon afterwards there
entered the door, and way was made for him up the
nave, the Marquis de Vaudreuil and his suite, with the
Chevalier de la Darante, the Intendant, and—to my
indignation—Juste Duvarney.

They had no sooner taken their places, than from a
little side door near the vestry there entered the Seigneur Duvarney and Alixe, who, coming down slowly, took
places very near the chancel steps. The Seigneur was
pale and stern, and carried himself with great dignity.
His glance never shifted from the choir, where the priests
slowly entered and took their places, the aged and feeble
bishop going falteringly to his throne. Alixe's face was
pale and sorrowful, and yet it had a dignity and self-
reliance that gave it a kind of grandeur. A buzz passed
through the building, yet I noted, too, with gladness, that
there were tears on many faces.

A figure stole in beside Alixe. It was Mademoiselle
Lotbinière, who immediately was followed by her mother.
I leaned forward, perfectly hidden, and listened to the
singsong voices of the priests, the musical note of the
responses, heard the Kyrie Eleison, the clanging of the
belfry bell as the host was raised by the trembling bishop.
The silence which followed the mournful voluntary played
by the organ was most painful to me.

At that moment a figure stepped from behind a pillar
and gave Alixe a deep, scrutinizing look. It was Doltaire. He was graver than I had ever seen him, and was
dressed scrupulously in black, with a little white lace

showing at the wrists and neck. A handsomer figure it would be hard to see; and I hated him for it, and wondered what new devilry was in his mind. He seemed to sweep the church with a glance. Nothing could have escaped that swift, searching look. His eyes were even raised to where I was, so that I involuntarily drew back, though I knew he could not see me.

I was arrested suddenly by a curious, even sneering smile which played upon his face as he looked at Vaudreuil and Bigot. There was in it more scorn than malice, more triumph than active hatred. All at once I remembered what he had said to me the day before: that he had commission from the King, through La Pompadour, to take over the reins of government from the two confederates, and send them to France to answer the charges made against them.

At last the bishop came forward, and read from a paper as follows:

"*Forasmuch as the well-beloved child of our Holy Church, Mademoiselle Alixe Duvarney, of the parish of Beauport and of this cathedral parish, in this province of New France, forgetting her manifest duty and our sacred teaching, did illegally and in sinful error make feigned contract of marriage with one Robert Moray, captain in a Virginia regiment, a heretic, a spy, and an enemy to our country; and forasmuch as this was done in violence of all nice habit and commendable obedience to Mother Church and our national uses, we do hereby declare and make void this alliance until such time as the Holy Father at Rome shall finally approve our action and proclaiming. And it is enjoined upon Mademoiselle Alixe Duvarneg, on peril of her soul's salvation, to obey us in this matter, and neither by word or deed or thought have commerce more with this notorious and evil heretic and foe of our Church and of*

*our country. It is also the plain duty of the faithful
children of our Holy Church to regard this Captain
Moray with a pious hatred, and to destroy him without pity; and any good cunning or enticement which
should lure him to the punishment he so much deserves
shall be approved. Furthermore, Mademoiselle Alixe Duvarney shall, until such times as there shall be peace in
this land, and the molesting English be driven back with
slaughter—and for all time, if the heart of our sister incline to penitence and love of Christ—be housed within
the Convent of the Ursulines, and cared for with great
tenderness."*

He left off reading, and began to address himself to
Alixe directly; but she rose in her place, and while
surprise and awe seized the congregation, she said:

"Monseigneur, I must, at my father's bidding, hear
the annulment of my marriage, but I will not hear this
public exhortation. I am only a poor girl, unlearned in
the law, and I must submit to your power, for I have no
one here to speak for me. But my soul and my conscience I carry to my Saviour, and I have no fear to
answer Him. I am sorry that I have offended my
people and my country and Holy Church, but I do not
repent that I love and hold to my husband. You must
do with me as you will, but in this I shall never willingly yield."

She turned to her father, and all the people breathed
hard; for it passed their understanding, and seemed scan-
dalous that a girl should thus defy the Church, and answer the bishop in his own cathedral. Her father rose,
and then I saw her sway with faintness. I know not what
might have occurred, for the bishop stood with hand upraised and great indignation in his face, about to speak,
when out of the desultory firing from our batteries there
came a shell, which burst even at the cathedral entrance,

tore away a portion of the wall, and killed and wounded a number of people.

Then followed a panic which the priests in vain tried to quell. The people swarmed into the choir and through the vestry. I saw Doltaire and Juste Duvarney spring swiftly to the side of Alixe, and, with her father, put her and Mademoiselle Lotbinière into the pulpit, forming a ring round it, preventing the crowd from trampling on them, as, suddenly gone mad, they swarmed past. The Governor, the Intendant, and the Chevalier de la Darante did as much also for Madame Lotbinière; and as soon as the crush had subsided a little, a number of soldiers cleared the way, and I saw my wife led from the church. I longed to leap down there among them and claim her; but that thought was madness, for I should have been food for worms in a trice; so I kept my place.

XXVI.

THE SECRET OF THE TAPESTRY.

THAT evening, at eight o'clock, Jean Labrouk was buried. A shell had burst not a dozen paces from his own door, within the consecrated ground of the cathedral, and in a hole it had made he was laid, the only mourners his wife and his grandfather, and two soldiers of his company sent by General Bougainville to bury him. I watched the ceremony from my loft, which had one small dormer window. It was dark, but burning buildings in the Lower Town made all light about the place. I could hear the grandfather mumbling and talking to the body as it was lowered into the ground. While yet the priest was hastily reading prayers, a dusty horseman came riding to the grave and dismounted.

"Jean," he said, looking at the grave, "Jean Labrouk, a man dies well that dies with his gaiters on, aho! . . . What have you said for Jean Labrouk, m'sieu'?" he added to the priest.

The priest stared at him, as though he had presumed.

"Well?" said Gabord.   "Well?"

The priest answered nothing, but prepared to go, whispering a word of comfort to the poor wife. Gabord looked at the soldiers, looked at the wife, at the priest, then spread out his legs and stuck his hands down into his pockets, while his horse rubbed its nose against his shoulder. He fixed his eyes on the grave, and nodded once or twice musingly.

"Well," he said at last, as if he had found a perfect virtue, and the one or only thing that might be said, "well, he never eat his words, that Jean!"

A moment afterwards he came into the house with Babette, leaving one of the soldiers holding his horse. After the old man had gone, I heard him say, "Were you at mass to-day?   And did you see all?"

When she had answered yes, he continued: "It was a mating as birds mate, but mating was it, and holy fathers and Master Devil Doltaire can't change it till cock-pheasant Moray come rocketing to 's grave.   They would have hanged me for my part in it, but I repent not, for they have wickedly hunted this little lady."

"I weep with her," said Jean's wife.

"Ay, ay, weep on, Babette," he answered.

"Has she asked help of you?" said the wife.

"Truly; but I know not what she says, for I read not, but I know her pecking.   Here it is.   But you must be secret."

Looking though a crack in the floor, I could plainly see them.   She took the letter from him and read aloud:

"If Gabord the soldier have a good heart still, as ever

he had in the past, he will again help a poor, friendless woman. She needs him, for all are against her. Will he leave her alone among her enemies? Will he not aid her to fly? At eight o'clock to-morrow night she will be taken to the Convent of the Ursulines, to be there shut in. Will he not come to her before that time?"

For a moment after the reading there was silence, and I could see the woman looking at him curiously. "What will you do?" she asked.

"My faith, there's nut to crack, for I have little time. This letter but reached me, with the news of Jean, two hours ago, and I know not what to do, but, as I stand scratching my head, here comes word from General Montcalm that I must ride to Master Devil Doltaire with a letter, and I must find him wherever he may be, and give it straight. So forth I come; and I must be at my post again by morn, said the General."

"It is now nine o'clock, and she will be in the convent," said the woman tentatively.

"Aho!" he answered, "and none can enter there but Governor, if holy Mother say no. So now goes Master Devil there? 'Gabord,' quoth he, 'you shall come with me to the convent at ten o'clock, bringing three stout soldiers of the garrison. Here's an order on Monsieur Ramesay the commandant. Choose you the men, and fail me not, or you shall swing aloft, dear Gabord.' Sweet lovers of hell, but Master Devil shall have swinging too one day." He put his thumb to his nose, and spread his fingers out.

Presently he seemed to note something in the woman's eyes, for he spoke almost sharply to her: "Jean Labrouk was honest man, and kept faith with comrades."

"And I keep faith too, comrade," was the answer.

"Gabord's a brute to doubt you," he rejoined quickly, and he drew from his pocket a piece of gold and made her take it, though she much resisted.

Meanwhile my mind was made up. I saw, I thought, through "Master Devil's" plan, and I felt, too, that Gabord would not betray me. In any case, Gabord and I could fight it out. If he opposed me, it was his life or mine, for too much was at stake, and all my plans were now changed by his astounding news. At that moment Voban entered the room without knocking. Here was my cue, and so, to prevent explanations, I crept quickly down, opened the door, and came in on them.

They wheeled at my footsteps; the woman gave a little cry, and Gabord's hand went to his pistol. There was a wild sort of look in his face, as though he could not trust his eyes. I took no notice of the menacing pistol, but went straight to him and held out my hand.

"Gabord," said I, "you are not my jailer now."

"I'll be your guard to citadel," said he, after a moment's dumb surprise, refusing my outstretched hand.

"Neither guard nor jailer any more, Gabord," said I seriously. "We've had enough of that, my friend."

The soldier and the jailer had been working in him, and his fingers trifled with the trigger. In all things he was the foeman first. But now something else was working in him. I saw this, and added pointedly, "No more cage, Gabord, not even for reward of twenty thousand livres and at command of Holy Church."

He smiled grimly, too grimly, I thought, and turned inquiringly to Babette. In a few words she told him all, tears dropping from her eyes.

"If you take him, you betray me," she said; "and what would Jean say, if he knew?"

"Gabord," said I, "I come not as a spy; I come to seek my wife, and she counts you as her friend. Do harm to me, and you do harm to her. Serve me, and you serve her. Gabord, you said to her once that I was an honourable man."

22

He put up his pistol. "Aho, you've put you head in the trap. Stir, and click goes the spring."

"I must have my wife," I continued. "Shall the nest you helped to make go empty?"

I worked upon him to such purpose that, all bristling with war at first, he was shortly won over to my scheme, which I disclosed to him while the wife made us a cup of coffee. Through all our talk Voban had sat eying us with a covert interest, yet showing no excitement. He had been unable to reach Alixe. She had been taken to the convent, and immediately afterwards her father and brother had gone their ways—Juste to General Montcalm, and the Seigneur to the French camp. Thus Alixe did not know that I was in Quebec.

An hour after this I was marching, with two other men and Gabord, to the Convent of the Ursulines, dressed in the ordinary costume of a French soldier, got from the wife of Jean Labrouk. In manner and speech though I was somewhat dull, my fellows thought, I was enough like a peasant soldier to deceive them, and my French was more fluent than their own. I was playing a desperate game; yet I liked it, for it had a fine spice of adventure apart from the great matter at stake. If I could but carry it off, I should have sufficient compensation for all my miseries, in spite of their twenty thousand livres and Holy Church.

In a few minutes we came to the convent, and halted outside, waiting for Doltaire. Presently he came, and, looking sharply at us all, he ordered two to wait outside, and Gabord and myself to come with him. Then he stood looking at the building curiously for a moment. A shell had broken one wing of it, and this portion had been abandoned; but the faithful Sisters clung still to their home, though urged constantly by the Governor to retire to the Hôtel-Dieu, which was outside the reach of

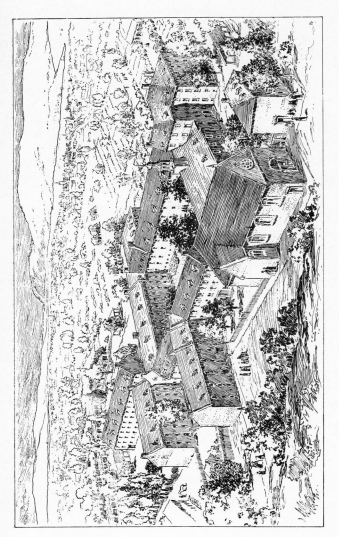

The Convent of the Ursulines.

shot and shell. This it was their intention soon to do, for within the past day or so our batteries had not sought to spare the convent. As Doltaire looked he laughed to himself, and then said, "Too quiet for gay spirits, this hearse. Come, Gabord, and fetch this slouching fellow," nodding towards me.

Then he knocked loudly. No one came, and he knocked again and again. At last the door was opened by the Mother Superior, who was attended by two others. She started at seeing Doltaire.

"What do you wish, monsieur?" she asked.

"I come on business of the King, good Mother," he replied seriously, and stepped inside.

"It is a strange hour for business," she said severely.

"The King may come at all hours," he answered soothingly: "is it not so? By the law he may enter when he wills."

"You are not the King, monsieur," she objected, with her head held up sedately.

"Or the Governor may come, good Mother?"

"You are not the Governor, Monsieur Doltaire," she said, more sharply still.

"But a Governor may demand admittance to this convent, and by the order of his Most Christian Majesty he may not be refused; is it not so?"

"Must I answer the catechism of Monsieur Doltaire?"

"But is it not so?" he asked again urbanely.

"It is so, yet how does that concern you, monsieur?"

"In every way," and he smiled.

"This is unseemly, monsieur. What is your business?"

"The Governor's business, good Mother."

"Then let the Governor's messenger give his message and depart in peace," she answered, her hand upon the door.

"Not the Governor's messenger, but the Governor himself," he rejoined gravely.

He turned and was about to shut the door, but she stopped him. "This is no house for jesting, monsieur," she said. "I will arouse the town if you persist.—Sister," she added to one standing near, "the bell!"

"You fill your office with great dignity and merit, Mère St. George," he said, as he put out his hand and stayed the Sister. "I commend you for your discretion. Read this," he continued, handing her a paper.

A Sister held a light, and the Mother read it. As she did so Doltaire made a motion to Gabord, and he shut the door quickly on us. Mère St. George looked up from the paper, startled and frightened too.

"Your Excellency!" she exclaimed.

"You are the first to call me so," he replied. "I thought to leave untouched this good gift of the King, and to let the Marquis de Vaudreuil and the admirable Bigot untwist the coil they have made. But no. After some too generous misgivings, I now claim my own. I could not enter here, to speak with a certain lady, save as the Governor, but as the Governor I now ask speech with Mademoiselle Duvarney. Do you hesitate?" he added. "Do you doubt that signature of his Majesty? Then see this. Here is a line from the Marquis de Vaudreuil, the late Governor. It is not dignified, one might say it is craven, but it is genuine."

Again the distressed lady read, and again she said, "Your Excellency!" Then, "You wish to see her in my presence, your Excellency?"

"Alone, good Mother," he softly answered.

"Your Excellency, will you, the first officer in the land, defy our holy rules, and rob us of our privilege to protect and comfort and save?"

"I defy nothing," he replied. "The lady is here

against her will, a prisoner. She does not desire your governance and care. In any case, I must speak with her; and be assured, I honour you the more for your solicitude, and will ask your counsel when I have finished talk with her."

Was ever man so crafty? After a moment's thought she turned, dismissed the others, and led the way, and Gabord and I followed. We were bidden to wait outside a room, well lighted but bare, as I could see through the open door. Doltaire entered, smiling, and then bowed the nun on her way to summon Alixe. Gabord and I stood there, not speaking, for both were thinking of the dangerous game now playing. In a few minutes the Mother returned, bringing Alixe. The light from the open door shone upon her face. My heart leaped, for there was in her look such a deep sorrow. She was calm, save for those shining yet steady eyes; they were like furnaces, burning up the colour of her cheeks. She wore a soft black gown, with no sign of ornament, and her gold-brown hair was bound with a piece of black velvet ribbon. Her beauty was deeper than I had ever seen it; a peculiar gravity seemed to have added years to her life. Passing me her sleeve brushed my arm, as it did that day I was arrested in her father's house. She started, as though I had touched her fingers, but she only half turned toward me, for her mind was wholly occupied with the room where Doltaire was.

At that moment Gabord coughed slightly, and she turned quickly to him. Her eyes flashed intelligence, and presently, as she passed in, a sort of hope seemed to have come on her face to lighten its painful pensiveness. The Mother Superior entered with her, the door closed, and then, after a little, the Mother came out again. As she did so I saw a look of immediate purpose in her face, and her hurrying step persuaded me she was bent on some project of espial. So I made a sign to Gabord and followed her. As she turned the corner of the hallway just beyond, I stepped forward silently and watched her enter a room that would, I knew, be next to this we guarded.

Listening at the door for a moment, I suddenly and softly turned the handle and entered, to see the good Mother with a panel drawn in the wall before her and her face set to it. She stepped back as I shut the door and turned the key in the lock. I put my finger to my lips, for she seemed about to cry out.

" Hush ! " said I. " I watch for those who love her. I am here to serve her—and you."

" You are a servant of the Seigneur's ? " she said, the alarm passing out of her face.

" I served the Seigneur, good Mother," I answered, " and I would lay down my life for ma'm'selle."

" You would hear ? " she asked, pointing to the panel.

I nodded.

" You speak French not like a Breton or a Norman," she added. " What is your province ? "

" I am an Auvergnian."

She said no more, but motioned to me, enjoining silence also by a sign, and I stood with her beside the panel. Before it was a piece of tapestry which was mere gauze in one place, and I could see through and hear perfectly. The room we were in was at least four feet higher than the other, and we looked down on its occupants.

" Presently, holy Mother," said I, " all shall be told true to you, if you wish it. It is not your will to watch and hear ; it is because you love the lady. But I love her too, and I am to be trusted. It is not business for such as you."

She saw my implied rebuke, and said, as I thought a little abashed, " You will tell me all ? And if he would take her forth, give me alarm in the room opposite yonder door, and stay them, and——"

" Stay them, holy Mother, at the price of my life ! I have the honour of her family in my hands."

She looked at me gravely, and I assumed a peasant openness of look. She was deceived completely, and, without further speech, she stepped to the door like a ghost and was gone. I never saw a human being so noiseless, so uncanny. Our talk had been carried on silently, and I had closed the panel quietly, so that we could not be heard by Alixe or Doltaire. Now I was alone, to see and hear my wife in speech with my enemy, the man who had made a strong, and was yet to make a stronger, fight to unseat me in her affections.

There was a moment's compunction, in which I hesitated to see this meeting ; but there was Alixe's safety to be thought on, and what might he not here disclose of his intentions !—knowing which, I should act with judgment, and not in the dark. I trusted Alixe, though I knew well that this hour would see the great struggle in her between this scoundrel and myself. I knew that he had ever had a sort of power over her, even while she loathed his character ; that he had a hundred graces I had not, place which I had not, an intellect that ever delighted me, and a will of iron when it was called into action. I thought for one moment longer ere I moved the panel. My lips closed tight, and I felt a pang at my heart.

Suppose, in this conflict, this singular man, acting on a nature already tried beyond reason, should bend it to his will, to which it was in some radical ways inclined ? Well, if that should be, then I would go forth and never see her more. She must make her choice out of her own heart and spirit, and fight this fight alone, and having fought, and lost or won, the result should be final, should stand, though she was my wife and I was bound in honour to protect her from all that might invade her loyalty, to cherish her through all temptation and distress. But our case was a strange one, and it must be dealt with according to its strangeness—our only guides our consciences. There were no precedents to meet our needs ; our way had to be hewn out of a noisome, pathless wood. I made up my mind : I would hear and note all. So I slid the panel softly, and put my eyes to the tapestry. How many times did I see, in the next hour, my wife's eyes upraised to this very tapestry, as if appealing to the face of Madonna upon it ! How many times did her eyes look into mine without knowing it ! And more than once Doltaire followed her glance, and a faint smile passed over his face, as if he saw and was interested in the struggle in her, apart from his own passion and desires.

When first I looked in, she was standing near a tall, high-backed chair, in almost the same position as on the day when Doltaire told me of Braddock's death, accused me of being a spy, and arrested me. It gave me, too, a thrill to see her raise her handkerchief to her mouth as if to stop a cry, as she had done then, the black sleeve falling away from her perfect rounded arm, now looking almost like marble against the lace. She held her handkerchief to her lips for quite a minute ; and indeed it covered more than a little of her face, so that the features most showing were her eyes, gazing at Doltaire with a look hard to interpret, for there seemed in it trouble, entreaty, wonder, resistance, and a great sorrow—no fear, trepidation, or indirectness.

His disturbing words were these : " To-night I am the Governor of this country. You once doubted my power—that was when you would save your lover from death. I proved it in that small thing—I saved him. Well, when you saw me carried off to the Bastile—it looked like that—my power seemed to vanish: is it not so? We have talked of this before, but now is a time to review all things again. And once more I say I am the Governor of New France. I have had the commission in my hands ever since I came back. But I have spoken of it to no one—except your lover!"

"My husband!" she said steadily, crushing the handkerchief in her hand, which now rested upon the chairarm.

"Well, well, your husband—after a fashion. I did not care to use this as an argument. I chose to win you by personal means alone, to have you give yourself to Tinoir Doltaire because you set him before any other man. I am vain, you see; but then vanity is no sin when one has fine aspirations; and I aspire to you!"

She made a motion with her hand. "Oh, can you not spare me this to-day—of all days in my life—your Excellency?"

"Let it be plain 'monsieur,'" he answered. "I can not spare you, for this day decides all. As I said, I desired you. At first my wish was to possess you at any cost: I was your hunter only. I am still your hunter, but in a different way. I would rather have you in my arms than save New France; and with Montcalm I could save it. Vaudreuil is a blunderer and a fool; he has sold the country. But what ambition is that? New France may come and go, and be forgotten, and you and I be none the worse. There are other provinces to conquer. But for me there is only one province, and I will lift my standard there, and build the grand château of my happiness there. That is my hope, and that is why I come to conquer it and not the English. Let the English go—all save one, and he must die.   Already he is dead ; he died to-day at the altar of the cathedral——"

" No, no, no ! " broke in Alixe, her voice low and firm.

" But yes," he said ; " but yes, he is dead to you for-ever.   The Church has said so ; the state says so ; your people say so ; race and all manner of good custom say so ; and I, who love you better—yes, a hundred times better —than he, say so."

She made a hasty, deprecating gesture with her hand. " Oh, carry this old song elsewhere," she said, " for I am sick of it."   There were now both scorn and weariness in her tone.

He had a singular patience, and he resented nothing. " I understand," he went on, " what it was sent your heart his way.   He came to you when you were yet a child, be-fore you had learned the first secret of life.   He was a cap-tive, a prisoner, he had a wound got in fair fighting, and I will do him the credit to say he was an honest man ; he was no spy."

She looked up at him with a slight flush, almost of gratitude.   " I know that well," she returned.   " I knew there was other cause than spying at the base of all ill treatment of him.   I know that you, you alone, kept him prisoner here six long years."

" Not I ; the Grande Marquise—for weighty reasons. You should not fret at those five years, since it gave you what you have cherished so much, a husband—after a fashion.   But yet we will do him justice : he is an honour-able fighter, he has parts and graces of a rude order.   But he will never go far in life ; he has no instincts and habits common with you ; it has been, so far, a compromise, founded upon the old-fashioned romance of ill-used cap-tive and soft-hearted maid ; the compassion, too, of the superior for the low, the free for the caged."

"Compassion such as your Excellency feels for me, no doubt," she said, with a slow pride.

"You are caged, but you may be free," he rejoined meaningly.

"Yes, in the same market open to him, and at the same price of honour," she replied, with dignity.

"Will you not sit down?" he now said, motioning her to a chair politely, and taking one himself, thus pausing before he answered her.

I was prepared to see him keep a decorous distance from her. I felt that he was acting upon deliberation; that he was trusting to the power of his insinuating address, his sophistry, to break down barriers. It was as if he knew himself at greater advantage, making no emotional demonstrations; so allaying her fears, giving her time to think; for it was clear he hoped to master her intelligence, so strong a part of her.

She sat down in the high-backed chair, and I noted at the moment that our batteries began to play upon the town—an unusual thing at night. It gave me a strange feeling—the perfect stillness of the holy place, the quiet movement of this tragedy before me, on which broke, with no modifying noises or turmoil, the shouting cannonade. Nature, it would have seemed, had forged a mood in keeping with the time, for there was no air stirring when we came in, and a strange stillness had come upon the landscape. In the pause, too, I heard a long, soft shuffling of feet in the corridor—the evening procession from the chapel—and a slow chant:

"*I am set down in a wilderness, O Lord, I am alone. If a strange voice call, O teach me what to say; if I languish, O give me Thy cup to drink; O strengthen Thou my soul. Lord, I am like a sparrow far from home; O bring me to Thine honourable house. Preserve my heart, encourage me, according to Thy truth.*"

The words came to us distinctly yet distantly, swelled softly, and died away, leaving Alixe and Doltaire seated and looking at each other. Alixe's hands were clasped in her lap.

"Your honour is above all price," he said at last in reply to her latest words. "But what is honour in this case of yours, in which I throw the whole interest of my life, stake all? For I am convinced that, losing, the book of fate will close for me. Winning, I shall begin again, and play a part in France which men shall speak of when I am done with all. I never had ambition for myself; for you, Alixe Duvarney, a new spirit lives in me. . . . I will be honest with you. At first I swore to cool my hot face in your bosom; and I would have done that at any price, and yet I would have stood by that same dishonour honourably to the end. Never in my whole life did I put my whole heart in any—episode—of admiration: I own it, for you to think what you will. There never was a woman whom, loving to-day "—he smiled—" I could not leave to-morrow with no more than a pleasing kind of regret. Names that I ought to have recalled I forgot; incidents were cloudy, like childish remembrances. I was not proud of it; the peasant in me spoke against it sometimes. I even have wished that I, half peasant, had been——"

"If only you had been all peasant, this war, this misery of mine had never been," she interrupted.

He nodded with an almost boyish candour. "Yes, yes, but I was half prince also; I had been brought up, one foot in a cottage and another in a palace. But for your misery: is it, then, misery? Need it be so? But lift your finger, and all will be well. Do you wish to save your country? Would that be compensation? Then I will show you the way. We have three times as many soldiers as the English, though of poorer stuff. We could hold this place, could defeat them, if we were united and had but two thousand men. We have fifteen thousand. As it is now, Vaudreuil baulks Montcalm, and that will ruin us in the end unless you make it otherwise. You would be a patriot? Then shut out forever this English captain from your heart, and open its doors to me. To-morrow I will take Vaudreuil's place, put your father in Bigot's, your brother in Ramesay's— they are both perfect and capable; I will strengthen the excellent Montcalm's hands in every way, will inspire the people, and cause the English to raise this siege. You and I will do this: the Church will bless us, the state will thank us; your home and country will be safe and happy, your father and brother honoured. This, and far, far greater things I will do for your sake."

He paused. He had spoken with a deep power, such as I knew he could use, and I did not wonder that she paled a little, even trembled before it.

" Will you not do it for France?" she said.

" I will not do it for France," he answered. " I will do it for you alone. Will you not be your country's friend? It is no virtue in me to plead patriotism—it is a mere argument, a weapon that I use; but my heart is behind it, and it is a means to that which you will thank me for one day. I would not force you to anything, but I would persuade your reason, question your foolish loyalty to a girl's mistake. Can you think that you are right? You have no friend that commends your cause; the whole country has upbraided you, the Church has cut you off from the man. All is against reunion with him, and most of all your own honour. Come with me, and be commended and blessed here, while over in France homage shall be done you. For you I will take from His Majesty the dukedom which he has offered me more than once."

Suddenly with a passionate tone, he continued : " Your

own heart is speaking for me. Have I not seen you tremble when I came near you?"

He rose and came forward a step or two. "You thought it was fear of me. It was fear, but fear of that in you which was pleading for me, while you had sworn yourself away to him who knows not and can never know how to love you, who has nothing kin with you in mind or heart—an alien of poor fortune and poorer birth and prospects."

He fixed his eyes upon her, and went on, speaking with forceful quietness : "Had there been cut away that mistaken sense of duty to him, which I admire unspeakably—yes, though it is misplaced—you and I would have come to each other's arms long ago. Here in your atmosphere I feel myself possessed, endowed. I come close to you, and something new in me cries out simply, ' I love you, Alixe, I love you ! ' See, all the damnable part of me is burned up by the fire of your eyes ; I stand upon the ashes, and swear that I can not live without you. Come—come——"

He stepped nearer still, and she rose like one who moves under some fascination, and I almost cried out, for in that moment she was his, his—I felt it ; he possessed her like some spirit ; and I understood it, for the devilish golden beauty of his voice was like music, and he had spoken with great skill.

"Come," he said, "and know where all along your love has lain. That other way is only darkness—the convent, which will keep you buried, while you will never have heart for the piteous seclusion, till your life is broken all to pieces ; till you have no hope, no desire, no love ; and at last, under a cowl, you look out upon the world, and, with a dead heart, see it as in a pale dream, and die at last : you, born to be a wife, without a husband ; endowed to be the perfect mother, without a child; to be the admired of princes, a moving, powerful figure to influence great men, with no *salon* but the little bare cell where you pray. With me, all that you should be you will be. You have had a bad, dark dream; wake, and come into the sun with me. Once I wished for you as the lover only; now, by every hope I ever might have had, I want you for my wife."

He held out his arms to her and smiled, and spoke one or two low words which I could not hear. I had stood waiting death against the citadel wall, with the chance of a reprieve hanging between uplifted muskets and my breast; but that suspense was less than this, for I saw him, not moving, but standing there waiting for her, the warmth of his devilish eloquence about him, and she moving toward him.

"My darling," I heard him say, "come, till death . . . us do part, and let no man put asunder."

She paused, and, waking from the dream, drew herself together, as though something at her breast hurt her, and she repeated his words like one dazed—"'Let no man put asunder'!"

With a look that told of her great struggle, she moved to a shrine of the Virgin in the corner, and, clasping her hands before her breast for a moment, said something I could not hear, before she turned to Doltaire, who had now taken another step towards her. By his look I knew that he felt his spell was broken; that his auspicious moment had passed; that now, if he won her, it must be by harsh means.

For she said: "Monsieur Doltaire, you have defeated yourself. 'Let no man put asunder' was my response to my husband's 'Whom God hath joined,' when last I met him face to face. Nothing can alter that while he lives, nor yet when he dies, for I have had such a sorrowful happiness in him that if I were sure he were dead I would never leave this holy place—never! But he lives, and I will keep my vow. Holy Church has parted us, but yet we are not parted. You say that to think of him now is wrong, reflects upon me. I tell you, monsieur, that if it were a wrong a thousand times greater I would do it. To me there can be no shame in following, till I die, the man who took me honourably for his wife."

He made an impatient gesture and smiled ironically.

"Oh, I care not what you say or think," she went on. "I know not of things canonical and legal; the way that I was married to him is valid in his country and for his people. Bad Catholic you call me, alas! But I am a true wife, who, if she sinned, sinned not knowingly, and deserves not this tyranny and shame."

"You are possessed with a sad infatuation," he replied persuasively. "You are not the first who has suffered so. It will pass, and leave you sane—leave you to me. For you are mine; what you felt a moment ago you will feel again, when this romantic martyrdom of yours has wearied you."

"Monsieur Doltaire," she said, with a successful effort at calmness, though I could see her trembling too, "it is you who are mistaken, and I will show you how. But first: You have said often that I have unusual intelligence. You have flattered me in that, I doubt not, but still here is a chance to prove yourself sincere. I shall pass by every wicked means that you took first to ruin me, to divert me to a dishonest love (though I know not what you meant at the time), and, failing, to make me your wife. I shall not refer to this base means to reach me in this sacred place, using the King's commission for such a purpose."

"I would use it again, and do more, for the same ends," he rejoined, with shameless candour.

She waved her hand impatiently. "I pass all that by.

You shall listen to me as I have listened to you, remembering that what I say is honest, if it has not your grace and eloquence. You say that I will yet come to you, that I care for you and have cared for you always, and that—that this other—is a sad infatuation. Monsieur, in part you are right."

He came another step forward, for he thought he saw a foothold again; but she drew back to the chair, and said, lifting her hand against him, " No, no, wait till I have done. I say that you are right in part. I will not deny that, against my will, you have always influenced me; that, try as I would, your presence moved me, and I could never put you out of my mind, out of my life. At first I did not understand it, for I knew how bad you were. I was sure you did evil because you loved it; that, to gratify yourself, you would spare no one: a man without pity——"

" On the contrary," he interrupted, with a sour sort of smile, " pity is almost a foible with me."

" Not real pity," she answered. " Monsieur, I have lived long enough to know what pity moves you. It is the moment's careless whim; a pensive pleasure, a dramatic tenderness. Wholesome pity would make you hesitate to harm others. You have no principles——"

" Pardon me, many," he urged politely, as he eyed her with admiration.

" Ah no, monsieur; habits, not principles. Your life has been one long irresponsibility. In the very maturity of your powers, you use them to win to yourself, to your empty heart, a girl who has tried to live according to the teachings of her soul and conscience. Were there not women elsewhere to whom it didn't matter—your abandoned purposes? Why did you throw your shadow on my path? You are not, never were, worthy of a good woman's love."

23

He laughed with a sort of bitterness. " Your sinner stands between two fires—" he said. She looked at him inquiringly, and he added, " the punishment he deserves and the punishment he does not deserve. But it is interesting to be thus picked out upon the stone, however harsh the picture. You said I influenced you—well ? "

" Monsieur," she went on, " there were times when, listening to you, I needed all my strength to resist. I have felt myself weak and shaking when you came into the room. There was something in you that appealed to me, I know not what; but I do know that it was not the best of me, that it was emotional, some strange power of your personality—ah yes, I can acknowledge all now. You had great cleverness, gifts that startled and delighted; but yet I felt always, and that feeling grew and grew, that there was nothing in you wholly honest; that by artifice you had frittered away what once may have been good in you. Now, all goodness in you was an accident of sense and caprice, not true morality."

" What has true morality to do with love of you ? " he said.

" You ask me hard questions," she replied. " This it has to do with it : We go from morality to higher things, not from higher things to morality. Pure love is a high thing ; yours was not high. To have put my life in your hands—ah no, no ! And so I fought you. There was no question of yourself and Robert Moray—none. Him I knew to possess fewer gifts, but I knew him also to be what you could never be. I never measured him against you. What was his was all of me worth the having, and was given always ; there was no change. What was yours was given only when in your presence, and then with hatred of myself and you—given to some baleful fascination in you. For a time, the more I struggled against it the more it grew, for there was nothing that could in

fluence a woman which you did not do.   Monsieur, if you
had had Robert Moray's character and your own gifts, I
could—monsieur, I could have worshipped you!"

Doltaire was in a kind of dream.   He was sitting now
in the high-backed chair, his mouth and chin in his hand,
his elbow resting on the chair-arm.   His left hand grasped
the other arm, and he leaned forward with brows bent
and his eyes fixed on her intently.   It was a figure singularly absorbed, lost in study of some deep theme.   Once
his sword clanged against the chair as it slipped a little
from its position, and he started almost violently, though
the dull booming of a cannon in no wise seemed to break
the quietness of the scene.   He was dressed, as in the
morning, in plain black, but now the Star of Louis shone
on his breast.   His face was pale, but his eyes, with their
swift-shifting lights, lived upon Alixe, devoured her.

She paused for an instant.

" Thou shalt not commit—idolatry," he remarked in a
low, cynical tone, which the repressed feeling in his face
and the terrible new earnestness of his look belied.

She flushed a little, and continued : " Yet all the time
I was true to him, and what I felt concerning you he
knew—I told him enough."

Suddenly there came into Doltaire's looks and manner
an astounding change.   Both hands caught the chair-
arm, his lips parted with a sort of snarl, and his white
teeth showed maliciously.   It seemed as if, all at once, the
courtier, the *flaneur*, the man of breeding, had gone, and
you had before you the peasant, in a moment's palsy from
the intensity of his fury.

" A thousand hells for him!" he burst out in the rough
patois of Poictiers, and got to his feet.   " You told him
all, you confessed your fluttering fears and desires to him,
while you let me play upon those ardent strings of feeling, that you might save him!   You used me, Tinoir

Doltaire, son of a king, to further your *amour* with a *bourgeois* Englishman! And he laughed in his sleeve, and soothed away those dangerous influences of the magician! By the God of heaven, Robert Moray and I have work to do! And you—you, with all the gifts of the perfect courtesan——"

"Oh, shame! shame!" she said, breaking in.

"But I speak the truth. You berate me, but you used incomparable gifts to hold me near you, and the same gifts to let me have no more of you than would keep me. I thought you the most honest, the most heavenly of women, and now——"

"Alas!" she interrupted, "what else could I have done? To draw the line between your constant attention and my own necessity! Ah, I was but a young girl; I had no friend to help me; he was condemned to die; I loved him; I did not believe in you, not in ever so little. If I had said, 'You must not speak to me again,' you would have guessed my secret, and all my purposes would have been defeated. So I had to go on; nor did I think that it ever would cause you aught but a shock to your vanity."

He laughed hatefully. "My faith, but it has shocked my vanity," he answered. "And now take this for thinking on: Up to this point I have pleaded with you, used persuasion, courted you with a humility astonishing to myself. Now I will have you in spite of all. I will break you, and soothe your hurt afterwards. I will, by the face of the Madonna, I will feed where this Moray would pasture, I will gather this ripe fruit!"

With a devilish swiftness he caught her about the waist, and kissed her again and again upon the mouth.

The blood was pounding in my veins, and I would have rushed in then and there, have ended the long strife, and have dug revenge for this outrage from his heart, but that I saw Alixe did not move, nor make the least resistance. This struck me with horror, till, all at once, he let her go, and I saw her face. It was very white and still, smooth and cold as marble. She seemed five years older in the minute.

"Have you quite done, monsieur?" she said, with infinite, quiet scorn. "Do you, the son of a king, find joy in kissing lips that answer nothing, a cheek from which the blood flows in affright and shame? Is it an achievement to feed as cattle feed? Listen to me, Monsieur Doltaire. No, do not try to speak till I have done, if your morality—of manners—is not all dead. Through this cowardly act of yours, the last vestige of your power over me is gone. I sometimes think that with you, in the past, I have remained true and virtuous at the expense of the best of me; but now all that is over, and there is no temptation—I feel beyond it: by this hour here, this hour of sore peril, you have freed me. I was tempted—Heaven knows, a few minutes ago I was tempted, for everything was with you; but God has been with me, and you and I are now no nearer than the poles."

"You doubt that I love you?" he asked in an altered voice.

"I doubt that any man will so shame the woman he loves," she answered.

"What is insult to-day may be a pride to-morrow," was his quick reply. "I do not repent of it, I never will, for you and I shall go to-night from here, and you shall be my wife; and one day, when this man is dead, when you have forgotten your bad dream, you will love me as you can not love him. I have that in me to make you love me. To you I can be loyal, never drifting, never wavering. I tell you, I will not let you go. First my wife you shall be, and after that I will win your love; in spite of all, mine now, though it is shifted for the moment. Come, come, Alixe"—he made as if to take her hand—"you and I will learn the splendid secret——"

She drew back to the shrine of the Virgin.

"Mother of God! Mother of God!" I heard her whisper, and then she raised her hand against him. "No, no, no," she said, with sharp anguish, "do not try to force me to your wishes—do not; for I, at least, will never live to see it. I have suffered more than I can bear. I will end this shame, I will——"

I had heard enough. I stepped back quickly, closed the panel, and went softly to the door and into the hall, determined to bring her out against Doltaire, trusting to Gabord not to oppose me.

XXVII.

A SIDE-WIND OF REVENGE.

I KNEW it was Doltaire's life or mine, and I shrank from desecrating this holy place; but our bitter case would warrant this, and more. As I came quickly through the hall, and round the corner where stood Gabord, I saw a soldier talking with the Mother Superior.

"He is not dead?" I heard her say.

"No, holy Mother," was the answer, "but sorely wounded. He was testing the fire-organs for the rafts, and one exploded too soon."

At that moment the Mother turned to me, and seemed startled by my look. "What is it?" she whispered.

"He would carry her off," I replied.

"He shall never do so," was her quick answer. "Her father, the good Seigneur, has been wounded, and she must go to him."

"I will take her," said I at once, and I moved to open the door. At that moment I caught Gabord's eye. There I read what made me pause. If I declared myself now Gabord's life would pay for his friendship to me—even if I killed Doltaire; for the matter would be open to all then just the same. I could not do that, for the man had done me kindnesses dangerous to himself. Besides, he was a true soldier, and disgrace itself would be to him as bad as the drum-head court-martial. I made up my mind to another course even as the perturbed "aho" which followed our glance fell from his puffing lips.

"But no, holy Mother," said I, and I whispered in her ear. She opened the door and went in, leaving it ajar. I could hear only a confused murmur of voices, through which ran twice, "No, no, monsieur," in Alixe's soft, clear voice. I could scarcely restrain myself, and I am sure I should have gone in, in spite of all, had it not been for Gabord, who withstood me.

He was right, and as I turned away I heard Alixe cry, "My father, my poor father!"

Then came Doltaire's voice, cold and angry: "Good Mother, this is a trick."

"Your Excellency should be a better judge of trickery," she replied quietly. "Will not your Excellency leave an unhappy lady to the Church's care?"

"If the Seigneur is hurt, I will take mademoiselle to him," was his instant reply.

"It may not be, your Excellency," she said. "I will furnish her with other escort."

"And I, as Governor of this province, as commander-in-chief of the army, say that only with my escort shall the lady reach her father."

At this Alixe spoke: "Dear Mère St. George, do not fear for me; God will protect me——"

" And I also, mademoiselle, with my life," interposed Doltaire.

" God will protect me," Alixe repeated ; " I have no fear."

" I will send two of our Sisters with mademoiselle to nurse the poor Seigneur," said Mère St. George.

I am sure Doltaire saw the move. " A great kindness, holy Mother," he said politely, " and I will see they are well cared for. We will set forth at once. The Seigneur shall be brought to the Intendance, and he and his daughter shall have quarters there."

He stepped towards the door where we were. I fell back into position as he came. " Gabord," said he, " send your trusted fellow here to the General's camp, and have him fetch to the Intendance the Seigneur Duvarney, who has been wounded. Alive or dead, he must be brought," he added in a lower voice.

Then he turned back into the room. As he did so Gabord looked at me inquiringly.

" If you go, you put your neck into the gin," said he ; " some one in camp will know you."

" I will not leave my wife," I answered in a whisper. Thus were all plans altered on the instant. Gabord went to the outer door and called another soldier, to whom he gave this commission.

A few moments afterwards, Alixe, Doltaire, and the Sisters of Mercy were at the door ready to start. Doltaire turned and bowed with a well-assumed reverence to the Mother Superior. " To-night's affairs here are sacred to ourselves, Mère St. George," he said.

She bowed, but made no reply. Alixe turned and kissed her hand. But as we stepped forth, the Mother said suddenly, pointing to me, " Let the soldier come back in an hour, and mademoiselle's luggage shall go to her, your Excellency."

Doltaire nodded, glancing at me. "Surely he shall attend you, Mère St. George," he said, and then stepped on with Alixe, Gabord and the other soldier ahead, the two Sisters behind, and myself beside these. Going quietly through the disordered Upper Town, we came down Palace Street to the Intendance. Here Doltaire had kept his quarters despite his now desperate quarrel with Bigot. As we entered he inquired of the servant where Bigot was, and was told he was gone to the Château St. Louis. Doltaire shrugged a shoulder and smiled—he knew that Bigot had had news of his deposition through the Governor. He gave orders for rooms to be prepared for the Seigneur and for the Sisters; mademoiselle meanwhile to be taken to hers, which had, it appeared, been made ready. Then I heard him ask in an undertone if the bishop had come, and he was answered that Monseigneur was at Charlesbourg, and could not be expected till the morning. I was in a most dangerous position, for, though I had escaped notice, any moment might betray me; Doltaire himself might see through my disguise.

We all accompanied Alixe to the door of her apartments, and there Doltaire with courtesy took leave of her, saying that he would return in a little time to see if she was comfortable, and to bring her any fresh news of her father. The Sisters were given apartments next her own, and they entered her room with her, at her request.

When the door closed, Doltaire turned to Gabord, and said, "You shall come with me to bear letters to General Montcalm, and you shall send one of these fellows also for me to General Bougainville at Cap Rouge." Then he spoke directly to me, and said, "You shall guard this passage till morning. No one but myself may pass into this room or out of it, save the Sisters of Mercy, on pain of death."

I saluted, but spoke no word.

"You understand me?" he repeated.

"Altogether, monsieur," I answered in a rough, peasantlike voice.

He turned and walked in a leisurely way through the passage, and disappeared, telling Gabord to join him in a moment. As he left, Gabord said to me in a low voice, "Get back to General Wolfe, or wife and life will both be lost!"

I caught his hand and pressed it, and a minute afterwards I was alone before Alixe's door.

An hour later, knowing Alixe to be alone, I tapped on her door and entered. As I did so she rose from a prie-dieu where she had been kneeling. Two candles were burning on the mantel, but the room was much in shadow.

"What is't you wish?" she asked, approaching.

I had off my hat; I looked her directly in the eyes and put my fingers on my lips. She stared painfully for a moment.

"Alixe," said I.

She gave a gasp, and stood transfixed, as though she had seen a ghost, and then in an instant she was in my arms, sobs shaking her. "Oh, Robert! oh, my dear, dear husband!" she cried again and again. I calmed her, and presently she broke into a whirl of questions. I told her of all I had seen at the cathedral and at the convent and what my plans had been, and then I waited for her answer. A new feeling took possession of her. She knew that there was one question at my lips which I dared not utter. She became very quiet, and a sweet, settled firmness came into her face.

"Robert," she said, "you must go back to your army without me. I can not leave my father now. Save yourself alone, and if—and if you take the city, and I am alive, we shall be reunited. If you do not take the city, then, whether my father lives or dies, I will come to you. Of this be sure, that I shall never live to be the wife of any other man—wife or aught else. You know me. You know all, you trust me and, my dear husband, my own love, we must part once more. Go, go, and save yourself; keep your life safe for my sake, and may God in heaven, may God——"

Here she broke off and started back from my embrace, staring hard a moment over my shoulder; then her face became deadly pale, and she fell back unconscious. Supporting her, I turned round, and there, inside the door, with his back to it, was Doltaire. There was a devilish smile on his face, as wicked a look as I ever saw on any man. I laid Alixe down on a sofa without a word, and faced him again.

"As many coats as Joseph's coat had colours," he said. "And for once disguised as an honest man—well, well!"

"Beast!" I hissed, and I whipped out my short sword.

"Not here," he said, with a malicious laugh. "You forget your manners: familiarity"—he glanced towards the couch—"has bred——"

"Coward!" I cried. "I will kill you at her feet!"

"Come, then," he answered, and stepped away from the door, drawing his sword, "since you will have it here. But if I kill you, as I intend——"

He smiled detestably, and motioned towards the couch, then turned to the door again as if to lock it. I stepped between, my sword at guard. At that the door opened. A woman came in quickly, and closed it behind her. She passed me, and faced Doltaire.

It was Madame Cournal. She was most pale, and there was a peculiar wildness in her eyes.

"You have deposed François Bigot!" she said.

"Stand back, madame; I have business with this fellow," said Doltaire, waving his hand.

"My business comes first," she replied. "You—you dare to depose François Bigot!"

"It needs no daring," he said nonchalantly.

"You shall put him back in his place."

"Come to me to-morrow morning, dear madame."

"I tell you he must be put back, Monsieur Doltaire."

"Once you called me Tinoir," he said meaningly.

Without a word she caught from her cloak a dagger and struck him in the breast, though he threw up his hand and partly diverted the blow. Without a cry he half swung round, and sank, face forward, against the couch where Alixe lay.

Raising himself feebly, blindly, he caught her hand and kissed it; then he fell back.

Stooping beside him, I felt his heart. He was alive. Madame Cournal now knelt beside him, staring at him as in a kind of dream. I left the room quickly, and met the Sisters of Mercy in the hall. They had heard the noise, and were coming to Alixe. I bade them care for her. Passing rapidly through the corridors, I told a servant of the household what had occurred, bade him send for Bigot, and then made for my own safety. Alixe was safe for a time, at least—perhaps forever, thank God!—from the approaches of Monsieur Doltaire. As I sped through the streets, I could not help but think of how he had kissed her hand as he fell, and I knew by this act, at such a time, that in very truth he loved her after his fashion.

I came soon to the St. John's Gate, for I had the countersign from Gabord, and dressed as I was, I had no difficulty in passing. Outside I saw a small cavalcade arriving from Beauport way. I drew back and let it pass me, and then I saw that it was a company of soldiers bearing the Seigneur Duvarney to the Intendance.

An hour afterwards, having passed the sentries, I stood

on a lonely point of the shore of the Lower Town, and, seeing no one near, I slid into the water. As I did so I heard a challenge behind me, and when I made no answer there came a shot, another, and another; for it was thought, I doubt not, that I was a deserter. I was wounded in the shoulder, and had to swim with one arm; but though boats were put out from the shore, I managed to evade them and to get within hail of our fleet. Challenged there, I answered with my name. A boat shot out from among the ships, and soon I was hauled into it by Clark himself; and that night I rested safe upon the Terror of France.

XXVIII.

"TO CHEAT THE DEVIL YET."

My hurt proved more serious than I had looked for, and the day after my escape I was in a high fever. General Wolfe himself, having heard of my return, sent to inquire after me. He also was ill, and our forces were depressed in consequence; for he had a power to inspire them not given to any other of our accomplished generals. He forbore to question me concerning the state of the town and what I had seen; for which I was glad. My adventure had been of a private nature, and such I wished it to remain. The General desired me to come to him as soon as I was able, that I might proceed with him above the town to reconnoitre. But for many a day this was impossible, for my wound gave me much pain and I was confined to my bed.

Yet we on the Terror of France served our good General, too; for one dark night, when the wind was fair, we piloted the remaining ships of Admiral Holmes's division above the town. This move was made on my

constant assertion that there was a way by which Quebec
might be taken from above; and when General Wolfe
made known my representations to his general officers,
they accepted it as a last resort; for otherwise what hope
had they? At Montmorenci our troops had been repulsed; the mud flats of the Beauport shore and the St.
Charles River were as good as an army against us; the
Upper Town and Citadel were practically impregnable;
and for eight miles west of the town to the cove and
river at Cap Rouge there was one long precipice, broken
in but one spot; but just there, I was sure, men could
come up with stiff climbing, as I had done. Bougainville
came to Cap Rouge now with three thousand men, for he
thought that this was to be our point of attack. Along
the shore from Cap Rouge to Cape Diamond small batteries were posted, such as that of Lancy's at Anse du
Foulon; but they were careless, for no conjectures might
seem so wild as that of bringing an army up where I had
climbed.

"Tut, tut," said General Murray, when he came to
me on the Terror of France, after having, at my suggestion, gone to the south shore opposite Anse du Foulon, and scanned the faint line that marked the narrow
cleft on the cliff side—" tut, tut, man," said he, "'tis the
dream of a cat or a damned mathematician."

Once, after all was done, he said to me that cats and
mathematicians were the only generals.

With a belligerent pride Clark showed the way up
the river one evening, the batteries of the town giving
us plunging shots as we went, and ours at Point Levis
answering gallantly. To me it was a good if most anxious time: good, in that I was having some sort of compensation for my own sufferings in the town; anxious,
because no single word came to me of Alixe or her father,
and all the time we were pouring death into the place.

But this we knew from deserters, that Vaudreuil was Governor and Bigot Intendant still; by which it would seem that, on the momentous night when Doltaire was wounded by Madame Cournal, he gave back the governorship to Vaudreuil and reinstated Bigot. Presently, from an officer who had been captured as he was setting free a fire-raft to run among the boats of our fleet, I heard that Doltaire had been confined in the Intendance from a wound given by a stupid sentry. Thus the true story had been kept from the public. From him, too, I learned that nothing was known of the Seigneur Duvarney and his daughter; that they had suddenly disappeared from the Intendance, as if the earth had swallowed them; and that even Juste Duvarney knew nothing of them, and was, in consequence, greatly distressed.

This officer also said that now, when it might seem as if both the Seigneur and his daughter were dead, opinion had turned in Alixe's favour, and the feeling had crept about, first among the common folk and afterwards among the people of the garrison, that she had been used harshly. This was due largely, he thought, to the constant advocacy of the Chevalier de la Darante, whose nephew had married Mademoiselle Georgette Duvarney. This piece of news, in spite of the uncertainty of Alixe's fate, touched me, for the Chevalier had indeed kept his word to me.

At last all of Admiral Holmes's division was got above the town, with very little damage, and I never saw a man so elated, so profoundly elated as Clark over his share in the business. He was a daredevil, too; for the day that the last of the division was taken up the river, without my permission or the permission of the admiral or any one else, he took the Terror of France almost up to Bougainville's earthworks in the cove at

Cap Rouge and insolently emptied his six swivels into them, and then came out and stood down the river. When I asked what he was doing—for I was now well enough to come on deck—he said he was going to see how monkeys could throw nuts; when I pressed him, he said he had a will to hear the cats in the eaves; and when I became severe, he added that he would bring the Terror of France up past the batteries of the town in broad daylight, swearing that they could no more hit him than a woman could a bird on a flagstaff. I did not relish this foolish bravado, and I forbade it; but presently I consented, on condition that he take me to General Wolfe's camp at Montmorenci first; for now I felt strong enough to be again on active service.

Clark took the Terror of France up the river in midday, running perilously close to the batteries; and though they pounded at him petulantly, foolishly angry at his contemptuous defiance, he ran the gauntlet safely, and coming to the flagship, the Sutherland, saluted with his six swivels, to the laughter of the whole fleet and his own profane joy.

"Mr. Moray," said General Wolfe, when I saw him, racked with pain, studying a chart of the river and town which his chief engineer had just brought him, "show me here this passage in the hillside."

I did so, tracing the plains of Maître Abraham, which I assured him would be good ground for a pitched battle. He nodded; then rose, and walked up and down for a time, thinking. Suddenly he stopped, and fixed his eyes upon me.

"Mr. Moray," said he, "it would seem that you, angering La Pompadour, brought down this war upon us." He paused, smiling in a dry way, as if the thought amused him, as if, indeed, he doubted it; but for that I cared not, it was an honour I could easily live without.

I bowed to his words, and said, "Mine was the last straw, sir."

Again he nodded, and replied, "Well, well, you got us into trouble; you must show us the way out," and he looked again at the passage I had traced upon the chart. "You will remain with me until we meet our enemy on these heights." He pointed to the plains of Maître Abraham. Then he turned away, and began walking up and down again. "It is the last chance!" he said to himself in a tone despairing and yet heroic. "Please God! please God!" he added.

"You will speak nothing of these plans," he said to me at last, half mechanically. "We must make feints of landing at Cap Rouge—feints of landing everywhere save at the one possible place; confuse both Bougainville and Montcalm; tire out their armies with watchings and want of sleep; and then, on the auspicious night, make the great trial."

I had remained respectfully standing at a little distance from him. Now he suddenly came to me, and, pressing my hand, said quickly, "You have trouble, Mr. Moray. I am sorry for you. But maybe it is for better things to come!"

I thanked him stumblingly, and a moment later left him, to serve him on the morrow, and so on through many days, till, in divers perils, the camp at Montmorenci was abandoned, the troops were got aboard the ships, and the General took up his quarters on the Sutherland; from which, one notable day, I sallied forth with him to a point at the south shore opposite the Anse du Foulon, where he saw the thin crack in the cliff side. From that moment instant and final attack was his purpose.

The great night came, starlit and serene. The camp-fires of two armies spotted the shores of the wide river,

24

and the ships lay like wild fowl in convoys above the town from where the arrow of fate should be sped. Darkness upon the river, and fireflies upon the shore. At Beauport, an untiring General, who for a hundred days had snatched sleep, booted and spurred, and in the ebb of a losing game, longed for his adored Candiac, grieved for a beloved daughter's death, sent cheerful messages to his aged mother and to his wife, and by the deeper protests of his love foreshadowed his own doom. At Cap Rouge, a dying commander, unperturbed and valiant, reached out a finger to trace the last movements in a desperate campaign of life that opened in Flanders at sixteen; of which the end began when he took from his bosom the portrait of his affianced wife, and said to his old schoolfellow, " Give this to her, Jervis, for we shall meet no more."

Then, passing to the deck, silent and steady, no signs of pain upon his face, so had the calm come to him, as to Nature and this beleaguered city, before the whirlwind, he looked out upon the clustered groups of boats filled with the flower of his army, settled in a menacing tranquillity. There lay the Light Infantry, Bragg's, Kennedy's, Lascelles's, Anstruther's Regiment, Fraser's Highlanders, and the much-loved, much-blamed, and impetuous Louisburg Grenadiers. Steady, indomitable, silent as cats, precise as mathematicians, he could trust them, as they loved his awkward, pain-twisted body and ugly red hair. " Damme, Jack, didst thee ever take hell in tow before? " said a sailor from the Terror of France to his fellow once, as the marines grappled with a flotilla of French fire-ships, and dragged them, spitting destruction, clear of the fleet, to the shore. " Nay, but I've been in tow of Jimmy Wolfe's red head; that's hell-fire, lad! " was the reply.

From boat to boat the General's eye passed, then shifted to the ships—the Squirrel, the Leostaff, the Seahorse, and the rest—and lastly to where the army of

Bougainville lay. Then there came towards him an officer, who said quietly, "The tide has turned, sir." For reply the General made a swift motion towards the maintop shrouds, and almost instantly lanterns showed in them. In response, the crowded boats began to cast away, and, immediately descending, the General passed into his own boat, drew to the front, and drifted in the current ahead of his gallant men, the ships following after.

It was two by the clock when the boats began to move, and slowly we ranged down the stream, silently steered, carried by the current. No paddle, no creaking oarlock, broke the stillness. I was in the next boat to the General's, for, with Clark and twenty-two other volunteers to the forlorn hope, I was to show the way up the heights, and we were near to his person for over two hours that night. No moon was shining, but I could see the General plainly; and once, when our boats almost touched, he saw me, and said graciously, "If they get up, Mr. Moray, you are free to serve yourself."

My heart was full of love of country then, and I answered, "I hope, sir, to serve you till your flag is hoisted on the citadel."

He turned to a young midshipman beside him, and said, "How old are you, sir?"

"Seventeen, sir," was the reply.

"It is the most lasting passion," he said, musing.

It seemed to me then, and I still think it, that the passion he meant was love of country. A moment afterwards I heard him recite to the officers about him, in a low, clear tone, some verses by Mr. Gray, the poet, which I had never then read, though I have prized them since. Under those frowning heights, and the smell from our roaring distant thirty-two-pounders in the air, I heard him say:

> " The curfew tolls the knell of parting day ;
> The lowing herd wind slowly o'er the lea ;
> The ploughman homeward plods his weary way,
> And leaves the world to darkness and to me."

I have heard finer voices than his—it was as tin beside Doltaire's—but something in it pierced me that night, and I felt the man, the perfect hero, when he said :

> " The boast of heraldry, the pomp of power,
> And all that beauty, all that wealth e'er gave,
> Await alike the inevitable hour—
> The paths of glory lead but to the grave."

Soon afterwards we neared the end of our quest, the tide carrying us in to shore ; and down from the dark heights there came a challenge, satisfied by an officer, who said in French that we were provision-boats for Montcalm : these, we knew, had been expected ! Then came the batteries of Samos. Again we passed with the same excuse, rounded a headland, and the great work was begun.

The boats of the Light Infantry swung in to shore. No sentry challenged, but I knew that at the top Lancy's tents were set. When the Light Infantry had landed, we twenty-four volunteers stood still for a moment, and I pointed out the way. Before we started, we stooped beside a brook that leaped lightly down the ravine and drank a little rum and water. Then I led the way, Clark at one side of me, and a soldier of the Light Infantry at the other. It was hard climbing, but, following in our careful steps as silently as they might, the good fellows came eagerly after. Once a rock broke loose and came tumbling down, but plunged into a thicket, where it stayed ; else it might have done for us entirely. I breathed freely when it stopped. Once, too, a branch cracked loudly, and we lay still ; but hearing nothing above, we pushed on, and, sweating greatly, came close to the top.

Here Clark and I drew back, for such honour as there might be in gaining the heights first I wished to go to these soldiers who had trusted their lives to my guidance. I let six go by and reach the heights, and then I drew myself up. We did not stir till all twenty-four were safe; then we made a dash for the tents of Lancy, which now showed in the first gray light of morning. We were discovered, and shots greeted us; but we were on them instantly, and in a moment I had the pleasure of putting a bullet in Lancy's heel, and brought him down. Our cheers told the General the news, and soon hundreds of soldiers were climbing the hard way that we had come.

And now, while an army climbed to the heights of Maître Abraham, Admiral Saunders in the gray dawn was bombarding Montcalm's encampment, and boats filled with marines and soldiers drew to the Beauport flats, as if to land there; while shots, bombs, shells, and carcasses were hurled from Levis upon the town, deceiving Montcalm. At last, however, suspecting, he rode towards the town at six o'clock, and saw our scarlet ranks spread across the plains between him and Bougainville, and on the crest, nearer to him, eying us in amazement, the white-coated battalion of Guienne, which should the day before have occupied the very ground held by Lancy. A slight rain falling added to their gloom, but cheered us. It gave us a better light to fight by, for in the clear September air, the bright sun shining in our faces, they would have had us at advantage.

In another hour the gates of St. John and St. Louis emptied out upon this battlefield a warring flood of our foes. It was a handsome sight: the white uniforms of the brave regiments, Roussillon, La Sarre, Guienne, Languedoc, Béarn, mixed with the dark, excitable militia, the sturdy burghers of the town, a band of *coureurs de bois* in their rough hunter's costume, and whooping Indians, painted and furious, ready to eat us. At last here was to be a test of fighting in open field, though the French had in their whole army twice the number of our men, a walled and provisioned city behind them, and field-pieces in great number to bring against us.

But there was bungling with them. Vaudreuil hung back or came tardily from Beauport; Bougainville had not yet arrived; and when they might have pitted twice our number against us, they had not many more than we. With Bougainville behind us and Montcalm in front, we might have been checked, though there was no man in all our army but believed that we should win the day. I could plainly see Montcalm, mounted on a dark horse, riding along the lines as they formed against us, waving his sword, a truly gallant figure. He was answered by a roar of applause and greeting. On the left their Indians and burghers overlapped our second line, where Townsend with Amherst's and the Light Infantry, and Colonel Burton with the Royal Americans and Light Infantry, guarded our flank, prepared to meet Bougainville. In vain our foes tried to get between our right flank and the river; Otway's Regiment, thrown out, defeated that.

It was my hope that Doltaire was with Montcalm, and that we might meet and end our quarrel. I came to know afterwards that it was he who had induced Montcalm to send the battalion of Guienne to the heights above the Anse du Foulon. The battalion had not been moved till twenty-four hours after the order was given, or we should never have gained those heights; stones rolled from the cliff would have destroyed an army!

We waited, Clark and I, with the Louisburg Grenadiers while they formed. We made no noise, but stood steady and still, the bagpipes of the Highlanders shrilly challenging. At eight o'clock sharpshooters began firing on us from the left, and our skirmishers were thrown out to hold them in check, or drive them from the houses where they sheltered and galled Townsend's men. Their field-pieces opened on us, too, and yet we did nothing, but at nine o'clock, being ordered, we lay down and waited still. There was no restlessness, no anxiety, no show of doubt, for these men of ours were old fighters, and they trusted their leaders. From bushes, trees, coverts, and fields of grain there came that constant hail of fire, and there fell upon our ranks a doggedness, a quiet anger, which grew into a grisly patience. The only pleasure we had in two long hours was in watching our two brass six-pounders play upon the irregular ranks of our foes, making confusion, and Townsend drive back a detachment of cavalry from Cap Rouge, which sought to break our left flank and reach Montcalm.

We had seen the stars go down, the cold, mottled light of dawn break over the battered city and the heights of Charlesbourg; we had watched the sun come up, and then steal away behind the slow-travelling clouds and hanging mist; we had looked across over unreaped cornfields and the dull, slovenly St. Charles, knowing that endless leagues of country, north and south, east and west, lay in the balance for the last time. I believed that this day would see the last of the strife between England and France for dominion here; of La Pompadour's spite which I had roused to action against my country; of the struggle between Doltaire and myself.

The public stake was worthy of our army—worthy of the dauntless soldier who had begged his physicians to patch him up long enough to fight this fight, whereon he staked reputation, life, all that a man loves in the world; the private stake was more than worthy of my long sufferings.   I thought that Montcalm would have waited for Vaudreuil, but no.   At ten o'clock his three columns came down upon us briskly, making a wild rattle ; two columns moving upon our right and one upon our left, firing obliquely and constantly as they marched.   Then came the command to rise, and we stood up and waited, our muskets loaded with an extra ball.   I could feel the stern malice in our ranks, as we stood there and took, without returning a shot, that damnable fire.   Minute after minute passed ; then came the sharp command to advance.   We did so, and again halted, and yet no shot came from us.   We stood there inactive, a long palisade of red.

At last I saw our General raise his sword, a command rang down the long line of battle, and, like one terrible cannon-shot, our muskets sang together with as perfect a precision as on a private field of exercise.   Then, waiting for the smoke to clear a little, another volley came with almost the same precision ; after which the firing came in choppy waves of sound, and again in a persistent clattering.   Then a light breeze lifted the smoke and mist well away, and a wayward sunlight showed us our foe, like a long white wave retreating from a rocky shore, bending, crumpling, breaking, and, in a hundred little billows, fleeing seaward.

Thus checked, confounded, the French army trembled and fell back.   Then I heard the order to charge, and from nearly four thousand throats there came for the first time our exultant British cheer, and high over all rang the slogan of Fraser's Highlanders.   To my left I saw the flashing broadswords of the clansmen, ahead of all the rest.   Those sickles of death clove through and broke the battalions of La Sarre, and Lascelles scattered the soldiers of Languedoc into flying columns.   We on the right, led by Wolfe, charged the desperate and valiant men of Roussillon and Guienne and the impetuous sharpshooters of the militia. As we came on I observed the General sway and push forward again, and then I lost sight of him, for I saw what gave the battle a new interest to me: Doltaire, cool and deliberate, animating and encouraging the French troops.

I moved in a shaking hedge of bayonets, keeping my eye upon him; and presently there was a hand-to-hand *mêlée*, out of which I fought to reach him. I was making for him, where he now sought to rally the retreating columns, when I noticed, not far away, Gabord, mounted, and attacked by three grenadiers. Looking back now, I see him, with his sabre cutting right and left, as he drove his horse at one grenadier, who slipped and fell on the slippery ground, while the horse rode on him, battering him. Obliquely down swept the sabre, and drove through the cheek and chin of one foe; another sweep, and the bayonet of the other was struck aside; and another, which was turned aside as Gabord's horse came down, bayoneted by the fallen grenadier. But Gabord was on his feet again, roaring like a bull, with a wild grin on his face, as he partly struck aside the bayonet of the last grenadier. It caught him in the flesh of the left side. He grasped the musket-barrel, and swung his sabre with fierce precision. The man's head dropped back like the lid of a pot, and he tumbled into a heap of the faded golden-rod flower which spattered the field.

At this moment I saw Juste Duvarney making towards me, hatred and deadly purpose in his eyes. I had will enough to meet him, and to kill him too, yet I could not help but think of Alixe. Gabord saw him also, and, being nearer, made for me as well. For that act I cherish his memory. The thought was worthy of a gentleman of breeding; he had the true thing in his heart. He would save us—two brothers—from fighting, by fighting me himself!

He reached me first, and with an "Au diable!" made a stroke at me. It was a matter of sword and sabre now. Clark met Juste Duvarney's rush; and there we were, at as fine a game of cross-purposes as you can think: Clark hungering for Gabord's life (Gabord had once been his jailer too), and Juste Duvarney for mine; the battle faring on ahead of us. Soon the two were clean cut off from the French army, and must fight to the death or surrender.

Juste Duvarney spoke only once, and then it was but the rancorous word "Renegade!" nor did I speak at all; but Clark was blasphemous, and Gabord, bleeding, fought with a sputtering relish.

"Fair fight and fowl for spitting," he cried. "Go home to heaven, dickey-bird!"

Between phrases of this kind we cut and thrust for life, an odd sort of fighting. I fought with a desperate alertness, and presently my sword passed through his body, drew out, and he shivered—fell—where he stood, collapsing suddenly like a bag. I knelt beside him and lifted up his head. His eyes were glazing fast.

"Gabord! Gabord!" I called, grief-stricken, for that work was the worst I ever did in this world.

He started, stared, and fumbled at his waistcoat. I quickly put my hand in, and drew out—one of Mathilde's wooden crosses!

"To cheat—the devil—yet—aho!" he whispered, kissed the cross, and so was done with life.

When I turned from him, Clark stood alone beside me. Dazed as I was, I did not at first grasp the significance of that fact. I looked towards the town, and saw the French army hustling into the St. Louis Gate; saw the Highlanders charging the bushes at the Côte Ste.

Genevieve, where the brave Canadians made their last stand; saw, not fifty feet away, the noblest soldier of our time, even General Wolfe, dead in the arms of Mr. Henderson, a volunteer in the Twenty-second; and then, almost at my feet, stretched out as I had seen him lie in the Palace courtyard two years before, I beheld Juste Duvarney.

But now he was beyond all friendship or reconciliation—forever!

XXIX.

"MASTER DEVIL" DOLTAIRE.

THE bells of some shattered church were calling to vespers, the sun was sinking behind the flaming autumn woods, as once more I entered the St. Louis Gate, with the grenadiers and a detachment of artillery, the British colours hoisted on a gun-carriage. Till this hour I had ever entered and left this town a captive, a price set on my head, and in the very street where I now walked I had gone with a rope round my neck, abused and maltreated. I saw our flag replace the golden lilies of France on the citadel where Doltaire had baited me, and at the top of Mountain Street, near to the bishop's palace, our colours also flew.

Every step I took was familiar, yet unfamiliar too. It was a disfigured town, where a hungry, distracted people huddled among ruins and begged for mercy and for food, nor found time in the general overwhelming to think of the gallant Montcalm, lying in his shell-made grave at the chapel of the Ursulines, not fifty steps from where I had looked through the tapestry on Alixe and Doltaire. The convent was almost deserted now, and as I passed it, on my way to the cathedral, I

took off my hat; for how knew I but that she I loved
best lay there too, as truly a heroine as the admirable
Montcalm was hero! A solitary bell was clanging on the
chapel as I went by, and I saw three nuns steal past me
with bowed heads. I longed to ask them of Alixe, for
I felt sure that the Church knew where she was, living
or dead, though none of all I asked knew aught of her,
not even the Chevalier de la Darante, who had come
to our camp the night before, accompanied by Monsieur
Joannes, the town major, with terms of surrender.

I came to the church of the Recollets as I wandered;
for now, for a little time, I seemed bewildered and in-
capable, lost in a maze of dreadful imaginings. I entered
the door of the church, and stumbled upon a body.
Hearing footsteps ahead in the dusk, I passed up the
aisle, and came upon a pile of *débris*. Looking up, I
could see the stars shining through a hole in the roof.
Hearing a noise beyond, I went on, and there, seated on
the high altar, was the dwarf who had snatched the cup
of rum out of the fire the night that Mathilde had given
the crosses to the revellers. He gave a low, wild laugh,
and hugged a bottle to his breast. Almost at his feet,
half naked, with her face on the lowest step of the altar,
her feet touching the altar itself, was the girl—his sister
—who had kept her drunken lover from assaulting him.
The girl was dead—there was a knife-wound in her breast.
Sick at the sight, I left the place and went on, almost
mechanically, to Voban's house. It was level with the
ground, a crumpled heap of ruins. I passed Lancy's house,
in front of which I had fought with Gabord; it, too, was
broken to pieces.

As I turned away I heard a loud noise as of an ex-
plosion, and I supposed it to be some magazine. I
thought of it no more at the time. Voban must be
found; that was more important. I must know of Alixe

first, and I felt sure that if any one guessed her whereabouts it would be he : she would have told him where
she was going, if she had fled ; if she were dead, who
so likely to know as this secret, elusive, vengeful watcher?
Of Doltaire I had heard nothing ; I would seek him
out when I knew of Alixe. He could not escape me in
this walled town. I passed on for a time without direction, for I seemed not to know where I might find the
barber. Our sentries already patrolled the streets, and
our bugles were calling on the heights, with answering
calls from the fleet in the basin. Night came down
quickly, the stars shone out in the perfect blue, and, as I
walked along, broken walls, shattered houses, solitary pil-
lars, looked mystically strange. It was painfully quiet, as
if a beaten people had crawled away into the holes our shot
and shell had made, to hide their misery. Now and
again a gaunt face looked out from a hiding-place, and
drew back again in fear at sight of me. Once a drunken
woman spat at me and cursed me ; once I was fired at ;
and many times from dark corners I heard voices crying,
" *Sauvez-moi—ah, sauvez-moi, bon Dieu!* " Once I stood
for many minutes and watched our soldiers giving biscuits and their own share of rum to homeless French
peasants hovering round the smouldering ruins of a house
which carcasses had destroyed.

And now my wits came back to me, my purposes, the
power to act, which for a couple of hours had seemed to
be in abeyance. I hurried through narrow streets to the
cathedral. There it stood, a shattered mass, its sides all
broken, its roof gone, its tall octagonal tower alone substantial and unchanged. Coming to its rear, I found Babette's little house, with open door, and I went in. The
old grandfather sat in his corner, with a lighted candle
on the table near him, across his knees Jean's coat that I
had worn. He only babbled nonsense to my questioning,

and, after calling aloud to Babette and getting no reply, I started for the Intendance.

I had scarcely left the house when I saw some French peasants coming towards me with a litter. A woman walking behind the litter carried a lantern, and one of our soldiers of artillery attended and directed. I ran forward, and discovered Voban, mortally hurt. The woman gave a cry, and spoke my name in a kind of surprise and relief; and the soldier, recognising me, saluted. I sent him for a surgeon, and came on with the hurt man to the little house. Soon I was alone with him save for Babette, and I sent her for a priest. As soon as I had seen Voban I guessed what had happened: he had tried for his revenge at last. After a little time he knew me, but at first he could not speak.

" What has happened—the palace ? " said I.

He nodded.

" You blew it up—with Bigot ? " I asked.

His reply was a whisper, and his face twitched with pain : " Not—with Bigot."

I gave him some cordial, which he was inclined to refuse. It revived him, but I saw he could live only a few hours. Presently he made an effort. " I will tell you," he whispered.

" Tell me first of my wife," said I. " Is she alive ?—is she alive ? "

If a smile could have been upon his lips then, I saw one there—good Voban! I put my ear down, and my heart almost stopped beating, until I heard him say, " Find Mathilde."

" Where ? " asked I.

" In the Valdoche Hills," he answered, " where the Gray Monk lives—by the Tall Calvary."

He gasped with pain. I let him rest awhile, and eased the bandages on him, and at last he told his story :

"I am to be gone soon. For two years I have wait for the good time to kill him—Bigot—to send him and his palace to hell. I can not tell you how I work to do it. It is no matter—no. From an old cellar I mine, and at last I get the powder lay beneath him—his palace. So. But he does not come to the palace much this many months, and Madame Cournal is always with him, and it is hard to do the thing in other ways. But I laugh when the English come in the town, and when I see Bigot fly to his palace alone to get his treasure-chest I think it is my time. So I ask the valet, and he say he is in the private room that lead to the treasure-place. Then I come back quick to the secret spot and fire my mine. In ten minutes all will be done. I go at once to his room again, alone. I pass through the one room, and come to the other. It is a room with one small barred window. If he is there, I will say a word to him that I have wait long to say, then shut the door on us both—for I am sick of life—and watch him and laugh at him till the end comes. If he is in the other room, then I have a way as sure——"

He paused, exhausted, and I waited till he could again go on. At last he made a great effort, and continued: "I go back to the first room, and he is not there. I pass soft, to the treasure-room, and I see him kneel beside a chest, looking in. His back is to me. I hear him laugh to himself. I shut the door, turn the key, go to the window and throw it out, and look at him again. But now he stand and turn to me, and then I see—I see it is not Bigot, but M'sieu' Doltaire!

"I am sick when I see that, and at first I can not speak, my tongue stick in my mouth so dry. 'Has Voban turn robber?' m'sieu' say. I put out my hand and try to speak again—but no. 'What did you throw from the window?' he ask. 'And what's the matter, my Voban?' 'My God,' I say at him now, 'I thought you are Bigot!' I point to the floor. 'Powder!' I whisper.

"His eyes go like fire so terrible; he look to the window, take a quick, angry step to me, but stand still. Then he point to the window. 'The key, Voban?' he say; and I answer, 'Yes.' He get pale; then he go and try the door, look close at the walls, try them—quick, quick, stop, feel for a panel, then try again, stand still, and lean against the table. It is no use to call; no one can hear, for it is all roar outside, and these walls are solid and very thick.

"'How long?' he say, and take out his watch. 'Five minutes—maybe,' I answer. He put his watch on the table, and sit down on a bench by it, and for a little minute he do not speak, but look at me close, and not angry, as you would think. 'Voban,' he say in a low voice, 'Bigot was a thief.' He point to the chest. 'He stole from the King —my father. He stole your Mathilde from you! He should have died. We have both been blunderers, Voban, blunderers,' he say; 'things have gone wrong with us. We have lost all.' There is little time. 'Tell me one thing,' he go on: 'is Mademoiselle Duvarney safe—do you know?' I tell him yes, and he smile, and take from his pocket something, and lay it against his lips, and then put it back in his breast.

"'You are not afraid to die, Voban?' he ask. I answer no. 'Shake hands with me, my friend,' he speak, and I do so that. 'Ah, pardon, pardon, m'sieu',' I say. 'No, no, Voban; it was to be,' he answer. 'We shall meet again, comrade—eh, if we can?' he speak on, and he turn away from me and look to the sky through the window. Then he look at his watch, and get to his feet, and stand there still. I kiss my crucifix. He reach out and touch it, and bring his fingers to his lips. 'Who can tell—perhaps—perhaps!' he say. For a little minute— ah, it seem like a year, and it is so still, so still—he stand there, and then he put his hand over the watch, lift it up, and shut his eyes, as if time is all done. While you can count ten it is so, and then the great crash come!"

For a long time Voban lay silent again. I gave him more cordial, and he revived and ended his tale. "I am a blunderer, as m'sieu' say," he went on, "for he is killed, not Bigot and me, and only a little part of the palace go to pieces. And so they fetch me here, and I wish—my God in Heaven, I wish I go with M'sieu' Doltaire!" But he followed him a little later.

Two hours afterwards I went to the Intendance, and there I found that the body of my enemy had been placed in the room where I had last seen him with Alixe. He lay on the same couch where she had lain. The flag of France covered his broken body, but his face was untouched—as it had been in life, haunting, fascinating, though the shifting lights were gone, the fine eyes closed. A noble peace hid all that was sardonic; not even Gabord would now have called him "Master Devil." I covered up his face and left him there—peasant and prince— candles burning at his head and feet, and the star of Louis on his shattered breast; and I saw him no more.

All that night I walked the ramparts, thinking, remembering, hoping, waiting for the morning; and when I saw the light break over those far eastern parishes, wasted by fire and sword, I set out on a journey to the Valdoche Hills.

XXX.

"WHERE ALL THE LOVERS CAN HIDE."

It was in the saffron light of early morning that I saw it, the Tall Calvary of the Valdoche Hills.

25

The night before I had come up through a long valley, overhung with pines on one side and crimsoning maples on the other, and, travelling till nearly midnight, had lain down in the hollow of a bank, and listened to a little river leap over cascades, and, far below, go prattling on to the greater river in the south. My eyes closed, but for long I did not sleep. I heard a night-hawk go by on a lonely mission, a beaver slide from a log into the water, and the delicate humming of the pine needles was a drowsy music, through which broke by-and-bye the strange crying of a loon from the water below. I was neither asleep nor awake, but steeped in this wide awe of night, the sweet smell of earth and running water in my nostrils. Once, too, in a slight breeze, the scent of some wild animal's nest came past, and I found it good. I lifted up a handful of loose earth and powdered leaves, and held it to my nose—a good, brave smell—all in a sort of drowsing.

While I mused, Doltaire's face passed before me as it was in life, and I heard him say again of the peasants, "These shall save the earth some day, for they are of it, and live close to it, and are kin to it."

Suddenly there rushed before me that scene in the convent, when all the devil in him broke loose upon the woman I loved. But turning on my homely bed I looked up and saw the deep quiet of the skies, the stable peace of the stars, and I was a son of the good Earth again, a sojourner to the tents of Home. I did not doubt that Alixe was alive or that I should find her. There was assurance in this benignant night. In that thought, dreaming that her cheek lay close to mine, her arm around my neck, I fell asleep. I waked to hear the squirrels stirring in the trees, the whir of the partridge, and the first unvarying note of the oriole. Turning on my dry, leafy bed, I looked down, and saw in the dim haze of dawn the beavers at their house-building.

I was at the beginning of a deep gorge or valley, on one side of which was a steep, sloping hill of grass and trees, and on the other a huge escarpment of mossed and jagged rocks. Then, farther up, the valley seemed to end in a huge promontory. On this great wedge grim shapes loomed in the mist, uncouth and shadowy and unnatural —a lonely, mysterious Brocken, impossible to human tenantry. Yet as I watched the mist slowly rise, there grew in me the feeling that there lay the end of my quest. I came down to the brook, bathed my face and hands, ate my frugal breakfast of bread, with berries picked from the hillside, and, as the yellow light of the rising sun broke over the promontory, I saw the Tall Calvary upon a knoll, strange comrade to the huge rocks and monoliths —as it were vast playthings of the Mighty Men, the fabled ancestors of the Indian races of the land.

I started up the valley, and presently all the earth grew blithe, and the birds filled the woods and valleys with jocund noise.

It was near noon before I knew that my pilgrimage was over.

Coming round a point of rock, I saw the Gray Monk, of whom strange legends had lately travelled to the city. I took off my cap to him reverently; but all at once he threw back his cowl, and I saw—no monk, but, much altered, the good chaplain who had married me to Alixe in the Château St. Louis. He had been hurt when he was fired upon in the water as he tried for freedom; had escaped, however, got to shore, and made his way into the woods. There he had met Mathilde, who led him to her lonely home in this hill. Seeing the Tall Calvary he had conceived the idea of this disguise, and Mathilde had brought him the robe for the purpose.

In a secluded cave I found Alixe with her father, caring for him, for he was not yet wholly recovered from his injuries. There was no waiting now. The ban of Church did not hold my dear girl back, nor did her father do aught but smile when she came laughing and weeping into my arms.

"Robert, O Robert, Robert!" she cried, and at first that was all that she could say.

The good Seigneur put out his hand to me beseechingly. I took it, clasped it.

"The city?" he asked.

"Is ours," I answered.

"And my son—my son?"

I told him how, the night that the city was taken, the Chevalier de la Darante and I had gone a sad journey in a boat to the Isle of Orleans, and there, in the chapel yard, near to his father's château, we had laid a brave and honest gentleman who died fighting for his country.

By-and-bye, when their grief had a little abated, I took them out into the sunshine. A pleasant green valley lay to the north, and to the south, far off, was the wall of rosy hills that hid the captured town. Peace was upon it all, and upon us.

As we stood there, a scarlet figure came winding in and out among the giant stones, crosses hanging at her girdle. She approached us, and, seeing me, she said: "Hush! I know a place where all the lovers can hide."

And she put a little wooden cross into my hands.

(1)

THE END.

A STORY OF THE PEOPLE'S POWER.

The Eternal City.

By HALL CAINE, author of "The Christian," "The Manxman," "The Bondman," "The Deemster," etc. 12mo. Cloth, $1.50.

"A vivid and moving picture of Roman life."—*Pittsburg Commercial Gazette.*

"Bound to exercise a great influence in the controversies now exciting the world."—*St. Louis Post-Dispatch.*

"One of the very strongest productions in fiction that the present age has been privileged to enjoy."—*Philadelphia Item.*

"The most ambitious work the author has so far undertaken, and may be regarded his greatest success."—*Cleveland Plain-Dealer.*

"A powerful novel, inspired by a lofty conception, and carried out with unusual force. It is the greatest thing that Hall Caine has ever attempted."—*Brooklyn Eagle.*

"The praise of the great men of letters—Ruskin, Collins, Blackmore, Gladstone—who hailed with delight the advent of 'The Deemster' and 'The Bondman,' should now be readjusted to meet present exigencies, for Mr. Hall Caine has done for the myriads of his English readers what Walpole did for a smaller yet not less discriminating public. . . . The true Italian spirit of Onuphrio Muralto we find revived after many years in 'The Eternal City.'"—*New York Times Saturday Review.*

D. APPLETON AND COMPANY, NEW YORK.

RECENT FICTION.

The Way of Escape.

By GRAHAM TRAVERS (Margaret Todd, M. D.), author of "Mona Maclean," "Windyhaugh," etc. 12mo. Cloth, $1.50.

"A classic."—*Philadelphia Item.*
"Exceptionally good."—*New York Tribune.*
"Undeniably clever."—*London Literary World.*
"Strong in dramatic incident."—*Boston Budget.*
"A work of unusual power."—*Chicago Record-Herald.*
"Vera is a marvellous piece of womanhood."—*London Star.*

Those Delightful Americans.

By Mrs. EVERARD COTES (Sara Jeannette Duncan), author of "An American Girl in London," "A Voyage of Consolation," etc. 12mo. Cloth, $1.50.

"A particularly clever and amusing book."—*New York Sun.*
"Full of clever, humorous, oftentimes subtle insights into the American character."—*Chicago Record-Herald.*

My Captive.

By J. A. ALTSHELER, author of "The Wilderness Road," "In Circling Camps," etc. 12mo. Cloth, $1.25.

"A spirited and interesting narrative."—*Philadelphia Press.*
"A mightily interesting little tale of the Revolution. . . . By all odds the cleverest tale Mr. Altsheler has written."—*Philadelphia Item.*

The Outlaws.

A Story of the Building of the West. By LE ROY ARMSTRONG. 12mo. Cloth, $1.25.

"Promises well for the literary career of its author."—*Philadelphia Press.*
"Full of life and picturesqueness, spirited and brimming with incident and character."—*Brooklyn Eagle.*

T' Bacca Queen.

By T. WILSON WILSON. 12mo. Cloth, $1.00; paper, 50 cents.

"Human passions are depicted with a vividness amounting to a triumph for the author, and the novelty of the plot, the strength of the characters in the book, and its forceful style will appeal strongly to the reader."—*Cleveland World.*

D. APPLETON AND COMPANY, NEW YORK.

RECENT FICTION.

The Man Who Knew Better.

By T. GALLON, author of "Tatterley," etc. Illustrated by Gordon Browne. 8vo. Cloth, $1.50.

"The best Christmas story that has appeared since the death of Charles Dickens. . . . It is an admirably written story, and merits warm welcome and broad recognition."—*Baltimore Sun*.

Under the Skylights.

By HENRY B. FULLER, author of "The Chevalier of Pensieri-Vani," "The Cliff Dwellers," etc. 12mo. Deckle edge, gilt top, $1.50.

The charming humor, delightful flavor, and refined quality of Mr. Fuller's work impart a peculiar zest to this subtly satirical picture of the extraordinary vicissitudes of arts and letters in a Western metropolis.

The Apostles of the Southeast.

By FRANK T. BULLEN, author of "The Cruise of the Cachalot," "Idyls of the Sea," etc. 12mo. Cloth, $1.50.

"Mr. Bullen writes with a sympathy and pathetic touch rare indeed. His characters are living ones, his scenes full of life and realism, and there is not a page in the whole book which is not brimful of deepest interest."—*Philadelphia Item*.

The Alien.

By F. F. MONTRÉSOR, author of "Into the Highways and Hedges," etc. 12mo. Cloth, $1.50.

"May be confidently commended to the most exacting reader as an absorbing story, excellently told."—*Kansas City Star*.

While Charlie Was Away.

By Mrs. POULTNEY BIGELOW. 16mo. Cloth, 75 cents.

Mrs. Bigelow tells a wonderfully vivid story of a woman in London "smart" life whose hunger for love involves her in perils, but finds a true way out in the end.

D. APPLETON AND COMPANY, NEW YORK.

RECENT FICTION.

Some Women I have Known.

By MAARTEN MAARTENS, author of "God's Fool," etc. With Frontispiece. 12mo. Cloth, $1.50.

"Maarten Maartens stands head and shoulders above the average novelist of the day in intellectual subtlety and imaginative power."—*Boston Beacon.*

The Wage of Character.

By JULIEN GORDON, author of "Mrs. Clyde," etc. With Portrait. 12mo. Cloth, $1.25.

Julien Gordon's new novel is a story of the world of fashion and intrigue, written with an insight, an epigrammatic force, and a realization of the dramatic and the pathetic as well as more superficial phases of life, that stamp the book as one immediate and personal in its interest and convincing in its appeal to the minds and to the sympathies of readers.

The Quiberon Touch.

A Romance of the Sea. By CYRUS TOWNSEND BRADY, author of "For the Freedom of the Sea," "The Grip of Honor," etc. With Frontispiece. 12mo. Cloth, $1.50.

"This story has a real beauty; it breathes of the sea. Fenimore Cooper would not be ashamed to own a disciple in the school of which he was master in these descriptions of the tug of war as it was in the eighteenth century between battle-ships under sail."—*New York Mail and Express.*

Shipmates.

A Volume of Salt-Water Fiction. By MORGAN ROBERTSON, author of "Masters of Men," etc. With Frontispiece. 12mo. Cloth, $1.50.

When Mr. Robertson writes of the sea, the tang of the brine and the snap of the sea-breeze are felt behind his words. The adventures and mysteries of sea life, the humors and strange complications possible in yachting, the inner tragedies of the foks'l, the delightful adventures of Finnegan in war, and the original developments in the course of true love at sea, are among the vivid pictures that make up a volume so vital in its interests and dramatic in its situations, so delightful in its quaint humor and so vigorous and stirring throughout, that it will be read by sea lovers for its full flavor of the sea, and by others as a refreshing tonic.

D. APPLETON AND COMPANY, NEW YORK.

RECENT FICTION.

A Nest of Linnets.

By F. FRANKFORT MOORE, author of "The Jessamy Bride," "A Gray Eye or So," etc. Illustrated. 12mo. Cloth, $1.50.

"That 'A Nest of Linnets' is bright, clever, and well written follows as a matter of course, considering that it was written by F. Frankfort Moore."— *Philadelphia Telegraph.*

The Eternal City.

By HALL CAINE, author of "The Christian," "The Manxman," "The Bondman," "The Deemster," etc. 12mo. Cloth, $1.50.

"A powerful novel, inspired by a lofty conception, and carried out with unusual force. It is the greatest thing that Hall Caine has ever attempted."— *Brooklyn Eagle.*

The Teller.

By EDWARD NOYES WESTCOTT, author of "David Harum." Illustrated. 12mo. Cloth, $1.00.

The publishers of "David Harum" have the pleasure of presenting the only other story written by the lamented Edward Noyes Westcott. Mr. Westcott's business life lay with practical financial matters, and in "The Teller" he has drawn upon his knowledge of life in a bank.

When Love Flies Out o' the Window.

By LEONARD MERRICK. 12mo. Cloth, $1.00 ; paper, 50 cents.

"The attention of the reader is held from start to finish, because the whole plot is original, and one can not tell what is going to happen next."— *Washington Times.*

The Beleaguered Forest.

By ELIA W. PEATTIE. 12mo. Cloth, $1.50.

"'The Beleaguered Forest' is not a novel—it is a romance ; it is not a romance—it is a poem."— *Chicago Post.*

D. APPLETON AND COMPANY, NEW YORK.

F. F. MONTRÉSOR'S BOOKS.

The Alien. 12mo. Cloth, $1.50.

Miss Montrésor has utilized incident and intrigue in this excellent story to give a vivid delineation of character. The scene is laid partly in England, and there are also glimpses of South America. The love of a mother for a prodigal, the self-sacrifice of a woman, and the mingled motives of an adventurer, who plays a leading part, are all sketched with the delicacy, penetration, and grasp of motives that have distinguished this talented author's work.

At the Cross-Roads. 16mo. Cloth, $1.50.

"Miss Montrésor has the skill in writing of Olive Schreiner and Miss Harraden, added to the fulness of knowledge of life which is a chief factor in the success of George Eliot and Mrs. Humphry Ward. . . . There is as much strength in this book as in a dozen ordinary successful novels."—*London Literary World.*

False Coin or True? 16mo. Cloth, $1.25.

"The tale never flags in interest, and once taken up will not be laid down until the last page is finished."—*Boston Budget.*

"One of the few true novels of the day. . . . It is powerful, and touched with a delicate insight and strong impressions of life and character. . . . The author's theme is original, her treatment artistic, and the book is remarkable for its unflagging interest."—*Philadelphia Record.*

The One who Looked On. 16mo. Cloth, $1.25.

"One of the most remarkable and powerful of the year's contributions, worthy to stand with Ian Maclaren's."—*British Weekly.*

"One of the rare books which can be read with great pleasure and recommended without reservation. It is fresh, pure, sweet, and pathetic, with a pathos which is perfectly wholesome."—*St. Paul Globe.*

Into the Highways and Hedges. 16mo. Cloth, $1.50.

"'Into the Highways and Hedges' is a book not of promise only, but of high achievement. It is original, powerful, artistic, humorous. It places the author at a bound in the rank of those artists to whom we look for the skilful presentation of strong personal impressions of life and character."—*London Daily News.*

D. APPLETON AND COMPANY, NEW YORK.